FRINGE BENEFITS

"Please sit down," Nancy said, taking one end of the couch. Sean followed her lead and lowered himself on the other end. He glanced up and noticed that she was examining him, as if to reassure herself that he was the same person she had met the previous night.

"Let me tell you about the job," she said, coming directly to the point. "It is perfect for someone with your skills, an actor that is. The hours are flexible and the pay is good, and there are a number of side benefits. Sound interesting?"

"So far," Sean replied. "What exactly do I do?"

"Debonaire provides an escort service to businesswomen visiting from out of town, wealthy single women who live here, any lady who needs what we provide: a distinguished male escort to accompany her to parties, events, the theater, and so forth."

Sean was flustered. "An escort service?" he said, unable to hide his incredulity.

Surely he would never stoop to such a job, no matter how much money it paid—no matter what the fringe benefits.

Would he?

For Women Only

Trevor Meldal-Johnsen

PINNACLE BOOKS
WINDSOR PUBLISHING CORP.

PINNACLE BOOKS

are published by

Windsor Publishing Corp.
475 Park Avenue South
New York, NY 10016

First printing: May, 1990

Printed in the United States of America

Chapter One

Things happen.

Normally the Power Company doesn't see anything much more exciting than a battle of odors between perspiration and deodorants, a battle invariably won by the hard-earned acrid smell of sweat. Invincible, it floods the large, one-room gym, permeating the wooden floor, the mats and pads and exercise equipment.

Beneath the high, bright fluorescent lights gleams black and chrome high-technology machinery, devices designed first to betray and then to build every muscle of the body. There are machines for biceps and triceps and shoulders and pectorals, for stomachs and thighs and calves, tens of thousands of dollars of smoothly moving hydraulic equipment dedicated solely to one mission: Improvement of the body.

And the bodies in the Power Company are indeed impressive. Dedicated, fit, and tanned, in spite of the weak spring sunshine, many with perfect muscular definition, they belong to corporate executives and actors, dancers and cabdrivers, waiters, hustlers, priests, and politicians. For the most part, however, these bodies do not sport rippling muscles — they are as solid and compacted as rocks.

The sounds, too, are concentrated and serious. There is the occasional clank of weights being released, the soft murmur of conversation, a short shout of triumph, the blend forming a total, harmonious symphony punctuated by a percussion of groans and grunts.

5

The Power Company is a gym for men, all kinds of men. Tucked away behind a corner shopping mall on Franklin Boulevard in Hollywood, it is not now and never has been a place for dilettantes. The men who go there tend to look down their noses at the YMCAs and coed gyms where other men loiter to pick up women, and vice versa. This was a place where you go to work out and improve. It had no other purpose, no distractions.

The events of the morning were therefore somewhat surprising.

First, there was a fire in the changing room. Apparently someone threw a cigarette in the paper towel wastebasket. There was more smoke than fire, but it took a company of firemen to find that out.

Next, Barry Shortridge, a relatively new member, ignored the advice of his trainer and tried to press 250 pounds. The barbell fell on his throat. Luckily someone heard the strange choking sounds and rushed over to help him before he died. As it was, at the very least he had ruptured his windpipe and was carted off to a hospital by an ambulance.

Finally, a fight erupted in the sauna when Dudley Carter apparently made a pass at Nick Valenti. Carter weighed in at about 180, while Valenti was close to 260. Eyewitnesses heard Valenti shout, "This isn't a fucking fag gym," just before the sauna door fell from its hinges, closely followed by Carter.

That Carter was already unconscious didn't stop Valenti from trying to kill him. It took three men, including "Tiny" Naylor, who outweighed Valenti by fifty pounds, to tear him off his hapless would-be suitor.

The police arrived toward the end of the melee and wisely stood back and waited for Valenti to calm down. Still, they drove the third siren-bearing automobile of the morning.

All of which prompted the fifty-two-year-old owner of the gym, Bob Fergusson, to scratch his bald head philosophically and say, "Things happen," when Sean Parker arrived at noon and asked with his normal cheerful smile how things were going.

Sean lay on his back on a bench, his chest burning as he fought for breath, his eyes closed. Beside him he could hear Billy, the trainer, tell someone, "Next week try and increase the number of sets to twenty-five."

Without opening his eyes, Sean knew that Billy would be writing as he spoke, keeping his usual perfect record of every customer's progress.

"Jesus," Sean managed to exhale. He hadn't come in for four days, and now he felt the consequences. Every muscle in his shoulders and arms ached. He should have been smart enough to anticipate the reaction and cut back a little. But he hadn't, and by tomorrow he'd not only be stiff but pain would accompany his every movement.

He thought he could just lie there and perhaps even fall asleep, but instead he opened his eyes to the glare of the overhead lights. He'd feel better if he took a sauna and a hot shower. Grimacing slightly, he sat, swinging his feet to the floor.

"How'd you do?" Billy asked. At 210 pounds and 5 feet 6 inches, he looked like a bulging fireplug with perfect definition.

"Did too much," Sean managed to say.

"You should know better," Billy said with a frown and walked away.

True enough. Sean had been diligently coming to the gym for almost two years; by now he should have learned to pace himself more intelligently, but the play in which he was starring had kept him away and the frustrations that came with being an actor had built up. He'd needed this outlet, and it wouldn't have been effective if he had pussyfooted around.

The play was due to open in a week and, as usual, the tension among the cast, between cast and director, between director and producer, among costume designers and lighting technicians and sound men and everyone else involved, was reaching a pitch that would soon become a frenzy. He didn't regret it — it went with the territory — but every now

7

and then he needed to uncap the pressure. For some reason, it was getting to him a little more than usual—probably, he'd decided, because the stakes were higher.

He gathered his towel off the floor, wiped his face, and stood, a tall, fair-haired man of twenty-nine, a little on the slender side compared to most of the others in the gym, but a standout because of his face. No matter how many weights the others pressed, none of them would ever be able to develop the same chiseled profile, the startling turquoise eyes, or the wide, strong mouth, creased at the edges by frequent laughter. It was one of those rare disarming faces that both men and women found attractive, as Sean had discovered at an early age, somewhat to his consternation.

Part of his attractiveness had to do with his genuine and obvious lack of vanity. He knew he was handsome—after all, he was an actor, a profession where good looks were a definite asset—but he was totally unself-conscious about it, without an arrogant bone in his body, so much so that it always shocked him slightly when someone complimented him on his appearance.

"Hey, Sean, how's it going?" A stocky, dark man in his forties gave him a smile as he passed, heading for the floor. Jimmy Fedora was a character actor, which is what they called actors who get only third or fourth billing yet earn the envy of their peers by working steadily.

Sean would have loved to be called a character actor if it meant steady work, but his looks were a definite hindrance. He had the face of a romantic lead, and there weren't that many parts available for romantic leads, unless you were a major star. Since arriving from Seattle three years earlier, he had done a couple of television commercials and had garnered supporting and then lead parts in a number of Equity-waiver stage productions—the official title for small theater where you get paid only in experience, praise, and admiration. All in all, his career had hardly taken off like a rocket.

He entered the sauna room and lowered himself to the wooden bench, sitting with his elbows on his knees. The heat was instant and relaxing and gave the illusion at least that it

8

was also healing.

Another man peered around the door to see if there was space and then bustled in, murmuring a greeting. He was Alex something-or-other, and Sean knew from previous conversations that he was an advertising copywriter.

"How's the acting coming along?" Alex asked. In his early thirties with a flat, swarthy face, his large brown eyes were perpetually rounded as if by surprise.

"Just fine," Sean said. "How's the advertising?"

"It's cool. Same old stuff. Are you appearing in anything now?"

"A play at the Outpost Theater. It's due to open in a week," Sean said.

Felix sat, groaned once, and said, "I don't know the Outpost. Where is it?"

"Los Feliz," Sean said, thinking that a large part of his problem was that nobody knew where the Outpost was. Little theaters generally had a core audience of subscribers. Usually run under a budget that didn't support advertising, they languished in martyrdom to their art without even being noticed by the general public. People rarely stumbled over theaters by accident.

"Is that where you're based?" Alex asked.

"Not particularly. I auditioned for the play and the producer rented the theater for its run." He was being polite, answering the questions but not creating the conversation further. Although normally social and outgoing, at this moment he wanted nothing more than silence.

Part of the problem was that the damn play was becoming too important to him, he told himself. A few months ago he had almost thrown in the towel as an actor. After all, how long could a person persist without winning the game?

He had seriously reassessed his goals. He wasn't getting any younger and all he had to show for it was a degree in drama, some nice reviews, and careers as a waiter, a chauffer, a telephone salesman, and a tour guide. Perhaps, he had argued with himself, he would be better off finding a real career, pursuing his love of acting as a devoted amateur.

In the final analysis, however, the thought appalled him. He was dedicated to this strange, egotistical craft, and good at it, even though his attempts to work as a professional had been less than successful. He decided to give himself two more years. After that, he would start to develop a career as a high school drama teacher, or something equally depressing.

And then this opportunity had come, an unsolicited gift from the gods. The play was written by a friend of his, Oscar van Houten, and also provided a big break for Oscar. Michael Falwell, the well-known film director, loved the play and wanted to direct, and Falwell's boyfriend of the moment agreed to put up the money to produce. What set this apart from other such vanity productions was that Falwell had started in theater twenty years earlier. He had gone on to acclaim as a film director and his return to the stage would doubtless be a heralded event in Hollywood.

It would be a showcase production of sorts. Half of the important people in Hollywood would be there during the first few shows, a plus not only for Falwell but for everyone one connected with the play. When Sean won the lead role he saw it as the best opportunity he'd ever had, a chance to really attract the kind of attention he needed, something to set him apart from the other thousands of hopeful semiprofessionals in Los Angeles.

The fact it was important to him was, of course, what added to the normal pressures.

The "normal" pressures included being out of a job and close to broke, being without a girlfriend, and about to be homeless after housesitting for a friend who would be returning from a location shoot sooner than expected. Add to that a director who was not only an asshole but who had also forgotten what he learned in the theater so many years before, and a producer who sat in on all the rehearsals and constantly whispered "advice" in the director's ear, more often than not also nipping at the lobe of said ear with sharp, affectionate teeth. It was all very distracting.

Sean must have sighed very loudly, because Alex looked over and said, "I've always admired actors. It takes a lot of guts to do what you do."

"Or stupidity," Sean said.

Alex grunted. "Who's stupid? You doing what you like, or me pulling down a hundred grand a year being a whore?"

Sean shrugged and said, "Who knows?" It wasn't a conversation he wanted to get into. He picked up his towel and said "See you later."

"Good luck with the show," Alex called after him.

Walking across the tiled floors toward the showers, he remembered the words of his drama teacher seven years earlier, "There are about four reasons people become actors: one, they want fame, which they think brings the Three P's — pussy, power, and prestige; two, they are too inept to do any real work; three, their monumental arrogance has led them to overestimate their attractiveness and abilities, and; four, they love acting before an audience. What's your reason?"

The answer he gave then was still the same. *God help me*, he thought as the water slashed across his face, *I love it*.

The Outpost Theater sat between a laundromat and a health food store on Vermont Avenue. The marquee in front of the building said, *"Princely Passion*, Directed by Michael Falwell, Starring Sean Parker and Janet Whittaker. Opening Soon."

Sean drove his battered Volkswagen Bug down the alley, swerving to avoid an overflowing garbage container, and parked in the metered city lot behind the theater. He looked at his plastic Casio watch. After six. He wouldn't have to pay for parking.

He had recovered his usual sense of optimistic well-being. The play was excellent, he knew that, and he was doing a good job with the part, as good as anything he had ever done. No matter what else was going on in his life, at least he had that.

He clambered stiffly from the car. In spite of the sauna, shower, a short nap in the afternoon, and another shower an hour ago, he was feeling the effects of his workout. He resolved to return the next morning and push through it.

The thought reminded him, however, that his membership in the gym was due to expire in a week. Bob Fergusson had discreetly taken him aside as he was leaving and pointed out that he needed to come up with another five hundred dollars for the coming year. It didn't seem very possible in the light of current events. Well, he thought, refusing to let realities depress him, he could always start jogging again.

There were a dozen people already in the theater: a secretary, the assistant director, the set director and his helpers, the sound technician. Most of them greeted him as he walked along the hall toward the stage.

Janet Whittaker stood on one side of the stage, her arms tightly folded across her chest, muttering lines to herself, oblivious to her surroundings.

He had worked with Janet in another play about a year before and had discovered then that she was very intense. She was also good, once she loosened up. A tall blonde, slim to the point of thinness, with an uneven nose and a slightly lopsided smile, she had a small crush on him, he suspected. While friendly and forthcoming with her, he hadn't encouraged more as was usually the case in his relations with women, it just seemed to happen, regardless of his desires.

She saw him then and smiled. "I was just going over the history scene in my mind. It doesn't feel quite right to me," she said, stepping toward him.

"What is it?" he asked.

"I think Michael wants us to play it a little soft. My instincts are to go harder," she said, troubled.

She was right. Falwell was looking at the scene as a film director. It didn't play the same way on the stage.

"Well, just go a little harder today, a little harder tomorrow, and so on. If you're subtle, he won't even notice."

She brightened up. "You think so?"

"I know it," he said. Falwell was not the most perceptive director he had ever worked with.

"I'm really enjoying working with you again," she said, her

voice growing softer. She had pale blue eyes and her skin smelled of peaches.

"Me too," Sean replied.

Two more members of the cast arrived, Josh Prophet and Patrick Crowell. They dodged three crew members carrying a long plywood prop and joined Sean and Janet on the stage.

"Hey, how's every little thing?" Josh asked.

"Still firm," Janet said.

"Mein Herr is not here yet?" Josh asked. He didn't like Falwell much and spoke derogatorily of him whenever he got the chance.

"We're a little early," Sean said mildly. He never liked to contribute to cast tensions and generally kept his likes and dislikes to himself.

"I've never had to work so hard in my life," Patrick complained, a definite feminine lilt to his voice.

"It's the price you pay for fame and fortune!" came a sardonic voice. Oscar van Houten, the playwright, stood near the bottom of the stage. He was a formidable figure, six-two in height with gray, shoulder-length hair and the battered face of a prizefighter. His nose had been broken three times, twice by ex-wives, as he was always proud to point out. Although only in his mid forties, he looked at least ten years older.

He jumped nimbly onto the stage and walked toward them. "Work was given to us by the gods so that we could retain our sanity in an essentially purposeless world," he said. He reached Janet and put an arm around her shoulder. "Actresses were given so that playwrights would have a reward for working. Have you decided to sleep with me yet?" he asked her.

Janet turned her nose up playfully at the familiar banter. "You're old enough to be my father," she said.

"A perfect blend of genius and experience," he said. "Food for the mind and satisfaction for the body."

"I'm not hungry," she said.

"The only result of wasted opportunities is regret."

"Yeah, but regret also comes from foolish acts," she said.

"Aagh," Oscar groaned. "You drive me to the level of cliche: Nothing ventured, nothing gained!"

Sean smiled at the exchange, as he always did. Janet, in her mid twenties, was more than a match for the older man. But he also knew that she was fighting a losing battle. He had known Oscar for two years, and the colorful playwright usually got what he wanted, particularly when it came to women.

"Protect me, Sean," she said with a warm smile at him.

Oscar raised an eyebrow. "You seek refuge with the gallant Sir Sean? That's like the chicken asking the fox for protection."

"With some foxes you don't mind," she said, taking Sean's arm.

He was rescued from comment by the noisy arrival of Michael Falwell. "Hi, ho, cast!" Falwell shouted from the door. Behind him was the producer, his boyfriend Glen Oakley, and a party of four well-dressed men and women.

"I have some friends who'd like to watch us rehearse today," Falwell said as he walked down the aisle. "I hope nobody minds."

Sean and Oscar exchanged looks and Oscar grimaced irritably. Falwell had breached protocol. He should have asked permission of the cast before bringing spectators. Everyone was nervous and highstrung at this point and a gallery of unknown onlookers wouldn't help.

Oscar swallowed whatever he was about to say and looked away, as if interested in what a stagehand to his left was doing. Although not normally reticent to express his opinions, he wasn't about the bite the hand feeding him. The production of this play was as important to him as it was to Sean, if not more so.

Sean shrugged. Falwell hadn't shown much consideration for anyone other than himself so far; it was probably unrealistic to expect him to change now.

His guests sat in the front row while Falwell joined the actors on stage. He was a tall and thin man in his early fifties, with a beaked nose, a sardonic, thin-lipped mouth, and hair

14

artfully silvered on the sides.

Seven years earlier, he had won an Oscar for a film called, prophetically enough, *Quality*, but since then the gods had deserted him. Nothing he had done remotely approached the success (or quality) of that movie, and in Hollywood, memories were unmercifully short. They stretched back two, perhaps three films, if you were lucky.

It was well known that Falwell was no longer offered the plum assignments, hence the true reason for his return to the stage. The attendant publicity wouldn't hurt, particularly if the play was a success.

None of this was openly stated, of course. Like everyone else, Sean had heard Falwell's public pose that he needed to flex his "creative muscles," because film was too confining. Everyone in the business knew it was a crock, but directors and other creative people were allowed to say things like that. Hollywood could afford to be indulgent toward its failures.

"You look in fine form tonight, my dear," Falwell said to Janet.

"I think it's coming along nicely," she said seriously.

"It's my job to see that it does," Falwell said, pomposity coloring his voice.

"What an asshole," Oscar muttered to Sean, who just shook his head.

Falwell clapped his hands together and beamed at his cast, "All right, children," he said gaily. "Let's take it from the top."

Owing mainly to the presence of the guests, it was an exhausting rehearsal, even though Falwell ended an hour earlier than normal. Janet had persistent trouble with a particular scene; Falwell launched a sarcastic barrage of criticism at Patrick, who then sulked for the rest of the evening, and Sean felt as if he was trapped in an asylum with the inmates.

Falwell sailed on unfazed, maintaining a superior attitude of pained patience through it all, demonstrating to his little audience what a masterful job he was doing in spite of the

15

dunderheads he had to work with. The fact that all the actors saw through the pose and resented it didn't help matters.

It was therefore with some relief that Sean heard the director force a cheerful tone and say, "That's it for tonight, kids."

For a moment Sean experienced the curious state of confusion that always came at the end of a rehearsal or performance: concentration lifted, and with it a certain reality was replaced by another. Unnoticed people appeared from the shadows in which they had been standing, the rows were suddenly alive with motion, doorways opened, lights changed, and harsh noises signaled the advent of it all. It was like moving from one dream into another.

Janet was talking in the aisle to one of Falwell's guests, a tall, affluent man in a black cashmere jacket. At the end of the stage, Oscar gesticulated to Falwell, explaining a point.

"You're very good," said a voice a little behind him.

Sean turned to see one of the women who had come in with Falwell. A tall brunette, she wore an immaculately tailored rose-colored suit. Her earrings were gold, as was the necklace that ringed her neck. Green-eyed, her mouth artful, her voice husky and intimate, she was a picture of California self-fulfillment — wealthy self-fulfillment.

"Thank you," Sean said, placing her in the mid thirties.

She held out a slim hand. "Nancy Hamilton."

He took it, surprised at the firmness with which she gripped his. "Sean Parker."

"I know," she said with a quick smile. "Jerry told us. I hope you didn't mind us sitting in on the rehearsal."

"Uh, no," he said automatically. "You're all friends of his?"

"Acquaintances," she said. "I think you are going to have a triumph with this part."

"Well, it's a good part," he said, a little uncomfortably, adding, "You work in the business?"

"Peripherally," she said with that same fleeting smile. "As a matter of fact, Jerry mentioned that you were looking for a job?"

"Well, I'm kind of in between things right now . . ."

A card appeared in her hand and approached him. He

16

took it, half looking down as she said, "Give me a call, I might be able to help you. In fact, I think I have a good opportunity for you."

"Really?" he said with interest. "What kind of—"

"Whoops, it looks like everyone is leaving," she said, interrupting him. "Please call and make an appointment to see me. I'll explain everything to you then."

"Well, thank you," he said.

"I recognize potential when I see it." Another smile, and then she turned and left the stage.

Sean looked at the card. The title of manager was below her name. The name of the company was Debonaire, and there was a telephone number. No address.

"Nice piece of ass," Oscar said, approaching him.

"What's Debonaire?" Sean asked.

Oscar looked at the card and shrugged. "Beats me. Was she hitting on you?"

"I don't think so," Sean said. "She said something about a job."

"Oh, sure," Oscar said with good-natured sarcasm.

Sean didn't bother replying. He had been approached by women often enough to know when sex was involved. Whatever her interest in him, it wasn't sexual. He slipped the card into his pocket and out of his mind. "What did you think of the rehearsal?" he asked.

"It was good," Oscar said. "You were good. I'm a little concerned about one scene, though."

"Oh, which one was that?" Sean asked, professional again.

Oscar was in the middle of explaining his concerns when Janet joined them and said she was uncomfortable with the very lines he was talking about.

"Well, we'll work on them," Sean said.

Janet's face was flushed and her eyes bright. It was amazing how alive she became after working. "I thought we could grab something to eat," she said to Sean. "We can talk about it over food."

Sean was about to refuse automatically, but in truth he had nothing better to do. "Sure," he said.

"Oh, good," Janet said, taking his arm.

"Watch out, Sean. The young lady has designs on you," Oscar said, watching with amusement.

Janet stuck out her tongue. "This is work," she said.

"It's always work," Oscar replied sardonically.

Sean had a sinking feeling that Oscar was right, but it was too late, and he was too well-mannered to back out.

Oscar winked at him. "Don't bend down to pick up the soap," he murmured.

Janet looked momentarily puzzled, but Sean knew what he meant. It was the punch line of a typically crude Oscar joke, a list of things you should never do in a homosexual community. Although not directly applicable to Janet, the connotation was unmistakeable.

"What?" Janet began, then tossed her head irritably at Oscar. "It doesn't matter," she said, adding perceptively. "It's probably something gross."

Still holding Sean's arm, she led him away.

Chapter Two

Sean heard a muted murmur of satisfaction as a warm, smooth leg curled around his. He lay still with his eyes closed. It took him at least ten seconds to realize he was in Janet's bed and to remember what had happened the previous night. He felt the urge to run, allowed it to subside, and replaced it with a distinct sense of regret.

It wasn't the act of sex, he told himself; that had been pleasant enough. It was the repercussions that would surely follow.

He suppressed the urge to groan and instead concentrated on keeping his breathing calm. He could only do it for so long and then he would have no choice but to open his eyes and wish her a good morning, to smile and submit to the display of affection that was also certain to come.

Dinner, as it had turned out, was at her apartment. There had also been two bottles of wine, a stream of conversation (mainly from her), and then the inevitable.

He hadn't exactly fought her off when she threw herself on him with statements of undying devotion, he thought wryly. In fact, it had been extremely pleasant. She was an attractive woman and lively company. When he cautioned her that he did not feel the same degree of attraction toward her as she claimed to feel toward him, she had laughed carelessly and said, "I'm not asking you to love me, baby, just to fuck me."

Fair enough. She'd read the warning label, he told himself, even though another little cautionary voice whispered better advice: Never believe what a woman, *any* woman, says in these circumstances. No matter how many strings she says aren't there, she really wants to be loved. The sex is just a ploy to gain the ultimate goal. No matter what she says, that's what she wants—what they all want.

Another groan beside him, and the leg grew more persistent, the sole of her foot running against his shin.

"Mmm," he said, as if in his sleep, and turned slightly to sink his head deeper into the pillow.

What was it Oscar had said on this subject? "Women talk about wanting truth, trust, and friendship. It's all bullshit. Women don't want to hear the truth. Can't stand it. All they really want is to know you love them, where you've been with whom, and when you're coming back." Cynical cocksman though Oscar was, Sean's own experience hadn't contradicted the basic validity of what he had said.

He felt a hand slide over his hip toward his groin, find its target, and gently stroke it. He sighed resignedly. No matter what his mind said at this point, his body would react as it wished to. Sure enough, even as the thought occurred, his penis begin to expand.

"Hi," he said, turning his head.

Raised on one elbow, Janet looked down on him with soulfully affectionate blue eyes and said softly, "Hello, darling."

And this comment, more even than his own fearful thoughts, chilled him. He forced a smile. "I'd die for a cup of coffee," he said.

"In a little while." The hand gripped him remorselessly now. "The coffee machine will turn on automatically. We still have time."

"I have to go to the bathroom," he said, and fled.

The bathroom did not prove to be a lasting refuge. Rescue finally came (too late, but it came) in the form of Janet's realization that she had an appointment for a casting call.

They had made love for a second time and were standing in the kitchen drinking coffee when she looked at her watch and shrieked. "Oh, God! I'm supposed to go on a call!"

She rushed out of the room to change, leaving Sean alone with a mug in one hand, in a bathrobe that reached above his knees. He sighed and sat at the table to contemplate his life in relative quiet — except for the sounds of muffled curses and crashing bottles that came from the bathroom.

This type of one-night stand would have to stop, he told himself. Quite understandably, women always wanted more, and for him to commit to nothing except a few hours of sex was not only a disappointment for them but a form of dishonesty on his part, a kind of cheating. The fact that they generally believed what they wanted to believe, in spite of anything he might or might not say, didn't really diminish his responsibility. He knew his intentions, and if they did not include any kind of long-range relationship, he would be better off just not getting involved.

Easy to say but hard to practice. Women liked him; women wanted him. It was so much easier to acquiesce to their desires.

He shook his head and sipped at the strong black coffee. Since his last long-term relationship, one that had ended in literal disaster, there had been a string of these "flings," for want of a better term. Some had lasted one night, a couple had lasted as long as a week. None had ultimately satisfied him.

Maybe everything would change if the play became a success. If it led to paying jobs he would have money in his pocket, the ability to meet a different circle of people. Right now, if he met a woman who attracted him, he wouldn't even be able to afford treating her to dinner. As for taking anyone back to "his place," in a few days he wouldn't even have the place he was currently borrowing. Perhaps if things changed he would meet someone who could hold his attention for longer than a week.

Janet dashed back into the kitchen. She wore high-heeled shoes, a black leather skirt, and a blue silk blouse. Her long blonde hair was tied up.

"What's the part?" he asked, raising his eyebrows.

"Hooker," she said, leaning down to kiss his cheek. "I've got to run. Let yourself out and be sure to lock the front door. My neighbor got robbed three weeks ago."

"Sure," he said.

"I'll see you tonight at rehearsal," she said. She stopped at the door and looked back at him with a frown. "Sean?"

"Yes?"

"Last night? It was fun for both of us, right?"

He nodded.

"Well, it's back to business tonight, right? I don't think we should get involved in a serious kind of relationship while we're working together, right?"

He stared at her blankly for a second and then nodded again. "Oh, yeah, right. I agree. You're perfectly right," he said.

Janet smiled with obvious relief and said, "I'll see you later," and disappeared.

He heard the front door close, then leaned back in his chair, his face now registering his surprise. And then he began to roar with laughter.

When the laughter subsided, he ruefully admitted to himself that he still had a few things to learn about women.

Back in his own apartment, after eating a boiled egg and a slice of slightly stale bread, Sean looked at the card the woman had given him at rehearsal last night.

"Nancy Hamilton, Manager, Debonaire."

Sean wasn't naturally cynical, but a few years in Los Angeles had cured him of his original wide-eyed optimism. Life was a two-way flow. People who wanted to give you something usually wanted something in return. And often, it seemed, they wanted something from you without giving anything in return.

And yet . . .

He reached for the telephone and dialed the number.

When the receptionist answered he asked for Nancy Hamilton and gave his name. A moment later the calm, husky voice came on the line. "Sean, I'm so glad you called."

"Well, I thought I'd find out a little more about the job," he said, a trifle cautiously.

"Hold on a second, will you? I have to take another call."

The line went dead for a moment and then she returned. "Could you come in and see me this afternoon?" she asked. "Right now it's difficult to talk. Would two o'clock be all right?"

"Couldn't you tell me what's involved?" he asked.

"I'm sorry, I have to take this call. Come in at two and we can talk at leisure. I guarantee it will be worth the trouble."

"Well . . ."

"See you at two," she said. "North Tower, Century City." And hung up.

Sean stared at the silent receiver and then replaced it, slightly irritated.

Maybe he should just forget it. He didn't like getting hustled and he had the feeling that it had just happened. On the other hand, he didn't have much to lose except an hour or two. Time was about the only thing he had in abundance.

The North Tower in Century City was filled with banks, lawyers, theatrical agents, insurance companies, and a host of companies with names like Debonaire, none of which gave any clue to their activities.

Sean took the elevator up to the seventh floor and followed the signs, walking through a maze of corridors navigable only by moles and rabbits. Finally, after stopping twice for directions, he reached a door with a sign that simply said "Debonaire."

The reception area consisted of comfortable chairs, a couch, a table strewn with magazines. On the couch, two men in their twenties, both good-looking and casually dressed, idly flicked through magazines. A pretty blonde receptionist of about nineteen leaned over a desk, speaking softly into the telephone. She finished the conversation she was having on the phone, something about a man named

Jerry and his future, which she was unsure of, then asked Sean how she could help him.

"Sean Parker to see Nancy Hamilton," he said.

She took in his face and then the rest of his body and smiled. "Just a moment, please," she said, picked up the phone again, and spoke his name into it. "She'll be right out," she said, replacing the receiver. "Please sit down."

He stood in the center of the room, optimistically assuming that "right out" meant fairly immediately. Sure enough, a moment later the door opened and Nancy appeared.

She wore a dark business suit that did nothing to hide her slim legs, and her hair was tied back, adding to the professional look. "Come in," she said, holding the door open. He smelled a faint perfume as he walked past her.

She led him down another small corridor and then through the first door into her office. There was a desk, two chairs opposite it, a telephone with a dazzling array of buttons and blinking lights, a couch against one wall, two pictures above it, and a view of Beverly Hills through the only window.

"Please sit down," she said, taking one end of the couch. He followed her lead and lowered himself on the other end. "Would you like some coffee or anything?"

"No, thank you," he said, looking up and seeing that she was examining him, as if to reassure herself that it was the same person she had met the previous night.

"Let me tell you about the job," she said, coming directly to the point at last. "It is perfect for someone with your skills, an actor that is. The hours are flexible, the pay is good, and there are a number of side benefits. Sound interesting?"

"So far," he said. "What exactly do I do?"

"Debonaire provides a service to businesswomen visiting from out of town, wealthy single women who live here, or any lady who needs what we provide: a distinguished male escort to accompany her to parties, events, the theater, etcetera."

"An escort service?" Sean said, unable to hide his incredulity.

"A very distinguished agency for distinguished people," she

24

said, her eyes wary as she watched him.

Sean began to smile, amused at the idea. He shook his head. "I'm afraid this isn't for me," he started to say.

She held up her hand. "Let me explain," she said. "Debonaire is exactly what it claims to be, an escort agency. The agency books the date, sets the fee, pays an hourly fee to the escorts. You are not required to do anything except be the perfect gentleman. We do not advertise. We have a very high-class clientele who come to us through referrals."

"There's nothing else involved," he said dubiously. "No other demands. Just to escort these ladies places . . ."

Nancy smiled. "You're right to be suspicious. We can't guarantee the emotions of the clientele. There may be other . . . requests. But whether or not you comply is up to you. Completely. Nobody can force you to do anything against your wishes. I might add, however, that if there are *gifts* from satisfied clients, our escorts are allowed to keep them, over and above the salary. Some of our men make significant amounts of money."

"Yeah, well," Sean said doubtfully. "I don't think I'd be comfortable with it."

"Think about it," she urged, adding persuasively, "When you really look at what's involved, all you have to do is act. You are the charming, gallant escort, the companion of a wealthy woman. You'll be playing a part, just as you do on the stage, except this will be much more interesting—more like improvisational theater, right? And you'll get paid very well for it. Nobody has ever complained that the work is boring here, and some of our escorts make a thousand, two thousand dollars a week. Can you afford to turn down an opportunity like that?"

He shook his head, but whether at the enormity of the money or at the concept, he wasn't sure. And then he stood.

"Well . . ." he said.

"At least think about it," she urged, also standing.

"I'll think about it," he agreed, and walked to the door. He stopped there and turned as a thought struck him. "How did you pick me? Do you scout all the little theaters in L.A. for suitable prospects?"

She smiled at the absurdity. "Someone gave me your name and told me I'd find you there."

"Who?"

"A woman I know," she said. "Marina White."

Sean drove inattentively along Santa Monica Boulevard toward Hollywood, his mind definitely not on the present.

He hadn't seen or heard of Marina in almost nine months. More than a year earlier they had been in love. But after living together for a while, they had ended their affair in an abrupt explosion of recriminations.

Marina was an actress, a good one. Originally from New York, she appeared in numerous off-Broadway, regional, and stock productions. Her television work included guest appearances on shows such as "LA Law," "The Wonder Years," "Star Trek," and more. A couple of years earlier she had won a Los Angeles Drama Critics' Circle Award for her appearance as Isabel in *Period of Adjustment*, the Tennessee Williams play.

They met at a party and fell in love almost immediately. She was exciting, funny, and sophisticated, and, of course, beautiful. For the first two months, everything was wonderful between them.

And then . . .

Sean took Crescent Heights up to Sunset Boulevard, still hardly noticing his surroundings. He hadn't thought of Marina for a while, and was unpleasantly surprised to find that there was still a painful sense of loss associated with the memories.

. . . And then he had discovered the truth of the cliche: Love is indeed blind. After those first months he began to notice cracks in the idyllic picture. The problem was that although Marina was a good actress, she hadn't had a job in five months, and it was eating away at her. Unlike Sean, she wasn't able to handle rejection very well.

The first signs were evident in her increasingly negative

26

attitude. She'd go out on calls and come back filled with the bitter conviction that she hadn't got the part. As these turned out to be self-fulfilling prophecies, her resultant anger was somewhat surprising and certainly inappropriate.

The second stage was more serious. She began to hang out with a crowd Sean didn't care for: fringe celebrities, lissome young models who were too naive to see how they were being used, associated wanna-be's, and, of course, the dealers who found these insecure people suitable prey.

When she first started using cocaine she laughed at his concern. "It's recreational," she said. "What's wrong with getting high?" As he used nothing stronger than beer and wine, he didn't have a ready answer. But it soon became evident that there was something definitely wrong with getting high.

Her descent was almost too fast to chronicle. Marina became shrill, moody, and demanding — all in all, hell to live with. He tried his best to help her, but her anger and bitterness and blatantly manipulative behavior overwhelmed him. The bouts of manic anger, the euphoric highs and the deep depressions that invariably followed — they all became too much for him to handle. She had taken to cocaine like a hungry pig in a corn truck. Although he never touched drugs, he was sinking into despondency with her.

The last straw came when he found that she had stolen money from him. He moved out, terribly saddened, but his commitment to his own survival was too strong. He knew that it was being undermined and that sooner or later if he stayed with her that commitment would be dangerously compromised.

He wished her well and left. She cursed him. They hadn't spoken since.

Until now.

He called her as soon as he arrived at the apartment in which he was staying.

"Sean?" She sounded delighted and surprised to hear from him.

Once you lived with a druggie, suspicion stuck to you like a terminal disease, Sean thought. Who knew what chemical

27

was responsible for her current mood? He responded cautiously.

"Hi, how are you?" he asked.

"I'm fine. How are you?"

"Good, good. I got offered a job. Apparently you recommended me."

"Oh, Debonaire! Did you talk to Nancy? Did you take the job?"

"Why'd you recommend me, Marina?"

"I wanted to do you a favor. It's easy work, and the money's better than any of the jobs you've had."

"It's not my kind of thing," he said.

"Oh, Sean. You're so straight. It's just a high-paying acting job." She was echoing Nancy Hamilton's line. The difference was that her voice was hyper, embellished with a false brightness. He was sure she was high.

"You don't have to do anything you don't want to do," she continued into his silence. "You'll make great contacts. A lot of their clients are in the business. And you won't have to worry about money. At least try it. If you don't like it, you can always quit."

"Hiring myself out," he said.

"What do you think you're doing every time on stage?" she asked harshly. "Don't you need the money? Jesus! You can make at least a grand a week."

He avoided the issue and said, "How are you doing, Marina?"

"Will you come and visit me?" she asked.

"Are you still doing coke?"

She didn't answer.

"No," he said. "As long as you're driving yourself crazy, I can't see you."

He hung up and stood in the living room, staring down at the receiver. He realized that he'd forgotten to thank her for the job referral, but it didn't matter.

The theater was curiously still when Sean arrived for rehearsal that evening. He walked down the aisle and realized that the usual noise was absent: no carpenters or electricians, and nobody in the sound booth.

He looked at his watch. He was only five minutes early.

Janet arrived a moment later. "Where is everyone?" she asked, approaching the stage where he stood.

Sean shrugged. "Beats me. Maybe they weren't needed tonight."

"Well, I think we were just going to work on the scene with the two of us," she said uncertainly.

"How are you doing?" he asked, remembering the previous night.

"Oh, fine. The audition went really well. I have a feeling I got the part."

Apparently their tryst was no longer on her mind, but he wasn't hurt. "That's great!" he said. He really was happy for her. His peers so seldom worked, it was a pleasure for them all when one of them got a job.

"Yeah, it's not that big, but I think it's exciting. The director was there and I think he really liked me."

"Wonderful."

Oscar arrived next. He waited in the doorway and gazed at them for a moment before moving heavily down the aisle. "I bear bad tidings, children." He stopped at the foot of the stage and stared up at them.

"What?" Janet asked.

Sean examined his face and knew at once. Without hearing what Oscar had to say, he knew.

"Our gallant leader called me," Oscar said. He clambered up to the stage and then slumped down, half-facing them. "He did not wish to make an appearance due to a common condition known as cowardice. He wanted me to pass the news on to you."

"The play is cancelled," Sean said woodenly. He stepped forward and sat beside Oscar.

"What?" Janet shrieked.

Oscar nodded. "I'm afraid that's the truth. The play is no more."

"What happened?" Sean asked quietly.

"I think our heroic director refused to suck our generous backer's dick, or perhaps it was the other way around. In either case, there has been a lover's quarrel and there is no longer any money. *Ergo,* no longer any play."

"Jesus Christ," Sean said.

"How can they do this to us?" Janet asked, close to tears.

"Because we're only writers and actors," Oscar said, and for once the wry humor was missing from his voice.

"Shit, I'm sorry," Sean said. "This was a big break for you."

"Yeah. And you, too," Oscar said.

Indeed it had been, Sean thought ruefully. And he had made the amateurish mistake of counting heavily upon it. He should have known — *had* known — that the only certain thing in this business was the uncertainty. Who was it? Someone had said that Hollywood was a place that had no rules but that you broke them at your peril. Well, one of those rules was that nothing was in the bank until it was in the bank. Hell, you didn't even count a check until it had cleared, if you were smart. And he had thought he was smart.

But hope was some kind of narcotic. It blinded you to the realities, dulled your jaundiced edges, and left you open to the slings and arrows . . . So much for hope, he thought, with an uncharacteristically sharp jab of cynicism.

"Is there anything we can do?" Sean asked finally.

"Not unless you can raise the money for the play," Oscar said.

"It's not impossible. There's a lot of money around. Maybe we could put on a final rehearsal, invite some backers . . ."

"Do you know any backers?" Oscar asked cruelly. "Face it, man. We're out of here. The bills haven't been paid and we're not even going to be able to stay here another hour before the owner asks us to leave."

"The little shit," Janet said of their director.

Oscar shrugged and looked tired. "He's just another victim."

"Goddamn!" Janet said emphatically. "You can be as un-

30

derstanding as you like. I think he's a little shit!"

"Well," Sean said uncomfortably, swinging his legs to the floor, "there's no point in staying around here, I guess."

"Come on," Oscar said, putting an arm around each of them. "Let's go get drunk. On me."

"I don't think so," Sean said. "I think I'll just head on."

"Come on, it'll do you good."

"We can celebrate my audition today," Janet said almost cheerfully, and then seemed to have second thoughts about the tastefulness of her comment. "I mean . . . at least that gives us something to be happy about. I know you're both happy for me, right?"

"Of course," Sean said, "but let me take a raincheck. I'm not in the mood to go out. I need to go home."

"See you soon," Oscar said.

"Sure. I'll call you."

"Call me too," Janet said.

"I will," Sean promised.

He drove slowly back to the apartment. It was a warm night with only a faint breath of wind from the desert, enough to clean the smog out of the basin and drive the fog back out to sea. Normally he loved nights like this, but now he wasn't up to appreciation of anything much.

Shit! he thought, fighting an unexpected onslaught of tears, so close and then . . . He smiled grimly instead of crying. He should be used to it by now. Rejection and loss were the mainstays of an actor's life. Why should his be any different?

He went into the small, stuffy apartment and opened windows. He'd have to move in a couple of days when his friend came back. He could probably sack out on the couch for a day or two after Bert's arrival, but any longer than that would wear out his welcome. Time also to start looking for another job.

The thought made him shudder. Waiting tables, driving cabs. God, he was sick of it! He slumped in a living room chair. It was time for a change, some kind of major change.

He took his wallet from his pocket and removed the card

31

from it: "Debonaire."

Why not? Hell, why not? What was that Dylan line? "When you got nothin', you got nothin' to lose."

Without even thinking further about it, he reached for the telephone on the table beside him and dialed the number.

"Is Nancy Hamilton in?" he asked.

Surprisingly, she was. When he was put through, he said, "Miss Hamilton, I'd like to talk to you about the job."

Chapter Three

The girl finished the last lap and then effortlessly hoisted herself out of the pool, spinning nimbly around to sit on the side. Her long brown legs dangled into the water, artificially pale against the royal blue tiles.

"Susanne."

Her face suddenly adopted a bored expression and she lazily turned her head halfway toward the sound, as if not willing to acknowledge it. About 5' 5" and slim, in her mid twenties, with wet brown hair dangling to the small of her back, a slightly petulant mouth, and penetrating hazel eyes, she was not beautiful in a classical sense. For one thing, the strong nose was a shade too large. And yet somehow the total sum of her attributes—the flawless skin, athletic body, and the sense of vitality that emanated from her—worked together to create a strikingly attractive whole.

The woman who had spoken to her stood at the edge of the patio, framed by the sparkling French doors of the mansion. Tall, with black hair, Annette Lowell still looked at least ten years younger than her fifty years. She had obviously once been beautiful but would now be called merely a "handsome" woman. There was a severity to her face, one that came from determination and will, and it gave her an imposing presence.

"Barry Dobbs will be here in half an hour," Annette said.

Susanne looked directly at her mother and sighed. The senator would be here with his son David for one reason—so that she and David would meet. It was another of Annnette's matchmaking inspirations. "Yes, Mother, I know."

"You need to get dressed for lunch."

"Why don't we eat on the patio and keep it casual," Susanne said.

"We are eating in the dining room. Please look your best," Annette said. She turned and went back into the house. *I have spoken. There will be no further discussion*, Susanne thought, mimicking her attitude.

Susanne sighed again and reached for a towel to dry her hair. She was twenty-five, what her mother considered "prime marriageable age." The fact that Susanne wasn't interested in marriage was insignificant when compared to her mother's plans. Nor did Annette want just any marriage. That wouldn't do for a Lowell. It had to be what she called a "strategic marriage," one that would complement her vast business interests, interests that Susanne would one day inherit and operate, as her mother so often reminded her.

Their discussions on this subject had been frequent and volatile. As Susanne often said, "These are the nineties, for God's sake. You don't arrange marriages anymore, Mother. I'll meet someone and fall in love and I won't care if he comes from a wealthy family or not." After unfailingly mentioning some of her daughter's earlier and undeniably obvious mistakes, Annette would point out: "There are plenty of eligible wealthy men. Why not fall in love with one of them, if you must exhibit that naive romanticism?"

And so it would go, Annette's determination matching Susanne's mounting anger. None of it affected the end result, which was never in doubt: Annette continued to parade before her daughter a battalion of what she considered eligible young men.

Susanne had grown used to this recurring irritation, consoling herself with the thought that even someone as resolute as her mother could not force her to marry someone she didn't want to marry. Luckily she had inherited the same trait. She could be just as resolute as her mother when she wanted to be.

Her father, Kenneth, was no help to either of them. He just looked at it all with a kind of tolerant bemusement, which was generally how he viewed life. A prominent judge in Los Angeles, he was being groomed for political life by Annette, and thus had his hands full with the machinations directed toward him. The most he had ever said to Susanne on the subject of marriage was a murmured, "Well, it's getting close to the time you should be thinking about finding a nice boy and settling down." When she asked him with barely disguised impertinence why he felt it was suddenly the right time, he had stuttered and said finally, "Well, it would make your mother happy." End of subject.

That was the problem with their family. All activity was directed toward her mother's happiness—a fact Annette would deny vehemently, saying that she had their welfare at heart, and where would they be without her?

Susanne studied the pool, the crimson flowers spilling over the patio, the glossy marble statues, the bubbling fountain, the lush, manicured lawns, the splendid blooming roses, and in the background, bordering the rear of the estate, the fruit trees. An acre in Beverly Hills. She wondered what it was worth.

Like everything, it had been bought with her mother's money. Kenneth had come from a fairly wealthy family, but by the time he met Annette, he had frittered most of it away. At that time he worked as a lawyer, earning perhaps thirty-five thousand a year in a mediocre law firm, with not much to look forward to except a partnership during his dotage. Annette had immediately taken charge of his future.

She had invested the remnants of what had once been his fortune into carefully chosen real estate and never looked back. Although leveraging their equity to dangerous levels, she had been blessed by a Southern California market that had no way to go but up, and they now owned immensely valuable property from San Diego to San Francisco. She, or rather, they, also owned or had a major financial interest in a chain of community newspapers, a chain of copy shops, liquor stores, and God knew what else.

It was not a subject that interested Susanne all that much. She apparently hadn't inherited her mother's business acumen. It was enough to know that they appeared to be enormously wealthy and that she got almost everything she wanted, including a substantial trust account that was coming her way when she turned thirty. "When you're mature enough to handle money properly," Annette had graciously explained.

Susanne had graduated from college a couple of years earlier, after majoring in English literature, and had not yet decided what to do with her life, in spite of her mother's desire that she enter the family business. The English major had been a major bone of contention between them, but she had gone with her affinities, in spite of Annette's protestations that she should get a degree in business administration.

Now she was, in essence, doing nothing, after working first as a secretary and then for a brief and frustrating period as a reader for a film development company. When she hadn't been avoiding the advances of her boss, she had spent her time wading through endless piles of miserable scripts written for the most part by illiterate and talentless "writers." It would not be, she decided, her chosen career. Before either of those jobs she had briefly tried teaching, but that too wasn't something that excited her. She was interested mainly in film, but it was a difficult business to break into at any responsible level even if you had money. And strictly speaking, she wouldn't have money until she turned thirty.

Well, enough maundering, she told herself, moving limberly to her feet. She'd better get ready for yet another command performance. It would probably be a disappointment—if she were foolish enough to expect anything. Most of the men her mother tried to fix her up with were either geeks or jerks, in spite of the "good families" they were descended from. Frowning slightly, she walked into the house.

Senator Dobbs's son, David, was tall, thin, bespectacled,

and nervous.

It was hard not to be nervous around Senator Barry Dobbs, Susanne thought. There was something awesomely inhuman about his unrelenting cheerfulness. He spoke in pronouncements, endowing each phrase with total certainty and a dazzling smile. These were not his opinions, he seemed to say—his utterances, no matter how trivial, were either divinely inspired or based upon decades of experience and wisdom.

With his tanned skin, beautifully styled gray hairs and patrician face, the senator made his son look like a nonentity. David had a large nose, an almost equally large Adam's apple, and his head seemed to wobble on a spindly neck. He was an attorney, Susanne had been told, but he spoke very little, somewhat of an anomaly for someone in that profession.

"The gang problem is a drug problem. That's what I'm trying to make them understand in Washington," the senator was saying as he picked carefully at his salad. "The gangs are funded by drugs and exist because of drugs. Until we can stop the flow of this stuff into the country, we're not going to get anywhere."

"Well, why don't we attack it at the source?" Susanne's mother said. She considered herself well-informed on current issues. "Why don't we cut off funding to Colombia. Even send soldiers down there?"

The senator smiled indulgently and waved a hand. "Politics, my dear. I'm afraid there are very complicated alliances and consequences to consider."

Condescending chauvinist, Susanne thought irritably, but her mother merely smiled and said, "Something effective should be done along that line."

"And ultimately it will," the senator said. "When the best minds in the federal government finally face up to the problem, there will be effective measures."

"Your faith in government is inspiring," Annette said, with just a trace of irony.

The senator gave her a keen look, but chose to let it pass.

37

"It's all we have to make things work," he said.

"And we are very grateful you are there," Annette said generously.

Jesus! And I want to barf, Susanne thought. She had heard similar conversations between her mother and powerful local and national figures a hundred times. These people had long since ceased to impress her.

She looked over and saw David watching her, a faintly conspiratorial smile on his lips. Behind the thick glasses, she suddenly realized, an intelligent pair of brown eyes were appraising her.

Well, well, she thought. A surprise. One that reminded her once again not to judge people totally by appearances.

After lunch, at her mother's suggestion, she took David outside for a walk around the estate, showing him the gardens, the pool, the tennis courts. After being suitably impressed, he concurred with her suggestion that they sit on the patio.

"I'm sorry about this," he said, angling his long body clumsily into the chair.

"What?" she asked.

He grimaced and gave a self-deprecating shrug. "About being here, being foisted off on you, this parental matchmaking. It wasn't my idea."

"I'm the one who should apologize," she said quickly. "I think it was my mother's idea. She's always trying to set me up with someone."

"Maybe it was mutual," he mumbled. "My father does the same thing."

Susanne put a what-can-you-do? expression on her face, then said, "You're not dating anyone?"

David looked embarrassed and spoke toward his chest. "I don't have much time. Besides, I'm not very good with women. They . . . I'm not very good at it."

"I think you're a nice man," Susanne said.

"But dull," David added.

"I didn't say that," she protested. "Not everyone can be the life of the party, thank God."

"Are you dating anyone?"

"No," she said. "Not at the moment. I can't seem to get very interested in anyone that way right now."

David cleared his throat. "Would you . . . er . . . would you like to go out sometime? A concert or something?"

She hesitated and then said, "As friends?"

David looked almost relieved. "Sure. Of course."

"That would be fine," she said.

He nodded and looked away. "Do you play tennis?"

"Yes, but not very well. You?"

"Uh, yes. I played in college."

There was a long silence, and David cleared his throat again. "I don't understand why you don't date a lot. You're very . . . uh . . . pretty."

Susanne sighed. "I was going out with someone for a while recently. It didn't work out." She shrugged. "I don't seem to need that right now."

Another pause, and then Susanne asked if she could get him anything to drink. David shook his head.

"Do you like being an attorney?" she asked, enviable of the fact that he had a career.

"It's all right," he said without enthusiasm. He shook his head morosely at some thought and then said, "Did you hear about the attorney in his thirties who was killed in an automobile accident?"

"No. Who?" she asked unsuspectingly.

"Well, when he got up to the gates of heaven, he bitched at Saint Peter, claiming a mistake had been made, that he was still too young and wasn't meant to die until he was at least sixty. He demanded the right to appeal.

"So Saint Peter pulls the data up on the computer and studies it and says, 'Hmm, you're right. Okay, tell you what. You just hang out here and I'll take the data before the tribunal.' The attorney agrees, certain that justice will prevail. After all, this is heaven, right?"

"Some time later, Saint Peter comes back and says, 'Sorry, your appeal was denied. Come on through.' "

" 'That's impossible,' the attorney shrieks. 'On what

39

grounds?' "

" 'Well' Saint Peter says 'we added up your billable hours and they show you're at least sixty years old.' "

When Susanne stopped laughing, David said mildly, "It's a sometimes ignoble profession."

There was another pause and then he said, "Speaking of which, you didn't like my father much, did you?"

"He and my mother are similar types," Susanne admitted.

"Power," David said with a nod. "It's what they live for." He gave her that small smile again. "It's all right, I don't much like him myself."

Susanne smiled. "Well, even though she's my mother and all that, Annette isn't exactly the type of person I'd choose to hang out with either."

"Parents," he said, shaking his head. "In their view we never grow up."

"Ain't that the truth," Susanne said. "I think my mother stopped perceiving me when I was fifteen. In her mind, she probably still sees me the same way."

And then the very devils they were speaking of arrived. Holding the senator's arm, Annette strolled out onto the patio and said brightly, "Are you children enjoying yourselves?"

Susanne and David looked slyly at each other and then burst out laughing.

As instructed, Sean arrived at the Debonaire offices in Century City in the middle of the afternoon on Monday. Once again, a couple of good-looking young men leafed through magazines in the reception area, and once again, the same pretty receptionist showed him directly into Nancy Hamilton's office.

Nancy rose from behind her desk and walked around to shake his hand. She wore an ivory-colored linen suit, white high-heeled shoes, a simple gold and pearl chain around her neck, and looked generally immaculate.

"I'm glad you decided to join us," she said, her smile momentarily warm. She waved at the couch. "Do sit down."

He sat and she followed, crossing her legs and knitting her hands across one knee. "Would you like anything?" she asked. "Some coffee?"

"No, thank you," Sean said. He cleared his throat. "I'm still a little nervous about this."

"Of course you are," she said understandingly. "Let me give you some background. Explain how things work here."

"Good," he said.

"Our clients are discriminating women, many of them repeat customers. They like the service we provide, and a lot of it has to do with the fact that we choose our escorts with great care. Of course, clients will complain, that's just the nature of any service-related business. And some in particular will just complain on principle. However, if an escort has three complaints entered from three different customers, we no longer use him."

Sean nodded. "So if a client doesn't like an escort, has a grudge against him in some way, that's discounted."

"Exactly. Up to a point, of course. Conversely, if three of our escorts complain about the behavior of a particular client, a judgement is made whether or not to accept that person as a client anymore. Naturally, it depends upon the circumstances. At any rate, the bottom line is that our business depends upon our reputation. We avoid issues that affect it whenever possible."

The telephone buzzed. Nancy excused herself and went to her desk, sitting down and opening what looked like a large appointment book.

"Nancy Hamilton . . . Hello, Mrs. Champion. How nice to hear from you again . . . Are you in town long? I'm sure Ted would be available. Would you give me the dates . . . ?"

Sean watched her write carefully in the book and listened as she said, "Give me the flight number and time and I'll see that he meets you at the airport . . . very good . . . Will this be credit card, as usual? May I have the number and expiration date, please?" She wrote again, repeated the number and date back to the woman, thanked her, reassured her that all the arrangements were made, and hung up.

"Another satisfied customer?" Sean asked as she came back to the couch.

"A very wealthy lady from Houston," Nancy said with a smile as she sat again.

"She always asks for the same escort?"

"Yes, and he doesn't mind. She's a charming lady and very generous and appreciative."

For the first time, the idea of what he was doing began to grow real to Sean. Women actually called up Debonaire and asked for escorts! Somehow the idea struck him as funny and he fought the urge to smile.

"How much do you charge for these services and how much do the escorts get paid?" he asked bluntly, getting to the important facts.

"That's one of the first questions all my men ask," she said maternally. "It varies. We are very expensive compared to regular escort agencies, a fact that allows our men to make more money. It depends on the length of time involved, but our average charge is $300 an hour. The company takes two-thirds and the escort gets a third, which works out to about $100 an hour for you. On top of that, of course, there are tips, and some of them can be generous."

A hundred bucks an hour! Sean could hardly believe it. But he forced himself to ask a calm question. "And how often is there work?"

She shrugged. "Weekends are heaviest, but sometimes we get a rush when we least expect it. It's difficult to predict— one of the problems involved in managing this business, as a matter of fact. I would think you should have at least three appointments a week. How are you fixed for clothes? Do you own a tuxedo?"

Sean shook his head. "No. Are we required—"

"Sometimes there are formal occasions. You will definitely need a suit and good sports clothes, including jackets and ties. In fact, we encourage our men to wear jackets and ties at all times, even in casual settings, unless the client specifically requests more casual attire."

"Well," Sean said uncertainly. "I'm a little short right now. I mean I have jacket and slacks, but I don't own a suit or a tux."

"I suppose you can rent a tux, if that comes up," she said, with a small frown. "But you need some good-quality clothes."

"I can't really afford to buy anything right away," he said uncomfortably. "I have to find a place to stay in two days, and . . ."

She rose gracefully and moved to her desk, saying over her shoulder, "I think I'll be able to help you on both accounts."

Picking up the telephone she dialed an extension and said, "Ted. Can you come into my office? I want you to meet the new man I mentioned to you."

A moment later the door to her office opened and a man walked in. He was about Sean's age, perhaps a year or two older, with dark hair, sparkling green eyes, and a bright smile. His cheerfulness was contagious.

"Ted Marshall, I'd like you to meet Sean Parker."

"Hey, pleased to meet you," he said enthusiastically and bounded over to Sean, his hand outstretched. "Welcome to our little coterie."

Sean stood and shook hands with him, smiling, unable not to respond to this good cheer. "Thanks."

"Sean is looking for a place to stay," Nancy said.

"Hey, good timing," Ted said. "We've just lost a roommate. Maybe we can work something out."

"Well," Sean said, thinking about his nonexistent bank balance.

"Why don't you two talk about it?" Nancy said diplomatically. "Ted, I'd like you to show Sean the ropes anyhow. Explain the paperwork, the rules to him, and answer any questions he has, okay?"

"Delighted," Ted said, with a wink at Sean. "Consider it done."

Nancy wasn't done. "Sean, I'm going to advance you a thousand dollars on your salary. Perhaps Ted can help you with your wardrobe as well. He has excellent taste."

"Thank you," Sean said, taken aback by the generosity.

She scrawled a check out and held it out. "Here," she said. "This will help you get started, and I want you to start as soon as possible."

"I appreciate it," Sean said.

"I know a winner when I see one," she said. The statement was also a dismissal.

"Come on," Ted said. "I'll fill you in on everything."

Starting to feel as disoriented and strange as he had felt during on his first day of high school, Sean followed him down the corridor to another door, which Ted opened with a flourish. "This is kinda like the employee lounge," he explained. "We can hang out here when we're in the office."

It wasn't luxurious. There was a couch, a couple of armchairs, a radio playing some easy-listening music, and a television set that was not on. A pot of coffee sat below a coffee machine. A man reading a paperback book occupied one of the chairs. He looked up when they entered, grunted what may have been a greeting, and returned to his book.

Ted sat heavily on the couch, looked up and said, "Don't worry about it. There's nothing to it."

Sean sat cautiously beside him. "It's a little strange . . . the idea . . ."

"It's only dating," Ted said. "That's really the basis of it all. That's how you have to look at it. We're dealing with women who, for one reason or another, don't have a date and want one. All you're doing is going on a blind date."

Echoes of high school reverberated again in Sean's mind. He remembered one of his first blind dates, Annie Moore — studious, intelligent, and extremely beautiful. He had been a stammering fool and the date, set up by his best friend's girl, had been a disaster. In some small way, he'd been in love with her ever since.

"We're providing a service," Ted continued, repeating something Nancy had said, but adding facetiously, "It's a small step for you but a large step for mankind, one that we are extremely well paid for by a grateful womankind."

"I guess that's one way of looking at it," Sean said,

guardedly.

Ted changed the subject. "Let me tell about the apartment. It's in Studio City, just over the hill. I share it with Danny Perez. Three bedrooms, dining room, living room, jacuzzi, game room, laundry facilities. It's a good deal."

"How much is it?" Sean asked.

"Six-fifty apiece. It's a great area. A real bargain for what you get."

"Six-fifty?" Sean said. It was far more than he could afford at the moment.

However, he allowed himself to be persuaded to at least see the place, and followed Ted's bright red Alfa Romeo over Laurel Canyon to Ventura Boulevard, and then back a little way into the foothills.

It wasn't, he learned, an apartment, but a condominium, a luxurious complex of buildings situated in a wooded area. The architect had created the artful illusion that each unit was separated from the one beside it.

After entering the locked gates, they parked and walked through a courtyard to a door on the ground floor. "Home, sweet home," Ted said, opening it with a flourish.

The condominium covered three floors. Downstairs were the living room, kitchen, and dining room. On the next floor were two bedrooms, each with a bathroom, and upstairs was another bedroom and a small loft study.

It was indeed luxurious, particularly by Sean's standards. The carpet was lush and peach colored, the drapes hung in sinuous folds, and the furniture was modern yet comfortable chrome and leather. In the living room there was also a bar, an enormous thirty-inch television set, a stereo system to make an audiophile weep, verdant plants, and what looked like original art on the walls.

"Nice," Sean said.

Ted said from behind the bar, "Time for a drink. What would you like?"

"What have you got?"

45

"Everything," Ted said. "I'm going to have a vodka and orange juice."

"If you have gin, I'll have the same with gin," Sean said.

Taking ice out of the small refrigerator, Ted deftly poured the drinks and handed one to Sean who perched on a barstool. He came out from behind the bar and sat beside him.

"So what do you think?" Ted asked.

"It's wonderful," Sean said. "It's just more than I can afford right now."

"I wouldn't worry about that," Ted dismissed. "You're going to be rolling in money before you know it. I've been at this gig long enough to be able to tell who's going to make it and who's not. You are."

"Yeah, that's what I'm told. But it's kind of hard to believe," Sean said. He sipped his drink. It was strong. "It seems such a lot of money. I've never made that much doing anything."

A morose expression flitted across Ted's face, almost too quickly to be seen. "You'll earn it, believe me. You'll earn it," he said. "Some of these women . . ."

"How long have you been doing this?" Sean asked.

"About three years." Ted smiled, his good cheer returning. "I don't regret it at all." He waved a hand around the room. "It got me all of this—and more."

"Well, what's it like? I mean, what are the women like? These are women who pay men to take them out. It's weird."

"They're lonely," Ted said. "And for the most part they can afford to pay not to be lonely. They vary. Most of them are pretty nice. Harmless, you know. Every now and then you hit a real bitch on wheels, but that makes a nice change of pace." He laughed.

"Like what?" Sean prompted.

"Well, a couple of weeks ago, for instance, I have this woman I'm supposed to pick up, right? She lives in a condo in Marina del Rey. It's a penthouse condo, not just any condo. A million bucks of condo, if not more. She reeks of money. She comes to the door, she's about forty-five and pretty, and she's wearing a fur coat—in L.A. in summer, what's more—and diamonds are dripping from her neck.

46

And she takes one look at me, a really good up and down look, and tells me to come inside for a drink."

"You have to understand, I'm not in this business to argue with the customer, right? So I go inside for a drink. She asks what I want, I tell her, she pours me a drink, all the time not taking her eyes off me. Man, I felt naked. After about ten minutes of small conversation I suggest that we get going. She looks at me like she's looking at a piece of meat. I mean, she does everything but lick her lips, and she says, 'We're not going anywhere. I changed my mind. We're going to stay right here and party.' "

Sean stared at him as if hypnotized while he spoke. He was wondering how he'd react in a similar situation. "So what did you do?" he asked finally.

"What did I do? I fucked her brains out. The woman had a gorgeous body. What's more, she tipped me five hundred bucks." He roared with laughter.

"Does that happen often?" Sean asked nervously.

Ted shook his head. "Nah. I wish. Most of these women just want companionship. They're lonely, like I said. They don't want to go places and be seen alone all the time. They want to be seen in the company of someone good looking and personable. It's understandable, a natural human trait. Most of them are just nice people."

"Well, what would happen if you had refused this woman who wanted you to stay there with her?"

"Hey, she's paying for my time. If she wants me to stay with her, I stay with her. If she wants me to fuck her and I don't want to, that's another matter. You can usually talk your way out of that. Use your charm. But you got to remember, your time is theirs, that's what you're there for, what they're paying for. But, shit, why turn down a good fuck? This lady may have been a little old, but she was hotter than hell."

The front door opened and they both looked up. "Perfect," Ted said. "I think Danny just arrived. You'll get to meet your new roommate."

The man who entered the room was a shade under six feet

tall, lean to the point of thinness, but with a peculiar grace to his movements. Thick black hair fell calculatingly over his forehead. He had unmistakably Latin features with a straight nose, a wide, sensual mouth, and coal-black eyes that carried a hint of tolerant amusement. It all combined to give him a faintly dangerous aura. It was a face that would be attractive to most women, Sean thought.

He looked a little surprised to see Sean, but then smiled politely.

"This is Sean Parker. Meet Danny Perez, my Mexican houseboy," Ted said.

"Ha, ha," Danny said tiredly. He shook Sean's hand while Ted said, "I'm trying to talk Sean into moving in with us. He's just starting work at Debonaire."

"Very good," Danny said. "When are you moving in?" There was only the faintest trace of a Mexican accent. As an actor, Sean could tell that his voice had been consciously cultivated over a period of time.

"Well, it's a nice place, but it's a little beyond my reach. I'm kind of broke right now," Sean explained.

"Hey, don't worry about the money," Ted said. "We can carry you until you get rolling here. Can't we Danny?"

"No problem," Danny said. "The room's empty and we'd rather have someone from the business fill it. You'll have money pretty quick if you're starting work soon."

Sean looked at each of them. "Well, I really appreciate it," he said.

Ted beamed. "Then it's settled. You're here. Welcome."

"Well," Sean looked at them and then around the room. "I guess I am."

Chapter Four

Ted Marshall gunned the motor before turning off the engine of the sports car and relinquishing it to the parking valet. He enjoyed the powerful roar and the curious stares of people in the vicinity. He checked the creases of his trousers when he climbed out and then strolled toward the entrance of the pink Beverly Hills Hotel. He wore gray slacks, striped tie and navy jacket, and looked as if he belonged there.

Entering the luxuriously carpeted lobby, he walk unerringly to one of the house phones and dialed the room number he had been given.

A woman's voice answered, soft and husky, an intriguing voice.

"Good evening," he said politely. "This is Ted Marshall, here to escort you for the evening."

"I'll be down in five minutes," she said. "What color jacket are you wearing?"

"Navy," he said. "I have dark hair and green eyes."

"I'll recognize you," she said. "Just wait in the lobby."

He sat in an overstuffed chair on one side of the lobby and watched the parade of wealthy and famous. He was unawed, no stranger to this kind of life, even though his means were now somewhat limited.

The youngest son of a prominent Irish-English family in Boston, Ted had been born with the proverbial silver spoon in his mouth. His father had been quick to point out, however, that like everything else Ted touched, it soon grew tarnished. Ted had been, and still was, the black sheep of the family, a disappointment to father, mother, grandparents, uncles, and aunts. Expelled from three schools before he was seventeen, and finally kicked out of college for a carnal incident involving a dean's young wife, Ted had essentially lived on his wits since being forced into the world.

His heritage had gifted him with an Irish charm and a cold-blooded English practicality — a combination that bequeathed him a certain skill at exploiting others for his own benefit. The fact that he came in an attractive package hadn't hurt his effectiveness. On a social level, at least, he was genuinely likeable. He had discovered very early in his life that women, particularly older women, tended to adore him, a fact he took full advantage of.

He hadn't seen his father for seven years, a fact for which they were both grateful. They were separated by much more than distance. In fact, among the last words his father had spoken to him were, "You're not fit to carry the family name." Having been close to the subject, however, Ted knew that the family name was not exactly up there with the Kennedys and Cabots, and so he didn't take the admonishment too seriously. His father, who made in excess of a hundred million, had been able to buy his respectability. Nonetheless, his own beginnings had been rough, and he had attained his wealth through a combination of business acumen and an unprincipled ruthlessness.

While waiting in the lobby, Ted suddenly remembered something else his father had told him shortly before he finally left home: "You have the same ruthless nature I have, boy, but you lack an essential ingredient for success — discipline. Without that, your drive will just lead you into profligate ways."

Ted smiled, undisturbed by the memory. The old bastard had been right. He was incorrigibly profligate, but by God, he was having a good time doing it. It sure beat working twelve to eighteen hours a day as his father had done.

Fifteen minutes had passed before the tall, red-haired woman approached him. He guessed that this was his client and stood, plastering a smile on his face.

"Miss Kelly?" he said holding out his hand.

She flicked a glance over him with sparkling green eyes and took his hand in hers. "Ted, I'm pleased to meet you," she said in that husky voice.

He guessed she was somewhere in her mid forties, although she looked about five years younger than she probably was. Regardless of her age, she was a looker, with long legs, the firmest breasts money could buy, and a wide red mouth.

"You're Irish, are you?" he asked.

She raised an eyebrow. "I was once."

Ted laughed. "So was I." He put on a brogue. "And happy to forget it, I am."

"Well," she said, placing her arm through his. "We already have something in common."

They chatted pleasantly on the drive along Sunset Boulevard. They turned up Highland Avenue toward the Hollywood Bowl, where they were to attend a Mozart concert performed by the Los Angeles Chamber Orchestra.

It wasn't Ted's choice. He preferred clubs, dancing, and loud rock music. But as he knew the client was always right, he hid his feelings, talking glibly about his favorite Mozart pieces, knowledgeably salting his conversation with the names of other classical composers. Although outwardly attentive during the concert, he simply closed off the music and turned to his own thoughts.

Occasionally they talked. Miss Kelly, he discovered, came from Manhattan, where she was a headhunter for a large Wall Street investment banking firm. "Such boring people," she described them, with her low, attractive laugh. She worked there, she said, not because she had to (after all, her husband's death had left her well cared for) but because "I need the daily interaction with people. I just can't spend my life shopping and going to charity events. That's even more boring. Besides," she added meaningfully, "the job has some interesting perks."

She didn't have to spell it out. Ted had already figured out

51

that she was a woman with appetites. And many of the men she interviewed were probably attractive, and willing to put in a little extracurricular effort if it enhanced their chances of landing a better job.

The diamond choker around her neck, the bracelet on her arm, and the large stone on the slender ring on her finger all distanced her from her beginnings as the only daughter in a relatively poor Bronx family. Her father owned a grocery store and lived in fear of his life from hoodlums and thieves. "I knew I had to get out of there," she said. "I never wanted to find myself standing behind that counter past the age of sixteen."

Her husband's name had not been Kelly; it had been Whitehead, a name associated with old East Coast money. After his death, she had taken a perverse pleasure in reclaiming her Irish maiden name. "A little spit in the eyes of his family, who thought I was never good enough to marry him," she said with enjoyment.

Ted found himself liking her. In many ways, there was a strong similarity between them. He too had that rebellious streak, one that had led him into trouble as surely as any compass.

The thought made him recall his new roommate. He had taken Sean shopping that afternoon, helping him procure a new and more suitable wardrobe. Now there was someone who didn't know the meaning of trouble. Sean's naivete was unbelievable. Which was probably why Nancy had given him the job of whipping Sean into shape. It was an uphill struggle.

Hell, the guy still lived according to some ancient moral code, and wasn't even ashamed to talk about it. Stuff like women shouldn't be treated as objects, honesty in relationships, fair dealings with others, and crap like that. What a dweeb! There was no way to live according to an irrelevant code like that in this world and still make it. People like that got stepped over by those who were making it.

You had to use your wits, you had to take advantage of the situations that presented themselves to you, and above all you had to look out for yourself. Nobody cared as much about you as you did. It was a lesson he had learned early in life and one he never forgot. He was a living testament to the success of that strategy. Except for the odd unavoidable lean period, he lived well. His home was a luxurious condo, he drove a nice car, mixed in the best circles. He had the money, the women, and the drugs he needed, and he was unhindered by remorse. Life was a lark, to be attacked with energy and skill.

It would be difficult, but Sean would change. He knew that. He couldn't help but change. He'd meet people of the wealth and status that he had only read about, and he would find that with wealth and status came temptation. Sooner or later he would begin to succumb to temptation, and with that would come change.

During the concert, Ms. Kelly proved to be a toucher. Every now and then she would lean toward him to whisper a comment, her breast touching his shoulder, her hand resting lightly on his for a tantalizing second, her knee brushing his. It was subtle yet expected, the normal game between men and women — those initial forays into the other territory — one that Ted always found both erotic and arousing. He began to look forward to the remainder of the evening.

After the concert, when they returned to his car, he asked where she would like to go next. "Perhaps some supper?" he suggested.

She leaned her head against the window and looked lazily over at him. "Where would you like to go?" she asked.

Ted smiled. "Well, I should show you the town. However, even though I know it's very selfish of me, there's nothing I'd like more than to return to your hotel with you."

His unmistakable intention brought a warm chuckle from her. "There's nothing more I'd like than that either," she said, and the matter was settled.

When they reached her suite she tossed her jacket carelessly over a chair and continued toward the bathroom. "Why don't you order us a drink while I make myself presentable?" she suggested.

53

"What would you like?"

"A single malt scotch on the rocks."

"My favorite drink," Ted lied. "I think I'll have the same."

"Then order a bottle and a lot of ice," she said over her shoulder, and left the room.

The drinks arrived before she emerged from the bathroom, probably according to her design, but the wait was worth it. She wore a black silk robe belted at the waist and her hair fell down below her shoulders. The diamond bracelet had been taken from her wrist and now sparkled on her left ankle. The choke still encompassed her neck.

Ted stood up when she entered and looked at her with frank admiration. "You're beautiful," he said unoriginally.

She continued walking, stopping finally just inches away from him. "So are you," she said.

He reached down to the table and picked up the glass of Scotch he had poured for her. She shook her head. "Later," she said. "There's something else I want right now."

He had already taken off his jacket and tie, so now she began to unbutton his shirt. Running her hands below the shirt across his chest and down to his stomach, she pulled the tails of the shirt out, murmuring approvingly, "Very nice." Then she undid his belt and unhooked the top of his trousers and pulled the zipper down. Sliding her hands underneath his briefs, she found what she was looking for. "Mmm, *very* nice," she said, smiling a long, slow, lascivious smile as he grew hard in her hands.

Leading him by the cock, she moved backward out of the living room and into the adjoining bedroom, until the back of her legs hit the bed. And then she fell and lay there looking up at him. "Do me," she ordered. "Do me good. I want to feel your tongue."

"Where?" he asked.

"Everywhere." She undid the belt on her robe and put her hand between her legs. She pulled back the skin of her vagina and the pink clitoris stood up like a small peak in a folded valley.

Ted fell to his knees beside the bed and lowered his head

54

and listened to the beginnings of her satisfied moans. It was great, he thought. Not only would he get a large tip out of this, she'd probably be pleased enough to give him a gift.

His tongue moved faster as she writhed below him, her breath growing shorter as small cries of pleasure erupted from her throat. Her eyes stared unseeingly at the ceiling.

This was great, he thought again, wondering how many people enjoyed their work as much as he did.

While Ted was picking up his date at the Beverly Hills Hotel, Sean stood nervously in front of the mirror in their apartment. He was, as Ted had enthusiastically pronounced after their shopping expedition, "Ready for action." He wore a navy blue cashmere jacket, a Brooks Brothers cotton shirt, a striped tie, gray wool trousers, and Italian brown leather shoes. He hadn't been dressed as well as this since his college days. Nor had he ever looked as prosperous.

Danny appeared in the doorway and nodded. "Looking good," he said.

He himself wore a white linen suit with a dark blue tie. He looked immaculat — as suave as the archetypical Latin lover.

Nancy Hamilton had arranged for Danny and Sean to share their duties during Sean's first time out. "He'll show you the ropes," she had said. Two women, who were friends, needed escorts that evening.

They took Danny's car, a small, luxuriously appointed BMW, and drove toward a Beverly Hills residential address, where they were to meet their clients. From there they were to go by chauffeured limo, provided by one of the ladies, to Club Twenty/20 in Century City, where a fundraising dinner and fashion show was being held.

During the drive, Sean asked Danny how long he had been working for Debonaire. "About a year," Danny replied.

"So you like the work."

Danny shrugged eloquently. "It beats working the bars. Nice class of people. Now and again there's someone you'd rather not be with, but you just glow through that, you know."

"You from L.A.?"

"Yes," Danny said, his voice suddenly curt. He fiddled with the radio dial and settled on KROQ. Peter Gabriel's mournful voice filled the car.

"Still have family here?"

Danny avoided the answer and said, "Where are you from?"

"Seattle, originally, but I've been here a few years."

"An actor, huh?"

"Yeah. Well, right now I'm an escort," Sean said.

"You'll get used to it."

The house was on a wide boulevard in the flatlands, about three blocks north of Santa Monica Boulevard. Set back from the road, it was surrounded by a high metal security fence and barred by a locked gate.

Danny pressed the buzzer and announced their names into the speaker. The gate creaked open on hinges that needed oil, and they drove down a long curved driveway to the front of the house, a two-story Spanish-style mansion.

Sean's date was Doris Winston, a small, dark-haired women in her fifties. She had dark hair, a ready smile, a girlish giggle, and shrewd brown eyes. As soon as they entered, she poured them what she called "a glass of Chardonnay for the road," chattering away good-naturedly at them both, a genial hostess.

Her friend was Catherine Vaughn, tall, rangy, and around the same age. She had brown hair, a slow but warm smile, and didn't hold her years quite as well as Doris. She carried more weight and there were somber lines around her mouth. From the quick sidelong glances at Danny, however, it was obvious that she was both nervous and excited.

They were so old, Sean thought. He couldn't help it. How was it going to look, he and Danny in the company of these women? People would think they were mothers and sons.

"You're almost the spitting image of my husband when he was younger," Doris said, handing Sean his drink and plopping down in an armchair opposite him. "He died ten years ago. Too much work and not enough fun."

"What did he do?" Sean asked politely.

"He was a film agent, had his own agency, then got into production. He made a fortune but never had time to spend it. No kids and no time to play."

"I see," Sean said, not knowing what else to say.

"You're an actor?" she asked giving him a knowing glance. It was then, as he met her eyes, that Sean realized he was not dealing with a stupid woman. Doris didn't miss much and knew how to evalauate what she saw.

"Yes," he said, volunteering no more.

"Well, for tonight, should anyone ask, please say you're a friend of the family, that I knew your parents. Where are you from?"

"Seattle, Washington."

"Aerospace?"

"Yes. My father's an engineer at Boeing."

They finished their drinks and left the house. As promised, a long black limosine waited in the driveway. When they stepped in, Doris opened a small bar and poured them each another glass of chilled wine.

Her friend, Catherine, it turned out, was a divorcée. Her ex-husband, also in the "business," also an agent, had left her three years earlier and moved in with a young actress client, thirty-five years his junior. "Catherine's been moping around ever since, haven't you dear? Tonight is her formal declaration of independence."

"Well, hardly moping," Catherine protested. "I've been out on a few dates."

"Going to dinner with a man who already has one foot in the grave hardly qualifies as a date," Doris said sarcastically. She shot Danny an admiring look. "Danny here is a date."

Danny inclined his head at the comment. "It's hard for me to believe that you haven't been besieged by men since your divorce," he said graciously to Catherine, lightly touching her hand as he spoke.

"Oh," she responded, flustered, while Doris giggled approvingly, darting a sly, conspiratorial glance over at Sean.

He couldn't help but smile back at her infectious good spirits.

Doris presented their tickets at the door of the club, and as soon as they entered she was greeted by a dark-haired Frenchman she called Fernaud, apparently the manager or owner. He showed them into Le Prive, the smaller and more private dining room, where four black musicians played soft blues from a small stage.

"What's the charity?" Sean asked, as soon as they were seated.

"It's for battered children," Catherine said seriously. "I always support them. They work with the county to place the kids in good foster homes and provide counseling. It's very important."

"Two hundred bucks a ticket, they'd better do good work," Doris said, unimpressed.

Sean didn't comment, but the thought of dinner and a fashion show for two hundred bucks impressed him. As did the fact that drinks from the bar were extra, in spite of the hefty ticket price.

The other clientele were obviously wealthy, the men well-dressed and the women resplendent. A couple of people nodded at Catherine, but other than that, nobody paid any attention to them.

"Let's dance," Doris said taking Sean's hand. She led him on to the floor just in time for beginning of a slow blues number. She took one hand in hers and placed her other on his back. She was a surprisingly good dancer, easy on the feet with an excellent sense of rhythm.

"How long have you been doing this?" she asked, looking up at him.

He hesitated, remembering Danny's earlier warning during an indoctrination session. "Never let them know you're just a beginner," he had said. "If they ask how long you've been doing this just say a while." Which was exactly what Sean said.

"Well, I suppose it would be a silly question to ask why you're doing this. Obviously, your acting career is coming along slower than you'd like and you're doing it for the money."

"Yeah, well, acting hasn't been that kind to me since I've been here."

"It's a tough business," Doris said. "I've seen those that make it and those that fall by the wayside. Are you any good? I mean at your craft?"

"I think so," Sean said. "I've been told so and it feels good to me, even though I'm always learning. But being good really isn't enough. I mean, it takes persistence to stay out there and be seen. It also seems to take a little bit of luck."

"Good luck," Doris said, "always seems to come when you least expect it and never when you want it or desperately need it."

The dinner was excellent, but, as Doris explained, Twenty/20 and the Mustache Cafe were owned by the same people. The Mustache chef came to the club on special ocassions and prepared the food. "Obviously, it's not as good as places like Citrus and Le Dome, but generally speaking, the quality is always high, usually for a very reasonable price," she said.

They had more wine with dinner and then carried their glasses into the main room for the fashion show. The tables were already taken so they stood near the bar with a distant view of the stage.

It was very modern — antiseptic yet chic. The ceiling of the seating area around the stage was decorated with what looked to be photographers' umbrellas and other paraphernalia suggesting a fashion/photography motif.

Then after a short welcoming speech and a thanks to the attendees by the head of the charity, the emcee took over and the parade of rail-thin models began. The clothes were hideous, mainly pastels that lacked any vibrancy or personality. The girls all had shoulders that stuck out like longshoreman's, while the pale young men wore clothes that made them seem of even more indeterminate gender.

Doris seemed to think so to, because she took Sean's hand and said, "Let's go back to the music." The four of them went back to the Le Prive, where they drank more wine and chatted.

Doris told them about the owner, how he had arrived from France with a family and less than $100 and worked as a dishwasher, then a waiter, then a maitre'd, before starting his own restaurant. "He's worth millions now," she said.

While listening and participating, Sean formulated some opinions about Danny. He noticed that Danny carried a veneer of sophistication, but he was sure it was only a veneer. Danny said the right things, smiled at the right times, and yet his politeness was almost barren in its lack of depth. His mission, apparently was to have others perceive him as beautiful man, correction, a polite, charming, and beautiful man. And at that he was certainly good.

Sean also noticed that commensurate with the amount of wine she drank, Catherine grew increasingly relaxed. At one point, while dancing with Danny she became positively amorous, curling both arms around his neck and pressing her body against his. Doris, who noticed Sean watching them, cocked an eyebrow, "Catherine seems very satisfied with my choice," she said.

"You're doing this as a favor for her?"

"As a favor for me," Doris said tartly. "I can't stand listening to the woman's misery much longer. I thought I would get her out of her damn house and show her a good time."

When the dance was over Catherine drew reluctantly away from Danny, looking up with suddenly limpid eyes.

Half an hour later they left, returning to Doris's place for a drink—or so Sean thought. But when the limosine stopped in the driveway, Doris looked at Danny and said, "The driver will take Catherine home. Why don't you accompany her." Danny nodded as if this was totally expected.

Sean stood beside the car not knowing what to do. "Come on in," Doris said, "and we'll have a nightcap." He followed her into the house.

This time he was more observant, noticing the original artwork on the walls, Persian carpets in the hallway, the odd piece of sculpture beside doorways, and the sumptuous furnishings in the living room.

He was feeling as nervous as he had on his first date, but he tried to hide it and, after fidgeting with his feet, finally sat on the sofa. She asked him what he would like to drink. "Um, a glass of wine would be fine."

"How about something a little stronger?" she asked over her shoulder from the bar. "A B&B? After that dinner and all the wine we had tonight, it'll do you good."

"Well, all right," he agreed.

She poured the brandy and benedictine into two huge snifter glasses and brought them back, sitting not far from him on the couch. Lifting her glass, she said, "To a fun evening."

"To a fun evening," Sean said.

They drank in silence for a few moments. She was right. It did do him good. He had never had B&B before, but it was delicious and suddenly became his after-dinner favorite. He lowered his nose to the snifter and found the smell alone satisfying.

Doris stared at him mischeviously over the rim of the glass. "I can think of only one way to make this evening even more delightful," she said.

"Oh?" Sean said clumsily, a sinking heart telling him that he knew what was coming.

"Yes. Why don't we go to bed?" she suggested.

Sean felt his face redden. He cursed himself, he cursed her, he cursed his situation. Goddamn, what was he doing here? It was too much! On his first night he was getting hit on.

Determined to handle it with at least an appearance of aplomb, he attempted to hide his consternation. "I'm afraid that won't be possible."

"Oh," she said, her voice suddenly cool, and placed her glass on the oak table. "And why is that?"

It was a quandary he had faced before, fairly often: how to turn down a woman he liked but didn't want to sleep with. And yet tonight the circumstances were far different. He was being paid to be here. In essence, at least for the moment, he was owned by her — certainly his time was.

"Well," he said, struggling to find the right words, "it has been a delightful evening, and of course my time is yours, but, um, I'm afraid, you know it's just, uh, for me to be here to be your escort and I mean, anything else it's not really . . ." And the stammered words trailed off.

The beginnings of irritation in her eyes were replaced by amusement. "This is your first night on the job, isn't it?" she said.

Sean nodded, embarrassed to be caught in the earlier lie. "Yes, um, this is actually my first date," he admitted. He sighed.

"Well, this is also my first time, the first time I've used a service, I mean." Her voice grew a little sharper. "I was led to believe from a friend who recommended it that part of the service included more than just escort duties."

"Look," Sean said. "You are a real nice lady, but uh, that's not part of my job as I understand it."

She looked back at him for a long moment and then a wistful look entered her face. "Tell me something, Sean. If the position was exactly as it is, but instead of being a fifty-five-year-old woman, I was thirty and still beautiful, what would you say then?"

He looked back at her and somehow felt a sadness. "Uh," he began, constructing an evasion, but her eyes demanded an honest answer. "I truly don't know. But I think I'd say exactly what I'm saying to you now. It's not your age, I mean, yes, of course that does have something to do with it, I mean." He stopped, juxtaposed a few words in his mind and said, "I'm young enough to be your son, Doris. Besides, you don't need to do this. You're an attractive, bright, and intelligent woman. You can find men closer to your own age."

"Men closer to my own age are old and tired. And dating is an old and boring game. Anyway, why shouldn't I have the right to find somebody younger, more exciting?"

Sean scratched his head. He really didn't have an answer. She had every right. So he said it. "I've got nothing against people of different ages dating," he said. "I mean, not really. It's not something I'd do, but I guess you do have that right. But you shouldn't have to buy it."

"I'm afraid I do," she said, a note of self-pity entering her

62

voice for only a second. Then her voice grew harsh. "I am, as they say, over the hill. It's fine for men to have younger women, but society still frowns on older women being with younger men. It's a bum rap, don't you think?"

"It doesn't seem fair," Sean said. "But then life isn't particularly fair, I suppose."

She cupped her glass in both hands and looked up at him. "Thanks for your honesty. Even though it's a dose of reality." She fluttered one hand toward him. "No, you're right, I'm a foolish old woman, unable to let go of dreams of youth."

"You're not that old," he protested. "You're very attractive. Not only that, but I think you are a wonderful person. You enjoy life so much, it makes it a pleasure to be with you. You'll find someone, I guarantee it. You'll find someone."

"It's been a long time," she said.

"It'll happen, I know it," he said encouragingly.

She reached out and patted his hand. "And you are a nice young man, Sean. I just hope you know what you are doing here in this business."

"I'm just trying to earn a living."

She nodded. "I know, but sometimes it costs more than money to get money." There was a sound of a car in the driveway. "That'll be the chauffeur. I'll have him take you home," she said.

"What about Danny? His car is still here."

She stood and looked down at him with a strange expression in her eyes. "Don't worry about Danny, I'm sure Catherine will arrange in the morning for him to come by and pick it up. Danny doesn't have the qualms that you have. Danny is not as nice a man as you."

She stopped at the front door before opening it. "I have something strange to ask of you."

"Yes," Sean asked.

"I'd like to see you again as a friend." He looked momentarily worried and she hurried on. "It has nothing to do with the agency, nothing with dating, just as a friend. I'd like us to stay in touch. I enjoy your company. Maybe some of your youth rubs off on me."

Sean was undecided. "Well, I'd kind of like that too, but it's really against the rules of the agency. We're not supposed to be in private contact with any of the clients."

"They won't know. At least I won't tell if you won't," she said, a mischevious look entering her eyes again.

Sean nodded. "Well, I'd really like that."

"Call sometime. I'm listed under my initial in Beverly Hills. I'm not famous enough to have an unlisted phone number," she said.

"I'll call you," he promised.

She opened the door. "You do that," she said as he slipped past her, "and take care."

The driver held the door of the limo open for him. Sean slid in and looked through the tinted windows. Doris lifted her hand once and turned and went back into the house.

He sank back into the seat and twisted his face into an expression appropriate to the feeling of mental cringing that he was experiencing. In truth, it hadn't been that dreadful, but it had been difficult. He realized that the ordeal had left him sweating profusely. Automatically he reached for the bar. Another drink certainly wouldn't hurt.

Chapter Five

"My father was a tough mick," Ted was saying. "Grew up in the slums and never forgot it. He even used to boast about it. 'I never would have been able to appreciate wealth if I hadn't lived on potatoes for three meals a day,' he used to say."

"That's like the old, 'I used to walk five miles to school in the snow every day,' that parents tell their kids," Sean said with a smile.

They were having a rare breakfast together, each with a grapefruit and a bowl of cereal on the table before them. For some reason Ted was expansive, willing to talk about his life. "He made his money in construction. It had to do with the fact that he was tied into the Democratic party power structure in Boston. He supported them and they supported him. The contracts came his way. And, naturally, the unions never seemed to fight him. There's probably more than one body buried in the concrete foundations of some of the buildings he put up."

"Sounds like quite a formidable man," Sean said.

Ted looked pensive, twirled his fork between his fingers. "He was an asshole, a hard man. Didn't have a loving bone in his body. He started beating the shit out of me when I was six and didn't stop till I was seventeen and too big for him to take on."

"And your mother?"

Ted's face grew lighter. "She came from an English family . . . lost all their money in the Depression and lived their life in genteel poverty. Still at one of the best addresses in town, of course, but never admitting that they were on the edge. Too proud for that."

"That's a weird combination, I didn't think the Irish and English got along," Sean said.

Ted smiled. "They don't. But Dad had the money and the power to overcome her father's and mother's reservations. When he offered his hand in marriage, her father had no choice but to say yes. He couldn't afford to send her to college, and people of his own class who still had money didn't want to be saddled with her. He thought this was the best solution for her—to marry a wealthy man, even if he was Irish scum."

Ted scooped a wedge of grapefruit up and plopped it in his mouth. "I've got to admit that she loved him," he said. "I don't know what she saw in the old bastard, but she loved him. Even though I know he fucked around. God, did he fuck around! He'd go after any piece of tail that swished by him. She continued to love him. I asked her about it once, just before I left home. She said men had needs that women did not and could not understand. All she had to understand, she said, was that she loved him."

"And you look like her, not your father, right?"

"Yeah, I've got her looks, thank God. My father is short, bulging all over. He has a blotchy red face, typically Irish. What about your family?"

Sean thought of his father—quiet, dedicated to his work, studious. He liked nothing more than confronting some engineering problem and losing himself in it until he discovered the key and unlocked the door. His mother was a short brunette. She had put on weight in recent years but still had the energy of a fifteen-year-old. She was always involved in something, some charity work, some community benefit.

"They're just ordinary people," Sean said. "Not very exciting. Third generation West Coast. My grandfather was a gold miner in Oregon. My great-grandfather was a cowboy. My other grandfather was a merchant. My parents are just ordinary, nice people."

"Well, maybe you were luckier than I was," Ted said. "Nice wasn't a part of my life. I was always being pushed around somewhere. From one school to the other, one house to another. My mother seemed to move to a bigger and better house every three years. Of course, each time my father sold he made a killing."

Ted lapsed into a thoughtful silence. Sean got up and poured himself a cup of coffee from the stove and returned to the table.

"So, how are you liking the job?" Ted asked.

Sean shook his head and said, "I'm not sure yet."

He had almost quit after his first date, but after a short bout with his conscience he had talked himself out of it. After all, he hadn't compromised himself, and in fact the evening had even turned out well, with Doris becoming a new friend. He hadn't gone into this with total naivete. He had known that at times he would have to struggle to maintain his integrity, and so far he had been able to do it.

As part of the argument Sean also considered the fact that he was finally making his looks pay off. All his life women had been attracted to him. Consequently, he had spent a lot of time avoiding their often unwelcome advances. Unlike some other handsome men he knew of, he never used his looks to manipulate women into having sex with him.

He remembered how one of his best friends during college days, Derrick Arrow, had made a career out of bedding women, sometimes seeing how many different women he could date and conquer in a particular week. Sean had never been attracted to the promiscuous lifestyle. It didn't suit his personality. The regrets and repercussions when he had indulged himself were enough to warn him off further such conquests. Now, however, he was using his looks to please women, not sexually, but by gracing them with his company—and he was getting paid for it. If this

67

wasn't utilizing your resources, what was? And if Hollywood didn't want what he had to offer, there were apparently plenty of women willing to pay for an evening of his company. Not that it was the same amount of money as a working actor made, but it wasn't too shabby. And it sure beat waiting tables.

On his second date for Debonaire, his arguments seemed well justified. The woman had thought him sweet. She was about sixty and he had taken her to a play and then taken her home. She had invited him in for a nightcap and thanked him for a delightful evening. After a motherly peck on his cheek with thin dry lips, she had tipped him a hundred dollars.

His third date had been more difficult, but ultimately not disastrous. An edgy woman of about fifty, she apparently had not cared much for his company for most of the evening. During the first half of the time they spent together she had criticized him for what he was doing and, in effect, for who he was. Some of it was subtle, some of it wasn't. It came in comments like, "Yes, I have a son, he's a lawyer. He works very hard for a living. Have you ever done that?"

"Been a lawyer?" Sean had asked.

"Oh, no, dear. Worked very hard."

Finally, while they were having dessert in a cafe on Sunset Plaza, he had politely asked her why she didn't like him. Taken aback for a moment, she finally said, "Because you're too damn good-looking and I don't trust good-looking men."

Somehow it had cleared the air between them and the rest of the evening had been relatively pleasant. She had not, however, tipped him.

He told the story to Ted, who laughed. "Yeah, you run across a sour old bitch like that every now and again. It's nothing to worry about. They're harmless. They just need somewhere to spray their venom. But they're paying for it, so what do you care? Just let it slide off your back."

"I guess you're good at that, huh?" Sean ventured.

"Yeah, I've gotten good at it," Ted said. "I don't show my real feelings to these broads that often."

"But sometimes you do?"

"Sometimes," Ted said soberly. Then his face cracked into a smile. "Don't take this stuff seriously. I'll tell you what happened to me yesterday. I picked up this woman, real loaded, dripping diamonds. She lives in a mansion in Pasadena. She wants me to take her to the races, right?

"So we go to the track and we don't sit, well, first of all, we don't stand down at the railings and we don't even sit in the stand. We go to her private box. You know how many of those there are? The goddamn things must cost a fortune. People can't look in, the glass is darkened on the sides and the front looks down at the track. It's great!

"All right. We go into the box and there's a picnic basket waiting for us with champagne, caviar, paté, crackers, all sorts of good stuff. But she's not interested in nibbling, and it turns out she is not all that interested in the races.

"We get in the box and the first thing she does is start taking off her clothes. Well, I think, not a bad looking woman. This could be interesting. And then the speakers blare out that a race is starting. Then she says, 'My horse is in that race.' 'What's its name?' And she says 'Special Order.' "

Ted stopped his story to laugh and look over at Sean to see how it was going over. "Now it gets really weird," he said with a final chuckle. "She gets down on the floor on her hands and knees, naked you understand, and in her hand is a leather riding crop, the kind the jockeys use. She hands it to me. She says, 'I want you to ride me. When the starting gun goes off, I want you to ride me.' I look at her and say 'What do you mean, ride you?' 'Ride me, and I want you to use this,' and she hands me the whip. 'But take off your clothes first' is her last order.

"What the hell, I take off my clothes, riding crop in my hand, the gun goes off and she says, 'Now!' I mean, is she excited, or what? Her eyes are just about popping out of her head. 'Now!' she shouts again, and I realize I am

69

supposed to be sitting on her. So, I sit on her. She says, 'Ride me.' So I start moving like I am on a horse or something and she says, 'Okay, make me go faster.' And the announcer is going, you know how they talk, 'Red Fling. Red Fling is taking the lead. Queen's Crown is right behind. Special Order. Coming up fast is Special Order.' And she says, 'Go Special Order! Okay, ride me hard now! Make me go faster. Make me win!'

"So it's obvious to me that she wants me to hit her, so I tap her with the whip, but she says 'Harder, faster, harder, faster!' So I'm slashing her thigh with this goddamn crop, and this woman is beside herself. I expect to see foam pouring out of her mouth. She's totally gone. So finally the race ends and guess what?"

"What?" Sean said.

"Special Order comes in first. This lady is sitting there panting and sweating just like she's run the race herself, and she turns back to me and says, 'Now really ride me.' And so I do.

"Now, how can you take something like that seriously?"

Sean couldn't help laughing. The picture of Ted naked at the race track with a woman asking him to ride her was indeed too bizarre to be taken seriously.

When Sean stopped laughing, he glanced at his watch and said, "I guess I better get it together."

"You got a day job?"

"Yeah, I'm supposed to pick this woman up at about eleven."

"Well, maybe it'll be a little more exciting than your last date," Ted said. "Hey, it might even be a pleasant surprise.

"Catch you later, cowboy," Sean said.

Sean was more than pleasantly surprised, he was delighted at the vision waiting for him in the lobby of the Century Plaza Hotel.

She was about thirty-five, give or take five years, and in her prime. Almost as tall as he was, she looked an ex-

70

model who had thankfully put on a few pounds. She wore tennis shoes, blue jeans, and a T-shirt, with a sweater and a bag slung around her shoulders. She was shapely enough not to wear a bra, Sean noticed admiringly. Long black hair fell below her shoulders and large hazel eyes watched him approach with approval.

"Ms. Kaplan?" he asked.

She held out a hand and shook his firmly. "Call me Kate," she said. "I assume you're Sean Parker?"

"Yes, I am."

She raised an eyebrow. "You're certainly an improvement over the last one they sent me. He was a Hispanic who thought he was God's gift to women."

"Well, I'm pleased you're pleased," Sean said. If that was Danny she was talking about, it wasn't a remark he'd pass on.

While they stood in front of the hotel and waited for the valet to bring his car, she asked how the weather was at the beach.

"It's in the 70s, rather like it is here."

"Oh, good. I haven't been to the ocean for ages."

A minute later the convertible Nancy had told him to rent drove up. "She's paying a lot of money, all day and into the evening," Nancy had said. "Go ahead and rent an expensive convertible." And so he had, settling on a Mercedes.

The valet jumped out and opened the door for her while Sean walked around to the other side. "Nice car," she said, as he slid into the seat. "I rented it," he informed her guilelessly. She gave him a small smile of approval and they sped smoothly away.

There was a jaunty air of confidence about her, a kind of "I like who I am and fuck you, buddy," that Sean found most attractive and refreshing. He discovered that she was owner of her own advertising agency in Chicago, here to pitch a new client. "I've been rehearsing a presentation for days and the meeting is tomorrow," she explained, "so I am doing what I always do, which is take a day off and just forget about it. That way I walk in relaxed and unconcerned."

Sean asked if it was a big agency. "It's getting bigger," she said. "We do about seven million dollars a year. It started off with nothing four years ago. There is a lot of stress but I love it. At least now I can afford distractions when I need them."

They reached Venice, and after finding a parking spot walked out onto the beach. Kate took off her shoes, rolled up her jeans, and cavorted in the shallows like a young girl, while Sean walked more sedately on drier ground.

"God, I love L.A." she shouted exuberantly. "If I could live here I would."

"Why can't you?" Sean asked.

"Responsibilities," she said, as if he had asked a foolish question. "I have seven full-time people working for me and clients who depend upon me. I just couldn't up and leave, nor would I want to. God, the idea of starting all over again in a new city. Yuk."

She tired of the beach after about an hour and they walked up into Venice and window-shopped for a while. They stopped in at Dudley Moore's restaurant, 72 Market Street, for a late lunch. Kate was disappointed not to find the actor playing the piano, but it did nothing to spoil her appetite or her conversation.

"The advertising business is the apex of American civilization," she said cynically. She sliced her calamari and took a bite. "In advertising you have the ultimate blending of art, commerce, and technology, and it's a blend that keeps this country moving forward. It's what sells, it's what causes people to consume, it's what turns the wheels of commerce, and, in fact, the wheels of the very cars right here on the freeways of Los Angeles."

"Are you proud of what you do?" Sean asked.

"Are you?" she asked pointedly.

He took a bite of his pasta and chewed it without answering the question. She seemed to sense his embarrassment and continued talking. "Every client I've ever had, as

72

a matter of fact, thinks that his product is the most important product in the world. It's my job to make the world think so too. It's not always easy. I mean, how seriously can you take flea collars?"

"Well, I guess dogs take them pretty seriously," Sean said.

"Dogs don't give a shit; they've always had fleas. No, it's the public, the buying public that has to take them seriously, and that's the gig. People are worried about their dogs; people should be worried about their dogs; people will be worried about their dogs; we make people worry about their dogs." She started to laugh.

Sean joined her. "Doesn't your cynicism make your job a little hard," he asked.

She looked startled. "Cynicism? I'm not cynical, this is just reality. I just try to be lighthearted about it. If I took it seriously, God, I'd be a wreck within a year. I've got to have fun at what I do, or what's the point?"

"And you like the money?" Sean said.

"Yes, and I like the money."

"Well, so do I," Sean said. "That's why I do what I do."

After lunch they entered a small boutique, where Kate saw a silk blouse she simply had to have. The pale blue suited her well. She modeled it for Sean, twirling around in the small showroom.

She was immensely attractive, he thought for about the tenth time in a couple of hours. It wasn't just her physical appearance, it was the energy she put into everything she did, the enjoyment she seemed determined to get from it. He felt a rush of affinity for her. God, this was so different from the other experiences with women he met through the agency. This was like being on a date with a girl you liked.

She must have felt the same way, because when they returned to the street and started walking back to the car she very casually took his hand in hers and made some innocuous remark about where she'd like to live in Los Angeles. After the initial shock, Sean was flattered, and when that wore off, it simply seemed natural — and pleasant.

"What would you like to see now?" Sean asked when they got back to the car.

"The hotel," she said. "I'd like to change."

When they reached the hotel and entered the lobby, Sean suggested he wait there for her. "No, no," Kate said, "that won't be necessary. Come on up. I have a suite that has its very own bar. You can sit down and have a drink while I decide what to wear."

Her room was peach colored and comfortable, with a large color television set, a comfortable couch, a desk, and chairs. Sean sat on the couch and then wandered to the bar, opened the small refrigerator, and retrieved a beer. He wandered back to the couch, sipping reflectively.

He wondered where they would go next. When relatives came to Los Angeles, there were standard places to take them. They all wanted to see Disneyland, Knotts Berry Farm, Universal Studios, Grauman's Chinese Theatre, the stars on the sidewalk on Hollywood Boulevard, and the homes of the stars in Bel Air and Beverly Hills. But he knew Kate wouldn't want any of that. She was not exactly a tourist and not particularly predictable.

He looked back over his shoulder and noticed the bedroom door was ajar. "Where do you want to go now?" he called out.

"What?" came a muffled voice.

"Where do you want to go?"

"Come here, I can't hear you."

He stood, beer in hand and walked to the door, stopping a few feet away so he wouldn't be able to look in and said, "Where do you want to go next?"

"Come here and let's talk about it," she said. "Come on in, I won't bite."

Feeling a little foolish, he pushed the door open and stepped in.

She stood before the closet, staring at the available clothes. She wore nothing but brief, almost transparent

74

panties.

She had wonderful body, long, slim legs, a bottom rounded but still firm, and breasts that were starting to become heavy but had not yet lost their shape. Her nipples were large and brown. He stared; he couldn't help it.

"Sean, what do you think I should wear?" She turned and saw him looking at her. Undisturbed by the frank admiration in his eyes, she smiled and said, "You're not bad looking yourself, you know."

"You're beautiful," Sean said, "you really are."

"Then come here and let's really admire each other."

Slowly he walked across the room and stopped inches away from her. He could feel the heat between them and see something change in her eyes as they stared into his.

He reached a hand out and touched her shoulder, sliding it gently down the soft skin of her arm. And then, almost without noticeable movement, they were in each other's arms and he was kissing her.

Her mouth opened immediately and her tongue searched for his while he ran his hands down her back, across the curve of the small and over her rising buttocks.

She pressed against him and then drew back and attacked his belt and the buttons of his shirt, her eyes fierce with sudden need. Moments later they were on the bed, limbs tangling, mouths exploring, breath mingling, both driven beyond thought by an urge that had been building to this all afternoon.

And then they both exulted in fulfilling their mutual desire.

Afterward, when they lay sated in bed, he asked a question that had been bothering him all afternoon. "Why," Sean asked, running a finger lazily around a softened nipple, "did a beautiful woman like you want an escort?"

"Because I like company, I don't like to be alone."

"You must have friends."

"I don't have friends here. I have associates. And my rule, my very first rule, is I never date clients, ex-clients, or possible clients. And they are the only people I know here. So what better than an escort when I'm here? I don't have time to go out and pick someone up or to sit in a bar and have some married man sidle over to me and tell me how attractive I am and how lonely he is. This is the easiest way. It's perfect."

"Well, I'm very glad," Sean said, kissing that collapsed nipple.

She reached one hand across his stomach and down. "Now, the only question is . . ."

"What?"

"Whether you are as energetic in bed as you are skillful?" She kneaded him with her fingers and then giggled. "Oh, how the mighty rise again," she said.

After they made love again, he asked if she wanted to go out to dinner. Almost asleep, she opened her eyes and looked at him, shaking her head. "I think we should call it a day. I must be suffering from jet lag. I'm exhausted. Or maybe it's just extreme sexual satisfaction. But I've got to get enough rest to be together for the presentation tomorrow."

Sean felt a slightly disappointed feeling well up inside him.

"Will I see you again before you leave?" He rolled over and sat on the edge of the bed.

"I don't think I have time for that. The next time I come."

"That would be nice," he said, leaning over to kiss her on the shoulder.

She turned quickly to kiss him lingeringly on the mouth. "It was a good day," she said.

"Yeah, I enjoyed it too," he said, and began to dress.

After tying his shoelaces, he stood and looked down at her. "Well, I guess . . . goodbye," he said.

"Oh, wait," she said, rolling quickly out of the bed and walking over to her handbag. She rummaged through it, saying, "I'm sorry, I almost forgot."

She took out her wallet and took withdrew two one-hundred-dollar bills from it. "This is for you," she said.

"For services above and beyond the call of duty."

Sean felt his face flush and shook his head. "No, that's not necessary," he said.

She pushed the money at him, and said, "You've got to take it. I want you to."

Again, like a stubborn child he shook his head.

She looked at him, her eyes widening with sudden understanding. "My God, you forgot! You forgot, didn't you?"

Sean just stood there, his face hot.

"I'm sorry," she said. "But that's the way it was. That's all it was. Now, please take the money. It doesn't mean anything, it's just something I want you to have."

He stared at her, almost hating her for a moment, but then the feeling faded. There was no point in being angry at her. She had understood all along. He had been the fool. Unwillingly he put out his hand and took the bills. Then, without speaking, he turned and walked out of the room.

He stood in the corridor outside her door, leaned up against the wall, and closed his eyes. He felt dreadful — soiled and, even worse, stupid.

What a fool he'd been, he told himself, what an idiot. It wasn't until just a minute ago that he remembered what he'd been doing, what he had been there for, what he had done, what he was. For most of the day he had forgotten. Now he couldn't. He had just been bought and paid for.

Danny Perez loathed these Sundays, when once a month he paid a courtesy call on his parents. As he drove through East Los Angeles and the graffiti-scarred buildings of Boyle Heights, where he had grown up, he realized again that his dislike of these events was twofold. One was going home to face the eternal disapproval of his parents, the other was to be back in a neighborhood and a past that he preferred to forget.

He'd shoplifted groceries at that store on the corner

there. He had lost his virginity in the back of a car down that alley. He had painted that message on the wall, a message only a blur now as he passed it. He had fought his first fight at the high school right there. And in that park, in that grubby park, on his right, he had been initiated into the gang as a homeboy. He smoked his first joint in that park and later sold lids of grass there to younger kids.

It was a tough Mexican neighborhood, and he had been a tough Mexican kid, a gang member until twenty, but even though he had dropped out of high school in his senior year — an act his father had never forgiven — Danny had two things going that would get him out of the barrio before he turned twenty-one. He had been natively bright, a quick learner, naturally curious about all aspects of life. And he had been very handsome, even at that age.

He pulled up on the garbage-strewn street, opposite the small two-bedroom bungalow he once called home. Mother, father and three children had lived there — two boys and a girl in one room, mother and father in the other. Now, since the kids had moved out and his grandfather had died, his grandmother lived in the room where he had once slept.

He turned off the engine and automatically glanced in the rearview mirror. A small blue Toyota pulled alongside the curb, half a block behind him. Danny frowned slightly. He'd seen a blue Toyota near his condo and again on the freeway.

It was ridiculous. He'd seen too many movies. Blue Toyotas abounded in L.A. by the tens of thousands. Besides, there was no reason in the world anyone would be following him.

He got out of the car and, as usual, walked apprehensively toward the house. The picket fence had been painted recently and the grass was immaculate, green and short. The rosebushes were blooming.

He climbed up the creaking wooden steps and stood on the slanting porch, hesitating at the door as he always did.

Then he rang the doorbell, opened the door, plastered a smile on his face, and stepped in.

His mother bustled out of the kitchen, her sleeves rolled up, an apron around her waist. A large woman, overweight ever since he could remember, yet still carrying it well, she held her arms out, a smile of welcome on her face. He walked over and hugged her and said, "How's my favorite lady?"

She looked up at him with her creased face, genuine joy there. "Very good Danny. And how have you been? Working hard?"

"Yes, Mama," he said.

"Well, today you can relax. Enjoy a good, home-cooked meal, a meal you can't get on that side of town."

"You know how I always look forward to it, Mama."

"And so you should," she said. "You probably eat gringo food all the time—it's not good for you. It's not what you were brought up on."

"Where's Papa?" he asked.

She rolled her eyes, "In the living room reading the Sunday paper, watching the baseball on television."

"I'll say hello to him," he said. He went down the narrow hall toward the sound of the television set. He stepped into the living room, with its frayed and sagging furniture, and saw his old man in the recliner, his feet propped up on the footstool, the Sunday paper like a fan on the floor around him and a beer in one hand.

"Hey, Papa," he said from the doorway, "how's the Dodgers doing today?"

His father shrugged without looking up. "They got no pitching staff," he said. "They need pitchers."

"Yeah, it's been a tough season." He walked a little further into the room and said, "How you been?"

"Good, good." his father said. "And you?"

"Just fine."

As always, they had very little to say to each other. When he was a kid most of his father's communication consisted of a series of orders, and when he went off the straight-and-narrow most of the communication consisted of accusations and recriminations. Little had changed since those days. His father still considered him a lost soul.

He went to one end of the couch, half watching the television, until finally his father spoke again. "So," he said, the irony unmistakable in his voice. "It's good of you to come. It's been what, five weeks, six weeks?"

Danny shrugged. "I'm real busy, Papa. I come when I can, you know."

"Yeah, well, your sister comes once, twice a week. She lives just as far away as you do, but she knows how happy it makes your mama."

It wasn't that big a deal, Danny thought sardonically. Anna was in her third year at USC and had a lot of spare time on her hands, so it was easy enough for her pop over to the house. His younger brother, Jesus, who was studying to be an auto mechanic, shared an apartment with some other guys not far away. He visited all the time, generally because he could get free meals.

"So," his father said, breaking the silence. "How's the work? What is it? Selling office supplies?"

"It's coming along fine." Danny said.

His father grunted. For years after moving out, in answer to the query of what he was doing, Danny always replied. "A little bit of this and a little bit of that." His father had not unjustifiably suspected that he was probably doing something verging on, if not actually, criminal. And he had complained incessantly.

When he started working for Debonaire, Danny gave them a new story, one that hinted at stability in his lifestyle, telling them he worked as a telephone salesman, selling office products across the country. It covered a lot of bases—for instance, that he worked shifts, sometimes at night, sometimes days, and was thus never readily available. Of course, his mother wanted to know why she couldn't call him at work, but he explained that being in the telephone business they couldn't tie up the lines with incoming calls and therefore it was impossible for her to reach him there. Without deliberately calling him a liar, his father had made plain his disbelief in the story.

His father, Carlos, had a gardening business and had worked hard all his life, six days a week, twelve to fourteen hours a day—until a back injury had left him in a supervisorial capacity, one that had reduced his income but also freed his time somewhat. His mother had worked as a domestic all her life and now brought in almost much money as Carlos.

They had bought the house ten years earlier, and it was really all they owned, that and a rusting old van. They were devout Catholics, decent if unimaginative people, but they were proud of what they had accomplished. Proud of the fact Anna was in college and Jesus was studying in the community college. Danny was their failure and their source of shame. It was something he was always reminded of, even though it no longer took the form of angry accusations. Since those early years in high school, when he started using drugs and hanging out with the tough crowd, his father had despised what he knew of his life.

His mother called out from the kitchen and they went into the small dining room. His grandmother, bent, gray, almost totally deaf, already sat at the table, inspecting her plate as if she expected something to jump out at her. Danny got himself a beer from the refrigerator, patting his mom on the shoulder as he walked past her to sit.

"How are you, Grandma?" he asked, kissing her on the cheek. She looked up at him almost as if not recognizing who he was. "It's Danny, Grandma." he said with a grin. She greeted him and returned to her inspection of the plate.

"So, Danny, you got any steady girlfriend yet?" His father asked while his mother bustled around, dishing out the pork and placing the freshly made corn tortillas on the table.

"No, nothing steady, Papa. I see a couple of women every now and again, but nothing serious."

"You never have anything serious," his father grumbled. "About time you settled down and raised a family. I'd like to have grandchildren in my lifetime." They were the same tired old remarks he always made.

"Well, I'm working on it." Danny said. "How's the gardening business?"

His father shrugged, "Slow, you know. It's hard to find good help. The kids these days, all they want to do is go smoke marijuana in the back of the van. Nobody wants to work anymore; they want everything to come for free. Most of the kids are willing to steal for money. I don't know what this place is coming to. I started working when I was thirteen and I'm sixty now and I've never stopped. Six days a week, twelve-hour days, and I worked for what I got. Yes, I remember when I was a kid . . ."

Danny tuned out the speech, he had heard it many times before, what an educated friend of his had once called this Horatio Alger story with a twist: from rags to rags.

His family, like most of the people in the neighborhood, were suckers. People who worked themselves so hard they were old before their time. They could never understand that they had been exploited and used by Anglo society and by their money-grubbing church. Look at his father. All he had to show for it was a back injury, a small rundown house in a lousy neighborhood, and a beat-up old van. All his life he had worked, and this was all he had. But he was too stupid to see it. He wanted Danny to be the same, to work and work and work and marry some fat Mexican broad and have a bunch of kids he couldn't afford to feed and to get old fast. Not for him, no way.

And yet, on some level that even he was aware of, Danny loved his mother and respected his father. The man was honest, he had his standards, he was uncompromising. He never did anything he didn't feel good about doing, no matter how much money he was offered to do it. Stupid, but still to be admired. He would never admit it to anyone, and seldom admitted it to himself, but Danny wanted

82

their approval, probably more than just about anything.

He was twenty-seven now, earning good money and saving a lot of it. What he really wanted to do one day was to get into some legitimate business. But to do that, something better than what he was doing had to come along. Still, it was a possibility he was always aware of, even looking for, but so far there had been nothing to attract him away from his present lifestyle.

The words at the table jolted him from his reverie. As usual, his mother was protecting him. "Of course he's listening. Why shouldn't he be listening?" she was saying.

"Because he doesn't want to hear you have to work hard for money. He doesn't want to hear it again," his father said glumly.

"I'm listening, Papa." Danny said. "I work for my money, I work hard."

Selling what is it?" his father said ironically.

"Office products."

It was ordeal those three hours, evading his father's jabs and sly digs, his mother's concern as to whether he was eating properly, seeing nice girls, living in a nice place, doing well at his job. What future was there? When was he going to get married? Could he afford that nice car? Why didn't he think about going back to school and getting his diploma, etc, etc, *ad nauseum*. But it was something he always endured, perhaps out of guilt.

Finally, with relief, he said his goodbyes, put up with his mother's hugs, his father's "See you when you feel like dropping by again," kissed his lifeless grandmother on the cheek, and trotted toward his car as if it offered salvation and a refuge.

Driving back, he felt the predictable anger that descended upon him after one of these Sundays. Nobody had the right to think that they were better than he was. They weren't. His father was an idiot, a peasant. He made more money in a couple of months than his father made in a year. Who was he to take this condescending position? Shit, he was out of the barrio and they were still there.

He reached the Hollywood Freeway and accelerated out into the fast lane, enjoying the smooth power of the car. He was doing all right, he told himself, he was doing okay.

He thought back to his escape from the barrio. Naturally enough it had been a woman who had shown him his path out.

He had driven over to Hollywood with a friend and was hanging out on the boulevard with a few lids of grass to sell. But Danny was more interested in the people there than the business at hand. They ranged from the sublime to the preposterous, young and old, wealthy and poor. The hustlers and the hustled. He was standing at the newsstand at Las Palmas when the woman came up beside him. She picked a magazine off the rack and leafed through it. But somehow he knew her attention was on him.

She was in her thirties, blond, tanned, and affluent. It wasn't the three rings on her fingers that told him that, or her clothes—which were after all just the usual jeans and T-shirt. It was an aura she carried with her, something in the way she stood and in the bold way she looked at him, as if knowing she could buy anything she wanted, including the good-looking young Mexican boy beside her. And Danny Perez knew in that moment, before any word was spoken, that he was willing to be bought by the likes of her.

It lasted a couple of months, two appointments a week at a hundred bucks a throw. Her husband worked in the downtown garment district. "I think he spends his time fucking models because he sure as hell doesn't have shit left for me," she told him when he first started visiting her. He didn't care how she justified her actions. She had a great body and he was getting paid to enjoy it. When it started to cool off, she had introduced him to a friend.

Within a year Danny had moved to Hollywood and was servicing an average of three different women, a number of times each a week. They were all married of course, but that didn't bother him. In fact, he liked it that way. It kept the usual complications to a minimum.

From there it had been simply a hop, skip and jump to Debonaire, where the fees were larger and the clientele classier. He had few complaints. He was making good money and he could put up with his work. In fact, sometimes he even loved it.

"Fuck him," he said of his father as he crossed Cahuenga Pass and started to speed down the hill into the Valley. He wouldn't end up a loser like that. No way. All that disturbed him at that moment was a quick glimpse of a small blue Toyota in his rearview mirror as he took the Lankershim exit.

Chapter Six

San Pedro creeps up the western slopes of Los Angeles Harbor and overlooks pleasure boats, military and merchant craft, and one of the largest fishing fleets in Southern California. It is connected by a curving steel bridge to the thriving metropolis of Long Beach, famous for its convention center, oil refineries, and offshore oil wells, clumsily disguised as miniature subtropical island paradises.

San Pedro was once little more than a sleepy fishing village, but in recent years it has become chic, attracting developers and property-hungry yuppies with its relatively inexpensive bargains. It also boasts one of the largest Samoan populations outside of Samoa and New Zealand. This dislocated and sometimes violent social group works for the oil industry and the fishing fleet.

But it was not Samoans Marina had come to see. She was looking for another immigrant, a Vietnamese fisherman by the name of Ho Trig Man.

Wearing boots halfway up her calves, tight blue jeans, a beige silk shirt, and a red silk scarf, Marina looked as if she belonged anywhere but on the waterfront. Still, the stares she attracted were not unappreciative, and occasionally whistles followed in her wake.

After asking a half-dozen people, she finally found Ho's boat, a rusting, weatherbeaten, thirty-footer. Ho, a small and wiry Vietnamese man, was bustling around doing something with ropes.

She stopped on the edge of the dock and took out a camera. "Hi," she shouted.

The man, who appeared to be in his sixties, glanced up quickly and took her in. He had a lined face and sharp black eyes. Then he looked down and continued winding his rope. In the background, a younger Vietnamese washed the deck down with a hose.

According to the directions it was almost certainly Ho. As she had been told, the boat was named *Saigon 2*, but she had to be certain.

"Are you Mr. Ho?" she called.

He stopped what he was doing and looked at her suspiciously. "Yes, it's me. What you want?" he asked.

She looked at her camera. "Could I take a picture of your boat?"

"What for," he asked.

"It's a very pretty boat," she said. "I hear you are a good fisherman."

"Who talked to you of me?"

She shrugged her slender shoulders and said, "Just some fisherman down there," waving her hand. "Can I take a picture?"

"No, no picture," he said and turned his back.

She looked through the camera and got a shot of the boat's name and his bent figure.

He must have heard the click, because he spun around, his expression furious. "No, no picture," he shouted, waving his arm. She clicked again, getting his face this time.

He took a long fishing knife from his belt and waved it in the air. "No picture. Not allowed, no picture," he said.

This time she got a shot of him with the knife in his hand. Then he came toward her, still waving the knife, hurrying down the gangplank.

One more shot? she wondered. She decided against it, turned and hurried away, avoiding puddles of fishy water on the dock. She had what she had come for.

Susanne Lowell lightly brushed mascara on her long eyelashes and then stepped back from the mirror to examine the result. She wrinkled her nose, thinking as always that it was too large. All in all, however, the effect was fairly pleasing. She wore a tight and short black leather skirt, a pink T-shirt partially covered by a man's waistcoat, oversized crescent-shaped silver earrings, black stockings, and a pair of high black heels.

She was reaching for the lipstick when Annette's voice came from the door. "Where are you going, Susanne?"

She put a dab on her lips to check the color before answering. "There's a party. Bob's taking me."

"A party? Where?" Annette asked, entering the room and addressing her daughter's reflection in the mirror.

"Barry Donaldson's house."

"You shouldn't be going there," Annette "Donaldson is trash. It doesn't do you any good to be seen in a place like that, Susanne. You should know how important appearances are by now."

"He's just another producer, Mom, like half the people in this town," Susanne said impatiently.

"Those low-budget slasher films can hardly be called movies. Besides, it's a well-known fact that Donaldson is a heavy cocaine user and an indiscriminate womanizer."

"I don't do drugs, you know that. I've told you before."

"If you hang around with pigs you're liable to get dirty."

Susanne turned from the mirror to look at her mother. "I'm twenty-five years old, you know, and where I go should be of no concern to you. I passed the age of consent a long time ago."

"I'm your mother and I care about you. Besides, you're living here on my money, which gives me the right to be concerned."

It was an old argument, one that led up a blind alley. Rather than get into it, Susanne shrugged her shoulders and turned back to the mirror. "Well, I'm not getting into any trouble. Bob's a nice enough guy."

"Bob Coleman is another spoiled Beverly Hills brat," Annette said uncharitably.

In truth, Susanne couldn't argue that point. Bob wanted to be an actor and had appeared in one of Donaldson's films, a low-budget epic. His family was in real estate and immensely wealthy — wealthy enough, at least, to indulge his fantasies. They had sent him to acting school, reputedly invested in Donaldson's film, and generally done what they could. The fact of the matter, however, was that Bob had very little talent and would probably never make it in the business. Susanne knew all that, but he was still fun to hang out with. Even though she had refused to sleep with him, he still asked her out. He seemed to enjoy her company.

Annette moved backward and leaned against the doorjamb folding her arms across her chest. "While we are on the subject of you living here, what exactly are you planning to do with your life? At least, what's this week's plan? Don't you think it's time you took a serious look at that?"

Another shrug from Susanne. "I don't know, Mom. How about you fund a movie for me, let me produce it?" she said lightly.

"Get serious. If you really wanted to get into the film business, you should have stayed where you were and worked your way up, gained some experience."

"All I learned from the reading job was how to tell a good script from a bad one," Susanne said. "Once I knew that, there wasn't any point in staying there, no potential for advancement."

"Well, why don't you try and get a job in development? I could make some calls for you."

"Maybe I will if the right opening comes up," Susanne said.

"It's about time you started creating that opening, working for it instead of just waiting for something to fall in your lap. Life doesn't work that way. It takes hard work and dedication in this world. It takes drives and persistence."

"Spare me a lecture tonight, will you," Susanne said flippantly. "Bob's going to be here any moment and I still have to finish getting ready."

"Don't speak to me in that tone," Annette said, her voice rising. She glared at Susanne's reflection in the mirror. "I will not tolerate disrespect."

Susanne swung back around to her. "You force it on me. You push me and push me. You leave me no other way to turn. Why do you keep doing it? You know that I don't respond well to this kind of pressure."

Annette glared at her. "You don't respond well to anything that counters your desires. You're a self-indulgent, spoiled little child still, in spite of your age. And that's exactly how I am going to treat you." She turned and moved away.

As she went through the door, she said harshly over her shoulder. "Don't be in too late, I've had just about enough of this. You'll find yourself out on the street on your ass without a cent from me."

"Maybe that would be better," Susanne called out after her, her voice ragged with emotion.

She was still feeling upset by the time Bob picked her up in his white Mercedes convertible.

"Hey, Bob," she said, and hopped over the door, not waiting for him to open it.

"How goes every little thing?" he asked with a wide smile. He had fair hair, blue eyes, and a generally handsome face marred by a slightly receding chin.

"Let's get out of here," Susanne said.

He accelerated and the car leaped forward. "Trouble on the home front?" he asked, looking over at her.

"There's always trouble on the home front, if you can call it a home. It's a goddamn battle zone. That woman makes me sick sometimes."

"Your mother, huh? They can do that, can't they?" And then he changed the subject, indulging in some gossip about a mutual friend of theirs.

Barry Donaldson's house in Bel Air was a low-slung American ranch-style bungalow, nothing much to look at but probably worth a million and a half bucks in the remorselessly appreciating market. They parked on the street because the driveway was already full and walked in to the strains of raucous rock and roll, loud laughter, breaking glasses, yelps, and general mayhem.

The problem was, Susanne thought bleakly as she looked around at the chaos, her mother was right—Donaldson was trash, and so were most of his friends. She wondered what she was doing here, but it was a rhetorical question; the answer was that it was preferable to being at home. Anything was better than sitting before that forbidding and critical presence.

The host bounced joyously across a room to welcome them. Obviously he was already four sheets to the wind.

"Hey," he said, arms outstretched to hug them both. "I'm glad you could make it." A jocular bundle of sleaze, Susanne thought, suppressing a shudder. Donaldson was short, over-weight, and balding, with thick glasses that enlarged his eyes. He wore a gold chain around his neck, in defiance of both contemporary fashion and taste, a shirt unbuttoned halfway down his chest, tight blue jeans, and snakeskin boots. Susanne grimaced. He was a repulsive old man, no doubt about it.

"Make yourselves at home," he waved his hand. "Booze in that room, pharmaceuticals in the bedroom down there, lots of beautiful people all here to have a good time." Then he moved away to welcome a couple who had followed them in.

They made their way through the crowd to the room with the bar, chatting with a few people they knew along the way. When they reached it, Susanne poured herself a gin and tonic. Usually she drank white wine, but tonight she needed something to salvage the remainder of the evening.

She gulped half the drink down and looked around. It was the usual crowd: would-be actors, over-the-hill actors, bogus producers with naive and hopeful starlets, thin and insolent models, the usual drunks and cokeheads.

"You want to go into the other room and do a line?" Bob asked.

"You always ask that question and I always say no, Bob," she said, leveling an irritated gaze at him. "Why do you always ask that question? I tried it once and I didn't like it.

I've told you that."

"Well, maybe it wasn't good stuff," Bob said.

She turned away from him, and walked across the room toward the patio.

"Hello, there. How's it going?" The man who spoke to her seemed familiar. He was short, about 5' 5", hair greying at the temple yet handsome in a rakish sort of way. He smiled crookedly at her, an appraising look of admiration in his eyes.

"Just fine," she said, and continued out the doors to the patio.

Half a dozen people frolicked in the pool; two of the girls were already topless. She watched them from the patio door and then downed the remainder of the drink. She stood there with the empty glass in her hand, gloomily consulting the night sky for signs.

The trouble was, she told herself again, that her mother was right. She really needed to do something. She needed to find an activity that would catch her imagination, something exciting enough to motivate her, to which she could devote her energy. This kind of frivolous life wasn't for her. She knew it, but somehow to have her mother constantly point it out to her made the pill more bitter to swallow. There was no way for Annette to give her advice without making her seem stupid or incompetent in some way. It probably wasn't intended, it was just Annette's manner. As a business tycoon of some note, she was used to bossing people around. Unfortunately, the members of her family were also subjected to it.

"Oh, God, Gordy Winston is here," said a voice at her elbow. She turned to see a blond girl in jeans and tanktop with a rapturous expression on her face. She was about her own age or a couple of years younger. It was not someone she had met before.

"I beg your pardon," Susanne asked.

"Gordy Winston's here. God, he's so awesome! I can't stand it. I cream myself every time I look at him," the girl said, beside herself with excitement and glee.

"Oh, you mean the actor?"

"Yeah, Gordy. He's on TV, on 'Flight Patterns.' It's the hottest show going. He's even better looking in person than he is on television."

"Well, I'm glad for you," Susanne said drily.

"Be glad for me by the end of the night. I swear I'm going to find a way to fuck his brains out," the girl said.

"Yeah, well, good luck," Susanne said and stepped further out onto the patio.

She stood there for a moment, looked at the empty glass in her hand, and turned and went back into the main room. She headed for the bar and poured herself another gin and tonic.

Bob stood in the hallway talking earnestly to a slim brunette wearing a leather skirt similar to Susanne's and what seemed to be the same high heels.

The conversation in the room reeled around her in the same monotonous, never-ending patterns.

"I swear to God he was wearing a toupee. It wasn't real, it wasn't even an expensive one. You'd think he could afford an expensive one or a hair transplant or something."

"She has AIDS, everybody knows it."

"Yeah, well, we're just waiting for the final answer from the money men and expect to begin shooting in the fall."

"I just took a meeting earlier today with Richard Gere. He's been into Tibetan Buddhism, but he's about to make a big comeback, a real big comeback. He's gonna knock this town on its ass."

"She's hot, she's hot. She's going to be as big as Elizabeth Taylor was in her heyday."

"Hey babe, why don't we go snort a few lines and then go back your place and get naked."

"Why don't you fuck off, asshole."

They weren't even really conversations, Susanne realized as she listened. They were poses, assertions, glib statements. Very little real communication took place at parties like this.

The man with the crooked smile who greeted her earlier came up to her again. "You don't remember me, do you?"

"I'm sorry," she said.

93

"We met at a party about six months ago, Daryl Hannah's place."

"Oh, well, nice to see you again," she said.

"We talked. I thought there was a certain chemistry between us. Don't you remember?"

"Chemistry?" she said.

"Well, I find you very attractive and I thought you felt the same way about me."

"I'm sorry, you must be thinking of someone else," she said coolly.

"Well, why don't we just chat and see if it's still there," he suggested, leaning closer to her.

"I know you're thinking of someone else," she said tartly.

"Well, I certainly find you attractive and maybe you find me the same way. Why don't we go outside and talk," he said persistently.

"I don't find you the slightest bit attractive," she said and walked away.

She approached Bob and interrupted him while he was in midsentence with the brunette.

"Bob, I'd like to go now."

"What do you mean go? We just got here."

"The party's a drag," she said stiffly. "Why don't we go somewhere else."

Bob looked at the brunette and looked back at her. "Look, let's just stay a while longer."

"I really want to go," she said.

"Look, I want to stay," Bob said. "Why don't you just give it a chance. Sit down and relax somewhere and have another drink."

"I want to go," she said firmly. "Why don't you take me home then and you can come back."

Bob took another look at the brunette, who was listening to all this with an interested expression; Bob obviously had designs on her. With Susanne out of the way, he might even realize them.

"All right," he said quickly, "I'll take you home."

"Or we can go somewhere else," Susanne said maliciously.

94

Bob stood his ground. "I don't want to go anywhere else. I want to come back here. There are a lot of people here that I haven't talked to that I want to talk to. I'll take you home or you can stay a little while longer."

Susanne shrugged. "Take me home."

It wasn't a very social journey at first, but after five minutes Bob relented and made pleasant enough small talk. He dropped her off at her house and tore away—back to the brunette, no doubt, she thought cynically.

She let herself in the front door and went through the hall toward her bedroom in the back of the house. Her mother came out of the living room where she had been sitting with Susanne's father and said, "Back so soon?"

"The party was a drag," Susanne said. "I didn't see any reason to stay there. Besides, you were right. Donaldson is a creep."

She continued walking as her mother said behind her, "I usually am, aren't I? If you kept that in mind, your life would be a lot easier."

Susanne fought a rising rage. She wanted to turn around. She wanted to scream, "Fuck you" to her mother.

She had made a concession, a small one, but she had made a concession, and somehow Annette couldn't accept it. She had to throw it back at her, to make her feel wrong, to rub her face in the dirt.

Instead of saying anything, she just squared her shoulders and kept walking toward her room.

Marina called and asked Sean if he would have lunch with her.

It had been a week since he had started working for Debonaire. He had already repaid Nancy Hamilton the advance and still had more than a thousand dollars in his pockets. His situation had changed drastically. From penniless actor to affluent man of the world. He still felt uncomfortable about what he was doing, particularly his last date with Kate Kaplan. But there was no denying that affluence was a more desirable condition than poverty. And, to a large degree, he owed his current good fortune to Marina.

Still, experience urged him to treat her suspiciously. "What do you want?" he asked cautiously.

"I just want to see how things are going, whether the job is working out."

He hesitated. She sounded virtually normal—cheerful, bright, with no ulterior motive immediately evident. "Is that all?" he asked.

She laughed, a light tinkle on the other end of the phone. "Of course it is, Sean. Listen, I'm straight now. I'm getting my act together. I just wanted to see you for old times' sake, see how things were."

They met at the Hamburger Hamlet on Sunset Boulevard. He arrived first and took a booth. When he saw her being ushered down the aisle by the hostess, it struck him that perhaps she had been telling the truth. She looked radiant, almost as good as when he first met her.

Her brown hair was lustrous, her skin flushed and healthy, her eyes bright. There was a bounce to her step again. She wore boots, a short skirt, and a satin blouse, and he had to admit she looked quite lovely.

"Hi," she said. She bent to kiss his cheek, then slid in to the booth opposite him. "How are you, Sean? You look good."

"I'm fine. You look pretty good yourself. I'm glad."

"Yeah, well, I'm feeling fine, like I said. I'm getting straight and everything's looking better."

"Doing any work?" he asked.

A momentary flicker clouded her eyes. "I'm trying out for a few things, but nothing's happened yet."

"Well, I'm glad to hear you're active again," he said.

"How about you, how's the job going?" she asked.

Sean shrugged. "It's all right, I guess. The money is good."

"Yeah, real good," she said.

"How did you hear about it?" he asked. "I mean, how do you know Nancy Hamilton?"

"Well, Debonaire is a male escort service, right? The company also runs a female escort service called Panache. I

96

worked there for a little while, got friendly with Nancy. Didn't last too long, I didn't like the work."

"Oh." Sean said, slightly bewildered by this news. "I didn't know that."

"I'm sorry about your play," Marina said. "Are you going out on any calls now?"

Sean shook his head, trying to suppress the guilty feeling. No, he hadn't gone out on any calls. His agent had telephoned him once to set something up, but he had begged off saying the part didn't sound like it was for him. Since starting work at the escort agency, his drive or need to go and subjugate himself before casting directors had somehow diminished. Perhaps it was the fresh money in his pocket, perhaps it was something else.

They ordered and during the desultory talk while they waited for their food Sean thought back to his relationship with Marina. She truly was a beautiful woman; he had been more than a little in love with her at first. Initially, her spirit had attracted him, a kind of gusto with which she approached everything, a certain *joi de vivre*.

In the early days of their relationship the communication between them had been almost adolescent, it was so high-spirited. There was a lot of laughter, physical tumbling around, and crude references to bodily functions and parts — all done in an exhilarating spirit of play. He had never really had a relationship like that with a woman before. And it had been an exhilarating experience.

But then, like clouds against a blue sky, the shadows had come. First a new kind of desperation came over Marina, a shrillness, an edge. Then came the evasions, the lies, and finally the betrayals.

"I think the new Pacino movie was wonderful," she was saying. "Now there's an example of someone who blew it but was able to come back."

"Eric Clapton's another," he said.

"Greg Allman," she suggested.

He looked across at her in a sudden moment of clarity and wondered if she had really changed again. If not, she was putting on a good act. Still, as an actor he knew it was possible. Even the healthy appearance could simply be due to the marvels of makeup. He hated himself for thinking such thoughts, for distrusting her so. And yet one lesson he had learned the hard way was that a coke addict could not be trusted. An addict had only one loyalty — to the habit. Trust, kindness — they were never returned and never appreciated.

During their coffee she broached her real reason for the meeting. "I wonder if you could do me a favor?" she asked.

"What?" he said, suddenly alert.

"Well, you know my friend Sue?"

Sean nodded.

"Sue Winston," she added unnecessarily. "Well, she had herself pregnant, and apparently the guy who did it has skipped town and she wants to try and find him; get some kind of support out of him. But she can't."

"That's too bad," Sean said. "But how can I help?"

Marina looked away quickly and then back at him. "Well, the guy used to work for Debonaire," she said. "His name's Varney. He hasn't worked there for a while, but they may have some information on him."

"You want me to ask Nancy?" Sean said. "Why don't you just call her and ask her yourself."

Marina just shook her head. "No, I don't want you to ask and I can't call. She's very protective toward her employees. Their files are like gold to them. They don't let anybody see them and they don't give out the information."

"So?"

"Well, I was wondering if you could get a look at the files," Marina asked.

"You mean sneak into their files, like a spy, and look up this guy's record?" Sean asked, feeling once again betrayed by Marina. "Is this why you got me the job there, Marina? Is that why you wanted to help me out — 'cause you wanted to get me into the company so I could look up this *file* for you?"

"No, not at all," she said, outraged. "For Christ sake, Sean, what do you think I am? I only found out about this yesterday. And she only found out about her pregnancy last week. I just thought you might be able to help out. Christ, the poor chick has been left in a lurch. She is scared, she is pregnant, and she doesn't know what to do. All she wants to do is contact this guy. God, Sean, how could you think I'd do that?"

Sean wanted to believe her even though he knew he shouldn't. But he wanted to. He really did. And he felt himself wilt before her convincing defense. She was looking at him guilelessly, her eyes suddenly innocent, waiting to see what his reaction would be.

He wanted to sigh, but instead he said, "I don't think I can help you, Marina."

She reached across the table and touched his hand, a quick gesture before withdrawing. "Sean, this is no big deal," she said. "I just want you to look in the file and see if there is an address on the guy, a forwarding address or phone number or anything like that. It will take you a second. It's the last favor I'll ask you. I'm not even asking you for myself. I don't want anything out of this for myself. I'm asking for Sue. She's the one that needs help."

Sean toyed with his spoon for a long moment, then he looked up at her. "I'm not promising anything; I'm not going to risk the job to do this for you. You understand that, don't you?"

"I wouldn't want you to do anything that would put you at risk," she said quickly. "But if the opportunity comes up, just to have a look at the file. Really, that's all I want you to do."

"All right," Sean said. "If the opportunity comes up and only if it presents itself. I'm not going to go out of my way to do this and I'm not going to take any chances. If it comes up, I'll see what information I can find out for you."

Again she reached across the table and clasped his hand in hers. "Thanks, Sean. Thanks a lot. I won't forget this."

He stared into her bright and beautiful eyes and wondered why he felt he had just been taken for a ride.

Chapter Seven

She could only be described as angelic. Correction, Ted thought, saintly was an even better word.

Her perfectly formed features were serene, the azure eyes calm and placid, showing no hint of expression. And yet in almost shocking contrast, there was a deeply sensual curve to the full mouth. Blonde hair fell in waves to her shoulders. A draping blue dress hinted at hidden curves and swells.

She stood in front of his table and looked down at him without speaking. He noticed that she was tall, almost his height.

And then, as he faced the curious void in her eyes, she said, "You'll do."

Ted grinned more confidently than he felt and said, "I'm glad to hear it."

She slid opposite him into the booth, her eyes still examining him. He had been waiting, as instructed, in the dim corner of the bar in the Hollywood Holiday Inn.

The waitress came over and asked for their order. The lady raised an inquiring eyebrow at him.

"I'll have a beer. What about you?"

"A 7-Up", she said.

"My name is Ted Marshall."

"You may call me Cecelia," she said, her voice thin yet clear and powerful.

Ted cleared his throat and said, "Well, Cecelia, are you

100

visiting town?"

"Yes."

"And where have you come from?"

"It doesn't matter," she said. "We don't have to make small talk."

The waitress arrived with their drinks and placed them on the table. She stood there for a moment and Ted realized he would have to pay. He pulled a ten-dollar bill out of his pocket and handed it to her. He sat in silence while she counted the change and placed it back on the table. He held out a dollar, "For you."

When she had gone, he felt the woman's eyes still on him and returned her gaze. That placid look was on her face again, but somehow it seemed that the eyes were looking right into him, expressionless as they were.

"Well, what shall we talk about?" he asked, a trace of irritation in his voice.

"Do you belong to a church?" she asked.

"What?" Ted said. The non sequitur question was both incongruent and incomprehensible. "Church?"

"Yes," she said. "Do you have a religion, a church you go to?"

"No." Ted shook his head. "I was raised . . . I mean, my family was Catholic so I was raised that way, but I stopped going a long time ago."

"You should go to a church," she said.

"I'm not the churchgoing type." Ted smiled. "I like sin much too much."

"All the more reason you should go to church," she said. "A person like you, you need to balance things out. If you were still a practicing Catholic you could sin all you wanted to and then go to confession. Isn't that what Catholics do?"

Ted shrugged. "I suppose so, I don't see the need for it, though."

"Everyone has a need for forgiveness." she said mildly. "Sinners in particular have a need for forgiveness. Surely you can see that."

He didn't know what to say. He couldn't believe he was sitting here with this beautiful woman having a discussion about religion in a place like this, on a night like this, knowing what they were going to do. He looked around the bar, almost as if to see whether anyone was watching them. He turned back to her. "And what about you? Do you get forgiveness for your sins?"

"I *am* forgiven," she said with utter certainty. "Shall we go now?"

Ted looked down at his beer and said, "Where are we going?"

"I have a room down the street at the Roosevelt," she said. "I'd like you to walk down there with me and wait outside for about two minutes while I go in. Then you can follow me in. I'll give you the number. Suite 634."

"Sure, whatever you like," Ted said. He drained the rest of his beer.

They both stood and he held out his arm. When she took it, her hand felt as light as air. "Cecelia, right?" he asked.

She nodded regally, as if to one of her subjects, and they walked out through the bar.

As they left the elevator and entered the lobby, a woman standing ahead of them in front of the bookstore grew suddenly excited. She was in her sixties, with a leathery brown face, and was wearing a frock covered in large floral prints. She looked at them, swung her head back to the shop window and then back at them. Then she hurried over to intercept Cecelia.

Cecelia slowed as the woman cautiously touched her arm. "Sister Cecelia," she gushed. "It's so nice to meet you. I just want to let you know how inspired I get from you. Bless you for the example you provide us."

Almost imperceptibly, Cecelia increased the pace. "Thank you," she said, smiling over her shoulder at the woman. And then, in a moment, they were out of the lobby.

"My God," Ted said as soon as they stepped into the cool

night air. "You're Sister Cecelia, the evangelist, aren't you? I've seen you on television. You get on stage with little angel wings and a choir and all that stuff and you preach, right?"

"That is correct," Cecelia said.

He walked silently beside her down Highland Avenue toward Hollywood Boulevard, his mind extremely active. This was hard to believe. He had seen her on television. She was nationally famous, probably even internationally, as far as he knew. She packed them in wherever she went, spreading the Word of Christian love, accompanied by the normal evangelical tirades against sin and sinners. Presumably she made a fortune doing it.

He found himself automatically wondering how he could turn this to his advantage. Nothing came to mind immediately. But he knew subconsciously he would keep turning the problem over until it resolved—hopefully to his benefit.

As they had planned, he waited on the sidewalk while she went inside. After a couple of minutes he entered and walked through the deeply carpeted lobby underneath glistening chandeliers to the elevators. He went up to the sixth floor and down the corridor to the room number she had given him.

He knocked on the door. "Come in," he heard the voice say. He turned the handle and pushed the door open. There was only a dim light in one corner and no sign of Cecelia in the living room.

"In here," came a voice from the bedroom.

He took off his jacket and draped it over one of the armchairs and then walked to the other dimly lit room. He stopped at the doorway and saw a movement beside the bed.

She was kneeling there, her elbows resting on the mattress, her hands clasped in prayer. And she was totally naked except for a pair of silver angel's wings that were strapped to her back.

He stood frozen in the doorway, not believing what he was seeing. Ted had certainly confronted his share of bi-

103

zarre sexual encounters during his lifetime, but this one took the cake.

"Amen," she said, stood up and turned to face him.

She held her hands out to him, palms raised as if in supplication, that serene expression still on her face.

"Now, ravish me," she said.

Jesus, Ted thought, for the first time in many years, I hope I can. This was distracting—too, too weird.

Ted thought that Sister Cecelia must have had God on her side, providing her with supernatural energy, because she proved to be virtually insatiable, possessed of inextinguishable appetites.

Over breakfast, brought to the suite by room service while he waited in the bathroom, she told him more about herself. She was, he thought, the strangest, most fascinating woman he had ever met. Particularly when she told him who she really was.

"Aimee Semple McPherson."

"I beg your pardon?" Ted said. "Wasn't she an evangelist as well. Didn't she die?"

"Well, yes, she died in 1944, but I was born a few months after she died. I'm Aimee reincarnated. I knew it by the time I was fifteen." Gone was the inscrutable serenity, replaced by an energized zeal.

"Really?" Ted said, not knowing what else to say.

Cecelia nodded firmly. "When I was about fifteen I saw some old newsreel footage showing some of her ceremonies and some other scenes, and there was this achingly familiar feeling, like I knew what she was about. And then before the end of the documentary, I knew she killed herself with an overdose of sleeping pills. There were other things that I just knew. And then it came to me that this had been me."

"Really?" Ted said again, and began to examine his egg.

She gave him a scornful look. "You don't believe me? Well, that doesn't matter. I know the truth myself."

"No, no," Ted said hastily, "it's not for me to believe you. It's just something I don't know anything about. I mean, I don't know. What do I know? If you believe that, that's fine."

Cecelia nodded. "I read everything about her. How she started out, getting married at the age of seventeen, going to China where her preacher husband died, how she had a daughter and came back to the U.S., got married again and had a second son, and then packed up her kids in a large tent and started her career as a traveling revivalist.

"It was a hard time for her until she came to Southern California and discovered she could heal people. She always used to say, 'I'm not a healer, Jesus is the healer. I'm only the little office girl who opens the office door and says come in.' And then she opened the Angelus Chapel in Echo Park and started Foursquare Gospel, sending it around the nation, around the world, by radio. I know it all."

"I don't know much about her, but wasn't there some kind of scandal?" Ted said.

Cecelia's mouth grew hard. "Yes, there was. There was a disappearance and the press tried to crucify her. She claimed that she had been abducted and held prisoner, but a bunch of newspaper reporters decided that she had actually gone off with her lover, a married man who operated her radio station. It was a terrible scandal."

She smiled triumphantly. "But that was in 1926. Aimee overcame it. Even though she didn't have the same number of followers, she had the loyal ones until she died in 1944 in a hotel room."

"And she killed herself?"

"Yes, so it is said."

"Well, how you can be the reincarnation of her? I mean, Christians don't believe in reincarnation, right?"

"Dogma," she spat the word out. "How can they know? You Catholics believe that someone who commits suicide is condemned to hell, right? Well, why couldn't that condemnation to hell be a return to earth, to live life again.

105

Isn't that a kind of hell, compared to going to heaven?"

"I suppose so," Ted said growing bored with the conversation. He had never struggled with questions like these, not for a minute in his life. He had always been interested in the here and now and what it could give him.

Still, he thought he could create some mischief. "And you're a little like Aimee, too, aren't you—in that you partake in the pleasures of the flesh?"

"Why wither on the vine? A woman is supposed to have love with a man. It says so in the Bible," she said.

"But this isn't what you tell your congregation," Ted said slyly. "From what I've heard, you preach against the sins of the flesh outside of wedlock."

"Not all of us can be married. Besides, I am a disciplined person. My congregation is not as lucky. I can control my desires." Ted thought back to the previous night and the frenzy with which she had made love and wondered if now she even remembered it. In any case, control of her desires had not been a major factor.

"Well," he said, pushing himself back from the table. "I guess I had better get going."

"I'd like to see you again when I'm back in town," she said.

"That will be fine, just call the agency."

"I'd prefer a more direct method."

Ted shook his head. "I'm afraid that's not allowed."

"I'm a very wealthy woman. I'll make it worth your while. Why don't you give me your telephone number? I'll call you directly."

"I'd get fired if anyone found out," Ted said.

"You have my word that nobody will," she said insistently. "Besides, for obvious reasons, we will never go out in public. And if for any reason you got into trouble for seeing me, you also have my word that I'll make it worth your while financially."

Ted looked at her for a moment. Crazy as she was, he believed her. "All right," he said.

Five minutes later he walked out of the apartment, well

satisfied and five hundred dollars richer. Hell, by pocketing the agency fee as well in the future, he'd make a fortune off her. Still, he couldn't dispel the nagging thought he might later have reason to regret this arrangement.

Susanne's father, Kenneth Lowell was sitting in an armchair, a sheaf of papers on his lap, glasses perched on the end of his nose as he studied them.

She stood in the doorway of his office and watched him for a moment. He looked so vulnerable, so open to the disturbances of the world at moments like these, it brought a strange motherly feeling to her.

He was in his late fifties, with gray hair receding at the temples, brown eyes and slightly rounded shoulders, probably from sitting and reading too much, just like this. All in all, however, at 5'11", with a long straight nose and a wide chin, he was a distinguished if not exactly handsome man.

He must have sensed her presence, because he looked up over his glasses. "Oh, Susanne. Hi, what are you up to?"

She ambled further into the room, then slipped into the chair across from him, her legs over the side of the armrest. "Just wanted to have a chat," she said.

He took the papers off his lap and placed them on the table beside him, then removed his glasses. "Yes?" he said patiently.

"Well," she began, "you know Mom's been after me to do something with my life, as she calls it?" Kenneth nodded and she continued. "I've been thinking about it and I think I've decided what I want to do. I'd like to get into the film business and I need your help."

"As an actress?" he asked, a hint of disbelief in his voice.

She shook her head. "No, I want to get into production, to become a producer. I think it's something I'd be good at. You may not know it, but I do have organizational

107

skills. I also have a literary sensibility that I think would help me find good properties and develop them."

"It's not something I know too much about. Your mother would probably be more help than me. She knows all kinds of people in the film business. I mean, she could probably get you a job in a studio. I think she has offered to do that before. Either that or with an independent producer."

She shook her head again. "That's not what I want. I don't want a job, Dad. I don't want to *work* for a producer, I want to *be* one. I know a lot of people in the business myself and I know a lot of producers or people who call themselves producers. I'm brighter than most of them. I know more. I have more energy. In fact, I probably have even more contacts if I actually sat down and wrote them all on a piece of paper. I don't need to start somewhere at the bottom. I'm not a kid anymore. I think I could handle the business side of things pretty well. I'm planning to take a course at UCLA in production, financing in particular."

He looked impressed. "Well, that's very good. But what do you need my help with?"

"With Annette," she said. "I need some capital to get started. I have my eye on three books that haven't been optioned. All three of them would be good commercial films — quality, but commercial, which is the way I want to go. I'd like to option them and try to get a package together and also come up with a little development money to get at least a first draft screenplay out of a writer."

"What kind of money are you talking about?" he asked with a frown.

"I probably need about five thousand for the option and probably could get away with about ten thousand for a first draft screenplay, which I'd option instead of buy outright."

"I see," he said. "Why don't you just ask her for the money?"

An irritated look marred Susanne's pretty face. "You know what she's like; she doesn't think I can do anything.

She doesn't think I have any value whatsoever. And all my money is tied up in the trust. Sure, she can afford it, fifteen thousand is nothing to her. A hundred thousand wouldn't be anything to her, but with the attitude she has toward me . . ."

Kenneth nodded almost imperceptibly, probably even unconscious that he was doing it, she thought. "So what do you want me to do?" he asked.

"I'd just like you to talk to her, to prepare her for it. Not to mention money, but to tell her this is an area I'm getting interested in and encourage her, let her know that you think that I can do it. Kind of lay the groundwork. Tell her you think that it's a good thing. I mean, do you?"

"Yes, I think it's a good thing, and yes, I think you can do it. You're a bright girl with a lot of energy. All you've needed is direction, and if this is something you really want to do . . ."

"I do," she said emphatically. "There is nothing else I am really interested in. I think I could make an impact in this field. I don't expect to, you know, be a producer, make a hit movie, right away. But I think I can build a career."

"Well, when you have a screenplay, what are you going to do? You're going to need funding to get a movie done."

"Well," she said. "I've thought of that. And I know I don't have the money and I know I won't get it from either you or Annette so I'll go to another production company or studio with the project. I mean, if the project is hot enough, based on a book other people want to get their hands on but which I get my hands on first, I can carve myself some sort of a niche in the project. At the least, I'll get a credit as producer, executive producer, associate producer, something—whatever I can negotiate. If somebody goes for the project, I'll also get back my original investment, which I'll then be able to return to Annette. I'll be working on a film and I'll have a title and I'll have a credit. From that point on I can do the same thing, each time learning a little more and going a little further."

"You've really thought this out, haven't you?"

"I have."

"Well, I'll talk to her, try to break ground for you," he said. "But you know you are going to have to sell yourself when it comes down to it. You've just sold yourself to me, but your Mother is a much harder nut to crack."

"Thanks," she said, "that's all I need right now." She got up, walked over to his chair, and kissed him on the cheek. "You're not such a bad father," she said.

"Who said I was?" he said in mock indignation. "Anyway, I suspect I'm a better father than I'm going to be a politician."

She went back to her chair. "What do you mean? Is Mom after you to run for office again?"

"Annette has been grooming me for years to run for office. You know that. It's getting close to that time. She actually wants me to do it."

Kenneth had started his career as a lowly lawyer in a large firm. The appointment as judge had been politically inspired through Annette's many contacts in the local Democratic party establishment. He had been a judge for almost seven years and he seemed happy with it. Now she wanted him to run for Congress, then for a senate seat that was opening up when Senator Dobbs retired. It was all planned, carefully orchestrated, each step along the path.

"Do you think you have a chance of winning?" she asked.

He smiled briefly. "With your mother behind me, how could I lose? I'm just not sure about it now."

"Is it something you want to do? I thought you were happy being a judge."

He looked at her and once again she saw that sadness in his eyes, a sadness she first noticed months ago. It seemed to grow each day—some regret, misgiving, or fear.

"Whether I want to do it or not seems to be beside the point," he said quietly.

"If you don't want to do it, don't do it. I mean, for God's sake, if you're happy doing what you are doing, why

110

change?"

He looked at her with something like puzzlement and then finally said, "It's too late. It was too late a long time ago."

She gazed back at him, somehow knowing what he meant, yet not knowing what to say to make him feel better.

He picked up the papers from the table beside him, placed them back on his lap. "I better get on with this. It's supposed to be due in the morning. I'll talk to your mother about your movie ambitions, don't worry."

She looked at her feet, wondering if there was anything she could say to him, but there wasn't. "Okay, thanks. Goodnight."

"Goodnight" he said, putting his glasses on again.

She walked out the door, and it seemed as if the weight of his sadness was on her shoulders.

Sean had a 7:00 p.m. appointment with Nancy Hamilton. It was what she called his ten-day review. "Just to go over how things are going for you and to give you any feedback I've got, and generally to see if everything is okay," she had told him over the phone.

During the drive over he had wrestled again with the decision facing him: to quit or not to quit? Aye, that is the question, he thought mockingly to himself as he crested Mulholland Drive and began the descent on Laurel Canyon.

He wanted to quit and yet he didn't. Well, not exactly. He wanted to quit, but he didn't want to lose the nice cushion of cash the job was bringing him. There were all kinds of pros and cons, too many to allow an easy decision. Too many gray areas.

The truth of the matter was that although there was much he disliked about this life, there was also much he disliked about "working" as an actor. "Struggling" was more like it, he thought. While there were indignities to be

111

faced now, there were just as many as an actor. Going out on endless and futile casting calls, begging for parts, suffering sometimes callous and degrading rejection, keeping the smile on his face because who knew when he might be up again for another part before the same casting director. Yessuh! Yessuh! May I kiss your ass again? God, he hated that part of the business. And what about the results? No work, no money, and some menial job for an almost living wage.

At least now he was making money. His "fuck you" money. If he kept this up for a few months, even a year, he'd have a nice nest egg. Money to dress with, to go to the right places where he could make the contacts an actor needed, money with which to say "fuck you" to the next asshole casting director who gave him a hard time.

God! He didn't know what to do. What he really wanted to do was quit. But he didn't want to quit a pauper. On the other hand, would these injuries to his pride have deleterious long-term effects? Probably.

He drove down Sunset Boulevard, half noticing the billboards advertising the latest movies. Once he had envisioned his face up there; now it seemed a distant possibility. No matter how he needed money, he seemed to be retreating from that goal instead of advancing toward it.

He'd quit the job, he suddenly decided. The hell with it. He'd quit and go back to pounding the pavement. Probably. Almost certainly . . .

When he arrived, Nancy was seated in the reception area with a thin, pasty-faced young man. Dry blond hair hung almost to his shoulders. "Oh, good evening," she said to Sean. She looked at her watch. "You're right on time, but I'm afraid that I'm not."

She stood up and waved her hand at the man she was talking to. "Gary, this is Sean. Sean, why don't you go on into my office while I finish up here. I shouldn't be more than five minutes."

"That's fine," he said and went through the corridor and down to her office. There was nobody around in any of the rooms, he noticed.

He entered her office and stood uncertainly in the center of the room. Behind her desk were three filing cabinets, which reminded him of Marina's plea that he look up the file on Alex Varney, the father of her girlfriend's baby.

He wondered nervously if he should do it now, and almost immediately felt a surge of adrenaline. He stepped back to the door, listened, heard nothing and quickly went over to one of the filing cabinets. He opened it and saw what looked like accounts, credit card numbers. This wasn't it. He opened the next one. Alphabetized names he didn't recognize, possibly clients. He looked for Danny's name and for his, not there.

His nervousness growing, he went back to the door and listened again. He probably only had a minute or two left, he thought, and moved quickly back to the third and last cabinet.

He opened it and immediately saw Ted Marshall's folder. Moving up the alphabet past Sean Parker, Danny Perez, someone named Paul Quance, he saw an Alex Varney. That was it. Without taking the folder out, he opened it and glanced at the contents. A list of clients the man had taken out. Some other papers. There it was: an address on Carlton Way in Hollywood—6040, and an apartment number. Mumbling it to himself, he quickly closed the folder and slammed the door shut.

He was just coming around to the side of her desk when he heard a noise in the hall. Quickly he turned and looked out the large window as if just admiring the evening view.

"Hi, thanks for waiting."

He looked around as if surprised. "I was just looking at the city. It's pretty here at night," he said, his voice feeling thick and clumsy in his own ears.

Nancy didn't seem to notice anything out of place. "Yes, it's nice," she said, coming around to the other side of the

113

desk. He moved back to one of the armchairs facing her. "Well, let me see," she said standing there for a moment, tapping her fingers on the oak top.

She turned and opened the very filing cabinet he had just been looking through and took out his folder. She went back to her desk and opened the folder. Then she looked up at him. "Well, how do you like it so far?" she asked.

Sean took a deep breath, gathering himself, repeating once more in his mind—6040 Carlton Way. "Well," he said finally, "I don't know if I'm cut out for this kind of work."

"Oh," she said with some surprise. "You've been having problems?"

Sean shrugged. "Well, not exactly. It's just doing what I'm doing. I don't know if it's really something that suits me."

"I see," she said, scanning the few sheets of paper before her. "According to this you have been doing very well. You've had five or six assignments, and what's unusual is that three of them have called to say how pleased they were with you and that they'd like to use you as an escort again.

"Now, we always ask our customers to let us know how the evening was, how the escort was, so that we can keep on top of our guys and maintain some sort of quality control, but it's not that common that they take the trouble to do it. Three out of six is pretty good." She looked up at him and smiled.

"Which three were those?" Sean stammered.

"Doris Winston, Mavis Batten, and Kate Kaplan," she said.

"Well, I guess that's gratifying," Sean said. "It's just that I'm not very comfortable with this, you know."

"Have there been any demands to make you uncomfortable, any situations that you'd like to tell me about?" she asked.

Sean felt his face warm. "No," he said, not meeting her eyes. "No, nothing like that."

"Well, look," she said, "why don't you just give it a try a little longer. The money's good enough, isn't it?"

"Yes," he said, "the money's fine." It had been a long time since he had had this much disposable income.

"So why not give it another week? See how it goes," she said. "I would hate to lose you. I think you are really cut out for this kind of work and would be a valuable asset to this company."

"Well," he started to say uncertainly.

"Three more assignments," she said with a persuasive smile. "Give me three more and then we'll talk again. Don't make up your mind yet. I would hate to see you throw a very promising career away."

"Well, it not exactly a career," he ventured. "It's more a job; careers lead somewhere."

"Who knows where this could lead?" she said. "What contacts you'd make as an actor? Who's to say what could happen? In any case, job or career, I think it has more value to you than you realize, even more than just fulfilling your immediate needs. So just give me those three more assignments and then we'll talk again. Okay?"

Sean wavered. "Well, I suppose so. There's not much harm in that," he said.

"Good," she said, rising behind her desk. "Then I'll arrange something for you tomorrow and you will get a call in the morning to let you know the details. And then we'll get the next two set up. And then we'll have a nice chat."

"Okay," Sean said. "Thanks."

"You're doing well," she said. "Keep it up."

When he reached home only Danny was there. He was sitting in the living room listening to the jazz station, KKGO, a drink in his hand. "You got the night off too," Danny said.

"Yeah, I just had a meeting with Nancy," Sean said. He went to the refrigerator, got a bottle of beer, and opened it.

"Your review, huh? Gee, I forgot about those. How did it go?" Danny asked.

"Boy, she is a slick one," Sean said sinking into a chair. "I feel like I've been conned."

"Why, what happened?"

"Well, I don't know if I really like this gig, you know. And I sort of tried to tell her that, but she just wasn't having it. So she got me to agree to go on three more dates and then reconsider."

Danny smiled. "Well, she knows how to handle men, that one. She used to be a hooker, man. She should."

"Really?" Sean asked. "Nancy Hamilton, a hooker?"

"That's what Ted told me and he's pretty tight with her. He told me that when I first started. But she is a classy lady, no doubt about that. We're not talking about working the streets here, we're talking about a high-class call girl. Anyway, apparently she used to do that before starting Debonaire."

"Jesus, that's weird," Sean said.

Another shrug from Danny. "Hey, not so weird. You can only be a hooker for so long, man, then you get burned out. You get old and you get sick of it. She's gone up in the world. Now she's a madam. A high class one, but a madam."

Sean felt the casual words thud against him like the blows of a hammer. It wasn't that he was stupid, he wasn't. And it wasn't that he was naive, he had been around too long for that and seen too much. It was just that he'd been lying to himself. He had been refusing to look at what really was. He knew that now. Nancy *was* a madam. To hear it so plainly and casually stated somehow made it irrefutable. In that case, what was he, what was Ted, what was Danny? What were all the men who worked for Debonaire?

It was an ugly thought. A hard thought to confront, the one he had been shunting aside and rationalizing ever since first considering this job. So far he had not compromised himself . . . well, to be honest, he had compromised himself once. But that was excusable. In spite of that feeling of degradation at the end of the evening, there had

116

been pleasure with Kate before that moment. But how long could he continue? How long could he shrug aside the real issue?

"So why do you want to quit?" He heard Danny's voice if from a distance. He almost had to shake himself to return.

"What?"

"Why do you want to quit Debonaire? You told Nancy you wanted to quit."

"I'm not very good at this," Sean said.

"Hey, practice makes perfect, man."

Sean looked at him then. "Danny, when these women want you to sleep with them, do you ever turn them down?"

Danny narrowed his eyes. Carefully he took a cigarette from the pack before him and lit it.

"No," he said, exhaling a lung full of smoke. "I'm hired to perform a service, man, that's what I do. You don't tell a customer you don't feel like it."

"Never?"

Danny's mouth twisted. Was that self-revulsion?

"No, I don't turn them down. I'm doing them a favor and I get paid well for it." He looked over at Sean finally meeting his eyes. "Is that what bothers you?"

"I didn't know it would be like this." Sean said slowly. "I thought I'd be able to drift through, without . . ."

"Hey, man, you're making more money than you've ever made in your life. You had better think twice before you give that up," Danny said, his voice suddenly harsh.

Sean just shook his head in dumb silence. He felt ashamed, as big a fool as he had ever felt. All right, he told himself, he'd made a commitment and he'd keep it. Three more dates, and that would be it. Then he'd quit. No discussion, no doubts, no reservations.

Chapter Eight

Danny put the telephone down and began to chuckle. "Hey, guess who I got a date with?" he said to the room at large.

Ted glanced up from the kitchen counter where he was spooning sugar into a cup of coffee. Sean had just entered, still half awake, his hair tousled. He wore blue jeans and no shirt and walked somnambulistically over to the coffee machine.

"Who?" Ted asked disinterestedly.

Sean poured himself a cup of coffee.

"Bobbi Peters," Danny announced.

"No shit?" Ted said, coming alive. "You mean the lady who has that radio talk show? The shrink?" Danny nodded, still grinning.

"What?" Sean managed to ask.

"Dr. Bobbi Peters. Radiobitch extraordinaire," Ted said. He turned back to Danny. "How do you know? Nancy told you who it was?"

Nancy normally gave them as little information about the clients as possible, particularly if they were celebrities. Discretion, she said, was Debonaire's most valuable commodity. "She couldn't resist, she couldn't stop laughing herself." Danny said. "I mean, can you believe it?"

"Who is she?" Sean asked. He didn't usually listen to radio talk shows.

"Christ, she's like the Dear Abby of the airwaves!" Ted

said. "Actually, she's worse. She's a real ball buster."

"Yeah, yeah," Danny said. "She's the one that's always down on men, right? Talking about women's lib and stuff like that."

Ted began to mimic the voice of a woman. " 'Yes, dear, you must understand the needs of men are sometimes extremely selfish. But it is the dawning of a New Age and women are demanding their space. Consequently, men are currently very insecure.' That's what she was saying the other day, and here's another one I heard her say, 'Uh, Mary I'd really like to acknowledge your stand. There's nothing wrong with celibacy—even if you are married and a mother. Particularly if all a man has to offer you is physical lust.' Oh, God, you're going to have a real ball with this one, Danny."

"I've heard her," Danny said. "She's a real war horse, man. She's probably about sixty and ugly as sin, like that other broad. What's her name? Dr. Ruth someone. Oh, man, what a night this is going to be."

"Well, if she is a man-hater, why is she going out on a date with an escort?" Sean ventured as his head began to clear with the help of the coffee.

"Who knows," Danny said.

"Maybe she's doing research," Ted guessed.

"Well, maybe she's lonely. Or maybe it's legit and she really just needs to be seen with someone. Where are you supposed to meet her?" Sean asked.

"At a residence in Los Feliz. I don't know where we're going. Nancy said she would tell me when I got there."

"Better you than me," Ted said with a nasty chuckle.

"Hey, she specifically asked for a Latino male," Danny said. "Maybe I'm just what she needs."

Later that evening Danny discovered that Dr. Bobbi Peters was neither fat nor ugly nor sixty years old. She was a small blond woman who could have been quite pretty except for the thin and disapproving line formed by her mouth. And from what he could see of her figure, she seemed to be thin and shapely. She wore blue jeans, a baggy T-shirt, and a thin, knee-length silk jacket.

"Perez?" she asked when she opened the door.

"Yes, Danny Perez," he said.

"Shall we go?" she said, stepping out. He led her to his car, opening the door for her. He went to the driver's side and got in himself. "Where would you like to go," he asked.

"I'm dreadfully hungry, so how about some sushi? And then you can take me dancing. I'd like to go somewhere where there is Latino music."

"Good," Danny said. "I know a sushi bar in West L.A., and there's a club nearby that features South American salsa. Is that all right?"

"That would be fine," she said.

He took Franklin Boulevard to Hollywood and then went down La Brea Avenue to Olympic Boulevard and turned west.

Danny attempted polite conversation on the way, but she wasn't particularly receptive. Every now and then he sensed her glance on him, and once when he turned and caught her eye. She looked at him for a moment, then turned her head back to her window.

God, he wondered, was this tough lady shy or did she just have a chip on her shoulder? Sooner or later he'd find out, he knew that much. "Do you like Latin music?" he asked, trying once more to get a conversation going.

"No, not particularly. At least, I don't know. I haven't heard very much of it," she said.

"I see," he said, and lapsed in silence for another few minutes. He tried again with, "Are you originally from Los Angeles?"

"No, I'm from a small town in the midwest, but I've lived here for ten years," she said. "I like California. I don't think I could ever go back."

"What state are you from?"

"Ohio. Akron, actually."

"Not much going on there, is there?"

"No, it's nothing like L.A.," she said. Then for the first time she asked a question. "Are you from here originally?"

"Born and bred, one of the few natives," Danny said.

The conversation had apparently exhausted her reserves. She turned her head and looked out the window again. He didn't mention that he knew who she was until they were seated at the sushi bar, and he could resist no longer. "I listen to your radio show sometimes," he said.

"Oh," she said coolly, "and do you like it?"

Danny cocked his head. "To be honest, I don't listen to it too much. It's for women, I gathered."

"Well," she said primly, "most of my audience does consist of women, that is true. However, I think that any sensitive male could probably learn a lot by listening to it."

"Well, I'll make it a point to listen more frequently," Danny said. A moment later he asked a question that had been puzzling him. "There is something I am curious about," he began, wondering if he should even say it. "You asked that your escort be Latino and you wanted to hear Latin music. Why is that, especially if you don't know too much about it?"

For a moment she looked flustered and then gathered her composure. "Well, there's something passionate about Latino music. I just wanted to experience that," she said.

Danny nodded. She had only answered half his question, but he let that part of it pass. "Yeah, that's Latinos. We're all emotion. You know how it is, Blacks got rhythm, Latinos got emotion, whites have got intellect and most of the money."

She gave him a sharp look. "I didn't mean that racially," she said defensively.

Danny smiled. "I didn't mean that to be anything other than a joke. I am what I am. I don't care about other people's stereotypes one way or another."

"That's a very healthy attitude," she said.

He watched her eat sushi. She had delicate hands with long tapered fingers. When she smiled, which she had

121

done only twice this evening, she was actually pretty. Her hair was tied back, but he thought that if she let it fall to her shoulders, used a little more makeup, and wore more feminine clothes, she would actually be quite a pretty woman. But it was as if she were consciously hiding her attractiveness. He wondered what she was hiding from.

They drank saki with their sushi. He noticed that she kept up with him, drinking with quick nervous gestures, each little cup in one gulp. They had drunk three jugs each by the end of dinner and by the time they left he was beginning to feel a warm glow.

It seemed to be carnivale night at the salsa club on Pico Boulevard. Women wore skimpy costumes and feathers, while many of the men wore masks, glittering waistcoats, and tight pants. The main room was filled with flashing lights accompanied by bursts of conversation, peals of laughter, and the clatter of glasses. The music was provided by a live band with a large horn section. The atmosphere was festive.

"Let's dance," Danny said exuberantly, before they even found a seat. He took one of her hands and led her to the floor.

"I don't know how to dance this way," she said nervously.

"Don't worry, I'll show you."

They reached the floor and he began to move his hips. She tried to follow, but couldn't, stiff and uncomfortable. He put his hands on her shoulders and gave them a rub.

"Now relax, the first thing you have to do is relax," he said. "There. Okay, now let your shoulders move like this." He showed her. "Now your hips. Move your hips. Listen to the music, listen to the rhythm here. Okay, that's it, now let your hips move like this, side to side. There you go, forward. Good. Look at me."

And he rolled his hips. "Good," he said. "That's very good. Now, this is a step. Watch my feet. One, two, three, four, one, two, three, four, good. Okay, that's good. Okay, now remember to just relax, feel the rhythm. Just move now. There you go. Good."

He lifted his hand above his head and clapped in time to the music. "Good! Excelente!" he said with a broad grin. She smiled back at him, her eyes bright, her body moving easily now to the rhythm.

"All right," he said, "you're doing just great. You're born to do this. You're born for salsa. All right!"

After the music ended, they found a table and ordered drinks. An almost naked waitress brought the drinks in two tall glasses. Bobbi grabbed hers and drank it thirstily while Danny paid. "This is fun," she said. "I'm glad we came. This is really an exciting place."

"It's just getting warmed up," Danny said. "They haven't let their hair down yet. Wait another hour or so, it's going to get real wild."

"I feel real wild already," Bobbi said.

"Stick around, it's going to get crazy," Danny smiled.

At 1:35 a.m., when the music stopped and the waitress announced the last call, Bobbi Peters looked very different from when she had entered. Her hair was untied and floating around her shoulders, her eyes were still bright, but her voice had become slurred. Perspiration beaded her forehead, but she didn't seem to care.

"One for the road?" Danny asked.

She shook her head. "No, let's go. We can have a drink at my place. We could even dance some more there."

During the drive home, Danny asked her why she had hired an escort. "You shouldn't have any problem finding men to date. You're a pretty woman," he said.

She grimaced. "I have more trouble than you think. The problem is I intimidate men. They never ask me out, or else they're duds—other shrinks, older guys. I just don't get asked out that much. So, I thought tonight, what the hell, I'd do this. So far, I don't regret it."

When they parked in her driveway, she stepped out of the car and took his arm. "A big house," she said, looking up at the looming mansion, "Big lonely house. Come on. Let's go liven it up."

She took him into the living room, turning on the lights

123

as they moved through the hall. Danny thought she had to be doing pretty well in the radio business. The furnishings were obviously expensive, as if they had been chosen by a decorator. And yet there was something cold and barren about it, something not lived in.

"What would you like to drink?" she asked. He noticed she was teetering in her high heels. She must have been aware of it too, because she suddenly kicked them off.

"I think I'll just have a cup of coffee."

"All right, coffee coming up. Sit down and make yourself comfortable." She left the room and he heard her footsteps recede down the hallway. He stood for a few minutes longer looking around the room.

All the art on the walls was expensive and modern— abstract geometric patterns. He had never understood this kind of art. As far as he was concerned a painting was supposed to be a picture and a picture was supposed to represent something recognizable, something that you could understand.

Also on the wall was a golden plaque, framed of course. Some kind of radio award. The bookcase was filled with autobiographies, biographies and self-help books: *How To Be More of a Woman, How To Make a Man Love You, How To Survive as a Woman in The 1980s and Beyond, Orgasm—Is It Possible?*

She returned with two cups of coffee on a tray and took them over to the bar. "I'm going to put Grand Marnier in mine. Would you like some?"

"Sure, that would be fine, with milk and sugar, if you have it."

She poured a healthy slug of liqueur into each cup, then added the milk and sugar and brought the tray over to the coffee table in front of the couch.

"Um, very good," Danny said after the first sip.

She was nervous suddenly, peering at him over the rim of her cup, clearing her throat before she spoke. "Where do you live?" she asked, exhibiting a sudden willingness to make small talk.

124

"In the Valley. Studio City."

He had experienced enough of these encounters to know what she was going through—should she ask him to stay, would he stay, did she want to ask him to stay, what would happen if he stayed? An endless litany of questions that would remain unresolved until something was actually said. He finished half of his coffee and then helped her with his own question.

"Would you like me to go now, or stay?" he asked.

Her eyes widened, her tongue licked nervously over her top lip, but her eyes already held the answer. "I'd like you to stay," she said finally.

He put his cup carefully on the table, leaned along the couch toward her. She put her cup down as well and stared at him with expectant eyes. He brought his head closer and closer, and finally, when he was only inches away, her eyes closed and her head lifted slightly and her lips parted.

He kissed her slowly and sensuously, without any overt display of passion, sensing that was what she wanted. After a minute of this, when their tongues finally slid against each other, she opened her mouth wider and put an urgent arm around his neck and pulled his face hungrily against her, as if she couldn't get enough of it.

When they drew apart he lifted her shirt up over her head and unsnapped her brassiere with one practiced flick of the finger and lowered his head to her darkening nipples, feeling them stiffen against his tongue.

And then, because he knew it was exactly what she wanted, he slid his arms under her legs and arms and picked her up and carried her into the bedroom.

"That's never happened to me before," she said, her face totally flushed and relaxed for the first time that evening. Perhaps, Danny suspected, for the first time in a long time.

"What's that?" Danny asked. He was lying on his back staring at the ceiling.

125

"An orgasm. I've never had an orgasm like that," she said.

"You've never had an orgasm, or an orgasm like that?" he asked curiously.

She shook her head, not answering.

"How many men have you been with?" he asked.

"Well, I was married after high school and divorced five years ago, and then there were two more."

"That's it? Three men in your whole life?"

"Yes."

"And you never had an orgasm with any of them?"

"No, not until now. I didn't know it could be like this. I didn't know my body could respond this way. It was fabulous! It's like my body took complete control and I was just there watching it. It was such pleasure. I can't believe it."

Danny smiled to himself. No wonder Sean had called her a ball buster. No wonder her radio show had gained her the reputation of someone unsympathetic to men. The woman had never had a real man. He wondered how this would affect her show. He promised himself he would listen on Monday morning.

Her hand snaked across his belly and she said almost shyly, "Could that happen again?"

"With a little help from you," Danny said.

She looked at him, uncomprehending for a full three seconds. "Oh, you mean . . ." Her voice trailed off and she flushed.

"You've never done that either?" Danny asked.

She shook her head.

He reached up, put his hand behind her head and pulled it down toward him and asked, "Do you remember how to suck a lollipop?"

Winding up through the Hollywood Hills above Laurel Canyon, Sean found himself wondering what it would be like to be in love again. The fact of the matter was, in spite of the frequent company of women lately, that euphoric, all-encompassing feeling of adoration was something he missed, an absence, he admitted, that left him feeling strangely incomplete.

A soft fog drew hazy rings around the street lights. The car in front of him took the corner too quickly, tires squealing.

He wasn't in love with Marina any more. He knew that now. He'd known that when he saw her in the restaurant the other day. She was still beautiful and still desirable, but that feeling of wanting to be with her every minute, of wanting to touch her for no particular reason, of wanting to hear everything she had to say, and to tell her everything, no matter how trivial — all those feelings had died. And all that was left was a kind of distant affection. He still liked her, how could he not? No matter what she had done once, he had also loved her. But that wasn't what he needed again, not from her. That wasn't what he wished he had.

He turned left on Stanley Hills Drive, a narrow, steep street. A car coming down pulled over so that it wouldn't obstruct his upward climb. It was the unspoken rule of canyon living, an unexpectedly civilized courtesy, or perhaps it was the law. He wasn't sure.

In the dim light of the instrument panel he looked at the paper on which he had written the address and the name, Alyssia Havenhurst. "Two S's," the secretary at Debonaire had said. He pulled up in a small driveway before a two-car garage.

A small, dark-haired woman answered the door at the first ring. She was about 5'3", and thin. She wore tight jeans, and a thin blouse established the lack of a brasseire. She had a sharp face and a small, somewhat discontented mouth. "You're from the agency?" she asked breathlessly.

"Yes, my name is Sean. Alyssia Havenhurst?"

"Yes," she said, "come in."

Like many of the homes in Laurel Canyon, it was an older house, but it was larger than most, perched on the

127

side of a hill. The furniture looked expensive, of some antique vintage. Freshly cut flowers adorned a small table in the center of the living room and huge blowups of scenic photographs covered one wall. They could have been the work of Ansel Adams.

"Well, what would you like to drink?" she said, standing fairly close to him.

"A glass of wine would be fine," he replied.

"Good," she said. "That's what I'll have, too. Be right back." She hurried from the room and less than a minute later returned with two glasses and a bottle of wine in an ice bucket.

"It's an Edna Valley chardonnay," she said. "I hope you like it." She handed him his glass and held out her arm. "Well, shall we toast something?" she said. "How about fun and games?"

"Fun and games," Sean said. He noticed a pale area on the tanned third finger of her left hand. Either she was recently divorced and hadn't been in the sun much or she was married and had only just taken off her wedding ring.

"So, tell me about yourself," she said. "Do you do this full time?"

"No, I'm also an actor," Sean said.

"Oh, have I seen you in anything?"

"I doubt it," he said. "I've done a couple of commercials. That's about it. It hasn't been that easy to get work."

"So, that's why you do this?"

"I suppose you could say that," Sean commented. "Where would you like to go tonight?"

"I thought we could just stay here," she said.

"Oh." There was a muffled sound from the deeper recesses of the house.

"Is there someone else here?" Sean asked. "I thought I heard someone."

She sipped her drink and looked at him with something like amusement. "Yes, it's my husband."

"Your husband?"

"Um," she said. "He likes to be here."

Sean was almost afraid to ask what she meant, but felt he had to. "What do you mean he likes to be here? For what?"

"You don't mind, do you?" she asked innocently.

"Excuse me?" Sean said.

"He's what they call a voyeur," she explained, her voice as casual as if she were discussing the weather. "He likes to watch me make love to other men. That's okay with you, isn't it? I mean, he doesn't even have to be in the room as long as he can see in."

Sean put his glass down on the table. A growing feeling of dread that had started in his stomach was now coursing through his body. "You've got to be kidding," he said.

"No, of course not," she said, irritation seeping into her tone. "We've done this before."

"I don't do this," Sean said flatly. "I was here to escort you somewhere. Not to provide a circus for some sick man who gets off seeing his wife in bed with someone else."

"Well, there's no need to talk like that," she said resentfully. "It's a perfectly natural urge. He loves me and he likes to see other men enjoying me and me enjoying them. God, this is the 90s, you know."

"Not my 90s," Sean said getting to his feet. "I don't do this act."

She stood as well. "What is it—the money? I mean, we'll double your fee. Or at least give as much as the fee in addition as a tip for you."

"It's not the money," Sean said. "I just don't do this. Now if you'll excuse me, I'm leaving." He turned and walked toward the door.

"Well, what about my date?" she wailed after him. "We hired you."

"I just resigned," Sean said. He opened the front door and let himself out.

Sean sat in his car, furious not at the stupid woman or her depraved husband but at himself for getting into a situation like this. How could he not have anticipated it? The very nature of what he was doing demanded this kind of degradation. How could he think that he alone could remain untouched by it? It pervaded everything. It was part and parcel of the job. It was something that everyone else who was involved in the business probably put up with willingly. But it was not something that he could stomach, not any longer.

For some reason he thought of a childhood incident. He was no more than twelve at the time and there was a gang of boys at school who persecuted him mercilessly. And yet they were generally acknowledged to be the "cool kids," and he so wanted to be a part of that group he put up with their torture rather than avoid them.

Then one day, the leader of the group, Bobby, offered to show him a "fort" they had built in the hills behind the school. Sean had been both thrilled and scared. He didn't trust Bobby and yet he so much wanted to be a part of that group he put aside his distrust and followed him up there one hot dry afternoon after school. They took a dirt path through the woods until they reached a small clearing. There, six of Bobby's gang leaped out from behind bushes and beat the shit out of him.

Why think of this now, he wondered? And then it came to him. When you wanted something badly enough, you were willing to put aside your doubts and misgivings. You were even willing to put aside your integrity. You were willing, in effect, to become stupid.

That's exactly what he had done. The lure of easy money, the prospect of a job that needed little effort for a potentially large return, had drawn him in like a bee to honey. He had pushed aside the little voices, suppressed them, laughed at them, scorned their warnings. And, of course, they had been entirely prophetic.

He started the car and began to drive down the hill. There was only one thing to do, and that was to quit. What was the worst that could happen? Working as a waiter, a parking valet, a messenger even . . . any lowly job would keep him in food and lodging. And at least he would feel better about himself.

His mood improved during the journey home. He vowed to start calling people the very next day. In the meantime, until something turned up, he had enough money to move out of the condo into an apartment more suited to his station in life. Well, he'd been stupid, but at least he'd gained a small stake out of the experience. It had helped him escape the financial hole in which he had been sitting. Now he could make a fresh start, only this time he would be a little smarter about it.

Neither of the other two were home when he arrived, which was just as well. He needed time to think and strategize, to go over his checkbook, see what his resources were, and plan how he would handle the coming weeks. He poured himself a beer, took out his little solar calculator and his checkbook, and began to add and subtract figures.

The telephone rang. He got up and caught it before the answering machine came on.

There was an edge of panic to the voice. "Sean, is that you? Thank God you're there." It was Marina.

"Yeah, what's happening?" he asked, concerned.

"Can you come over right now? I need to see you."

"Why don't you just tell me what's going on?" he said in a calming voice. "It's getting late and I'm just settling down here."

"I can't," she said. "I need to see you, I've got to give you some stuff to look after for me. I've got to tell you what's been going on. You've got to get over here. Sean, I wouldn't ask you unless it was urgent."

He looked at his watch: 9:00 p.m. It wasn't that late, but he wondered if this was a drug-induced emergency. He asked, "Are you having a paranoid attack? Have you been doing coke again?"

"No, I told you I quit dope and I did. It's not that and

131

I'm not being paranoid. I've just gotten on to something and I think it's dangerous and I need to talk to someone about it. You've got to help me figure this out, Sean. You're the only one I can trust. Listen, there's a lot of money involved. Please, Sean I need your help."

"All right," Sean said resignedly. "I'll take a shower and be over there in about half an hour."

"You can't leave right now?"

"I'll be there in about half an hour."

"Okay. Thanks, Sean, I knew I could count on you. I'll see you then," she said, and hung up.

As he drove back over Laurel Canyon again, he wondered what Marina had gotten herself involved in. She had a wealthy family back East, and they generally kept her in enough money to live on. But once the dope habit started she had needed a lot more than they had been willing to provide, and she had begun to get involved in a number of strange schemes: multilevel marketing of one kind or another, a plan that had something to do with selling American cars in South America—which he vaguely suspected to be illegal, signing people up for various services for which she got a commission; and even wilder schemes that he turned a deaf ear to.

Nothing ever seemed to last. Somehow, in spite of her optimism, the schemes never made as much money as she thought they would and she quickly moved on to the next thing. Once, through utilizing her numerous social contacts, she had helped raise money for a new restaurant in Santa Monica, ostensibly for a piece of ownership, but that too hadn't materialized. Although she had raised over a hundred thousand dollars for the entrepreneurs, she got cut out of her percentage and walked out of the deal with a miserable three-thousand-dollar finder's commission. Business acumen wasn't a gift she had inherited from her wealthy father.

Sean reached her apartment and rang the buzzer at the mailboxes. He also suddenly remembered that he had forgotten to call her with the address of that Varney guy.

Well, now was as good a time as any to give it to her. He leaned his head toward the speaker to say his name. There was no answer. He pressed the buzzer. Still no answer.

For the first time he began to feel nervous. She said she was in danger . . . He jabbed at the buzzer one more time, but nothing happened. He remembered a movie he had seen on television where the detective had wanted to search the bad guy's apartment while he was away. He used the same trick, pushing six buzzers at random. When the voices came through, he mumbled, "Delivery" and waited. Sure enough, someone buzzed the gate open.

He took the elevator up to the third floor and went down the long hall to her apartment. He knocked on the door, but again there was no answer. On the slim chance it was unlocked, he turned the handle. After a slight push, the door swung open.

Sean stepped in warily, quickly glancing around the room. "Marina," he said, and then louder, "Marina."

He walked further in. The apartment looked messy as usual, books and magazines strewn all over the place, records and tapes on the floor. He called out her name again. There was only silence.

Quickly now, with a mounting sense of urgency, he strode across the living room into the small hallway that led to her bedroom. He turned into the bedroom and stopped in mid stride. Marina was lying on the bed, her eyes closed. Beside her was a syringe, some needles, a bottle with liquid in it.

"Jesus Christ," Sean said. She was totally out of it. Stoned out of her mind. He went over to her and said her name out loud. "Marina." There was no response, no movement.

My God, he thought suddenly, the fear tearing at him. She was not breathing. He sat quickly on the bed beside her and felt her wrist for a thread of life. Nothing.

"Jesus Christ," he said aloud.

He grabbed the telephone beside the bed and dialed 911. "Ambulance, I need an ambulance." he said quickly.

133

"I have a drug overdose over here." He gave the address and his name when requested.

"Just get the paramedics here. Fine, tell the police if you have to, but just get the paramedics here."

He hung up and sat there, staring at the quiet, lifeless face of the woman he had once loved, feeling more helpless than he had ever felt.

Chapter Nine

Afterward, when the medics had removed Marina's body, Sean sat in the living room with Lieutenant Roger Glenn of the Beverly Hills police department.

Glenn did not look like an employee of Beverly Hills. He looked as if he lived in that city. He wore a suit that must have cost a thousand dollars. His fair and perfectly cut hair was blow-dried back. His blue eyes and manicured fingernails were flawless.

"Does she have any relatives locally?" Glenn asked.

"Not any that I know of. Her parents are back East, I don't know where."

"Well, we'll look around and find some letters, phone bills . . . stuff. We have to notify the next of kin."

"Yeah, I know she was in touch with her parents. There should be something around here," Sean said.

"Tell me more about your relationship with her."

"I already told you," Sean said.

"Just tell me again for the record," Glenn said.

"We were lovers, we used to live together, and then we broke up. I found out she was doing drugs, I didn't like it and so I left her. And I didn't hear from her until recently."

"Why did she contact you?"

"Well, I called her. She had recommended me for a job and I called her to find out, to thank her."

"Find out what?" Glenn said, picking up on what he wasn't saying.

"Why she recommended me for a job, I mean, we had broken up and all."

"And what did she say?"

"She wanted to do me a favor."

Glenn looked across the room and then back at him. "You said you were an actor. This was an acting job?"

Sean shook his head. He felt foolish. In fact, he felt almost like a criminal. And yet there was no point avoiding it. The cop could find out easily enough if he wanted to.

"I work for a male escort agency," he said. He winced as the policeman raised his eyebrows. "It's a legitimate job. You get paid to escort women to things like movies, parties, the theater."

"You just escort them?" Glenn said, not bothering to hide his disbelief.

"Yes, I do," Sean said. "I just started over a week ago. And that's what I do—escort them. It's good money."

"And what is the name of this agency?"

"It's called Debonaire. Over in Century City."

"I see. Who owns it?"

"I don't know." Sean said. "There is a woman by the name of Nancy Hamilton who runs it. Look, why are you asking me all these questions? What I do doesn't have any bearing here."

"Don't get defensive, Mr. Parker. I'm just trying to get the whole picture here."

"I know, I know, Sean said apologetically. "Actually, it's a dumb job and I'm embarrassed about it. I just made up my mind tonight to quit."

"That's probably a good idea," Glenn said.

"Yes."

"So, tell me again what she said to you on the phone," Glenn said.

Sean repeated the conversation for the second time, adding, "She was scared of something, I know. Either that or she was just incredibly paranoid. She told me she wasn't on drugs, though." But even before he finished speaking, the policeman seemed to lose interest.

"Since when can you believe a junkie?" Glenn asked, with a cynical shrug. "They'll say anything. You should know that. You lived with her for a while, right? That's what you said?"

Sean nodded. "Yeah, until it got too bad. And you're right, I couldn't trust her. But she told me she quit and I really believed her this time. I don't know why, but it was different."

"It's always different. A different story each time," Glenn said.

Sean looked around the room. "Aren't you going to fingerprint the place or anything?"

"What for? It's a drug overdose. There's no need to investigate further. Her works are on the bed beside her, and she either shot up too much or she probably got a bubble in the syringe and she shot that into her blood. The coroner will tell us exactly what happened."

"But what if there was more to it than that?" Sean said. "What if she was in some kind of danger and not just paranoid? What if somebody . . . I don't know."

"Look, don't worry about it," Glenn said. "I know she is your friend and I don't want to sound callous, but as far as we're concerned she's just another dead junkie. Plus, she had a record."

"A record?" Sean asked, surprised. "A record for what?"

"Soliciting. She was picked up twice in Beverly Hills. She was out on bail, of course, and finally she was just fined. That's still a record. She wasn't a nice girl, this friend of yours."

Sean stood up, walked over to the liquor cabinet and poured himself a scotch. Shit, he thought, if they weren't going to fingerprint he might as well make himself at home. He took a large swig and began to cough and as soon as he settled down he took another gulp and returned with the glass to the couch.

"She didn't start out like that. She was a nice girl," he said. "Somebody did this to her, somebody made her a

137

junkie, helped her become one, supplied her with dope. Aren't you interested in that?"

"Look, Mr. Parker, let me give you the facts of life. Every day somebody OD's, every day dozens of people sell hundreds of people dope, every day in this grand city thousands of people buy cocaine and heroin and ludes and grass and whatever else you care to name. Drugs are not even my concern, for Christ's sake. I'll pass it on to the right guys, but nothing will happen. There are no leads here that will go anywhere."

Sean looked down at his suddenly empty glass and said heavily. "God, how could this have happened? How can this be ignored? A human life . . . I mean, how can this happen?"

Glenn stood up. "It happens every day, my friend. You get used to it. If there is anything else you can tell us, any real lead that you remember, that would help us in any way, call me. Otherwise, I suggest you just suffer this lesson and get on with your life. For now I suggest you go home and get some sleep."

"I don't know if I can sleep," Sean said.

"You might surprise yourself," Glenn said. "Sleep is one way of not having to face up to inner turmoil. I highly recommend it."

"Well," Sean said standing up, "you have my number. If I can be of any other help . . ."

"Good," Glenn stood as well, took a card from his jacket pocket, and handed it to Sean. "Call me if you think of anything you think I should know."

"Sure," Sean said. He took the card and put it in his pocket. He almost shook hands with the policeman, then changed his mind and turned around and left the apartment.

An apartment of death, he thought in the elevator. What a waste, what a terrible, terrible waste. When he first met her Marina had so much going for her, so much potential. And it had ended in what? Nothing. There was nothing left of her now. Just that body they'd taken out on a stretcher.

It meant nothing, her whole life meant nothing. Her so-called friends would forget about her in a matter of days, and her family would grieve for a while, but they had probably given up on her a long time ago. He'd grieve for a while, but he too had given up on her, months before. Shit, in fact he'd known that something like this would happen. You could only play chicken with life for so long. How many times could she run full tilt to the edge of the cliff and then slam on the brakes without going over the edge? He'd known it, and she had certainly known it. He had done everything he could to help, but it hadn't been enough.

Outside he climbed into his car, his mind still filled with thoughts of her. I did everything I could, he told himself. But the words had a hollow ring. Whatever he had done obviously hadn't been enough. There must have been something else he could have done to prevent this from happening, something he hadn't thought of, something he hadn't cared enough to do. Damn, he said, slamming his hand against the dashboard. Damn.

Sean went to the Power Company as soon as he woke up. He attacked the weights as if they were enemies, using every ounce of available muscle, purposely exceeding his limit in order to exorcise the demons that had been crowding his mind since finding Marina.

He hadn't been able to fall asleep till almost 3:00 a.m., and then awoke at 8:00. He wasn't tired or energized, just buzzing, his mind active and his emotions stretched to the breaking point. Yet in spite of this mental turmoil, Sean felt strangely empty inside. There was a space somewhere in him that something had left.

It wasn't simply the connection he had with Marina. In truth, that had died a long time before. It was something of himself that seemed to have disappeared. Perhaps it was inappropriately selfish to be so concerned with himself

139

now, but the previous twenty-four hours, in particular Marina's death, had caused him to examine himself in a new and harshly critical light. The suddenness of her passing shocked him. She was here and then she wasn't, and she had left nothing to show for the time she had spent here.

What would he leave behind if something happened to him tomorrow, the next day, next week, next month? What legacy would he leave behind? *Sean Parker, Struggling Actor,* his headstone would read. He had accomplished nothing. Worked in a couple commercials, not even national commercials but local ones, seen at the most by a few hundred thousand people. It wasn't what he had envisioned when he was younger, filled with the energy and zeal of his dream, unhindered by limiting factors, ignorant of the handicaps that others would beleaguer him with. He had seen so much more for himself. *Actor:* a word that resonated with tradition and honor. *Actor:* one who starred in films that would move hearts, change minds, and influence cultures. *Actor:* a man who would endow the writer's words with life and hopefully do work that was good enough to play a part, however small, in revitalizing a culture on its legs, tearing apart at the seams with greed and hedonism.

How close was he to that dream? A few stage plays that nobody would even remember, if anybody even remembered them now. A few television commercials that would certainly not bestow honor upon him. Actor? No, Sean Parker, escort and would-be actor.

He hadn't called the agency yet with his resignation. Somehow that seemed trivial in the light of what happened. He hadn't called anyone. He had avoided both Ted and Danny at the house and had gone directly to the gym. What would her parents think? Were they grieving for her now, he wondered? Did they still see her as a bright and hopeful young girl, talented, attractive, ready to conquer the world? Would that be how she remained in their memory? He hoped for their sakes that it would be so, because what she had become was a far cry from that vision. And what he was becoming was a far cry from his vision.

He strained at the weight, pressing up with his arms, his mouth twisted in a grimace, veins bulging in his forehead, but before he fully extended his arms he could feel them start to collapse. Too much. He let the weight down as gently as possible and lay there breathing hard, staring up at the lights on the ceiling, listening to the clatter of the equipment around him, a cough here, a voice, a shout.

God! Sue Winston, he remembered suddenly. He rolled the weight away and sat up on the bench. She was the closest thing to a real friend that Marina had. Pregnant and deserted, involved in her own problems, no doubt, she would still want to know. Had anybody told her? Would she have heard? Doubtful. Marina was a nobody, her death would make no headlines. There wouldn't even be a paragraph in the local paper, let alone the *Los Angeles Times*. Another junkie dies. Big deal. It happened all the time. Probably none of her friends knew. He had better call Sue and let her know what happened.

He rose from the bench and groaned, then stretched and rubbed his back. He'd overdone it, and yet he felt a little better, a little less stuck inside his ricocheting thoughts.

He went into the dressing room and opened his locker and pulled out his telephone book. He was pretty sure he still had Sue's number because sometimes he'd had to call her when trying to track Marina down. There it was. He hoped it was still operational.

Sue was also an actress and tended to move around from apartment to apartment, depending on how much money she had at the time. When she wasn't acting or shacking up with some guy, she worked as a word processor to make money. Nothing seemed to last long. She was as mercurial as Marina. In fact, they were alike in many ways. Although he had to admit that Sue had a sensible streak when it came to her own survival, a quality that Marina had never demonstrated.

He looked uncertainly at his book and wondered if he should change first. No, he thought he'd better call her

141

now and get it over with. Taking a quarter from his wallet, he closed his locker again and went to the public telephone and dialed her number.

A sleepy voice answered.

"Sue, it's Sean Parker. Hi, how are you?"

"Sean," the voice began to come awake. "Haven't heard from you in a long time. How's everything?"

"Sue, I have some bad news for you." There was a moment of stillness, and then she said "What?"

"It's Marina. Something happened."

"Oh my God, is she all right?"

"I'm afraid not, Sue. She OD'd last night. I'm sorry, but she's dead." There was a longer silence, then a small voice. "Marina dead? Marina, she OD'd? Are you sure? Where did you hear this?"

"Yes, I'm sure," Sean said as gently as he could. "She called me last night and wanted me to come over. When I got there I found her. I called the paramedics, but they were too late. They tried everything, but they couldn't save her. I'm sorry, Sue, but she's gone."

"Oh, my God."

"I thought I'd let you know before you heard it somewhere else," Sean said uncomfortably. "I'm really sorry to have to tell you this."

"No," she said, "it's all right. I mean . . . well, you know what I mean. My God, I can't believe it. Yes, I can. Marina was always flirting with this. I don't know why I'm surprised."

"Yeah, well," Sean said.

"Is there anything I can do? I mean, what about . . . what's happening with the funeral, and I mean. . . ." Her voice trailed away.

"The police are going to notify her parents. I'm sure they're taking care of all that," he said. "You might want to get in touch with the police and find out. The guy I talked to from Beverly Hills, a Lieutenant Roger Glenn. I have his number somewhere, but you can get him at the police department there."

"Yeah, I'll call. Okay, Sean. Thanks. How are you doing?"

Sean shrugged and said, "I'm all right—at least I'm alive."

"Yeah," she said soberly, "me too."

"And the baby. You have a child coming. That's something to live for."

She hesitated, "What? A child? What are you talking about?"

Sean frowned. "Marina told me that you were pregnant, that some guy had gotten you pregnant and then left the scene. In fact, she wanted me to find out his address for you. I assumed you knew that."

"I don't know what you're talking about," she said. "I haven't been pregnant for about five years, and then I got an abortion. I'm not planning on having kids right now. Jesus, all I need on top of my other problems is to be is a single mother."

Now it was Sean's turn to be silent. There was no mistake. That was what Marina had told him. But there was a mistake . . . What did it mean? The only thing it meant was that Marina had been lying. Which was not surprising, she'd lied often enough before. But why?

"Sue, I think I'd better talk to you more about this. Can I come over?"

"Yeah, I guess."

"I'll come over right now if I can. Are you still living at the same place on Wilcox?"

"Yes," she said. "Apartment 111."

He told her he'd be there in twenty minutes and hung up.

Where Marina was dark and mercurial, Sue was blond and mercurial. They could have been sisters. They were the same height and build and had somewhat similar features, strikingly attractive and sensual. She was wearing jeans and a T-shirt. Her hair was still disheveled and she wore no makeup. She looked as if she had been crying, her eyes swollen.

"Hi," Sean said, kissing her on the cheek.

Sean had met Marina through Sue, whom he had been dating casually before. She was the one who had taken him to the party where he first met Marina. He followed her into the living room and she asked if he wanted coffee. "I've got a pot on," she added.

"Yeah, I'd like some," he said, suddenly feeling tired.

She went behind the counter into the small kitchen. "Well, what was all this crap about me being pregnant?" she asked.

"I don't know," Sean said. "Marina told me your boyfriend got you pregnant. Alex Varney was the name she gave me."

She shook her head. "I don't even know anyone by that name."

"Then she was using me for some other reason," Sean said.

"She could do that," she said bitterly, then her face crumpled. "How can I say that now? In spite of her faults, I loved her."

"It's okay," Sean consoled. "That's no reason to avoid the realities."

"I'm still shocked," she said. "I can't believe this happened. She was so alive. She was just getting her life in order."

"How? What was happening?" Sean asked.

"She'd given up drugs completely. You know she spent some time in the Boswell sanitarium in Santa Monica? Detox program. She came out about a month ago and she stayed clean and she was real determined to stay clean. I mean, that's another reason that it's such a shock, y'know. She said she'd never do drugs again, that she had learned her lesson. I guess she hadn't. It really pisses me off."

Sean walked over to the kitchen counter and sat on the stool facing her. "Are you sure about that?" Sean said.

"Well, as sure as I can be. I saw her two days ago and

144

she was still clean then, and she wasn't real nervous. You know how fractured she gets when she doesn't have a hit of something? She wasn't like that at all. She seemed . . . she was excited, but she was more laid back than before. Anyway, that isn't what she was excited about. It was some kind of deal she'd run across."

"What kind of deal?" Sean asked.

She poured the coffee and said, "Cream?"

"Please, and sugar." He watched her fix both coffees and took the one she handed him.

"I don't know what it was. You know how she is. Some scam or another. Was, I should say, how she was." She stopped and her eyes filled with tears. "God, I feel so terrible about this. If only I could have done something."

Sean shook his head. "I feel the same way, and yet I don't know what I could have done. And it seems really silly to beat myself over the head for this . . ."

"It's just such a waste," she said, echoing his earlier words. Her hands cupped around the mug as if for warmth, her eyes staring hollowly at him. "She had so much going for her, you know. She was one of the most intelligent people I know, and really talented as an actress."

Sean shook his head, "I know, but I guess that wasn't something she wanted badly enough." He sipped at his coffee and then said again. "What's this deal she had going, I wonder? She called me about something, too. She said she was in danger."

"Danger? I don't know, she told me that she had just found out something, or come across some information that could lead to a lot of money for her. When I asked her what it was she just clammed up and got a little sly look in her eyes and said 'I'll tell you when it's time.' I have no idea what it was."

"And she wasn't doing drugs?" Sean said.

Sue shook her head. "Like I told you, she said she was clean. I know when she's lying. God, I've known her long enough to know that. I always know it when she lies to me. I know she wasn't lying about that."

"Well," Sean said. "Something must have happened to make her change her mind. She had pumped herself full of heroin."

"It's weird all right," Sue said, a small frown narrowing her forehead. "I mean, let's say she was going back to dope. I mean, she'd go back to coke or ludes or something else. She occasionally used to sniff heroin, but she never used to shoot up, you know."

"She didn't?" Sean said. "I just assumed that was something she had graduated to since I left her. She didn't?"

"I've never known her to use a needle."

"There were marks on her arms," Sean said. "The cop remarked on them too."

"Which arm?" she asked.

And then Sean got the picture. It flashed into his mind like a full-color slide. Marina on her bed. Syringe lying beside her right hand, and the puncture marks on the veins—of her left arm.

"Jesus Christ," he said, slamming his hand on the counter. "Marina was left-handed, wasn't she?"

Sue hesitated for a moment and said, "Yeah, I think so. Yeah, she used to write with her left hand."

"The needle marks were on her left arm," Sean said. "Why would she have done that? Why would she have used her right hand to hold the syringe?"

Sue got a distant expression in her eyes. "I told you I saw her two days ago, right? She was wearing a short sleeve T-shirt, cut up here, ya know." She marked a spot just above her shoulder. "There were no needle marks on her arms, I'd have seen them; I'd have noticed them."

Sean got up from the stool and said, "Can I use your phone?"

"Yeah," she said. "What does all this mean? I mean, this is so weird, this is strange. How can this have happened?"

"I don't know," Sean said with his back to her, "but I'm going to let the police know." He reached the telephone and thumbed through his wallet for the card that Glenn had given him. After a moment he found it and dialed the

146

number. "Lieutenant Roger Glenn," he said when there was an answer. After a short wait, Glenn's clipped voice came on the line.

"This is Sean Parker," he said. "I'm the guy who was at the apartment last night. Marina White, you know, the overdose? Listen, I need to talk to you. I've realized that there is something weird about this."

"What do you mean?" the policeman asked at the other end of the line.

"Well, you know those needle marks on her left arm?"

"Yes."

"She was left-handed. If she had been shooting up, it should have been on her right arm. Not only that, a friend saw her the day before and there were no needle marks on her arm. And we saw quite a few, didn't we?"

"Yes, I guess so. On her left arm, you think? Well . . ." the policeman's voice trailed off for a moment, and then he said, "What are you saying?"

"I'm saying there is something weird about this. Her girlfriend also says that she didn't use a needle. She did cocaine, sure: and other pharmaceuticals, but she'd never been known for shooting up heroin and she'd just been through a detox program. Don't you think this is a little strange?"

"Well, yes, a little," Glenn conceded.

"There's something else I've just thought of. I know where she used to keep her stash at the apartment. Maybe we should have a look there."

Glenn seemed to grasp this, something positive to use. He spoke more strongly. "Can you meet me there?"

"Sure, I can be there in half an hour," Sean said.

After hanging up, he saw that Sue was staring at him, her arms across her chest, a strange expression on her face. "Do you think somebody did this to her?" she asked. "Do you think she was killed?"

"I don't know," Sean said. "But I'm going to try and make sure the police find out. Listen, I'll see you later, and if you need anything, here's my phone number." He went back to the phone and wrote his number on the small pad beside it. "You can reach me there most of the time. Give me a call if you need anything at all, okay?"

He left her still standing in the middle of the room, looking like a bewildered little girl.

It took him twenty minutes to reach Marina's apartment. He waited in his car until he saw a blue Pontiac drive up and Glenn clamber out of it. Then he hurried across the street to catch up with the policeman. Lieutenant Glenn nodded, but did not look all that pleased to see him.

Glenn led the way through the main doors to the elevator and then, as the doors closed behind him, he said, "Why didn't you tell me any of this last night?"

"I didn't think of it," Sean said. "It was somewhat of a shock, you know."

"Yes, of course, but the thing about her stash."

"It wasn't until I called you," Sean explained. "I went to see a friend of hers and we were talking about her and I was describing what had happened and suddenly it came to me that she was left-handed. And how strange it was. And then, when I was talking on the phone to you, I remembered the stash."

"Well, let's see what's there," Glenn said as the elevator doors opened.

Glenn took the apartment key from his pocket and opened the door, ignoring the sign that said "No entrance by Order of the Beverly Hills Police Department."

As soon as they entered Glenn said, "Where is it?"

"That picture over the mantel," Sean said, pointing to a painting with a thick wooden frame. "She used to keep her stash between the canvas and paper backing. It lifts up."

Glenn put a hand on each side of the frame and lifted it off the wall. It was as heavy as it looked. He lowered it gingerly to the floor and turned it over face down.

"Right here," Sean said, kneeling. He took the tape that

148

held the paper to the back of the frame and lifted it easily.

Glenn reached over, drew the paper back and pulled out some papers and a small notebook. "That's all there is here, no drugs," he said. He picked up the top of the frame and shook it in case there was something else stuck higher up, but nothing came out. "Just this notebook and these papers, no drugs."

"Her friend told me that she'd quit, that she'd gone to a private sanitarium somewhere and gone through detox. If she had any drugs, they would have been there."

"Unless all she had was what was on the bed beside her. Or she may have hid them somewhere else. We haven't searched the apartment thoroughly," Glenn said. He looked a little sheepish. "There seemed to be no reason to. It was cut and dried." He gave a Sean a slightly resentful look.

Sean bristled. "Would you have rather I said nothing?"

"No, of course not," Glenn said. "It's just that this complicates things. What seemed to be a suicide, or accidental death, suddenly could be more. And I emphasize *could*. All we have is your statement that she was a lefty. There could be other reasons she used her right hand."

"What about these?" Sean asked. He picked up the folded pieces of paper and opened them. There were only three sheets and he recognized Marina's scrawl on them.

At the top of the first page there seemed to be a headline that said MURDER PLUS SECRET EQUALS MONEY. Below it was a subheading: *Things To Check*. The things to check were numbered.

1. Research family—all members
2. Find fisherman who disposed of body
3. Check whereabout, if any, of Alex Varney, employed at Debonaire
4. Check ownership
5. Marion again
6. Financial records
7. Make preliminary contact with AL
8. Contact Sean

The second sheet of paper appeared to be a letter. It read,

"To Whom It May Concern. I, Marina White, in the event anything untoward should happen to me, want it to be known that I have learned of a murder. This murder, which took place . . .

The letter ended there. The third sheet of paper was blank.

The "To Whom It May Concern" letter was dated the day before, the day she died.

"It looks like she may have been interrupted in the middle of this," the policeman said.

"Yeah, and shoved it behind the picture," Sean added.

"Does any of this make sense to you?" Glenn asked.

"Apart from my name and the name of the agency, only one thing: the mention of Alex Varney," Sean said, explaining to Glenn how Marina had wanted him to find an address for him.

"But she's not pregnant?" Glenn said when Sean finished his story.

"That's right. It looks like she had her own reasons for finding out where he was."

"Well, that's the only thing worth following up here," Glenn said. "Did you find his address?"

"I did," Sean said. He looked in his wallet and took out the piece of paper on which he had written the address after leaving the office. "Here it is."

Glenn wrote it down in the notebook. "I guess I should talk to the people at Debonaire."

"I doubt you'll find out anything there," Sean said. "It was just a regular employee file I saw. Said he was no longer employed there."

"Well, she had some business with him apparently," Glenn said.

"It must have something to do with Debonaire, whatever

it was," Sean said thoughtfully. "It must have. It seems what connects me, what I have in common with this guy . . ." He stared thoughtfully at the pieces of paper and then looked at Glenn. "I was about to resign, in fact, I was going to resign today. But I think I'm going to stay on there. If you do talk to them, I'd like you to do me a favor."

"What?" Glenn asked.

"Don't mention me. Not in connection with this or anything."

Glenn returned his stare for a moment, then nodded. "If you find out something, let me know," Glenn said, "But don't do anything illegal."

"No," Sean said, "I'm just going to keep my ears open. I think there is something going on. I don't know what, but I'm just going to stay alert and see what I hear."

Chapter Ten

When Sean got home he found a message from Nancy Hamilton asking him to call her immediately regarding his appointment the previous night. In light of all that had happened since, he'd almost forgotten how he had burst out of the house in Laurel Canyon, calling either the client or her husband a degenerate.

He dialed Nancy's number and asked for her. "Sean, what happened last night?" she asked, coming directly to the point. "We have a complaint from a client that you insulted her and left."

Sean was unapologetic. "I'm afraid there are some things I'm not into doing. Maybe I could have handled it a little better, but . . ."

"What happened?"

"She wanted me to have sex with her while her husband watched," Sean said. "I'm sorry, but I'm not into weird sex. I didn't take this job to do things like that."

"Oh," Nancy said. "I see."

"I told her that wasn't a part of my job and I left," Sean said.

"I see," Nancy said again. She waited a second and then continued. "Sean, if something like that happens again, I need you to call me immediately and let me know. We can't just leave unhappy clients sitting around like this."

"What? You'll send someone else to take my place? Someone who's willing to do that kind of thing?" Sean asked, verging on insolence.

"Don't disappoint me, Sean," Nancy said firmly. "Just follow the policy if anything happens that you feel you can't handle. Call me and let me know exactly what happened and I'll take the steps needed to handle the situation, whatever they may be."

Sean remembered his decision to leave the job and almost felt like doing it right then, but the memory of Marina's still body on the bed prevented him. He needed to stay, to find out what, if anything, was happening. "All right," he said, his tone conciliatory. "I'm sorry if I mishandled it, but it was a little bit of a shock to me."

"I understand," Nancy said more gently. "I have another job for you tonight. I'm sure it won't be like that."

"Okay, what are the details?" Sean said and jotted down the information she gave him.

As he hung up, the front door opened and Danny came in. He stopped when he saw Sean and said, "Hey, what's happening, man?"

"Nothing much," Sean said.

Danny tossed his jacket off over a chair and walked into the kitchen. "I'm going to make some coffee. Do you want some?"

"Sure," Sean said.

"How did your date go last night?"

"It wasn't great," Sean said. "In fact, Nancy just called me, bitching about it."

"What happened?"

Sean told him and as he related the story, Danny began to laugh. "It wasn't that funny," Sean said disgruntedly.

Danny shook his head. "Talk about throwing you in the deep end, man. To be put in the middle of a weird scene like that after only a few days on the job! I don't know what I would have done back then when I first started."

Sean narrowed his eyes. "What would you do now, Danny?"

153

Danny suddenly grew quiet and busied himself with the coffee. "I don't know, man, it's a weird scene. I'd have probably done what you did." he said finally.

Sean nodded, even though Danny's words seemed to lack conviction. Maybe he would have and maybe he wouldn't, he thought to himself. "Do you get much weird shit like that?" he asked casually.

Danny shrugged, "Yeah, I get my share. You know how it is. The world is full of people looking for thrills. Sometimes I provide them, sometimes I don't."

"How do you feel about that, Danny?"

Danny turned and looked at him. "I count my money," he said. "That feels good."

Ted stumbled down the stairs, looking rumpled and sleepy. He walked into the kitchen, grabbed a mug, and poured himself coffee from the still percolating pot. "Jesus, what a night," he groaned. He looked at the other two and said, "Good morning."

"It's afternoon, it's 3:00," Sean said looking at his watch.

"Yeah, well, I didn't get to bed until 9:00 a.m." Ted said. He looked up at Danny. "What did you do to that chick on the radio?"

"What do you mean?" Danny asked.

"Well, I heard her this morning. She sounded different."

"Oh yeah?" Danny said.

"I couldn't believe it. She was going on and on about sexual fulfillment. Instead of her usual bitterness, this morning she was talking about how women should demand the right to have orgasms and demand that their partners be sexually capable, how wonderful it is for both when they are. Jesus, you must have done a real number on her."

Danny began to laugh. "No kidding? I meant to listen but I didn't get a chance."

"I swear, the woman sounded like she had just come back from a honeymoon."

"Well," Danny said, "she'd never been fucked properly before. That was her only problem."

"I got to hand it to you," Ted said. "You must have done a real primo job on her."

"Yeah, it was pretty good," Danny said and started to laugh again.

When Sean was fifteen years old, tall for his age, already good looking and extremely horny, he had done some yard work for Mrs. Janice Petinger, a neighbor who lived four houses down the street.

It was a hot day and he took off his shirt. He raked up the leaves, mowed the lawn, and raked up the grass and deposited it on the sidewalk neatly bundled in plastic bags. Afterward, he went to Mrs. Petinger to collect his pay. Mr. Petinger was employed by Boeing, and during this period usually worked a double shift, apparently leaving Mrs. Petinger alone and somewhat lonely.

She opened the door at his knock. A short, overweight woman in her thirties, with coarse black hair that stood from her head like blades of thin grass, she wore tight green pants and a white blouse with the three top buttons undone to show mounds of robust pink flesh. She invited Sean in for a cool drink.

"No, no, I really have to go," he said. "But thank you, I just wanted to get my pay."

"You have a drink. You've been working hard out there. I've been watching you," she said, not brooking any argument as she led the way into the kitchen. He followed and she handed him a glass of orange juice.

Politely he drank half of it while she watched him, a curious expression in her dark brown eyes. He put the glass down on the counter and thanked her and then mentioned his pay again.

"Oh, yes," she said, "just wait here and I'll get it for

you." A moment later she came back with some dollar bills in her hand. She stood close to him and held the money out. When he reached for the money she playfully pulled her hand back and giggled. Sean looked at her as if she had just burped and then let his hand drop and waited to see what she would do next.

"I'm only kidding," she said handing the money to him. When he took it, she added, "You know, you could earn a few extra bucks, a little more than that if you wanted."

Sean looked at her and said, "Is there something else that needs doing around here?"

She reached out her hand without any warning and placed it on the crotch of his jeans. Sean jumped back against the refrigerator as if he had just been touched by a cattle prod. But there wasn't much space for him to move and he could only stare with bulging eyes. "I need doing," she said. "You need doing, too?"

It was every horny teenager's dream: seductive older woman offering herself to do unspeakably dirty acts. But this wasn't a dream woman. This was Janice Petinger, who was married to Harry Petinger, who sometimes had a beer with his father. Not only was she the very married Mrs. Petinger, she was also not the girl of his fantasies. Mrs. Petinger was twenty pounds overweight; she had lines in her face; she wore garish red lipstick and painted her fingernails pink. She was not his dream girl.

His face crimson, words choking in his throat, Sean simply mumbled something, slid to the side, and headed to the front door as fast as he could. He never told anyone of this incident, not even his best friend. He pitied Mrs. Petinger, and he was mortified by his own embarrassment and flight.

Tonight in Los Angeles, sitting at the top of the Bonaventure Hotel having dinner with a lady by the name of Mary Roland, Sean vividly remembered his encounter with Mrs. Petinger, for Ms. Roland was a much-older

156

Janice Petinger.

A plump, dark-haired woman of about fifty, she too had pink fingernails. She too viewed Sean with that curiously avaricious expression in her eyes. And she too seemed totally without shame.

Mary Roland was a divorcée, "married and divorced four times," she told him gleefully, "and each time left richer than when I'd arrived."

Sean hardly knew what to think about her obvious pride in these accomplishments. He simply nodded and smiled.

"All my husbands were younger than I was," she gushed on. "What do you think of that?" She didn't wait for the answer and continued. "You know, our society thinks that guys with young women are fine, but older women with younger guys are some sort of perversion. Well, fuck them. I think it's just fine. I even belong to a club—Older women, Younger Men. It's a dating club. You'd be surprised how many guys like older women. How do you feel about it? I think it's quite natural. I mean, women live longer than men, so why shouldn't they have younger guys? I mean, how many women just sort of waste away as widows after their husbands die in their forties? And then what are they supposed to do? Get another old guy who's going to die before them? Hell, no. They should go for the young blood. What do you think?" This time she waited for the answer.

"I think it's just fine," Sean said. "Although I have to admit that my girlfriend is younger than I am."

"Your girlfriend," she asked, her face sinking. "How can you do this kind of work and have a girlfriend?"

"I'm simply an escort, Ms. Roland. I don't do anything except provide company for out-of-town visitors like yourself."

"You don't do anything, you mean?" she asked.

"I'm just an escort," Sean said.

The evening went downhill from that point on. She got

rid of him right after dinner, and he thought—uncharitably—that she probably went out to find a younger man, one who was more available than he had claimed to be.

The next day when he went in to see Nancy Hamilton at the agency to pick up his weekly check, he was a little concerned that Mary Roland might have called in to complain about his lack of desire. But apparently she hadn't because Nancy asked him how the date went. "Fine," he replied, "just fine."

She gave him his check and then asked him if he could do her a favor. She picked a package up from her desk and said, "Could you deliver this on your way home? I'd call a messenger service, but they've been real slow lately and it's urgent that I get this there. You are going over to the Valley, aren't you?"

"Yeah, sure," Sean said. "Where is this to go?"

"The address is on it. In Bel Air. Just drop it off there."

Sean looked at it, saw the name A. Lowell and a Bel Air address. "I'll be happy to do it," he said. She thanked him and told him she didn't have another date for him yet, but she would probably set something up within the next day or two. "That's fine," Sean said. "I'm not in a rush. I've got some things to do."

He drove down Santa Monica Boulevard and cut up through Beverly Hills. He entered the east gate of Bel Air and wound his way past the mansions and cultivated landscapes.

Sean remembered being on this very road on the first day he arrived in Los Angeles. He had driven down from Seattle in his little Fiat, which had blown an engine and transmission soon after and had gone to the big automobile graveyard in the sky. He had driven down Interstate 5, a thousand miles nonstop, leaving early one morning and driving all that night and arriving in Los Angeles shortly after sunrise.

He remembered seeing his first palm trees in the weak

morning light and growing almost giddy with the pleasure of the sight. Even early in the morning the sun was warm, and the skies had not yet filled with smog. He had no idea where he was going to stay, but rather than look for a room, he had taken the Sunset Boulevard exit off the San Diego freeway and driven in the west gate of Bel Air, eyeing the mansions, some Spanish, some Tudor and more, a crazy conglomeration of architectural styles set back from the road behind tall iron gates with burglar alarm signs posted everywhere. And on the road, of course, there were the Mercedes Benzes, the Jaguars, the Rolls Royces, and the BMWs.

He had whooped with exhilaration on that first day here. To be actually winding down the canyons of Bel Air was both a culmination and a beginning. It wasn't the obvious wealth that entranced him, it was what this place represented. The people who lived here today had made their money in the film industry, as actors, directors, producers, even writers. They had reached some peak of their profession in the industry and these were the symbols of what they'd attained. It was what he wanted more than anything. Not the wealth, not the celebrity, not the power. What he wanted, and what he had come to Los Angeles for, was to attain excellence in his craft; the rewards would naturally follow. The rewards weren't why you did anything in the first place, not if you were any good. You did it because you loved it. Because it was what you had to do in order to actually survive.

On that first day in Los Angeles, as the sun climbed slowly and the fumes from the three million cars on the freeways began to rise with it, Sean had been filled with his dream. It had never been more real to him. It had pushed him from security in Seattle down the coast to this city filled with dreamers. And it had energized him, kept him in motion for months after that day.

Now, years later, as he once again wound up a hill, past

palm trees and a dozen other species, the dreams seemed dimmer, shrouded in moments of failure and disappointment, obscured by what he was doing now with his life. It seemed a great distance from what he had originally intended.

He turned on Stradella Road and started looking at the numbers on the walls of the estates. There it was, like many others set behind tall iron gates. He pulled in and stopped a foot away from the gate and pressed a buzzer in a convenient speaker on his left. A tinny voice asked his business.

"Delivery," he said.

"Just a moment," came the voice. Slowly, soundlessly, the gate swung open and he drove through, taking it all in: a sweeping lawn, geometric beds of colorful flowers, the lemon and orange trees, the two palm trees in front of the house, the towering avocado tree which stood off to one side.

He stopped opposite the front door, picked up the package, and got out of the car. He rang the doorbell and, while he waited, looked more closely at the house. Two stories, Spanish stucco, balconies with iron railing, crimson bougainvillea crawling up the wall, a red tiled roof. It was beautiful, substantial, and extremely valuable. He wondered how much land stretched behind the house.

The door opened and a young woman looked at him with a quizzical expression on her face. It was a moment that Sean somehow knew he would remember forever. He stood there, his mouth open to speak, but no words came. He stared like a fool, unable to tear his eyes away from this woman's face. The expression in her hazel eyes changed from boredom to mild interest, and then they widened ever so slightly to reveal an almost shocked awareness.

Her eyes were set wide, the mouth had a strong curve, the nose was a shade too large. It wasn't only her beauty that captured him. He'd seen beautiful before. If you were an actor you saw many beautiful women and appreciated them less and less. No, it was something else, something almost indefinable, a presence, a form of deep recognition.

His eyes flickered to take in the rest of her—blue jeans, the white T-shirt, hair that was still wet, hanging in strands down to her shoulders, very little makeup, that wide mouth again. She was tall and slim and her dark damp hair was brown.

She recovered first and pointed to the package he was carrying. "Is that the package?"

"Yes," he said. "Yes, it is." and passed it over to her. "Are you A. Lowell?"

She took the package and said, "No, I'm her daughter, Susanne."

"I'm Sean Parker," he said. He held out his hand and she took it, shaking it firmly for a moment before releasing it.

Their eyes found each other again and held. It was probably only for a moment, but it seemed to Sean like a long time.

"You live here?" Sean asked and smiled at his own question. "Of course you do. That was a silly thing to ask."

She leaned against the jamb of the door with her shoulder. There was a delightful smile that brought humor into what had been serious eyes. Now they sparkled.

"Who are you?" she asked.

"Sean, Sean Parker. I'm an actor," he said.

She glanced down at the package she was holding and said, "This is just part-time work?"

Sean nodded. "Who are you?"

"Susanne Lowell, and like you said, I live here."

"Are you an actress?" he asked.

She smiled quickly and shook her head, "No, I don't have an ounce of talent in that area. I'm hoping to get into production one day, but that's not what I am doing now."

"What are you doing now?"

161

She shrugged. "Living the life of the idle rich, I guess. Leeching off my parents."

It was an unusual situation for Sean. He had never felt this speechless or helpless before a woman. His chest pounded and his breath plugged his throat. She was achingly beautiful. He wanted nothing more than to reach out and touch her.

She looked at him a moment longer, then pushed herself off the door and said "Thanks."

"You're welcome," he said, and stood there motionless.

She stood motionless as well, as if held by him, and then nodded, "Well, I guess I'll see you."

Sean suddenly grew afraid he was making her uncomfortable, and said, "Yes, I'll see you. Goodbye." He turned quickly and walked back to the car. When he reached it he opened the door and looked back over his shoulder in time to see the front door close. He stood there looking at it, almost climbed into the car, and then shook his head. He couldn't . . . absolutely no way . . . he couldn't just leave. He ran back to the front door and rang the bell again. She opened it almost immediately. "Yes," she said breathlessly.

"Can I see you?" Sean asked, "I mean, will you have dinner with me or go out with me? You know what I mean."

She smiled and said, "Sure."

"Tonight, would tonight be all right?"

"Sure", she said, "Tonight will be just fine."

"Shall I pick you up?"

"I have to go out. Let's meet somewhere," she said.

"Where would you like to eat? What kind of food do you like?"

She was momentarily bewildered. "I don't know. You decide."

"How about Le Dome on Sunset. Are you going to be anywhere near there?"

"That'll be fine," she said.

"8:00 okay?"

"That'll be okay," she said.

"Great," Sean said stepping backwards, his eyes still on her face. "I'll see you at Le Dome at 8:00."

"Good," she said.

"All right, that's good, that's really good," Sean said, continuing to step backward. "I'll see you then. Bye."

"Goodbye," she said, and, closing the door, released him from whatever spell of enchantment she had cast over him.

Sean finally turned and walked back toward the car and clenched his right hand into a fist and swung it against the air in a downward slashing motion. "All right," he said. "All *right!*"

When he drove out the gate he let out a whoop, much like the yell of exhilaration that had seized him on that very first morning in Los Angeles.

Chapter Eleven

Returning from the airport after delivering Mrs. Arlene Ford to her out-of-town flight, Danny thought with some amusement of her generous farewell. All perfume and powder, she had kissed him lightly on the cheek when he pulled up curbside and said, "That sho' was the best visit I ever had, sugar," before flouncing away, her long hair bobbing, her curved hips swaying.

Mrs. Ford was in her mid thirties, wife of a Houston real estate developer. She had come to Los Angeles before on shopping sprees, but now, after meeting Danny, she planned to return much more often, or so she had assured him.

Danny smiled at the memory as he drove up the San Diego Freeway toward the Valley. There was something about women with southern accents that tickled him. No matter what their net worth, there was somehow always something that struck him as basic and earthy about them. And so far, at least in the bedroom, he hadn't been proven wrong.

Just before stepping out of his car, she had pressed a very nice five-hundred-dollar tip into his hand with a casual, "Don't worry, sugar, my old boy can afford it."

Danny was feeling more satisfied than usual. He had visited his accountant the day before and confirmed that he was doing well. His monetary reserves had expanded at an astounding rate during the previous year. According to his latest calculations, he had almost fifty-eight thousand dollars spread among CDs, mutual funds, and stocks in a couple of stable companies. For a man who had left the barrio with nothing, it wasn't bad, he told himself with some pride.

The problem was what to do with it. The investments were, by intention, extremely liquid. He could cash them in at any time—once he found something else worthwhile in which to invest. The lure of real estate had always tempted him, particularly here in Southern California. He kept on bumping into people who had made their fortunes in that manner. The idea of buying decrepit houses, fixing them up, and then selling them, had always appealed to him, but it was not an area in which he had much expertise. And yet real estate maintained its fascination, as it did to virtually everyone in Los Angeles who had seen others make their fortunes in escalating property values. He knew enough illegals through the contacts he still retained in East L.A. to get any labor done very cheaply. But somehow, whenever he thought along these lines, the concept that really thrilled him was to own his own company, some kind of service business. And when he allowed himself the luxury of dreams, the thought of owning his own restaurant brought him a kind of desperate ecstasy— even though he lacked experience in that area as well.

Various permutations of this dialogue ran endlessly in his mind for months at a time. One of these days soon he would have to make decisions. While the money was appreciating nicely, he couldn't just let it sit there forever. Sooner or later he would have to decide what to do with his life.

He turned smoothly off the freeway and took the hill up to the condominium complex. As he turned left to enter the gates, however, he suddenly became aware that another car was filling his rearview mirror. He pressed the remote control and the gates opened. The car, close on his heels,

165

came in after him. It was only then that he noticed it was a blue Toyota and somewhere a picture tugged at his memory. Feeling uneasy but not sure why, he drove into his parking place.

The Toyota was right behind him. Eyes fixed apprehensively on the mirror, he saw a short, overweight man, balding, his jacket wrinkled, get out of the Toyota and approach his window. A moment later, as he sat there still wondering what was happening, the man's knuckles rapped sharply against his window. Cautiously he lowered it five or six inches.

"Yes?"

"Danny Perez?" the man asked.

"Yeah, what of it?"

A brown envelope suddenly appeared through the window and dropped in his lap.

"The papers are served, buddy," the man said, then swung on his heels and returned to his car.

"Shit," Danny said, and picked up the envelope. Still sitting in his car he opened it and scanned the contents. It was a subpoena requiring him to appear at the divorce hearing between Jonathan Cutter and Linda Bell.

When he met Linda Bell a year earlier Danny had fully realized for the first time the timeless artifice of women—the ability to disguise their weaknesses and enhance their strengths in order to create an aura of allure. Linda was a television soap-opera queen, beloved by millions. Although in her early forties, perhaps older, she represented the essence of glamor—not beauty, he soon realized, but glamor—a word that used to mean witchery or enchantment but now represented allure.

Linda, he saw in the disheveled aftermath of lovemaking and in the harsh morning light, had flaws aplenty—from the too-large mouth to the softening neck and heavy cheeks, to the drooping breasts and sagging ass. All told, her natural attributes were on the decline. But what she did have was a pair of striking eyes, a lustrous mane of red hair, perfect skin, and a smile that promised more than any female could possibly deliver, and she made the most of these. Through the skillful use of makeup, the highlighting of her strengths and downplaying of her weaknesses, through a hairdresser who could perform miracles, and with the help of an awesome selection of the most expensive clothes available on Rodeo Drive, she made herself exactly what she wished to be.

Her husband, Jonathan Cutter, was some ten years her senior, an extremely successful television producer. He had reached that status through the skillful packaging of blatant sex, toned down for television consumption. He and Aaron Spelling vied for the title King of T & A. But apparently their marriage was not as successful as either of their careers. Cutter liked to dip periodically into the infinite pool of eager starlets who paraded through his offices, while Linda, who had a far higher social visibility, had to choose less obvious methods of fulfillment. Hence Danny.

He had seen her about a dozen times and he thought he had satisfied her well. Suddenly, however, she had ended the relationship, not because of finances, for she was as rich as Croesus, but because she said it was getting too dangerous. She didn't explain the source of this danger, nor did he ask. It wasn't any of his business. Or so he had thought at the time.

When Danny reached his bedroom he immediately consulted his address book and found Linda Bell's unlisted telephone number. Still perturbed by what had just happened, he prayed as he dialed that the number was still the same and that she would be in. She was. Urgently, he explained what had just happened.

"Oh, sweetie," she wailed, "I'm sorry to drag you into this, but it seems that Jonathan has had some sleazy private detective following me around. He knows all about us, plus a few of my other indiscretions. After all these years, the cocksucker wanted a divorce! I wasn't about to give him one, so he set about finding reasons to get rid of me."

"What does this mean? That I'll have to appear in court?" Danny asked.

"Well, if you've been served with a subpoena, it means you're a respondent in the case. It probably does mean that you'll have to be there, unless we settle out of court," she said, and reiterated her apologies.

"This will be all over the newspapers," Danny said gloomily. "They'd love to get a story like this about you, especially the tabloids."

"Don't I know it," she moaned. "The asshole is counting on that to get me to agree to the divorce. But I'll be damned if I'm going to give in to him that easily."

"Well, you're fucked if you don't. Maybe it would be the wisest thing for you to do," Danny said. "I mean, you don't want to see your name dragged through the mud, do you?"

"Nor yours, dear boy," she said sweetly.

"Right," Danny agreed.

"Don't worry about it, I'll let you know as soon as something happens," she cooed. "Now I have to run. I'll talk to you later."

Danny sat on the edge of his bed, the telephone still in his hands, and stared abjectly at the floor. If this made it as far as the courts, his name would be linked to hers forever. The story would be at every checkout stand in every supermarket in the nation. They would both be drenched in a veritable thunderstorm of publicity. And who knew once they started digging how deep the reporters would go and what would be divulged.

And then, concurrent with that thought, Danny realized a strange thing. It wasn't his reputation he was worried about. In fact, the publicity wouldn't particularly hurt his business or his relationship with the agency. In some ways, it could even help it.

What really worried him were his parents. If the full story were to be released in a blitz of publicity, they were almost certain to see it, if not directly then at the hands of some well-meaning family friend. What would their reaction be? Disgust? Dismay? Disappointment? The thing that really tore at Danny as he sat alone in his bedroom was his awareness that their opinions were still so important to him. Would he ever grow up and escape them? It seemed unlikely.

Ted had been working on the waitress for three weeks now. Tonight he had the feeling his efforts were about to pay off in spades.

She was young, no more than twenty-three he guessed, but youth had its advantages. She was bursting with vitality, her flesh glowing with it. The entire package was attractive. Her legs were slim and shapely, among the best he had ever seen, and the rest of her matched that standard. More than anything, however, her face attracted him. She had a saucy mouth and eyes that danced with mockery. Altogether, she was a seductive young lady.

He had noticed her when she began working at the club three weeks earlier. He often came to the Flip Club late at night after dates, enjoying the luxury of not waiting at the door like the other plebeians due to his two-thousand-dollar-a-year membership. It was his home away from home. Here he could be himself, amid the hi-tech decor and glitterati of young Los Angeles society. These were people his own age, with his own interests. It was where he came to relax, to score coke from his dealer when he needed it, to drink quietly, or to date women who had nothing whatsoever to do with the agency.

The club claimed exclusivity. In fact, however, if you

were willing to pay the stiff membership fee or willing to wait outside the door for the favors of the doorman, who would allow you to enter for a hefty price, anyone was admitted. Inside was a hundred-thousand-dollar sound system, the flickering lights, and the flashy modern decor that most clubs of these types boasted. Unlike some, however, there was a dining room adjacent to the main area where late suppers were available.

The waitress's name was Lin, spelled that way to set her apart, she had explained to him. She'd come here from Colorado and, like so many hopeful actresses, was indulging in menial labor while waiting for the big break. Ted always made it a point to sit at her station, and through friendly conversation and noticeably large tips he had found out quite a bit about her.

She had graduated from high school five years earlier, after appearing in high school plays, making it as prom queen, the usual bullshit. She had "always wanted to be an actress," and, after appearing in a few television commercials in Boulder, had come to Los Angeles four years ago with five hundred dollars, one suitcase, two pairs of jeans, and three dresses.

Her career had not flourished as quickly as she hoped, and since being here she had held a number of jobs as a cocktail waitress. Six months earlier she had managed to secure an agent who did "absolutely nothing for me," and subsequently she descended into the fringe world of drugs, alcohol, and "making contacts." But, as she pointed out to him, she was tough, a survivor, although there was a small tremble in her voice even as she said it. She was determined to stay here and persist until her talents were recognized.

Her talents were probably minimal, Ted thought. Sure, she was pretty, but the town was filled with pretty girls like her. And some of them were genuinely talented. But that wasn't of concern to him. What did interest him was the way she walked, the sexually knowing look in her eyes, the sway of her firm young breasts, and the way her mouth pouted at him when she leaned forward to serve him or answer a question.

He knew her shift would end in about an hour and lifted his hand to signal for another drink. She sauntered over to his table, tray balanced in one hand, a smile on her lips. "Same again, Ted?" she asked. He crooked his finger toward her and leaned forward.

"What?" she said, her eyes flirtatious, stepping closer to him.

"I've got some fabulous coke," Ted said. "Want to get together with me after you get off?"

She looked at him, looked around as if to see if anyone was watching, and then back again. "Sure", she said, "I get off in an hour."

"You got a deal. And yes, I will have another drink."

"Coming right up," she said and walked away with a last smile over her shoulder.

An hour later he met her on the sidewalk outside the club. She came up to him and took his arm intimately. "God that was a terrible shift. My feet are aching."

"I'll give them a rub, if you like," Ted said.

She grinned slyly. "I'll bet you will."

He looked down at her, already anticipating the night.

"Wow, neat car!" she exclaimed as she slid into the front seat of his Alfa.

Ted flicked on the radio and invited her to punch the buttons for some music. She chose some loud rock and roll and then settled back into the leather seats. "God, I could use some blow," she said. "This job is just the pits. Do you have any on you now?"

Ted shook his head. "I never carry, especially when I'm driving. It's at my place, though, and we'll be there in ten minutes."

"I guess I can wait. How's the business going?"

He had told her earlier he was involved in raising money for film projects, a kind of a "deal-maker." As a behind-the-scenes power, he had given himself a lie difficult to contradict. Even this peripheral involvement in the film industry had guaranteed her interest. Possibly he knew people—producers, directors, casting directors, etc. He wasn't to be wasted as a contact.

"It's going just fine. I just raised some money for an indie. Casting hasn't started, although the rumor is that Michael J. Fox is going to be starring," he said.

"Do you think there's a part in it for me?" she asked, her eyes suddenly alert.

"I don't know, but I'll certainly mention you to the producer," he said. "We're real tight. I'm sure he'd be willing to consider you if there was."

"Oh, that would be great," she said, her excitement rising and then falling with her next thought. "Getting work in this town is just so hard. But I know so many people now, I'm sure something is going to break soon."

"I'm sure it will," Ted said.

When they reached his condo, Ted was relieved to see that neither of the other two were home. "Why don't you grab a seat," he said when they entered the living room. "I'll just go and get the coke. There's the stereo, TV, there's a bar in the kitchen. Help yourself," he said, pointing out each item.

Ted reached into his bedroom closet and pulled out the locked briefcase. He fingered the three-number combination and opened it. Inside was an assortment of pills in colored bottles, a plastic bag of grass, and four or five packages of cocaine, each weighing a couple of grams. He took one out and then relocked the suitcase.

He'd been doing cocaine on a limited basis for about two years now. He only took it when he felt like getting loaded. It was simply a recreational drug he told himself many times, and he'd proven that he could control it. He

172

could stay straight as long as he wanted to stay straight. Of course, recently he had been taking it a little more than usual, but that was because of the pressures of the job. Besides, why bother to stay straight all the time when you could get loaded? It was too boring. It didn't hurt to get high now and then. Other people did it with booze constantly. Of course, he drank as well, but sometimes it just couldn't get him up to where he wanted to be. At those times, some coke or ludes or grass or the odd tab of ecstasy filled in the blank spots for him. Anyway, he could take it or leave it, that much he knew.

He went back downstairs and saw her lying on her stomach on the living room floor examining four or five CDs. She heard him coming and said over her shoulder, "You've got some good sounds here."

"Yeah," he said, dropping to the floor beside her. "Put on what you like." She had a great ass, he noticed not for the first time, and he put his hand on it and gave it a squeeze. She gave him that coquettish smile, chose a CD, and stretched an arm out to put it on the player. "You've got a great body," he said, fondling her again.

"You're not bad looking yourself," she said rolling on her side and resting her head on her arm. "You've never been interested in acting?"

"Nah," Ted shook his head. "That's not where the money is. Too much of a grind. I don't think I could take the rejection."

She rolled her eyes. "Tell me about it. I've had more rejection than I knew existed. Anyway, looking at this place, it doesn't look like you're doing too badly."

"No, not too badly," he said. He got up and went to the glass table in front of the couch. "Come on, let's do some blow."

She joined him there saying, "I can't wait. I can really use it."

Deftly he opened the small bag, put the cocaine in a pile

on the table, withdrew a razor blade from his pocket, and measured the coke out into lines. Then he took two silver straws from his pocket and handed her one. "Ladies first," he said.

She leaned forward and took a line up a nostril in one gigantic sniff. Then she leaned her head back and breathed deeply.

"God, this is good blow," she said. "There's not much cut in this, right? Can I have another hit?"

"Go ahead," Ted said, watching her face begin to flush. She leaned forward and put the straw in the other nostril and took another line with equal zest.

"Wow!" she exclaimed, her voice constricted. "This is good shit."

Ted leaned forward and did the same, taking up two lines. After a few seconds, he felt the rush begin to hit. His heart began to bump around, palpitate.

"I'm really buzzing," she said, her eyes bright. "Thanks."

"Yeah, I only get the best," Ted said. He leaned back on the couch. "Now, come here," he ordered, holding one hand out.

Without hesitation, she slid toward him, her mouth already opening, and he kissed her, twisting his hand in her hair, his mouth devouring hers, their tongues sliding against each other. His hand found her breast and he saw that the nipple was already hard. Sliding his hand down to her knee, he ran it up her leg against the rough black stocking until it reached firm and warm flesh.

Finally she broke away, breathing heavily, "I need another hit," she said.

"Go ahead," Ted said. "Take another couple." She did and then sat back up on the couch, her face suddenly almost crimson.

"I'm really flying now," she said. She grabbed his hand, "Feel my heart. It's missing beats. It's jumping all over. Wow, this is too wild!" She took his hand and placed it against her heart. It was thumping wildly he noticed, but that wasn't unusual.

"God, I'm peaking now," she said. Her voice speeding up, the syllables stumbling over each other in their hurry to get out. "Listen, is it cool here? Is it safe? I mean who else is here with you? Are there people here? Are we alone?"

Ted had been with enough cokeheads and was experienced enough himself to recognize the onslaught of paranoia. He looked at her critically. "Are you getting paranoid?" he asked.

"No," she said, "Do I look paranoid? I'm not paranoid. I'm just a little nervous, that's all. It just makes me a little nervous. Do you have any ludes to get the edge off this? I could really use a lude."

"Yeah, I do. Let me go get some." He stopped at the bottom of the stairs and looked back. Her hands were clenched tightly at her knees and she was staring down at them. God knew what thoughts were going through her mind. He went back into the bedroom, opened the same briefcase and took a couple ludes out of a small packet. Then he went downstairs, got some water from the kitchen, and handed the glass to her with the two ludes.

"Here, take this. It'll make you feel better," he said.

Her hand shaking, she reached for the glass. "Yeah, it'll just take the edge off. You know how it is? I mean, it's not that this is bad shit or anything, but I've been doing a lot of coke lately and maybe I've been doing a little too much. God, this was good shit and I'm really flying, but it's just that I'm a little too high, I think and . . . God, do you have any percodan? My fucking nose hurts. I'm going to have to put vaseline in my nostrils, I think. Maybe I should do a couple more lines just to kind of take me over the edge."

Ted watched her ramble on. God, I hope she doesn't freak out on me, he thought, concerned now. She really was on the edge. Anything could happen.

He remembered being at a party a few months earlier where there was a mound of coke the size of a sugar bag on the table. Some chick had stuck her whole face in it and sniffed up the shit. Then she had gone to the balcony and jumped off. At least she had landed in bushes, suffering only a few broken bones. She could just as easily have landed on the concrete. It hadn't mattered to her; she was past caring.

"Here, just take the ludes," he said, touching the hand that still held them. She popped them into her mouth and swallowed quickly.

"My face is hurting," she said. "I did some blow at work tonight. It must have been some bad shit, a lot of cut in it or something. My face is hurting. Maybe I need another hit." Without asking she leaned forward and took the last line on the table up her right nostril. Then she leaned back and looked at him and tried to force a smile.

"I'm going to be fine," she said. "The ludes are going to help. Don't worry, I'm going to be fine. Can we put on some other music?"

"How much coke did you do at work?" Ted asked.

"Three or four lines," she said with shrug, and then shook her head at some silent reproach.

That probably meant four or five, Ted thought, struggling to make a decision. This could be bad news, he told himself. One of the others could arrive home at any moment. She could be heading for a major freakout. He had planned on having her in his bedroom by now, but fucking her in this condition wouldn't be much fun, and who knew what she would do next. He suddenly made up his mind, logic prevailing over lust, and stood and said, "Listen, we got to go. Where do you live?"

"What do you mean, we got to go? Aren't we going to ball?" she asked, looking up at him, suddenly plaintive and childlike.

176

"I just realized some people are going to be arriving here. Where do you live?" he repeated.

"West Hollywood. But I don't want to go home, I want to party some more," she said.

Ted shook his head. "I think you've passed the point of partying, sweetie. I think I just better get you home."

"God, you're no fun," she complained.

"Come on," he said, grabbing her arm and pulling her up. "I'll get you over to West Hollywood."

After twenty minutes of her nonstop babbling, an illogical stream of consciousness, he arrived at the corner of Fairfax and Melrose. "Where do you live?" he asked.

"Near here," she said. "Listen, do you have any more coke? I sure could use a couple more lines. I don't want to come down too hard here. God, my nose hurts."

"Where do you live? Where exactly do you live?" Ted said.

"Do you have any more coke?" she repeated.

Impatience driving him, Ted leaned over and opened the door on her side. "Out," he said.

"What, here? Where are we?" she asked.

"Out," he said grabbing her shoulder and giving her a push.

"Hey, all right, be cool," she said, suddenly scared at his show of force. "Don't be such an asshole. Just be cool, okay? I'm getting out." She got out of the car, staggering slightly, slamming the door as hard as she could behind her.

"You're an asshole!" she shouted, her face distorted, and then raised her finger to give him the bird.

Ted tromped on the accelerator and tore off in a squeal of rubber.

What a waste, he thought.

Sean hardly noticed what she was wearing, although it

177

was obviously expensive and fashionable. They sat at a table beside a window, but he saw only her face. Her cheekbones were angular, her mouth exquisite, her eyes magical. She was simply the loveliest woman he had ever met, although he couldn't have explained why he thought that.

"Well," they both began, and then laughed.

"You first," Sean urged politely.

"I was just going to say it's nice seeing you again."

"It's nice to see you, too."

Was that a flush on her cheeks? She looked away, examining the roomful of diners for a moment, then met his gaze again. "You come here often?" she asked.

"No," he said. "I've never been here before."

"Oh, then why did you choose it?" she asked.

Sean turned the palm of his hand up in a helpless gesture. "Because it was the first name that popped into my mind."

A solicitous waiter hovered over to their table. Susanne asked for a dry white wine and Sean ordered the same.

"You've lived in Los Angeles all your life?" Sean asked.

"I was born here. I've been away a few times, but I've lived here most of the time. What about you?"

They talked for an hour, hardly pausing, barely noticing the food. They talked about childhood, school, college days. They told each other about their families, their parents, their friends. Sean told her about Marina, about their break-up, and then about her death of "a drug overdose." He couldn't bring himself to mention his suspicions. He didn't want them to cloud the evening any more than the recent death did.

Yet more than anything, they talked about the movies and the passion they shared to enter that world and become a part of it.

"I've spent the last couple of years considering my opsions," she said intensely, leaning forward. "I've looked at

178

teaching, at running my mother's businesses. God knows what else I've looked at. Nothing else excites me as much as getting involved in the film business. It's the only thing going that I could get into that has planetary impact, that influences millions and millions of people. And yet the product is also its own reward. You work and you work and you work and at the end of it you have a film, something you're proud of, something you've helped to create.

"I'll never be an actress, and I've tried to write, but I'm not very good. What I can do is recognize what's good. Show me a script or a book and I'll tell you whether or not it will make a good movie. And I also know I have all the organizational ability to put everyone together to get that product made."

"I know what you mean," Sean said enthusiastically. "You know, I've done a lot of stage work, and it's tremendously satisfying and exciting to capture an audience and carry them along with you on this journey and then to hear their applause. But films have a different kind of impact. They change cultures, influence trends and reach millions. And the audience is growing all the time. What could be more worthwhile than that?"

Susanne smiled. "I think we both have a missionary streak in us. We both talk about reaching people. But what do we want to say to them?"

Sean shook his head in protest. "It's not what I want to say. I'm the actor. I interpret. The writer is the one that says, the director gives form to that message, and I'm the one who interprets it. The skill is to be able to do so in a way that touches people, that gets through all of the everyday mush that they are crawling in or fighting against. To actually get through all of that and reach the person and have an effect, a positive effect. God, what a thrill that would be."

Susanne giggled, a sound that delighted him with its

insouciance. "I can't help it. You sound like an evangelist when you talk about film."

"You don't sound so different," Sean said.

"Well," she said. "Maybe one day we'll get to do something together."

"I hope so," he said.

Sean felt he had known Susanne forever. As if they were continuing a conversation they had started a long time before, filling each other in on the intervening years. It had never felt this way with any woman, not even with Marina.

With Marina, there had been an undeniable attraction, particularly sexual attraction. He had been fascinated by her vivacity when they first met, but the love, or what he had come to think of as love, had developed over a period of time. His attraction to Susanne was instantaneous. This was meeting an old lover, seeing an old friend, a rejoining rather than a new beginning.

At one time during the conversation he partially expressed his thoughts. "I feel like we've always been friends. It's wonderful meeting you."

She looked at him with a strange expression, almost of surprise, and then said, "I feel the same way."

And then the waiter interrupted, asking if they needed anything else. Only then did they look around the room and notice they were among the last three or four people there.

"Perhaps, we should go," Sean said regretfully.

"I guess it's getting late," she agreed.

Outside, Sean walked her to her car. "I'd like to see you again," he said.

"Of course," she said, almost in surprise.

"Tomorrow?"

"Call me." She reached in her bag and pulled out a card. "My number is on that," she said.

He took it, his hand touching hers and then stood there

180

looking at her.

She stared back at him, a glint of amusement suddenly appearing in her eyes. "Are you going to kiss me or just stand there?" she asked.

Sean reached out and put his arms on her shoulders. They both stepped forward and then their mouths were touching. It was not a chaste kiss of first meeting. Their mouths melted into each other and opened and their tongues met. It was as if in this way they were communicating in a far more direct manner than words and on some deeper level.

When they finally pulled apart, both short of breath, Sean wanted to ask her to come home with him. No, he didn't even want to wait that long; he wanted to take her right there on the street, to get into her car and make love on Sunset Boulevard.

"I want to ask you to come home with me now, but I think it might be better if we took things a bit more slowly," he said finally.

"If you ask me, I'll come," she said seriously. "But maybe this is happening too fast. We shouldn't rush it."

Sean reached out a hand and gently ran it across her cheek and across her jaw. "You're remarkable," he said. "I've never met anyone like you."

They kissed again, without the urgency of that first kiss. It was a more gentle exploratory kiss, and yet infinitely satisfying.

"I'll call you tomorrow," he murmured.

He stood on the sidewalk and watched her get into the car. As she drove away the tail lights disappeared around the corner at the bottom of the hill. He took a deep breath, then crossed the street to his car.

Susanne gripped the steering wheel tightly as she drove away. Every now and again her eyes flickered up to the

181

rearview mirror to see Sean still looking after her.

Oh, my God, she wanted to shout to herself. I can't believe it!

She remembered their kiss, and found herself closing her eyes for a moment — until she remembered she was driving and opened them quickly. He was handsome and talented and he had a gentle side to him along with an obvious strength. When she was with him she yearned to touch him all the time; she felt there was no time, no space, except for that which they occupied together.

She found herself comparing him to David Dobbs, the senator's son. David was a nice man with a gentle nature. She had seen him only the day before when he had come over for a game of tennis. A mismatched game, it turned out. When he said he had played tennis in college he neglected to mention with his self-effacing modesty that he'd been considered for the United States Davis Cup team. Even though he played down to her as much as possible, it was strictly no contest.

The difference between these two men had something to do with a certainty of being. While David had a visible strength in spite of his shyness, essentially he was unsure of himself, probably because he had been under his father's influence for so long. He seemed to be watching himself all the time, living in a perpetual state of selfconsciousness. Sean, on the other hand, had a certainty of himself, he knew who he was and he didn't need to continually examine what he was doing. He was almost entirely un-self-conscious and at the same time, terribly open. There was a naivete, a kind of innocence to him. And yet it wasn't because of lack of experience she was sure, it was simply the way he was. In his approach to the world he was one of those people who expected the world to give him the best it had to offer and probably received it most of the time, she thought.

Her last boyfriend, Roger Curtis, had been quite different. He too was an actor, but like many actors, he was completely self-involved. He was always eager to talk about himself and rarely bothered to find out her feelings or opinions if it didn't concern his immediate problems. After six months she had finally dumped him. And the boy-friend before him didn't bear thinking about.

She shook her head and swerved to avoid a Mercedes Benz that cut into the lane in front of her. She felt as if she had known Sean for a long time. Funny how he had mentioned that during dinner. She been thinking exactly the same thing only a moment before he said it. She felt comfortable with him, something like she would with any old friend, in spite of the very potent sexual and romantic undercurrents. Over and above that, there was a feeling of being home, back where she belonged.

God, she thought, almost desperately. It was almost too good to be true.

Chapter Twelve

Oscar grinned wryly at Sean and said, "I've told you this before, but you obviously don't believe me — women don't want to hear the truth. If you told her about this it would be at your peril, my friend."

Sean had met him for breakfast at the House of Pies in Los Feliz to ask his advice. He would be seeing Susanne today and he was wrestling with his conscience. Should he tell her about his job at Debonaire? Should he mention that he was employed as a male escort?

He didn't want to keep secrets from her. He felt an overpowering need to be as honest and frank as he could be. But hell, he was afraid of what she would think of him.

"Anyway," Oscar said with another grin. "What I want to know is, what's the job really like? You must be getting more ass than a toilet seat."

Sean shook his head. "It's not what I'm doing. I'm trying the best I can to not get involved with these women. I'm just in it for the bucks."

"And I presume that you are doing okay in that department?"

Sean nodded. "Yeah, moneywise, it's all right."

"What are these women like?" Orson asked.

"Some of them are lonely, some of them are bored, some of them just want an easy way to get some company. They can afford to indulge themselves."

"And some of them are horny," Orson stated.

"Yeah, that too."

Orson shook his head, his shoulder-length gray hair swinging back and forth with the motion. "Man, it's hard to believe you are actually getting paid for this. Are they all old?"

"Well, none of them are in their twenties," Sean said sardonically. "They range from thirty on up."

"Up, like what? Fifties?"

Sean nodded, "Yeah, fifties."

Oscar shook his head again. "I never would have figured you for doing something like this. Mr. Clean, Mr. Straight Guy. I never would have guessed."

Sean looked at him, an angry surge rising in his voice. "I wouldn't have figured it either," he said bitterly. "Desperation drives one to do strange things, doesn't it?"

Oscar held his hands up as if to defend himself. "Hey, I'm not making a judgment here. I'm just saying I wouldn't have guessed. I mean, you're doing what you have to do, man, and that's fine. Besides, I don't think it's that big a deal, that there's anything wrong with it. During the times I've been down and out I'd have done the same thing if I had known such a job existed. God, it sure beats waiting tables."

"I don't know about that," Sean said glumly.

"I'm sorry to hear about Marina," Oscar said, changing the subject to one that Sean had brought up earlier. "I mean, I only met her twice, but she seemed like a bright girl."

Another shrug from Sean. "Yeah, but she wasn't bright enough, was she?"

"It's a bummer," Oscar concurred.

Sean looked at his watch. "I've got to go. I've got an appointment. Thanks for the advice, anyway."

"Hey, no problem," Oscar said. "Call me again sometime

185

and we'll have a beer."

Sean picked up the check. "I'll take care of it this time," he said.

"Man, what's the world coming to? I thought it was always my duty to buy for the starving actor," Oscar joked.

"Well, I'm not starving and I'm not acting," Sean said, and stood.

"I'm going to sit here and have another free coffee. I'll catch you later," Oscar said, waving his hand dismissively. His eyes thoughtfully followed Sean's departing back.

Sean pulled up his car in front of Doris Winston's house and pressed the buzzer on the locked gate. After he announced his name the gate swung open, still with creaky, protesting hinges.

Doris stood outside the front door, a welcoming smile on her face. She wore baggy brown pants and a denim shirt and looked as if she had been working in the garden. Her hair straggled over her forehead.

When he stepped from his car and walked toward her, she held out her hand to shake his. "I'm so glad you called, Sean," she said. "I thought you'd forgotten all about me."

"No, not at all," he said, genuinely pleased to see this cheerful woman again. "I've just been busy. And then, well, I had a problem, and I thought you might be able to help me for some reason. You're one of the first people who popped in my mind when I wondered who to go to for advice."

"Well, I'm glad," she said warmly. Taking his arm, she walked him into the house.

They chatted pleasantly for a few minutes, and then after she poured him a cup of tea and sat beside him on the couch, she asked what his problem was.

"I have a dilemma," Sean said uncomfortably. "I met this

186

girl, you see, not through the agency, but quite separately. Anyway, I met her and I don't know . . . I really like her . . ." His voice trailed away.

"Well, that's wonderful," she said sincerely. "What's the problem?"

"I don't know whether to tell her about what I do, I mean my job at Debonaire, at the agency. I don't know whether to tell her about that or not," Sean said.

"Oh?"

"I guess I'm afraid to tell her. I want to, but I'm afraid I'm going to lose her before I get her. She's someone I've been looking for for a long time and really important to me. Even though we hardly . . . I was going to say hardly know each other, but even though we've only met once, we do know each other."

"You've only been on one date?" Doris said.

Sean nodded.

"And you already feel this strongly about her?" she said with an understanding smile. "Must be something special, this girl."

"She's really remarkable," Sean said. "She's everything I've been looking for. I don't want to blow it."

"Well, have you thought about quitting the agency?" Doris asked.

"I can't do that," Sean said.

"Why? The money? It's that good?"

"No, it's not the money. I have another reason for staying there, which I'd rather not get into, but I do need to keep working there for a while. I just don't know whether to tell her or not."

Doris took a sip of tea and regarded him shrewdly over the top of the cup with her bright brown eyes. Then she put the cup back on the saucer and placed it on the table. "Sean, you are starting a new relationship, one that obviously means a lot to you. The only thing I can recommend is complete honesty. You can't start something good with a lie. It just won't work. The lie will be there like the faulty foundation on a building. And the first time there's an earthquake, the whole thing will come tumbling down."

"Oh, God, I know that," Sean groaned. "I know it, and yet I keep thinking that it might not matter, that it's not important. That I'm only going to do this for a short while longer and she'll never know."

"You know that's not true," Doris said. "That it's not important, I mean. It *is* important. You're just going to have to face up to it and tell her and then let the chips fall where they may."

"But what if they fall? What if she doesn't understand? What if she ends it before it's even begun."

"I know it doesn't sound like viable alternative, but that's the chance you have to take. You're suffering from a severe case of chickenshititis, that's all." She smiled to take the sting out of her words. "Listen, just keep one thing in mind. If this girl feels as strongly about you as you do about her, it's unlikely she is going to walk away from you."

"That's logic, not necessarily life," Sean said.

"Maybe. But I have to say it again. The best thing for you to do is to quit the job. I mean, do what work you have to do, but quit the job if she is that important to you. That way when you tell her about it, it can be part of your sordid past."

"I can't quit," Sean reiterated.

"Why not?" Doris asked insistently.

Sean hesitated and looked over at her. Somehow he had trusted Doris Winston from the moment he first met her. "I'll tell you," he said, and launched into an explanation of Marina's death. Doris sat silently and listened to him.

When he finished, she simply nodded and said, "So, it seems pretty clear to you that the agency had something to do with this?"

188

"It's the only thing connecting us," Sean said. "I mean all three of us—her, the guy she was looking for, and me."

"But the man she was looking for might not have anything to do with what happened to her."

"His name was on the list, my name was on the list, the agency's name was on the list."

Doris nodded again. "It *is* strange." she conceded. "And you haven't found out anything more?"

"I haven't had time, but I am going to start asking questions. I don't know exactly what to ask, but I guess I'm going to start with the guy Marina was looking for, see who knows what about him."

"It seems a good idea," Doris said. She tapped her fingers on the top of the couch. "And that leads us right back to your problem. All I can say is if you trusted me enough to tell me about this, about the reason why you are staying, perhaps you should trust her enough."

"Yes, but I don't want to complicate things," Sean said. "I don't want her to think she is walking into a big problem here. That's a lot to ask of someone."

"It is," Doris said, "but you don't seem to have much choice."

"I could not tell her anything," Sean said. "I could just stick to the story that I'm an actor. It's not as if I'm really hiding anything shameful from her."

"You're thinking of it as just another white lie, aren't you?" Doris said. "Because you're doing this for a good purpose you think it's fine to tell her a little lie. I'm sorry, Sean, but that's not the way it works. A lie is a lie. If you really want to start this thing out right, you're going to have to be really honest with her."

Sean looked at her with a small smile on his face. "Yeah, I guess I knew you'd say that. I guess I knew all along that that's what I'd have to do, even though I'm afraid. A friend who I also asked for advice told me to lie

189

like hell. His theory is that women don't want to know the truth."

"Some don't and some do," Doris said. "I have a feeling this one does."

"Well, I guess I'll find out."

"What's her name?" Doris asked.

"Susanne Lowell. She lives in Bel Air with her parents."

"Oh, I wonder if that's Kenneth and Annette Lowell? I've met them once or twice. He's a judge and she's in some kind of business."

"Yes, that's them," Sean said. "She does real estate and stuff like that and her father's a judge."

"They are a very powerful family," Doris said. "Her mother is heavily involved in politics, very well connected. I've met her at a few fundraisers."

"What are they like?" Sean asked.

"Rich," Doris said. "That's all I know."

"Yeah, I know that much," Sean said.

"Sean?" Doris said carefully.

"Yes?"

"This piece of investigative work you're embarking on . . . it could bring you trouble, you know."

"Yes, I know."

"Well, if at any time you need help, I want you to know you can count on me, okay? For whatever I can do."

Sean leaned over and kissed her softly on the cheek.

Ten minutes later after lighter conversation, he left. It was almost noon and he had arranged to meet Susanne at a restaurant on Sunset Plaza for lunch. He thanked Doris for her advice and allowed her to hug him. "Come back and see me again, she said. "And just do the right thing. It'll all work out."

"I've always envied people who had a middle-class upbringing." Susanne said. She looked at Sean sipping his cappuccino. "Like you, for instance. A middle-class family, middle-class school, a middle-class neighborhood in middle-class Seattle. How normal and refreshing."

They were sitting at a sidewalk cafe after finishing lunch, and were now drinking coffee. Sean gazed at her woefully, "Childhood never felt all that normal to me. Besides, I've always admired people who have been brought up in wealthy families," he said. "In a wealthy neighborhood, going to wealthy schools, with wealthy parents. Call me crazy, but somehow, when I've been struggling to make ends meet in college and struggling to make ends meet down here, well, wealth didn't seem such a bad fate."

"I know a ton of rich kids," Susanne said. "None of them, or at least very few of them, are happy."

"Why?" Sean asked. He couldn't keep his eyes off her. He hadn't been able to tear his gaze away since they had met an hour earlier. She was still beautiful to him, even more so in daylight. She wore gray slacks and a pale blue blouse and a brown leather jacket that was now draped over the back of the chair. Her bare arms were brown, the hair on them golden in the sunlight.

She narrowed her eyes thoughtfully. "It seems to fall into two camps. The wealthy kids that I knew either got everything from their parents with no strings attached, or whatever they got was tied up in knots it had so many strings attached. Do you know what I mean? It's like you're either spoiled or else because of your wealth the word *responsibility* accompanies everything. Every gift has its responsibilities and you're expected to repay it by fulfilling those, a kind of doctrine of *noblesse oblige*. You're expected to follow in the family footsteps. Wealth is always accompanied by some amount of power, and you are expected to learn how to exercise that power for personal gain and make it look like a benefit to society. It's all hypocrisy, of course."

"And which category do you fall into?"

She held up both her arms. "Don't you see the strings dangling?"

"They aren't too apparent," he said.

She grimaced. "Believe me, my mother gave me everything. I went to fine schools, I went to fine colleges, I was given cars, I was given wonderful clothes, I was given a generous allowance. But I was always expected to follow in her footsteps and take over the business. There was a terrible row in college when I displayed more interest in the arts than in business. She threatened to cut me off. I told her to go ahead. I think my father probably talked her out of it, although he has never admitted it. She earned everything she got and she doesn't give anything freely. She expects it to be repaid."

She looked away for a moment, her jaw clenched. "Her mother," she continued, "came from a poor background. They wouldn't even qualify as middle class."

She went on to explain that Annette had grown up in a small town in Arizona. Her father had worked on the railroad for a while, but then when he lost that job he had taken whatever he could get, which often wasn't much. Annette had managed to graduate from high school, but the only work she could get was waitressing. When she was sixteen, Annette had hopped on the Greyhound and left Arizona to come to Los Angeles.

It had been a hard life for her at first. But after about five years she had taken a job as secretary to a real estate developer and had gained more than a salary. She found she had a good business head, and she picked up every piece of knowledge she could. Then, after marrying Kenneth, she'd used what little money Kenneth had left, money that he hadn't "squandered," as she was fond of pointing out, to build her empire. Susanne said all this with a slightly derisory note to her voice, as if she either doubted the history or had heard the story too many times.

"She was smart, no doubt about it. And she used everything she had learned. She brought property, first in Los Angeles, then San Diego, then San Francisco. God knows where she owns it now—up and down the coast, I guess. She's built a fortune out of not very much. But in gaining all that, I also think she lost something. It's made her tough, I suppose. God knows how many people she had to walk over to get where she got. I know some of the deals have been pretty hairy. Anyway, every penny she has today is valuable to her.

"So when you're the son or daughter of somebody wealthy, money tends to not have the same kind of value, and this attitude always creates resentment from the parents. *They* earned it, you didn't. It's quite understandable, I know, but I still don't like it. It's not as if I asked to be born in a wealthy family. I don't care that much about money. All I want to do are the things I want to do."

Sean tapped his knuckle on the table. "Why is it that those who have it don't care about money?"

Susanne frowned. "I know, I know—it always sounds so superficial to say that. But what about you? You've had to work for everything. I suppose money is important to you?"

Sean shook his head. "It's not important," he said. "It's a means to an end. I've always looked at it that way. I've always been willing to work for money, but I've always been able to get that work and to get as much money as I've needed. Until Los Angeles . . . Here it's become a little harder. I mean, there's so much competition for the kind of low-level job that I'm qualified for. I could always teach, of course, but it's not something that interests me. Too much dedication demanded there, too much time."

193

He dropped his eyes suddenly and toyed with his cup, realizing that he'd reached the perfect point in the conversation to broach the subject he felt compelled to bring up. But it was hard to contend with the fear that suddenly filled him now that the moment was here. Maybe he should just forget it or wait for a better time, he thought miserably.

"What?" Susanne asked, interrupting his thoughts. "What are you thinking about?"

Sean cleared his throat. "There's something I have to tell you," he said. "I don't want any secrets between us. You're too important to me."

"I agree, there shouldn't be any secrets. What is it you want to tell me?"

"Well, it's what I do for a living," Sean began. "I have this job you see, and I'm not very proud of it and I did it because I needed the money. I just hope you understand."

"What kind of job?" she asked, bewilderment clouding her features.

"Well," Sean said, "You see, I work as a male escort. I work for this agency. It's an escort agency and I'm available for dates with women when they need somebody to take them to dinner or the theater or something like that. I've only been doing it for a little while."

Susanne seemed to grow pale. "An escort?" she repeated softly, as if unable to grasp the concept. But her next words showed that she had. "You mean you hire yourself out. I thought that those places were all fronts for prostitution."

Sean shook his head vehemently. "It's not like that. I'm just an escort. I accompany people for a fee."

She stared blankly at him, her eyes those of a stranger. And then her mouth twisted, "Don't you find that degrading?" she said harshly.

Sean looked away. "It's not something I want to do or

that I'm proud of. I was going to quit but I have my reasons for staying. I just really want you to understand I'm not doing anything wrong. It's not like I'm a hooker for hire—a male prostitute or something. It's just a job and I have a reason . . ."

Susanne shook her head as if to shake away his words. "I thought you were an actor," she said distantly.

"I am," Sean said. "Of course I'm an actor. But I have to make a living, too. This is a job that earns a lot of money. I was broke and a friend recommended me and I took it, not really knowing what it was about, and—"

"I don't think I can deal with this right now," Susanne said, her hands gripping the edge of the table. "It's not what I thought of you."

"Listen," Sean began.

"No," she said, "I've got to go. Look, I can't talk about this right now." She pushed herself away from the table and stood, her face flushed now. And then without a backward glance she turned and hurried away.

Sean watched her cross the busy street, heedless of the cars rushing down the boulevard. She ran from the median to the other side, still not looking back at him.

His stomach was knotted and he felt bile start to rise in his throat. This was exactly what he had feared. Oh God, how afraid he had been. And now his worst nightmare had come true.

"You know what you have to do?" Nancy said.

Ted, who stood in front of her desk like a soldier receiving his orders, nodded.

"You've done this before, but let me tell you again," she said. "As soon as you turn on the bedroom light the system is activated. If the ceiling bedroom light is off, turn on the bedside light. That also activates the system. But a light has to be on and you have to be in the bedroom. Understood?"

"No problem."

Nancy leaned back in her chair, wrists on her desk, and gave him a thin smile. "This should be fun," she said.

An hour later, as directed, Ted met the two ladies at the bar of the Beverly Wilshire Hotel. He stopped at the door for a moment to watch them. They were sitting under one of those ridiculous horseracing paintings.

Francine was tall and sleek, a knockout by any standards. She had a tough, taut body beneath the expensive blue silk jacket, high-necked blouse, and knee-length skirt. Her dark, closely-cropped hair was glossy, and her makeup impeccable. But there was a hardness to her pale blue eyes and curved mouth, a watchfulness. She looked to be about thirty-two.

The other girl, Emily, he guessed to be about twenty-four. Well-dressed in a tight black skirt and leather jacket, and obviously well-off, she was pretty but not striking—the type of girl who would always be called second for a date on a Saturday night. Still, she had a good body. Even though she was slightly overweight she looked well exercised and firm. She seemed slightly nervous, tapping the stem of her glass with long red fingernails.

Ted sat opposite the two of them at the small table, ordered a drink, and made small talk to break the ice, careful not to ask questions that were too personal. Anonymity was guaranteed this evening.

By the time he launched into an amusing story about a well-known film producer who had suffered a public mishap in the Polo Lounge the day before, being physically set upon by his wife, his mistress, and an actress he was sleeping with, the atmosphere had improved considerably. Both women were laughing.

Deciding that the timing was appropriate, Ted finished

his drink and suggested they leave.

"How far away is the place?" Francine asked, taking his arm when they stood.

"A few blocks," Ted said.

The condominium was in a small complex three blocks south of Wilshire in Beverly Hills. It was owned by Debonaire. It was elegantly furnished in modern Italian leather over a thick wool carpet of swirling patterns. The art on the walls was original, the ashtrays and glasses were made of crystal. In the living room was a large thirty-one-inch television screen and a two-thousand-dollar stereo system, complete with multiple CD changer. There was a fully stocked bar and a fully stocked refrigerator. But in spite of the obvious luxury, the condominium did not look lived in. It was too clean, too sterile. Even the magazines on the coffee table looked untouched. There were no dirty dishes in the kitchen, no cigarettes in the ashtrays, the towels in the bathroom were almost geometrically arranged, the soap was untouched, and the toilet paper roll was still sealed.

"Nice place," Francine said in the doorway. Emily stood hesitantly a step behind her, as if ready to take flight.

"Come on in," Ted said with an expansive wave of the hand. "What would you like to drink?"

"I'll have a vodka tonic," Francine said, "and Emily will have the same."

"Good, me too," Ted said. He went behind the bar, opened a small icebox, clinked cubes into three glasses and deftly poured the drinks. The women leaned against the bar took their drinks and sipped them.

"Perfect," Francine said.

Ted moved out from behind the bar and went to the stereo system. He put on a Tears For Fears CD and adjusted the volume so that it was just slightly louder than background music.

197

"Do you live here?" Francine asked, sitting on the couch and crossing her shapely legs.

"No, it belongs to a friend," Ted said. "I'm allowed to use it, however."

Emily moved from the bar to sit beside Francine, who chose that moment to open her purse and withdraw a plastic bag of cocaine. She waved it enticingly in the air. "Something for a little extra buzz," she said.

"Great," Ted said. "Let's save it for a little later."

Francine nodded and put her arms protectively around Emily's shoulders. "This is all very new to Emily. You must excuse her nervousness."

"That's quite all right," Ted said, and smiled at Emily. "There is nothing to be nervous about. You're among friends here."

"Yeah, I guess so," Emily said with a tentative smile back.

"Emily was getting a little bored, weren't you dear?" Francine said. "She's never done a three-way. I thought would be an exciting experience for her."

"For everyone, I hope," Ted said gallantly. "Shall we?" He stood and motioned toward the bedroom.

"Why don't you let us go first? Give us about five minutes," Francine suggested, also standing.

"Let me just make sure that everything is in order," Ted said. Without waiting for permission, he moved across the room, through the small hallway to the bedroom. He flicked on the overhead light at the switch beside the door and quickly moved over to the bed, also turning on the bedside lamp. It was a three-way bulb and he switched it down to the lower setting. After a quick glance around the room, he went back into the living room.

"Go ahead and make yourselves comfortable," he said. "I'll just finish my drink."

Francine took Emily's hand almost paternally and led

her into the bedroom. In the other hand she held a bag of cocaine and her purse. Ted sat on the couch and sipped ruminatively on his vodka. It was going to be interesting, he told himself. Without doubt, Francine was a tough case. She probably knew more about bedroom antics than most women he came into contact with.

After five minutes he put his glass down on the table, smoothed his hair back with one hand, and walked toward the bedroom. The door was closed. Slowly he opened it, noting the overhead light was off. The dim glow from the bedside lamp illuminated the two nude women on the bed. He stepped in, unbuttoning his shirt as he moved forward.

Francine had obviously been preparing Emily.

She leaned forward, hair falling over her face, and lightly kissed the younger woman's nipple. It was hard, straining upward, and her face was flushed, her breathing shallow.

"Look," Francine said, regarding the nipple seriously, "Emily can't wait for you. She's been looking forward to you joining us."

Shirtless, his cock straining against his pants, Ted sat on the bed beside Emily. Gently he brushed his fingers over her breast and down her trembling skin to her stomach and the bush between her legs.

Francine smiled lasciviously at him, her lips gleaming in the soft light.

And then Ted lowered his head to where his hand explored and heard Emily give a sudden gasp as her head jerked back against the pillow, knowing as he serviced her that the hidden video cameras and tape recorders were recording every movement and every sound.

Chapter Thirteen

Susanne stood on the edge of the Santa Monica pier and stared down at the green rushing water as it swept toward the sand. Surfers in wet suits sailed past, and farther out a light breeze brought white caps frothing to the surface.

Since her talk with Sean, she had felt physically ill and had come directly to the beach from the restaurant, feeling a need for some vast space in which to collect her thoughts.

His announcement had been as shocking as a punch in the stomach. Taken the air right out of her. It was probably her fault. Naively, she had built him up to be something else, not just an actor, but an idealist, a man of great integrity. And then this had happened. He was nothing more than a gigolo, a male hustler, the lowest of the low in her estimation.

She'd seen others like him before. It was unavoidable in the circles in which she traveled. They stood out like zits. Golden-haired boys with their top buttons undone to show gleaming brown chests, boys with their big condescending smiles and glossy politeness, hungry and wealthy older women on their arms. They were kept men, something like household pets, although not worth as much, for, unlike even a dog, they lacked any semblance of loyalty. Sooner or later they always moved on to easier or wealthier prey.

God, how could this be? she thought desperately. She would never have guessed. Tears pricked her eyes, blurring the mauve horizon.

"Great day, isn't it," she heard from behind. She didn't turn, but felt the looming presence move in beside her.

"Isn't this your favorite time of year?" the man asked.

She skimmed him with a quick sidelong glance. He was tanned with fair hair. He wore shorts and a blue demin shirt. Young, athletically built, handsome. Another hustler, just like the ones she had been thinking about, although of a different type. She turned away and looked back at the ocean.

"Hey, I'm just trying to be friendly. My name is Tim."

She turned and met his eyes with a hostile stare. "Why don't you drop dead, Tim?" she said pleasantly.

He lifted his hands in self-defense took a step backward. "Hey, no problem, like I said, I was trying to be friendly." He took off to find a more susceptible victim.

She pushed herself away from the rails and walked farther toward the end of the pier, past the restaurants and stores, the game booths and bumper cars, her thoughts morose.

What luck she had, she thought. You find a man that you think is perfect and then you find out he has feet of clay. How could she have been so naive?

She thought back to another time . . . a time she had tried not to think about. A time just over a year ago. It started at one of those boring Beverly Hills affairs where everyone was trying to sell something to someone.

When she first saw Alex, her breath caught in her throat. Oh, what a handsome man he was with his dark hair, a profile that could have been chiseled by a master sculptor, and brown eyes that laughed continuously at the world. She had never seen such a beautiful man.

She had fallen in love with him instantly. Well, at the

time it had seemed like love. Upon reflection, it was just an intense infatuation, some kind of hormonal onslaught before which she had been helpless. They began dating. She had slept with him almost immediately and the sex was, she had to admit even after this long period of time, extremely good. He was a man who knew what he was doing in bed.

Like Sean he was an actor and like Sean he took odd jobs to support himself. They had only been going together for about two weeks when it happened. Alex met Marion.

Normally she tried not to think of Marion, had not thought of her for weeks. At least, whenever some thought had intruded, she succeeded in pushing it out of sight. Today she could no longer avoid it.

Marion was her older sister, old enough to have already come into some of the trust fund that Annette had created for her two daughters.

Marion was a beautiful young woman with the same coloration as Susanne, although slightly taller. She was an actress, even more of a disappointment to their mother. Marion had never shown any aptitude for business or, for that matter, much else. More high-strung than Susanne and more self-centered, she had been a terrible student in school, hadn't gone to college, and instead entered the acting profession in which she subsisted marginally, more because of her looks and contacts than because of innate talent.

But her looks had apparently been enough to attract Alex, because Alex had quickly switched allegiances from Susanne to Marion. Susanne had suffered something of a broken heart at the time, although it was also mixed with intense anger, resentment, a sense of betrayal, sadness, regret, and a few other emotions. She had hated her sister when it happened. And apparently her mother had

202

hated Alex, because she had attempted to intercede almost immediately.

Alex disappeared for a while, but returned to the scene after a week of silence. Then, after a series of intense meetings with their mother, he disappeared again, this time for good. And this time it was Marion who was left with a broken heart.

Susanne discovered that her mother had paid him off. "You're a stupid girl," Annette had disdainfully told her. "I expect it of your sister, but not you. He was only after your money and your sister's. I gave him what he wanted and he left. He was just a gigolo. He sold himself to women. That's what he did for a living."

And that was how it ended, the suitor paid off and gone, the two sisters bereft and betrayed, although the repercussions had continued long after that.

But she didn't want to think about those, not now. It was too dreadful.

She had to think of the present. She had to think of Sean. Was he an opportunist like Alex? Was he after her for her money, for her trust fund? After all, that's what he did—he went with women for money. This was his trade, his craft, his art. Why should his purposes with her be any different?

Yet as she remembered Sean's words, his sincerity and openness, his eyes, the touch of his hand, the feel of his mouth, her anger began to melt. Sean wasn't like Alex, who had been glib and dishonest. Hadn't Sean told her himself what he was doing for a living? He had volunteered the information, and from the way he stammered and stuttered when he told her, it hadn't been easy for him. He had wanted, as he said, to start the relationship without any lies between them.

And what had she done? She had run away like a child from a nightmare, rather than try to understand, rather than listen to the reasons he had tried so hard to tell her.

The experience with Alex had left her bitter and cynical.

She looked out at the ocean and watched a small motorboat cut across the waves, stern bouncing high and then thumping down each time. A man and a woman were on board. They wore windbreakers, their hair swept back by the wind. But they were laughing.

She turned and walked quickly back down the pier, ignoring the cries of barkers, the smells of cooking fish, the music of the merry-go-round. She had to give Sean the benefit of doubt. She owed him that, and she owed herself that. She only hoped she wasn't letting herself in for more heartbreak.

Sister Cecelia was as angelic and saintly as ever—and still just as weird, Ted thought.

She had called him at home earlier in the day and asked him to meet at her hotel, giving him the room number and the time for his audience. Her voice on the telephone was regal and distant. When he arrived at the hotel, however, he found her to be neither.

She opened the door wearing a long, white, almost transparent gown, through which he could see the pale shape of her body. Her eyes were bright and feverish, burning with some energy, and she held out her hand to take his and pulled him through the door. He barely had time to push it closed behind him before she dragged him into the center of the living room.

"Take me now," she said. "Here. Now."

And so he had, his pants around his ankles, his shirt half on and half off, pushing her gown up around her neck to reveal her long sleek body thrashing below him on the carpet.

There was no need for foreplay. She was as wet as a sponge, her juices dripping on the inside of her thighs. And so, hard as a rock, he had simply plunged between them while she let out a sudden scream.

Through it all her eyes were rolled back up into her head and her disembodied voice beseeched him to do it ever harder, as if she wanted, needed, him to split her in two, to punish her with the force of his lust. When she came, she screamed, a sound that subsided gradually into a muttered "Amen."

She took him into the bedroom then and they lay naked on a large bed while she talked and he listened.

She told him how successful her latest tour had been. She had gone into the heartland of America, renting huge halls and appearing before vast audiences. The reception had been tumultuous everywhere. She had never been so popular. She had saved thousands of souls, she said.

"You must make a lot of money," Ted said, admiration evident his tone.

She corrected him. "My mission makes a lot of money."

"But this?" he said with a wave of the hand. "They pay for everything right?"

She leaned back into the pillow and smiled sweetly at him. "My hotel, my clothes, my chauffeurs, my cars, my homes . . . my home in Dallas, my home in Santa Barbara, all my vacations, all my trips overseas . . . Yes, they pay for everything." She raised herself up on her elbows and studied him, running a finger across his face. "You'd be good," she said.

"Good at what?" Ted asked.

"As an evangelist," she said flatly, as if stating the obvious.

Ted burst into laughter and then shook his head.

"You've got to be kidding."

"You could do it, and you could make a fortune. What you're making now is nothing compared to what you could be making. We get almost a hundred million dollars a year. That's as much as some of the Fortune 500 companies."

"A hundred million," he repeated, then shook his head again, as if to bring himself down to earth. "I don't think I'm angelic enough."

"Huh," she scoffed. "That's nothing. You're certainly handsome enough, and I bet you could create an impressive stage presence. You could even team up with me. I'd be willing to apprentice you. We could travel together."

"And I'd wear little angel wings?" he asked sarcastically.

She ignored his tone. She was serious about this. "No, you could create a new identity—a white suit, a hat perhaps, to add stature, rings on your fingers, a gold necklace around your neck. You could be the second Elmer Gantry."

Ted smiled at the image. "I really don't think I'm cut out for that kind of work. I don't think I could stand the public scrutiny, particularly from the media."

A look of displeasure crossed her face. "Oh, the media," she said, shifting her body on the bed. "I have a little man from one of those horrible tabloids following me around. He's been taking pictures of me everywhere. In fact, I had one of my secretaries distract him when I knew you'd be arriving. For all I know he might have been parked outside my door here with a nice shot of you coming into the room if I hadn't done something. They're such a nuisance, these people. Parasites. But you get used to them after a while."

"I don't think I'd ever get used to that," Ted said.

"Well, it was just an idea. I think you have a natural

inclination for this type of work."

"I think I have a natural inclination for the type of work that I do," Ted said, and ran his hand across her breast and down to the soft golden down on her stomach. She shivered slightly at his touch and smiled up at him, her pink tongue running across her top lip. "Praise the Lord," she said.

Later, after making love a second time, her thoughts returned to the media. "I think we have to be more careful. Do you have some place where we could meet? I don't like the idea of seeing you where I'm staying. Perhaps you could book us a hotel room somewhere else next time."

Ted was lying with his eyes closed, his mind on other things — in particular, her mention of the amount of money she made. It was an awesome sum, and somehow he wished a little more of it could float his way. "What?" he said, opening his eyes.

"Do you have some place we could go, some place more private next time?" she repeated.

Ted smiled. "Yes, yes I do, I have a perfect place," he said. "Just let me know a day ahead of time and we can meet there."

He had an idea, a brilliant idea. It would just take a little daring, a little entrepreneurship . . . They went together, and they were qualities he had in ample supply.

He kept smiling, hardly aware of the woman beside him now, thinking only of the potential she represented. The future suddenly looked a little brighter.

When Sean arrived home, still heartsick at what had happened earlier, he found a message from Susanne on his machine. All it said was, "Please call me." Scarcely taking the time to breathe, he called her back immediately. She picked up the phone on the first ring.

"I've been thinking," she said abashedly. "I was silly. I reacted without thinking. We need to get together and talk."

Sean's heart jumped, but he kept his voice calm. "Where would you like to meet me?"

"Can I come to your place? Would that be okay?"

He could tell she was nervous. Her voice was strained. "Of course," he said, and gave her directions.

Glancing quickly at his watch, Sean trotted upstairs for a quick shower and a change of clothes. He told himself not to hope for too much. She had thought things over, she said, but for now she was probably only willing to hear him out.

She must have driven like a demon, because he had just finished combing his hair when he heard the buzzer from the outer door. He took the stairs down three at a time, pressed the button to let her into the building and opened the front door.

She came down the corridor almost at a trot, then slowed when she saw him. Her expression was serious, but he felt an almost illogical delight when he saw her. This was his second chance, perhaps his last, and he prayed silently that he wouldn't blow it.

"Come in," he said, standing aside. She walked through the living room directly to an armchair and sat without an invitation. After closing the door he lowered himself onto the couch, suppressing the urge to offer her something. Judging from her expression, she wanted to get directly to the point.

"We've got to talk," she blurted out. "I'm sorry I left you like I did. It was wrong of me. I . . . I don't know. Something happened before to me and I guess I wasn't thinking too clearly and it reminded me of that. I just couldn't face talking about it then, but we've got to."

208

"What was it that happened?" he asked, a little taken aback by her rush of words.

"It was a guy who I thought I was in love with, and it kind of ended up a disaster. Like you, he wasn't who he said he was, who I thought he was." And then she told him the story of Alex and her sister Marion, and of her mother's involvement.

When she finished Sean looked at her for a long moment and then said, "I didn't know you had a sister."

"Had's the right word," she said tautly.

"What do you mean?"

"She had a nervous breakdown shortly after all this happened and she's been in an institution ever since."

"Do you see her, visit her?"

Susanne compressed her mouth before speaking. "I went there once." She looked away. "I don't ever want to do it again. I couldn't stand it to see her like that. She used to be . . . God, I mean she was my big sister and I always looked up to her. Before what happened with Alex, I loved her and wanted to be like her." She shook her head vehemently. "I haven't been back, and I don't think I'll ever go back."

He watched a small blue vein beat wildly against the skin of her throat, like a bird trying to escape. He wanted to reach over and take her in his arms and comfort her and make it all right again, but he knew that he didn't have that right yet.

"I'm really sorry," was all he could say.

"Anyway," Susanne said, " 'cause of all this crap I didn't give you a chance to tell me what you wanted to tell me, about why you took this job."

"Well, I took it for a reason," he said. "I mean, I took the job thinking I could stay ahead of the game, that I wouldn't get caught up in it, that I could just stay an escort and not become something else. But it's pretty

209

apparent now that that's impossible. In fact, I was all set to quit the job a few days ago. But then something happened, and I changed my mind." A mental image of Marina pale and motionless on the bed flashed into his mind.

"What happened?" she said. "Why not just quit? The money can't be that important."

"Well," Sean began. "Remember I told you about the girl that I was with, the last girlfriend I had, Marina."

"Yes."

"She died a few days ago. Supposedly she died of a drug overdose, but I think there's more to it than that. And I think it was something to do with Debonaire, the agency I work for. I'm sticking around until I find out what it is. I owe her that much. God knows she hasn't had much justice in her life."

Susanne leaned forward with her elbows on her knees and said, "I don't understand. I think you had better explain." Sean shrugged and immediately launched into his story.

"Are you saying that you think someone murdered her?" Susanne asked when he had finished.

Sean nodded. "Somebody did something to her. I don't believe she took those drugs and overdosed by herself. Something else happened and I want to find out what it is."

There was a long silence while Susanne considered everything he told her. He watched the various emotions flicker across her face. Her fingers entwined, knotting into each other, some unconscious aid to concentration. Finally she looked up and said, "This is too strange. I mean it's really weird, isn't it? It's like a movie."

"Except that it's not a movie," Sean said. "It's real life, and Marina was a casualty. And I've got to do something about it."

"So, what are you going to do?"

"I'm going to see what I can find out. I'm going to ask questions around the agency. I'm going to check up on this guy that she wanted me to find out about, find him if possible, and just kind of nose around."

"If what you say is true," she said, "then isn't it possible that this could be dangerous? To you, I mean?"

Sean shrugged. "I'll be careful."

She lifted her eyes then and looked at him with a different kind of seriousness. "Is there anything I can do to help you?"

"Just be my friend," Sean said.

She got up from the armchair and moved to sit beside him on the couch and put her hand on his. "I'm sorry I doubted you," she said. "Will you forgive me?"

Sean reached one hand over and placed it on her cheek and turned her face toward his and kissed her. It was a long lingering kiss, one that seemed to exorcise all the demons that had plagued them both in the last few hours, and one that sealed a new and enduring relationship.

Still silent, the agreement between them as tangible as words, he took her hands and pulled her from the couch. Arm in arm they walked through the living room and up the stairs to his bedroom.

Once there, he closed the door behind them and kissed her again. This time their bodies pressed against each other, the passion growing, their breathing ragged.

Sean wanted her with such an overwhelming desire that his fingers trembled as he unbuttoned her blouse and the top button of her jeans. She smiled at him with amusement and took over, and then unbuttoned his shirt and pulled it back over his arms and jerked at his trousers.

Almost as if they had jumped a few frames in a picture they suddenly found themselves on the bed and he was kissing the tanned length of her thighs. She laughed with delight and anticipation and ran her hands across whatever parts of his body she could reach, his eyes, his nose, his neck, his ears, down his back and up his chest, as if ensuring herself that it was there and hers while he did the same to her, scarcely believing this was happening.

When he entered her she shrieked, but it was the sound of song, a melody of pleasure. She wrapped her legs around his back and they rocked together in a changing rhythm, one that was first fast, then mellow and slow and then rising and rising as if to a crescendo, and finally, as he began to groan, she sobbed and kissed his face.

They held their arms tightly enough around each other to stop their very breathing. "Slow down a moment, just a moment," she said, a note of panic in her voice, and she thrust up at him in a sudden fury.

He paused, but only for a second. And then they caught up with each other and simultaneous waves of sensation swept over them, until they both let out long deep sighs and collapsed into each other's arms.

They lay there for a long time, tenderly nuzzling each other and murmuring words of endearment. And then, miraculously, he found himself growing hard again. This time he began to move so gently, so slowly, that she purred beneath him deep in her throat, her hands tightening on his back, her nails digging into him, until at the momemt of climax her eyes stared unseeingly at the ceiling, as if there was nobody there at all, only the force of their joint sensation.

Afterward, Sean felt as if everything in his life had brought him to this moment, inside this soft yet hard, tender yet fierce, and altogether most beautiful woman.

212

For the first time he knew the intensity of sex when it was transmuted by love, knowing that in spite of the silence between them she was feeling exactly the same way. It was something he never wanted to end. It was more precious to him than anything in his previous life. In fact, he felt as if he just died and been reborn to a new and more fulfilling life, the life that he had always wanted but that had somehow evaded him until this moment.

Sean was the first to speak. He lay on his side, elbow propping up his head, and looked down at her. "I think I'm going to say the L word."

"The L word?" she asked, opening her eyes.

"I love you," he said.

"Oh, yes, yes," she replied. "And I love you. That much we know."

Chapter Fourteen

On the night he fell in love, nobody was more surprised than Danny. Love had never been among his plans. On the contrary, it was something he had avoided all his life — at least, ever since high school, when he made the mistake of falling in love with a beautiful blonde by the name of Minnie Ripley. When he had made the further mistake of declaring his passion directly to her, Minnie had laughed at the impossibility of his dreams, saying, "What would I want with a beaner?" Since then Danny had been too busy using women to fall in love with them — until tonight.

He had accompanied a client to a party in Sherman Oaks. High in the hills, the spectacular two-story house overlooked the gridded lights of the San Fernando Valley below. A magnificent pool dominated the imaginatively landscaped grounds in front of the house, allowing the swimmers an unobstructed view of the city.

The client was a forty-year-old divorcée who had not wanted to come alone to this society event. Her name was June King and she was overweight and rich. She was obviously proud of her possession, namely Danny, introducing him to virtually everyone with the same coquettish smile as, "My good friend, Danny."

Danny was bored. The attractive women all wore clothes that cost more than most people earned in a couple of months. The men were fit and cleanshaven.

The rooms were filled with clouds of bright chatter. He knew too much about the foibles of the rich to be impressed. As usual, he found their conversational topics to be testimonials to banality.

After making sure that June was comfortably ensconced in conversation with a small group of people, he stepped outside and stood beside the pool. Once the valley below had consisted of orange groves and farms, now it was the site of constant gridlock, home to millions.

The voice just behind his shoulder seemed to be filled with secret amusement. "So, you're June's date."

Danny turned to face what was, to his mind, a breathtakingly beautiful brunette. She was tall, her eyes almost level with his. There was humor around the full mouth and in the bold brown eyes. Long black hair fell straight to her shoulders. She had a slim, tense body, small breasts, and long legs. She wore a silk jacket, a skirt and blouse, but he hardly noticed the clothes. She looked to be in her mid thirties.

"I'm Tamara," the woman said holding out her hand. He took it, cool against his, and felt a jolt of something close to panic. "Danny," he managed to say.

"I know," Tamara said and broke into a broad smile. "I understand June hired you. She really lucked out, didn't she?"

"I beg your pardon," Danny said stiffly.

She continued to smile. "It's all right, I'm a good friend of hers. We have no secrets. At least, she doesn't. She told me you were an escort and that she had hired you for the evening. It's just between us girls."

"I see," Danny said, and couldn't resist asking. "And who are you here with?"

"My husband," she said. "He's inside talking about the stock market to June's husband. That's all they ever talk about. The ups and down of the Dow, the hot new stocks, the bandwagons to jump on and the disasters to cut loose. Different names, same conversation, year in and year out, no matter where the party."

"He's a stockbroker?" Danny asked.

She shook her head. "He's too rich to be a stockbroker. He hires stockbrokers. He's a rich man. Family money, you know. All he does is invest it."

"An investor," Danny said.

She looked at him without speaking, her eyes searching his, suddenly tense and watchful. "I'd like to see you sometime," she said.

Danny's throat felt dry, he didn't understand what was happening, what this woman was doing to him. He felt clumsy and naive in front of her. It was definitely not a normal reaction for him. "You can call the agency. They—"

"No," she said sharply, "that's not what I have in mind. I want to see you privately." She reached out and took his hand, "Come with me."

She led him around the pool and across the lawn to the side of the house, where there was a small and empty unlighted patio. It was bordered by lush potted plants, palms and ferns and creeping vines. Her eyes glowed at him from the shadows on her face.

"What do you want?" he asked.

"Nothing much. Just you, all of you," she replied.

"You don't even know me," Danny said, but for some reason he felt a sense of mounting excitement, one that he hadn't experienced for a long time, one he scarcely remembered.

"I know you," she said certainly. "I've been watching you since you arrived and I know you. I know who you are and who you've been and who you want to be. And I can help you."

216

It was impossible, Danny thought, and some of his confidence returned. "You don't know anything about me," he said.

"I know you've turned into a walking dick, and what you need in your life now is love," she said.

"Love?"

"Yes," she said, a quick smile showing the white gleam of her teeth. "You need love in your life. You haven't had any and you want it even if you don't know it."

Danny choked on a short laugh. He looked at her more closely then and saw that she was absolutely serious. There was no humor in her face now. She just stared back at him, waiting. "What about you?" he asked.

"That's what I need, too. As soon as I saw you I knew you were the one."

"You're married." he said heavily.

"I'm sure that's never bothered you before," she said. "Anyway, it's only a piece of paper. It's a roof over my head, money in my pocket—that's all it means. You see these men here tonight? They are all the same. And the women? They're all the same as well, expensive whores, although they never think of themselves that way. They think of themselves as good wives or mediocre wives, mothers, pillars of society. But what they really are are expensive whores, paid to service the men they are married to. That's what I am and that's what they are. But I want more. I want you."

"You're very unusual," Danny said weakly.

She stepped closer to him then. Her mere presence felt like a cocoon around his body. He could feel the disturbances, the waves, the small impingements, something of her seeking to grow even closer to him.

"You're unusual yourself," she said. "I think that you just haven't discovered it yet."

For some reason her words zeroed in on something

217

deep inside him, something that he hardly knew existed or had perhaps been denying for a long time. He felt a wave of grief as if remembering something precious lost a long time ago.

He couldn't speak, he just stared wordlessly at her. She did the same, silently watching him, waiting for something, although he had no idea what. And then she reached out and placed a hand gently on his cheek. When she spoke her voice was gentle. "You think you're the one doing the using, Danny, but you're the one being used. Bought and paid for. You already know that, don't you?"

And still he couldn't speak. Any words he had were throttled in his throat.

She withdrew her hand and said, "I'm going to give you a gift." And then before he could move, she untied his belt and unzipped his pants and fell to her knees on the red brick patio floor and took him in her mouth.

She was skillful, energetic, and within two minutes he was shuddering, head back against the wall, hips thrust out in a climax, groans bubbling from his lips.

When she finished she stood, pulled up his zipper and tightened his belt. She took a tissue from the pocket of her jacket and wiped her mouth.

"There," she said finally. "You owe me one."

Tamara Bennett called Danny at ten o'clock on the morning following the party. Before he had left with his date the night before, Tamara had asked him for his telephone number and he had surprised himself by giving it to her. When she called she said, "I want you to come and see where I live today."

"What about your husband?" Danny asked.

"My husband's playing golf," she said impatiently, "and

218

after golf he's having lunch at the club, and after that he's having meetings with his stockbrokers. Don't worry about my husband. I don't."

Danny hesitated. Not only was this not a part of his job, but all his experience warned him away from this one. He knew it was heading for nothing but trouble. She was too wild, too arrogant, too beautiful, too rich, too spoiled, too careless.

But she wanted him and seemed to know him on a level deeper than any woman had known him before. And it all happened so quickly, there was something miraculous about it.

Her energy and determination carried him away, sweeping aside his cautions along with it. His hesitation only lasted a second.

He asked her for directions and said he would be there in an hour.

The house where she lived was farther down the Valley in Tarzana, surrounded by at least an acre of grounds. As he entered the long driveway, Danny saw a tennis court to the side of the house, a guest house on the other side. Behind it, no doubt, was a swimming pool. What looked like a greenhouse sat at the end of a long stone-paved path.

The door was opened by a uniformed Hispanic maid who looked slightly surprised to see him.

"I'd like to see Mrs. Bennett, please," Danny said.

Confusion flickered momentarily across the maid's face. To see an Hispanic man asking for the mistress . . . but a moment later, before she could decide what to do, a voice came from the hall behind her. "It's all right, Elsa."

Tamara wore a long, caftanlike dress in a rainbow of subtle colors. Her hair was pinned back, leaving her neck bare. She took in the scene at the door with some amusement and then stepped up to Danny, her hand outstretched. He shook it.

"Come in," she said and led the way down the hall to a living room almost the size of his condominium.

Danny had seldom seen such wealth. From the fine Louis XIV furniture to the art that was everywhere. Paintings adorned the walls, bronze sculptures stood tall on the floor, wooden Nigerian sculptures formed a tableaux in one corner of the room, while small bronzes were clustered in another. The carpet was Persian, and three crystal chandeliers hung from the ceiling.

She sat on the couch, crossed her legs, and patted the space beside her. "Come and sit with me," she said.

When he sat beside her, she immediately put her hand on his knee. "This is not me," she said with a wave of her hand, "this is my husband. He has attempted to become one of the most conspicious consumers in living memory."

"It's very impressive," Danny said.

"Yes, I suppose it is." Her eyes rested thoughtfully on him. "But it's not really who I am. You know who I am, don't you?"

"I'm not sure," Danny said with a smile, "but whoever you are, you're quite unique."

"But so are you," she said, giving his knee a little squeeze. "This is why we're attracted to each other."

"What do you want?" Danny asked bluntly. He waved a hand at the room. "Obviously, I'm not exactly in your league, am I? You have everything material that you need."

She lifted her hand from his knee. "And there you have it," she said. "I have everything material, but that's all. I don't have what I really need. It's you I need."

"Why me?" he said, truly puzzled.

"Let me tell you something about myself," she said. She stood. "Would you like a drink?"

Danny shook his head. "No, thank you. It's too early."

She walked across the room to a small bar. "Not for me," she said, her back to him. She went behind it and poured herself a glass of wine.

"I was born in San Francisco," she said, coming back to the couch, glass in hand. "My father was a drunk, my mother was a whore. I grew up in the Mission district. I was in trouble with the police by the time I was fourteen. I never graduated from high school, but I always knew who I was, and because of that I have all this today. I'm paying the price, but there are compensations. I am where I want to be. I see the same qualities in you. I knew they were there the moment I saw you. You're hungry, Danny. You want more and you're in a small game with this escort business. It's not worthy of your talents. You know that and I know that. Right?"

Danny was shocked at her perceptiveness, but he didn't show it. "Maybe you're right, but marrying money isn't a solution for me," he said. "Hispanic men don't marry money."

"There may be other alternatives," she said.

"And if you are right, what do we have for each other?"

She smiled. "I don't know. At least, I'm not sure," she said. "But I do know that we are each in our way incomplete people. Perhaps we can give each other something that will make us more whole, more powerful, more able to do those things we want and need to do."

"With sex?" Danny asked with a small smile, feeling more confident on familiar ground.

"No, with love," she said.

And suddenly Danny was on shaky ground again. Love was not something he knew anything about. Love was something that happened to other people. It was not something he had sought or felt he needed. He always

221

thought of the line in that song, "They're writing songs of love, but not for me." Love hadn't been something that he thought he could find, not in his circumstances. And now she was talking of it as if it were the most natural thing in the world. It confused him and left him with strange sensations, both physical and emotional. He didn't speak, just stared back into her dark eyes.

"You'll find out what I'm talking about," she said, without a trace of irony or amusement. And then she stood, still holding her wine, and held out her hand to him. "You owe me one, remember?"

He allowed her to lead him out of the living room. They went up the marble stairs and down another hall untill finally they stood in a bedroom. And then with a deft, almost imperceptible motion, she slid the gown off her shoulders and stood there naked before him.

Her passion was astounding. There was a tigress in that bed. Her nails clawed his back, her legs gripped him. She was a blaze of constant motion, now below, now on top, now administering to him, now demanding his attentions. Just before the end she burst into an uncontrollable laughter that pealed around the room, some expression of profound relief. And then, as she rose with him at the end, she screamed, an eerie sound that pierced him to the core. They collapsed, drenched and momentarily exhausted.

But less than ten minutes later, murmuring a litany of endearments, she touched him again and told him she wanted more. "I can't get enough of you," she said.

Later she surprised him by pulling a pack of cigarettes from a bedside drawer and lighting one. "I only smoke after sex," she said.

"Tell me about your life." Danny asked as he watched

the blue smoke curl up toward the ceiling.

"My life is exactly what I want it to be," she said without any satisfaction. "I do what I want, when I want, and I get what I want. Up until now the only thing that has been missing is you and now it's complete."

"What about your husband?"

"What about him?"

"What kind of a relationship do you have?"

"He's a child," she said. "He's a grownup little boy. He plays his business games, his investment games, and let me do exactly what I want. He adores me. I please him in bed, but he's not even interested in that any more. Maybe he has something going on the side, but I doubt it. He's interested in numbers, in watching his portfolio grow in leaps and bounds. He's interested in compound interest, in P.E. ratios, in deals, in multipliers. All he wants from me is to be the perfect hostess in public and the perfect wife in private. And I'm very good at it."

"I'm sure you are," Danny said. "I'm sure you're very good at everything."

"And you," she said. "What do you want to do when you grow up? I'm sure you have plans."

For a second Danny was silent. He never spoke of this to anyone. But she not only invited it, she demanded it. "I want to go into business," he said.

"What kind of business?"

He shrugged as he lay there and said, "What I really want is to own and operate a restaurant."

"That takes a lot of capital to get started. My husband tells me that more restaurants fail through undercapitalization than for any other reason. Do you have the money?"

His dream seemed far away at this moment, lying in this multimillion dollar house, in this down-covered bed, with this beautiful wealthy woman beside him. "I have

223

some, not enough," he said. "but I'll get it."

She took a deep drag on her cigarette and said, "Do you know what the worst thing is about dreams? Allowing them to die. They're like a plant. Unless you water them—act on them—they die."

"Not mine," Danny said. "I've saved a lot of money and invested it. I'll get out of this business and do what I want to do."

"What kind of restaurant do you want to have?" she asked, stubbing her cigarette out in a crystal ashtray.

"I want it to have the best Hispanic cuisine from South and Central America. Each national dish, something unique, something for everyone. I want it to be very chic and very casual—casual but selective. I'll open it in Beverly Hills or maybe on Melrose or somewhere else in West Hollywood."

"That's a good idea," she said. "Maybe I can help you."

"How?"

"I don't know, I'll think about it." she said.

Danny didn't pay much attention to her statement. People seldom went out of their way for others, he'd found out. He never did, so why would he expect someone else to? He had his plans, and somehow he'd find a way to bring them to fruition with or without anyone's help. "When does your husband get back?" he asked, changing the subject.

She leaned over and kissed his ear. "Not for a long time," she said. She kissed his cheek, then his mouth, then his neck, then his chest, and continued the downward path.

Soon they were clutching at each other again, two halves that formed a whole, pieces that had been rejoined.

When Sean arrived home at about eleven in the morning, he found Danny in an uncharacteristically pensive mood. His roommate was lying on the couch, arms behind his head, gazing at the ceiling, listening to some soft jazz on the radio.

"How ya doing?" Sean asked.

It took Danny a long time to turn his head or to realize where he was. "Fine," he said, "just fine." He swung up into a sitting position. "What's new?"

"Nothing much," Sean said, going into the kitchen and pouring himself a glass of cold water. "How about you?"

Danny looked at him over the top of the kitchen counter and shook his head. "Women sure are something else, aren't they?" he commented.

Sean grinned. "Is this something you just realized?"

Danny smiled sheepishly. "Well, in a way."

Sean now brought his glass of water around from the bar, and sat in an armchair. He hadn't been to the gym for a few days and his body could feel the workout he'd just put himself through. He stretched his legs out in front of him and listened to the kneecaps crack. "Uh, you want to tell me about it?" he asked.

Danny shrugged. "I don't know, man, I met this woman. I mean, what would you think of a woman who had everything. Rich, good looking, good husband, I mean *everything*, and she tells you that she loves you, right away, as soon as she sees you? The woman tells you she fell in love with you as soon as she saw you. I mean, what would you think of that? Is she crazy or what?"

"Well," Sean said. "I suppose that could be the first thought. On the other hand, maybe she just fell in love with you."

"I don't know," Danny said. "Nothing like this has ever happened to me before."

"What do you think of her?" Sean asked.

"She's very different. Special," Danny said admiringly.

"Well, must be something in the air," Sean said obliquely.

"What would you think if that happened to you?" Danny asked.

"I guess I'd think I was a lucky guy."

Yeah, you'd think that wouldn't you?" Danny said. "It makes you wonder, though."

Sean drained the water from his glass and then casually changed the subject. "Hey, do you know a guy by the name of Alex Varney, who used to work for the agency?"

Danny looked puzzled for a moment and then said, "Oh, yeah, yeah, there was a guy, it must have been about a year ago. He was there when I came and left soon after I started."

"Where did he go? Do you know what happened to him or anything?" Sean asked.

"Beats me," Danny said. "You know how it is—guys come, guys go. Maybe he got married to some rich broad. Who knows? Maybe he took off to greener pastures, maybe he went home, wherever that is. Some guys only last there a few weeks, you know. I think he was there longer than that, but I don't know. Why?"

"Uh, some client was asking about him. I guess he'd dated her a few times. I didn't know who he was."

Danny looked at his watch. "Well, I guess I'd better get it together. I've got an appointment soon."

"See you later," Sean said as Danny walked across the room to the stairs. Sean went into the kitchen and poured himself another glass of water and stood there drinking it and thinking about what Danny had just said about women. To tell the truth, he admitted to himself, he was feeling something of the same confusion over Susanne.

226

He felt unbelievably lucky, and yet somehow undeserving of such largesse from the gods. She was everything he had ever wanted in a woman and more. There were qualities in her that were so admirable he'd never even conceived of them. The degree of her honesty, her frankness, the totally uninhibited warmth that she displayed in her closest moments . . . there were times he felt as if they were one, the same person.

The last thing she had said to him as he stood outside her car and looked down at her through the window was, "I love you," and then she smiled radiantly and drove away. He had stood there for minutes, unable to fully grasp what had happened, a vibrant feeling of unrestrained elation encompassing him, a feeling as if he was about to burst with joy.

And then he remembered the other thing she had said just before she left: which had been, "I'll be back in the morning, if that's all right?"

He looked at his watch and saw that it was eleven. The doorbell rang. He got up to let her in, thankful that he had showered at the gym before returning home.

They kissed at the door deeply, hungrily, and then both broke away laughing, faces flushed and eyes glowing.

"I missed you," Sean said—an unoriginal but perfectly acceptable comment, one that those in the first flush of love had probably made for centuries.

"I missed you, too," she said.

"Come in." He took her hand and led her into the living room. "Do you want some coffee?"

"I'd love some," she said.

She followed him into the kitchen and, while he tried to make coffee, put her arms around him from behind and pressed herself against him and said, "Last night was the most wonderful night I've ever had."

For the moment he gave up on the coffee and turned and kissed her again.

Suddenly Danny appeared and said, "Hey!"

They broke apart, a little flustered. "Oh, Danny, this is Susanne. Susanne, Danny."

Danny stepped forward and shook her hand, his eyes appraising. "Nice to meet you," he said. "Well, I guess I'm off. Enjoy the day." With a last almost conspiratorial smile at them both, he left.

"One of your roommates," Susanne stated. "Also one of the guys from that agency?"

"Yeah, he works there too," Sean said as he turned the coffee machine on. "He's, okay. I think he's also in love."

"With a client?" she asked.

"I don't know," he said, "but he was looking something like the way I feel this morning, and musing about the mysteries of women."

"And what about the mysteries of women?" she said with a smile.

"They are very mysterious," Sean said and reached for her again. Once more they kissed and then Sean said, "Are you sure you want coffee now?"

She laughed and said, "It'll keep. In fact, it might even taste better afterward."

"Afterward?" he said innocently.

She grabbed him by the belt of his pants and tugged. "Don't play hard to get."

They went upstairs to his bedroom and once again made love. This time they were more relaxed, their love-making punctuated with laughter and delight in each other.

Afterward, as they lay in bed, she said, "I'd like you to come home for dinner tonight. Can you do that?"

"Uh-oh," Sean said.

"That's right, you'll be put under a microscope," she

teased him. "At least by my mother. My father is pretty cool, but she'll ask . . . well, let's be honest . . . she'll want your whole genealogical history."

"I don't know if I am ready for this," Sean said.

"It won't be so bad. I'd like you to meet them."

"Okay, but what do I tell her when she asks what I do for a living?" Sean said.

"Tell her you're an actor and that you work as a bartender or something." She looked thoughtful. "She'll probably ask me that question as soon as I say you're coming for dinner. We better decide on something acceptable."

"I'm uncomfortable lying," Sean said. "Why don't I tell her I'm an actor between jobs at the moment. I'm living on royalties from some commercial work."

"That's fine."

"Why do you want me to meet them, anyway?" Sean asked, running his hand across her hair, which was spread fanlike on the pillow.

"Because you need to," she said. "Just like I need to know everything about you. There shouldn't be anything hidden between us, and you need to know what you're getting into with me, warts and all. And that wart includes my mother. She's part of the package, like it or not."

"If she's anything like you, I'm sure I'll like her," Sean said.

Susanne snorted. "Annette is nothing like me, she's nothing like anyone. Let's not kid ourselves. I can guarantee you won't like her."

After a moment she said, "To tell the truth, I'd be disappointed in you if you liked her."

"Well, then I promise I won't. I aim to please," Sean said.

"Yeah!" she said, with a playful punch in his arm. "And there's only one person you have to please—me!"

"And I was just about to do that." His hand busily moved down her stomach to the wiry bush between her legs.

"Oh, good boy," she said. And then she closed her eyes and groaned with pleasure.

Chapter Fifteen

Ted was in a foul mood. And it didn't help matters to arrive home to see Sean usher an exquisitely beautiful girl down the hallway. Life wasn't fair. As he explained to Sean a few moments later while he sipped a beer in the living room, "The woman I was with was an absolute pig. I mean *oink! oink!* pig."

"Too bad", Sean said. He poured himself a cup of coffee.

"I don't know why I'm doing this, sometimes," Ted moaned.

"Probably because it's more attractive to you than a real job," Sean said. He poured milk into the coffee, took a spoon of sugar and stirred it.

"She didn't even tip me," Ted complained. "She said with what the agency was getting paid, she was sure I was getting enough. Bitch!"

"Well, we all have those days, I guess," Sean said without much sympathy. He on the other hand was feeling on top the world. The lovemaking with Susanne had been extraordinary and he was filled with a sense of well-being.

"Sometimes I think I would be better off hustling by myself." Ted said grumpily. "At least then I'd be able to pick and choose who I wanted to associate with. I mean, there are some people, man, that you just don't want to be with, no matter how much you're getting paid."

"Oh, yeah, that reminds me, do you remember a guy by the name of Alex Varney who worked for the agency?" Sean asked.

"Yeah, he worked there for a time. He quit. I don't know where he went."

"Were you friendly with him?"

"No, not particularly. I knew him of course. He was a hustler. Weird guy. Why are you asking?"

"A client was asking about him, if he was still around. I was just curious . . . uh, who this guy was that left such an impression."

"Well, he was quite something when it came to women." Ted said with a small smile of remembrance. "Real good looking, very smooth. He did well. I don't know why he quit. He was probably making a fortune."

"Then you wouldn't have any idea of where he went?"

"No, no idea. But you know how they come and go in our business," Ted said. Then he looked inquiringly at Sean. "Who was the girl that was here? Someone special?"

"A good friend," Sean said evasively.

"A real looker," Ted said. "Man, compared to what I was with last night—yuk!"

"Well," Sean said, "got to run."

Ted sat alone in the living room, beer in one hand, his thoughts morose. He needed something to change. Things were not going that well. For some reason he wasn't making as much money now as he had been a few months ago and the pleasure of his job had somehow lessened in recent months. There was a time when he had really enjoyed it. A feeling of power over these women, older, richer, better in every way, or so they thought, and yet with his smile, his touch, and ultimately the act of sex, he had been able to prove his superiority. But somehow it seemed an empty victory these days.

He took another swig of beer. What the fuck, maybe it was just getting too easy. Maybe he was just bored. Maybe he needed something a little more exciting.

The telephone rang as if in answer to his thought. He picked it up before the machine came on. "Ted?" said a woman's voice.

He recognized it immediately. "Hi, how are you?"

"I'm fine," Sister Cecelia said. "I'd like to see you tonight. Would that be possible?"

"I think so," Ted said.

"I can't talk long. You have a place where we can meet? You remember what I told you at the hotel?"

"Yeah, I have a place."

"Is it where you live?"

"No, it's a place I can use. You want to meet me there?"

"Yes," she said.

"Well, let me find out if it's free. Then I'll have to call you back."

"All right," she said. "When you call, my secretary will answer. Give your name as Mr. Lloyd and say that I'll know what the call is about and she'll put you through."

"Fine," Ted said. "I'll call you soon."

"I'm looking forward to seeing you," she said and hung up.

He began to pace the living room floor in a state of agitation. It was the answer to a prayer, he thought excitedly. But he had to figure it out carefully. He couldn't make any mistakes. A chance like this didn't come along that often.

The first thing that he would have to make sure of was that the condo would be vacant tonight. There was only one other person in the agency whom Nancy Hamilton trusted for operations in the condo and that was Barney Cole. If he wasn't going to be there, it would almost certainly be empty.

He went back to the telephone.

"Hey, Barney," he said when the man answered, and then proceeded with two minutes of small talk about the women he had been with lately, lacing his dialogue with complaints about the job. Finally he asked the key question. "What's your date tonight?"

"Some broad from out of town," Barney said.

"Anything interesting planned?"

"Nah, just the opera and then back to her hotel, I guess. I have to play it by ear. She's some wife of an oil guy."

"Well, I hope you have a lucky strike," Ted said. "Let's get together and have a drink soon."

"Sure thing," Barney said.

Ted hung up and went upstairs to his room. He withdrew his locked briefcase from his closet and opened it. In addition to the usual supply of drugs, this time it also held a video tape, a 120-minute cassette tape, and a key in a plastic pouch.

As soon as Cecelia had mentioned the need for somewhere private a few days before, he had begun to prepare for the eventuality. He'd had a copy of the condo key made. He had also examined the equipment there and bought the tapes as a result of that.

Four times in the past he'd used the condo for Nancy, for what she termed "special clients." The word "blackmail" had never been mentioned. He hadn't asked for details and she hadn't offered any. Obviously, however, the sexual indiscretions of individuals were not being captured on video tape simply for posterity. All he knew each time was that in these special cases he received a big bonus. But it had given him an idea: if the special facilities were available, why not put them to good use for the cause of personal enrichment? Now, the opportunity was here.

Forty-five minutes later he was entering the condominium in Beverly Hills. As always, it was immaculate. Without pausing to admire the decor, he went directly to the bedroom and opened the closet door. He turned on the inside light and moved down the long walk-in closet to the door on the false wall.

Opening it, he flicked on another light switch. It was a small space, just large enough to stand in. On a makeshift shelf, side by side, were a video camera and tape recorder. He followed the line of vision of the camera and looked through the one-way mirror at the bedroom. The tape recorder, he knew, was hooked to a microphone situated in the ceiling above the bed.

Quickly he took the existing tape out of the camera and replaced it with his. Then he did the same with the tape recorder.

He stood there for a minute, inspecting his handiwork, wondering if he had forgotten anything. He didn't think so. It was really very simple. And that simplicity was one of the reasons this plan had appealed to him so much.

He took the tape and the cassette he'd removed and placed them in a corner of the main closet under a pile of linen. As soon as he had done what he had to do, he'd replace them in the machine. Everything would be as it was before, and nobody would be the wiser. It was a perfect setup.

And it would make him very rich.

Sean found Alex Varney's apartment building without

much difficulty. It was a newer unit, only two or three years old, but already showed signs of Hollywood wear and tear. Old newspapers littered the front steps and the unkempt bushes around them. Empty wine and beer bottles had been planted in the undergrowth.

Presumably the police had already followed his lead and checked on Varney, but he wasn't counting on it. The lieutenant had been ambivalent enough about the matter not to fill Sean with confidence about the prospect of his diligence. Better he conduct his own investigation.

He reached the mailboxes at the top of the stairs and scanned the names. There was no Varney. He pressed the one marked "Manager" and finally a ghostly voice wavered through the squawk-box.

"Could I talk to you about a previous tenant?"

"Police?"

"No. Personal," Sean said.

There was a buzz as the gate unlocked and he pushed it open and went to apartment number one. A young woman in her twenties stood in the doorway. She was wearing shorts and a T-shirt and carried a baby less than a year old on one hip. "Can I help you," she said in a sociable enough tone.

"I'm trying to trace Alex Varney. He used to live here," Sean said. "I wonder if you could give me any information about him, such as a forwarding address."

"What's it about?" she said, adjusting the baby. She had stringy brown hair and wore no makeup over her pale face. Sean guessed that she was fairly newly married and managed the apartment to make ends meet. Her husband probably had a job while she looked after the building.

"I'm a friend of his parents from Seattle and they wanted me to track him down because they haven't heard from him for a while."

"What's the name again?"

"Varney. Alex Varney."

"I can't remember anyone by that name."

"How long have you been manager here?"

"A couple of years," she said. Then her face lightened with comprehension. "Oh, you're talking about the guy the cops were asking about."

"Apartment number five, I believe," Sean said.

"Oh, right, Varney, that's the one who disappeared."

"What do you mean disappeared?" Sean said.

"He disappeared. He just wasn't here anymore. Everything was in his apartment—his furniture, his clothes . . . And then after the first, when he didn't pay the rent, we contacted the police, who came by and asked some questions, but no one ever figured out where he went off to. Some cop was by here the other day asking questions again. He talked to my husband."

"You mean he left all of his stuff here?"

"Well, I don't know if it was all of his stuff, but it sure looked like most of it."

"Well, what happened to it?"

"We either put it into storage or more likely gave it to Goodwill. I think the police took the valuables."

"What police were these? Local?"

"I dunno. I guess Hollywood."

"Do you know if they filed a missing persons report?"

She shrugged. "Who knows. I mean, you know the way people move around Hollywood. Real bunch of transients here. We get people in and out all the time, ya know. I don't think the police were too worried about it. In fact, now that I think back, they thought we were dumb to even bother them with it. But we had to do something, the apartment was just sitting there. The owner doesn't like to lose the rent money."

"Yeah, sure," Sean said. "Do you remember this guy at all?"

"He was real good looking. Drove a nice car. Um, but I don't think I ever talked to him."

"Do you know if he was friendly with anyone here."

"I don't think so," she said. "People here pretty much mind their own business, ya know."

"Well, is there anything else you can think of that might help me find him?"

"I don't know. No, I suppose you could talk to the police and see if they ever found him or filed a missing persons report. Um, I'm sorry I can't help you any more."

Sean thanked her for her time and left.

Well, that was that, he thought as he stood on the front steps. Or was it? What she said was true: Hollywood was filled with transients, people who were on the move for one reason or another. But to leave all his stuff, he must have moved in hurry, driven perhaps by some compelling reason. Maybe he was scared, maybe he was involved in something, maybe anything. He decided to call Lieutenant Glenn when he got home. Before he bothered the Hollywood police, he'd see if Glenn had already done the job for him.

Sean put a call in to Glenn when he got home. Half an hour later, the policeman called back. Sean told him he had been to Varney's apartment and what he had discovered. "I assume you looked into it as well?" he asked.

"I did," Glenn said irritably, "and I don't know why you took the trouble to do this. This is verging on interference in an ongoing investigation."

"It didn't cause any trouble," Sean said. "I just went there to ask about him."

"Have you found out anything more about the

238

agency?" Glenn asked, his voice still disgruntled.

"No, not yet. Nobody knows much about Varney. I talked to some of the other guys that worked there. They just said he left and had no idea where. Was a missing persons report filed?"

"No," Glenn said. "Hollywood didn't take the trouble. People move around that area all the time and there was no report filed by a relative or anyone. They just let it drop."

"So, what happened to his belongings?"

"Who knows? The landlord probably sold them," Glenn said.

"So you think this is a dead end?"

"Yes," Glenn said. "Now, if you'll excuse me, I have more pressing matters to attend to. If you learn anything else, let me know. But I don't suggest you start some kind of private investigation. Just find out what you can at the agency."

Sean hung up thoughtfully. It was becoming apparent to him that Roger Glenn wasn't going to be much help in discovering what had really happened to Marina. Nor, obviously, did Glenn appreciate his interest. From now on, until he discovered something that was real, something in the way of proof of what had happened, he'd go it alone.

He looked at his watch. He didn't have time to think about it now. He had to get ready for his ordeal at Susanne's house this evening—the parental cross-examination and inspection.

At five o'clock, Nancy Hamilton called Sean and asked him to meet a client for dinner that evening.

"I'm sorry it's such short notice, but she just called and I only have a couple of people available. You were my first choice."

"I'm afraid I won't be able to make it," Sean said. "I . . . I seem to have caught the flu. I'm feeling lousy and I've got a fever."

"Oh," Nancy said. "You don't sound too bad."

"Well, it just started," Sean said. "I know how it goes with me . . . in a couple of hours my fever will be higher and I'll be feeling like a dog."

"I see," Nancy said. "Well, maybe Danny can fill in, if he doesn't have anything else planned tonight. Is he there?"

"I'm not sure," Sean said. "Let me go and check his room."

He ran upstairs and knocked on Danny's door. "Come in," came a voice. He opened the door to find Danny lying on his bed.

"It's Nancy. She wants to know if you could fill in for someone this evening?" Sean said.

"Oh," Danny said. "I guess so. Is she on the phone?"

"Yes."

"I'll pick it up here," Danny said, reaching for the instrument beside his bed.

Sean went downstairs and hung up the phone there.

A minute later Danny came down. "Nancy says you're sick?" he said, raising an eyebrow in obvious disbelief.

"A little flu," Sean said.

Danny smiled. "No problem, man. I've nothing to do tonight anyway." He winked at Sean. "I hope you have a good time."

The woman sitting on the beige sofa in the antiseptic hotel suite took a sip of her drink and then simpered at Danny's question. "I'm from San Francisco. It's nice to come to Los Angeles, where there are real men," she

240

said.

To make matters worse, Danny thought, she wasn't bad looking, about forty, thin and rich. She was a redhead, with full lips and greedy green eyes that had brazenly examined him before she suggested a drink in the suite prior to going out to dinner. Any other time, he would have been enjoying himself.

"And what kind of work do you do?" he asked.

"I'm vice president of a mortgage loan company," she said. "My position has nothing to do with the fact that it's owned by my husband—oops!" She cut herself off, raising a hand to her mouth, her eyes filling with mock humor. "I said the H word."

"That's naughty," Danny said with a smile. "You should never mention the H word when you're out of town on a business trip. Out of sight, out of mind. That's rule number one."

"And what's rule number two?" she asked coyly.

"When the cat's away, the cat should play," he said, grimacing inwardly at the dialogue. He had done it often, but it had never seemed so trite.

He finished his drink and put it on the table. Removing his arm from the back of the couch he said, "Shall we go and have dinner now?"

She looked into the ice on the bottom of her glass and twirled it around and said, "What if we went to dinner later? Much later?"

Danny took in the knowing look in her eyes, the way her tongue ran across her full upper lip, and saw the hunger and the need.

"That would be fine. We could call and change the reservations," he said smoothly. But inside he was cringing. He knew where this evening was going—to the same place that so many others had gone.

But tonight all he could think about was Tamara, and

241

he knew that once he was in bed with this woman, servicing her, listening to her cries and whispers and moans, feeling her flesh and allowing her to grasp at his, he would still be thinking of Tamara. She was there to haunt him, and from now on she would be there to haunt him. There was no escaping it.

"What a good idea," the woman said, looking up from her glass. "Why don't you just go ahead and do that."

"The mayor is in an untenable political position," Annette said. "That financial scandal has ruined his chances for the governorship and it's very unlikely he will be reelected."

Across the table her husband shook his head adamantly. "First of all, the financial scandal was simply a media scandal. Nothing was ever proven, no wrongdoing. And I don't think, frankly, that the public cares about it. So, I don't see that its going to be much of an impediment."

Annette's dark eyes flashed. "What the public cares about or doesn't care about is beside the point, my dear. The party establishment cares, and that's who holds his political future in its hands." Having made her point she seemed to deflate, then she looked across at Sean who was sitting beside Susanne. "Are you interested in politics, Sean?"

"I'm afraid not," Sean said. "I don't have a very high opinion of politicians."

They were sitting in a large dining room. The long table could have comfortably seated twenty, but the four of them sat at one end with Kenneth at the head, Annette beside him, Susanne and Sean beside each other. They were eating filet mignon, wild rice, and asparagus. The wine was a marvelously smooth French burgundy served in lead crystal goblets. The china was paper thin, the cutlery was silver, the tablecloth, linen. Soft classical music played on a stereo in the background.

"That's probably because you don't understand the dynamics of power," Annette said condescendingly. "Politicians are the exact animals they need to be to survive in that particular jungle. They are not nice people. If they were, they wouldn't last a day. It takes strength to wield power. It also takes cunning and the practice of hypocrisy and diplomacy and, above all, a will to survive in spite of all obstacles. We wanted a democracy, and these politicians are necessary to make it work."

"You didn't mention integrity. Surely that counts for something when the fate of other people is in your hands."

"There's only one kind of integrity, and that's the integrity of getting the job done."

"So, the end justifies the means?"

"Of course," she said. "No matter what people say, they all think that anyway and they all practice it. It's not such an evil concept. If the means are worthwhile and it takes a little rough and tumble to accomplish that end, most people are willing to do that . . . those with any guts, anyway."

"I see," Sean nodded.

Susanne had been watching this exchange intently. "Mother believes that only the strong survive," she said sweetly.

"Well, then shouldn't it be the responsibility of the strong to help the weaker ones survive better?" Sean asked. "After all, the politicians aren't acting for individuals, they're acting for country, state or city, a group."

"True," Annette said. "But in order to get into the position where one is powerful enough to effect change and take care of the weak, one sometimes has to do unpleasant things. It's a law of nature. In order to survive, one has to be fit."

"I think that the danger for those who practice that particular creed is that they can lose sight of the ends and that power itself becomes the end," Sean said.

Kenneth Lowell gave Sean an appreciative look. "That's very perceptive," he said. "I'm inclined to agree with you."

"Nonsense," Annette said. "Power only corrupts the weak, not the strong."

Kenneth changed the subject to what he thought more neutral ground. "Are you getting much work as an actor?" he asked Sean.

"I get parts now and then, but not as many as I want."

"I've always admired actors," Kenneth said. "It takes courage to put up with that kind of rejection on a daily basis. You've got to be tough, I suppose."

"Well, you get used to it," Sean said.

He felt Susanne touch his thigh under the table. And then her hand moved higher. He concentrated on her father.

"Well, you two must have a lot in common," Kenneth said, addressing both Sean and Susanne.

"What do you mean?" Annette asked him.

"Well, Sean being an actor and Susanne being interested in production, as I mentioned to you the other night."

"Oh, yes," Annette said acidly. "I hope Sean works harder at his career than she seems to be doing at hers." She leveled her gaze at Susanne. "I told you before, if you're really serious about that you should apprentice with somebody and start off at the bottom like everybody else does."

"Well, I understand your viewpoint," Susanne said mildly, "but I don't think we need to discuss it now."

Annette disengaged from her daughter and turned to Sean. "Do you make a living as an actor?" she asked.

"Not much, but I have a few residuals coming in from some commercials."

"Does your family support you in your endeavors as an actor," she asked.

"Not financially," Sean said, "But I do have their moral support."

"Well, that's very nice."

Although still polite, she appeared to lose interest in Sean from that point on and managed to steer the conversation back to politics, a dialogue she conducted mainly with her husband.

After dinner Sean and Susanne excused themselves, saying they were going out. As soon as they reached his car, Susanne fell into the seat and exhaled deeply, "God, what an ordeal."

"It wasn't so bad," Sean said as he slipped into his seat. "Except that I've been wanting to kiss you for hours." And he reached over and kissed her.

"You were great," she said. "I don't see how they can help but like you. I know my father did. You never know with my mom, though. She has curious ideas about people."

"She's a tough lady," Sean said.

Susanne snorted. "That's putting it mildly. It's like calling Attila the Hun a tough guy."

"Maybe you're a little hard on her," Sean said as he started the engine. "Although I must admit I find her somewhat . . . forbidding."

"Listen, we're talking about the original heart of steel here. You know how I told you she grew up in the Southwest? Well, she still has family there, brothers and

245

sisters around somewhere. I've never met them. She hasn't been in touch with them since she left home. I have aunts and uncles. I've asked her about them, you know. I said, 'Well, can I meet my aunts and uncles?' and she said, 'No, they're all trash and you'll have nothing to do with them.' That's it! She cut them off, dead. Her own immediate family. No contact, no communication, nothing."

"Well, I guess I'm lucky. I kind of enjoy my family," Sean said.

They had planned to go to a movie after dinner, but suddenly Susanne put her hand on Sean's arm and said, "Let's pass on the movie tonight."

"What do you want to do?"

"Let's go to your apartment. I'd just like to talk to you, and listen to you and make love to you two or three dozen times."

"Just can't get enough of me, huh?"

She giggled. "I'm an animal around you. All through dinner I kept remembering the last time we made love."

"I wondered what was going through your mind."

"Well, now you know."

They came to an intersection and Sean cut across a lane to take a fast left turn, his tires squealing. "Your wish is my command—and my desire," he said as she held onto the sides of her seat.

Chapter Sixteen

Cecelia had disappeared behind dark glasses, baggy woolen pants, and a floppy blue sweater. It was so unexpected a sight, Ted didn't recognize her when he opened the door of the condo in Beverly Hills.

"Oh, hi! It's you!" he said finally.

"My disguise," she said, entering the room. "People are so used to seeing me in long robes, the guy from the tabloid didn't even look twice at me in the hotel lobby. I walked right past him."

"Well, it suits you," Ted said.

"It's been a while since I've been out by myself in clothes like these," she said, a faint longing in her voice. She walked further into the room and quickly took it in. "It's a nice place. A friend of yours lives here?"

"Yes, he's out of town. Would you like a drink?"

"I'd love one. The last few days have been hell."

Somehow, the word *hell* coming from her lips struck Ted as being as incongruous as her clothes, and he couldn't help smiling. "What would you like?" he asked, moving behind the bar.

"A vodka tonic would be fine."

He poured two drinks and brought them around to her. They sat on the couch. She took a sip and gave him a quick, almost shy look. "I've missed you. I needed to see you again. I think you must be growing on me."

"Well, I've missed you, too," Ted said with as much

sincerity as he could muster.

Apparently it wasn't enough, because she smiled wryly and said, "Why don't we be honest with each other? I am paying you for your company, you know."

"But I like you," he said. "You're unusual. You're the only evangelist I date."

She laughed, a curiously girlish sound. "Well, I suppose that does make me kind of unique."

"What 'hell' has been happening in the last few days?" Ted asked.

"The media have been all over me like flies," she grimaced. "And they're not very friendly. My PR people agreed to a *People* magazine interview—reluctantly. What a mistake! I could tell immediately by the line of questioning that the reporter already had the story in her mind before she even spoke to me. She was out to slaughter me. God knows how it's going to finally appear. And then there are the tabloids. They've been following me relentlessly."

"I guess that goes with the territory," Ted said.

"I could live without it."

"Yes, but that's not the way it works when you have a high profile, money, power, followers. You have to expect it."

"I know that," she snapped, "but I don't have to like it, do I? Why don't we change the subject?"

Ted sipped his vodka carefully, then put it on the table. "It looks like you need a nice, relaxing massage," he said.

She sighed. "That's the best offer I've had for days."

He stood and held out his hand. "Come on, let's go to the bedroom. I'll have you relaxed in no time."

"I don't have a lot of time, just a couple of hours, so let's make the most of it," she said, rising.

"I'll do my part," Ted promised.

As soon as they walked into the bedroom, she put her arms around Ted's waist from behind and pressed herself against him. "You know, I love being wicked like this with you," she said. "It makes all the sanctimonious piety I have to put up with somehow a little more bearable. Smiling at everyone, being so saintly, giving them advice . . . to come here with you like this and do nothing but indulge my carnal fantasies is like a vacation. Exhilarating."

Ted turned, cupped her buttocks in his hands, and pulled her even closer. Gently but insistently he moved his hips against hers. "Well, carnal knowledge happens to be my specialty," he murmured. "You may be a minister of divinity, but I'm one of carnality."

"I know," she said. "That's exactly why I'm here."

Almost two hours later, when she looked at her watch, a sated Cecelia stretched in bed and said regretfully, "I have to go." She swung her long pale legs to the floor. As Ted made a move, she turned and placed a restraining hand on his arm. "You stay here," she said. "I'd better go first. I'd rather not be seen leaving the building with you, just in case."

"You don't think you were followed, do you?"

"No, I don't, but I'd rather be safe."

"That's fine," Ted said. "I should tidy up anyway."

Ten minutes later, fully dressed and having restored her makeup, Cecelia leaned over the bed and kissed him lingeringly on the mouth. "That was quite wonderful," she said.

"For me too."

She got up, opened her purse, and removed a stack of hundred dollar bills. Peeling off what looked to be ten or twelve, she put them on the dresser.

"I'll call you soon," she said over her shoulder as she left the room.

A moment later he got up and, still naked, walked quickly into the living room. He made sure the front door was locked and then returned to the bedroom. He entered the closet, opened the false door, took out the tapes he had put in the video machine and the cassette recorder, replaced them with the originals, and carried them into the bedroom.

He thumbed through the stack of money on the dresser. It was a nice amount, a profitable evening, but she would be paying him a lot more than that, he promised himself. A *lot* more.

Susanne had just arrived home after spending the night with Sean, and she was tired. She should have come home earlier, she knew, but they hadn't been able to get enough of each other and it hadn't taken much persuasion on his part to get her to stay.

She was drinking orange juice in the kitchen when her mother entered.

"I suppose you spent the night with that actor," Annette said brusquely.

"Sean. His name is Sean," Susanne replied in tart response to her tone.

"You should have called," Annette said, changing her approach.

"Yes, I should have," Susanne conceded. It was an unspoken agreement between them. If she wanted to spend the night with someone and called, no questions would be asked. At least it was that way most of the time; it depended upon her mother's mood.

Annette went to the coffee machine and poured a mug for herself. "He's not good enough for you," she said with her back to Susanne.

"You don't know him," Susanne said wearily. God knew she didn't need this discussion.

"He's just another pretty face without any substance. He'll never succeed as an actor. Then what?" she said, and

250

turned around, leaning against the cabinet.

"He is not without substance," Susanne said, trying to hold back the mounting anger. "He's sensitive and talented and one of the least superficial men I know. Compared to some of the guys you've laid on me, he's a genius!"

Annette simply ignored what she said and continued, "Then he'll want to live off you. On my money."

"God, sometimes you're despicable," Susanne said.

"What do you know about him? His background? Where he's really from and what he's really done?"

"I know enough."

Annette regarded her coldly over the top of her coffee mug. "I wonder if you'll ever learn," she said reflectively. "When there is money and power, there is responsibility — the responsibility to protect what you have from greedy strangers. You can't take anything or anyone at face value."

"I can't live with that viewpoint of people, the constant suspicion. I find it hateful," Susanne said. "And I could remind you that I have neither money nor power. As you so often point out, both of those are yours. I exist simply through your largesse. Isn't that right?"

"I'm simply trying to protect you," Annette said.

"From what? You see enemies everywhere. Barbarians at all the gates, even when they don't exist. And, believe me, Sean is not an enemy." Susanne slammed her glass onto the kitchen counter. "I'm a grown woman, Annette. Don't you think it's time you let me make my own mistakes, if indeed they turn out to be that?"

"When it comes to men you're a fool," Annette said flatly, unmoved by her daughter's emotion. "You've proved that before."

"You've got the memory of an elephant when it comes to my mistakes. So it'll always be that way, right? People never change. Circumstances never change."

251

"No, people don't change," Annette said.

"Oh, God!" Susanne said exasperatedly. She picked up her glass, put it down again, looked away, then back at her mother. "Don't you see?" she said plaintively. "Other people can change, do change. You just can't see it. All you can do is see yourself in them."

"I don't know what you're talking about," Annette said stiffly. "And I can't continue this discussion. There's a very important dinner for your father tonight and I need to start making the arrangements."

"Right," Susanne said. "Well, it's been nice talking to you." She turned and started to leave the kitchen.

"Don't you want to know what it's about?" Annette said, a curiously excited edge to her voice.

"What?" Susanne said, stopping.

"A group of very important political figures. Senator Dobbs is going to announce his retirement soon and your father's going to run for the vacant seat."

Susanne faced her. "Well, that's what you've always wanted, isn't it?"

"Yes."

"What about Daddy? What does he want?"

"Why, what I want, of course. What's best for him," Annette said, genuine bemusement in her voice.

Susanne shook her head and left the kitchen.

Danny decided that underneath the elegant and controlled veneer, Tamara was a very complicated woman. They had met for lunch at Le Chardonnay on Melrose Avenue — an impossibly difficult restaurant at which to get reservations on short notice, but somehow she had managed it. He had never eaten there before, but after the succulent duck he understood why she lauded it as one of the ten best restaurants in Los Angeles.

After spending a hundred dollars on lunch, she wanted to walk down Melrose and spend more on clothes. One leather skirt later she took his hand and said, "I've booked us a room at the Hotel Bel Air."

They each drove their own car, Danny following, up Stone Canyon into the always serene hotel grounds, and then checked in, no hint of subterfuge or embarrassment on her part. The room turned out to be a suite. After room service had delivered a bottle of chilled white wine, she undressed herself and then him, and they made love on the living room floor.

Lying in bed later, they drank the wine and talked.

Danny wanted to know what she had done before she was married. How did she come to Los Angeles?

"The movies, like every other dumb beauty," she said. "It didn't take me long to figure out what the odds were, though, and I didn't want to get into a game where losing was a foregone conclusion. I decided to get a rich husband instead. I started off waitressing and then moved up."

Up? So how had she met her husband? Considering her background, it was curious.

"I worked as hostess at a restaurant. He came in one day and I trapped him," she said calmly, looking to see his reaction.

"Come on, there must be more to it than that," Danny urged. "How did you trap him?"

"The way all intelligent women trap men," she said, with a slow smile. "You get him to notice you, to like you, and then you back off. When he comes running, you back off a little more, but not enough to cause him to stop. You play stop and go, stop and go, and before he knows it, he's in a corner and you're blocking the only exit."

Danny laughed. "Shit, it sounds like playing a fish!"

"It is. Hooking, playing, and landing." She gave him an incredulous look. "Come on, this isn't news to you."

Danny ran the back of his hand down her arm, then circled her thin wrist with his forefinger and thumb. "No, it's not, but most women aren't so honest."

"Not when they're young," she corrected. "Surely the women you come in contact with are blunt."

He withdrew his hand. "Sure, but that's because they know they have nothing to lose with me. I'm hired, and when I've done my job, I'm gone."

"I have nothing to lose with you either," she said carefully. And then noting the slight stiffening of his shoulders added quickly, "But not for the same reasons. Not because I've bought you."

"Then why?" he said.

"I believe in the present, Danny, not in the past or future. They don't exist. If there's no past or future, how can you lose anything?"

"That's too deep for me," Danny said.

She looked at him for a long moment, her brown eyes puzzled by her own thoughts, then slowly tipped her wine glass so that some of the liquid spilled onto his chest. She ran her finger across it, making patterns. "I love being with you. I love watching you, the way you move and look. I love touching you, making love with you. There's no guarantee it would be the same tomorrow, so I don't think about that. If I died right now, just keeled over in this bed, I'd have been happy for these moments. Do you understand that?"

Bending her head, she licked at the wine on his chest.

"Yes," he said, and stroked her head. His brown hand looked pale against the blackness of her hair.

Suddenly a totally unaccustomed feeling of tenderness swept over him. Shit, it almost felt as if he had tears in his eyes. Thank God she couldn't see him.

254

Sean spent part of the day sleeping. He had barely slept the night before in Susanne's company. Not that he regretted it; it had been one of the best nights of his life. In fact, it seemed that each time he saw her the relationship just got better and better.

When he wasn't thinking of her, he spent the remainder of the early afternoon wondering what to do next about the mystery of Marina's death. He seemed to have reached a point of futility. Essentially, all he had learned about Varney was that the man had disappeared suddenly. The other clues in Marina's note were still as puzzling as ever. Debonaire was a connection, but how? And how could he find out? He couldn't very well just ask, not if he wanted to maintain his low profile. And what was the murder she had written of? Could it have been Varney? The man had disappeared under what he (if not the police) considered suspicious circumstances. Or was it all just the rambling of a drug-fried brain?

He wasn't proceeding very well with his mission, and the distraction of Susanne wasn't helping. There were moments when he wanted to just quit—quit thinking about justice for Marina, quit the agency, and get on with his life. He had a future with Susanne ahead of him, one with a glorious potential for happiness. Why didn't he just get on with it?

The answer was simple: because this was something he had pledged himself to do.

He was sitting in the living room, alone with these thoughts, when Nancy called to tell him there was a job that evening for both him and Ted. Another "double date," this time to a fundraising party. For a moment Sean thought of refusing, but he couldn't, not if he wanted to find out Debonaire's connection to Marina's death.

He wrote down the information and promised to pass the details along to Ted, who had already been informed of

255

the assignment.

He sat there for a moment after hanging up, looking at the names and address he had scrawled down, and it came to him that there was one lead he could explore further.

Alex Varney had a folder in Nancy Hamilton's filing cabinet. When he had looked before, all he had concentrated on was the name and address. That was what Marina had wanted. There had been other papers in the file, but he had been too hurried to look at them. Right, there had been a list of clients. He remembered that. It might be helpful to see who they had been. Perhaps he would recognize a name among them.

He needed another look at the file. It would take luck for the opportunity to present itself again, but he resolved to be ready for it when it did.

Feeling much better now that he had a course of action, he began to get ready for the evening.

It was a black-tie event at the Beverly Hills Hotel, a benefit for some environmental/ecological group Sean had never heard of. It seemed, however, that a number of enormously wealthy and powerful people had. The women dripped wealth and the men exuded confidence. He didn't know how Ted felt—he looked quite comfortable and at home—but he felt out of place.

The ladies they were with also seemed to belong. They appeared to know most of the people there and were entirely unembarrassed by their young companions.

Both were in their fifties; one was named Dawn, the other Kate, reminding Sean of Kate Kaplan, the attractive advertising lady he had spent a day with. It seemed a lifetime ago. Also, this Kate looked nothing like the other. This one was overweight, and no amount of makeup could hide the lines in her face and the heavy rings of her neck.

She wore a choke diamond necklace, while her companion, equally unattractive, wore pearls.

Who was with whom? Although Ted sat with Kate and Sean with Dawn, it didn't seem to matter to the ladies. They apparently simply wanted to be seen with handsome escorts.

When dinner was completed and the speeches all made, the tables were pushed aside to reveal a dance floor. The piety on the stage was replaced by a six-piece dance band, and the liquor began to flow liberally. The good works had been done, now it was the good-time segment of the evening.

The first disturbing event of the evening occurred on the dance floor. He was dancing with Dawn and she had just put both arms around his neck when he saw Janet Whittaker sail past in the arms of a handsome young man. Sean hadn't seen her since the play had collapsed. She wore a silver gown and looked as blonde and beautiful as always.

She saw him a moment later and smiled over the shoulder of her companion. Then she noticed who he was dancing with and raised an eyebrow quizzically.

Sean felt his face grow hot with embarrassment. What was she thinking to see him dancing with this obviously possessive elderly lady? He immediately began to rehearse excuses. Dawn was an aunt. She was a friend of the family visiting from out of town. Or how about the truth? He was being paid to escort her.

As it turned out, Janet and her friend left the floor and he didn't see them again. However, he felt sure that she'd call him one of these days to ask who he was with, and would probably mention it as a curiosity to mutual friends.

Dawn possessed energy totally inappropriate to her age, or so Sean thought. She was tireless, endlessly dragging him onto the floor until he begged exhaustion and the need for a drink.

"All right," she agreed, adding relentlessly, "A fifteen-minute rest period and then we really boogie!"

And then, sitting at the table, the most curious event of the evening happened.

Sean was sipping a gin and tonic, trying to catch his breath while Ted chatted with the two women, when a young woman came up behind them. She was about twenty-four or five, not exactly pretty but definitely noticeable. She wore a low-cut pink gown, but what Sean really noticed was the white, angry line of her mouth.

She leaned over Ted, her eyes glaring, her voice tight, and said very distinctly, "You fucking blackmailing son of a bitch!" And then she scurried away, moving stiffly through the crowd, to the exit.

"What on earth was all that about?" Kate asked.

Ted raised an eyebrow. "I've no idea. I've never seen her before in my life. I don't know who she is," he said.

"I know her," Dawn said. "Dobbs. Emily Dobbs. The senator's daughter."

"Really?" Ted said. "Well, I've never met her. She must have had too much to drink. Either that or she's confusing me with someone else. Some old lover, perhaps."

"Wishful thinking," Kate said with a giggle, and placed a suddenly proprietary hand on Ted's arm.

They all laughed at that. Except Sean. He wondered what the hell had really just happened.

Propped up by pillows, Dirk Hunt looked down at his woman as she laved his testicles with her skillful tongue and then drew it up the shaft to take his thick penis in her mouth.

She wouldn't make him come this way. He knew that. She'd take him to a point where he was almost throbbing with anguish and then, as always, she would raise her head and look at him with that secret power in her eyes and then crouch above him, lowering herself down, inch by inch, not allowing him to thrust up, regaining control, maintaining command.

He loved it. No woman had ever manipulated him as skillfully. Finding her was the best thing he'd ever done. He knew that and so did she.

When he had arrived in Los Angeles five years earlier, fresh out of his twenty-year stint in the navy, she had been a high-class call girl without a pimp. At the time she was facing a few territorial problems that required male assistance. He'd acted quickly to fill the position. And then things had just gotten better and better until now they both had more money than they had ever dreamed of. She no longer had to turn tricks to earn her money, having moved on to a much more lucrative opportunity, and the strong-arm stuff wasn't required of him very often. When it was, he didn't mind. It helped relieve the boredom.

A large man with a thick neck and a brutal face, an almost Oriental slant to his cheekbones and eyes, Dirk had no doubts that she was the brains of their little enterprise. He was available when work of a more physical nature was required. Grunt work, just like he'd done in the navy. He was happy with that. The rewards were plentiful and equally shared.

Beside the bed, the telephone suddenly jangled, stiffening him and causing her to stop what she was doing and look up. "No, don't stop," he groaned. "Let the machine get it."

She smiled and lowered her head again while the machine clicked on.

They half-listened through her recorded greeting until the voice of a woman came on: "I need to talk to you. I've got a job for Dirk."

She lifted her head again.

"I'd better get it," Dirk said, and reached for the phone.

"Dirk here. No, she isn't. What do you need? Uh-huh." He reached over to the night table and picked up a pad and pen. "What's the name again? Do you have an address. No other information? Okay, I'll see what I can do. Soon. All right, I'll tell her you called."

He hung up and met her questioning glance.

"What did she want?" the woman asked.

He put the pen and paper back on the table and said, "Some guy dating her daughter. She wants me to check up on him. No big deal."

"Oh, God, not again," she said.

"Don't worry about it. Just some actor. Someone called Sean Parker. Now, why don't we get back to what we were doing?"

"Sean Parker?"

He glanced at the pad and then nodded. "Come on, babe, my balls are aching. Help me get rid of the pain before I start this job."

"Believe me, this job won't take you long," Nancy Hamilton said. "I know him. I can tell you everything you need to know." And then with a triumphant smile she licked the tip of his penis with her tongue.

"He's harmless," Nancy said later. "Real raw meat. Just your average nice guy." Her eyes grew distant. "But very good-looking. Robert Redford type."

Their lovemaking completed, Dirk had brought up the subject of business. "But he works for the agency," Dirk said. "He can't be *that* nice, baby."

"He needs the money. What pisses me off is that I'm going to lose him. He must have met the girl when I sent him to the house with a package once."

"Well, I'm going to have to tell her that he works for

260

you, aren't I?"

" 'Fraid so," Nancy said.

"Should I check up more? She said she wanted to know everything there was to know about him."

"There's nothing to know. Just tell her about him working at the agency. That'll fulfill all her expectations. She'll be satisfied to know she was right to be suspicious."

"And then what?"

"Then we see what she wants to do about it," Nancy said.

Dirk looked troubled, a heavy frown creasing his forehead. He rubbed the top of his head, as if to erase his uncomfortable thoughts.

"What?" Nancy asked.

"I don't like it. Normally she's smart, but when it comes to her daughters the woman's crazy. Things could get out of hand again."

"This is different, honey. Don't worry about it," Nancy said. "This guy will be easy to handle. He's a pussycat."

Her words didn't console him. Dirk continued to look worried. He'd been in enough street brawls over women to know that even pussycats had claws.

Chapter Seventeen

When the female secretary answered, Ted said, "This is Mr. Lloyd. May I speak to Sister Cecelia? She's expecting my call." She wasn't, but he was hoping she'd remember the coded name and come on the line.

After a short pause, there was a breathless, "Yes?"

"Hi, it's me," he said. "I need to see you."

"When?"

"As soon as possible."

"It's difficult."

"It's urgent. Besides, don't you want to see me?"

She hesitated, then said, "I'd like that. The same as before?"

"It's no longer available," Ted said, aware she was being circumspect because other people were in the room. "Perhaps we could meet in the same bar where we first met and go elsewhere from there."

"No, that wouldn't be practical," she said.

She was worried about being followed by the reporter in the lobby, probably. Excellent, he thought. Her concern about the media was quite appropriate for the moment. "All right, let me pick you up at the delivery entrance of your hotel. I'll wait outside and you can just hop in my car and we'll be off before anyone can see us. How about in an hour?"

"Fine," she said, and hung up.

An hour later he pulled into the alley and stopped beside huge double doors, his car engine idling. No more than a minute later one of the doors opened and Cecelia emerged, wearing the same baggy clothes and dark glasses she had worn before. She hopped quickly into the car and he took off down the alley.

"Hi," Ted said.

She removed her glasses and settled back in her seat with a sigh. "I'm so glad you called. I didn't realize how much I needed to get out of there. It's been another of those days. Everything that could go wrong did."

Not quite everything, Ted thought to himself.

He zigzagged onto Sunset Boulevard and turned right.

"Where are we going? Did you book a room somewhere?" she asked.

"It doesn't matter," he said, slowing down and pulling into a metered parking space.

"What?" she asked, looking with bemusement at the stores beside them. "You have to make a stop for something?"

He turned off the engine and faced her. "I have some bad news for you," he said. "Today's going to get worse."

"What are you talking about?"

What a fine looking woman, he thought. Those delicate features, the calm eyes, the luxurious body beneath the loose clothes . . . it was a shame to waste her. On the other hand, there was no shortage of fine women.

"Do you remember our last meeting?" he asked.

She nodded, a slight nervousness in her motions now.

"Well, I'm afraid the whole thing was videotaped and recorded. And—"

She interrupted sharply. "What the hell are you talking about, Ted?"

He reached back and got a package from the floor. Handing it to her, he said, "This is a copy. The original is in a safe place. Take a look at it when you get a chance. It's most . . . revealing."

Her face grew hard as understanding came. "Are you blackmailing me?"

Ted shrugged. "As far as the tabloids are concerned, the Rob Lowe tapes would be a B film compared to these. They'd be fighting among themselves in a bidding war to buy them. I'm not greedy, so the thought naturally occurred that you might want to buy them from me instead. Save yourself a lot of notoriety, save your church. You know what I mean?"

"You fucking bastard," she said, her voice low and tight. "I always knew you were a bastard, but I never knew how much. You fucker!"

Ted smiled. "If only your congregation could hear you now. The real Cecelia. Of course, the tapes will give them the idea. They'll—"

"How much?" she snapped.

"What's your mission, your reputation worth to you? You probably have a better idea than I do."

"I'll give you ten grand," she said. "Drive me now to where the original is and I'll give you ten thousand dollars."

Ted laughed. "You've got to be kidding. The tabloids would pay me ten times that. Is that all your business is worth? It makes a hundred million a year." His smile faded. "The way I figure it, one percent of a year's gross wouldn't be too much to ask. It wouldn't be greedy or unreasonable."

"A million dollars? You want a million dollars?" she hissed.

"Sounds good to me," Ted said calmly.

"Jesus Christ!" she said disgustedly and turned away from him to stare out at the sidewalk.

"Blasphemy! What next?" Ted said, realizing that he was actually enjoying himself.

"You're going to be sorry you ever thought of this," she said, swinging her head back around.

"I don't think you're in a position to threaten me," Ted said mildly. "Seems like I hold the cards. And you know what they say in the movies. If anything happens to me, someone has instructions, etc. How long will it take you to come up with the money? I don't want to put any undue pressure on you. How about forty-eight hours?"

She pulled the door handle and pushed her door open. "You'll hear from me," she snarled. She got out of the car and slammed the door and glared down at him, no trace of serenity in her face now.

Ted leaned over and rolled down the window. "Don't you want a ride back to your hotel?"

"Fuck you!" she said. She turned and stalked away, her back rigid, her arms swinging stiffly.

Ted smiled. Not exactly the reaction he'd expected, but it didn't matter—the result would be the same. She'd pay. She had other choice.

Danny met Tamara late in the afternoon at a bar not far from where he lived. Comfortable, neighborly, and quiet, except during the two nights a week it had music, Residuals was owned by a group of actors and others in the film business. If you were a writer or actor and received a residual check worth a dollar or less (an unexpectedly frequent occurrence) the management gave you a free drink and pasted your check on the wall with the other members of the honor roll.

She'd said on the telephone that she didn't have much time, so Danny had already ordered and a drink was waiting on the table for her when she arrived. They kissed before she sat, and once again he marveled at the feelings she could evoke in him—this time a kind of giddy pleasure.

"I missed you," he said.

"Since yesterday?" she teased, then took pity and said, "I

265

missed you too."

She wore a casual white linen suit and looked ravishing.

"Where do you have to be?" he asked.

"A meeting. Women in Film. I'm on a committee. Part of my wife job. 'Keep the family flag flying' sort of thing."

"Do you do a lot of charity kind of stuff?" he asked, realizing he knew nothing about her day-to-day life.

"Until I met you, I didn't have anything else to do, honey," she said wryly. "I'm on a couple of boards, a couple of committees. It helps kill the time, but it isn't too demanding."

He liked her cynicism. Some people might find it objectionable, but to him it showed a strong sense of realism. Besides, it was a quality he shared. In fact, he thought, he liked just about everything about her.

The thought made him shake his head.

"What are you thinking?" she asked.

"How I feel about you," he said with rare candor. "The fact that I can miss you in a day, that I want to be with you all the time. This is all very new for me."

She looked at him with a strange satisfaction in her eyes. "I told you that you needed love," she said.

"I didn't know."

"Do you know that hand-in-hand with love is misery? It has a price, you see."

"What do you mean?" he asked, misery being the furthest thing from his mind.

"I'm not going to leave my husband. We're going to have to be satisfied with this," she warned, narrowing her eyes.

He spread his hands. "Have I complained?"

"You will," she predicted.

"Let's worry about that when it happens," he suggested.

"Good idea," she said, her mood lifting.

They talked for fifteen minutes about each other, as lovers do, and the subject of his parents came up. This led to the problem uppermost on his mind: Linda Bell.

"When it makes the newspapers, *'Male Escort Cited in Star's Divorce,'* everything they've ever believed about me will be true, particularly to my father. My mother will just carry the shame like a knife wound in her heart," he said miserably.

"You're really worried about this, aren't you?" Tamara said.

Danny looked embarrassed. "I shouldn't be. I didn't know I would be, but I guess what they think is more important than I realized. I've never wanted to hurt them, just to live my own life."

"And you don't think she'll settle with her husband and give him the divorce?"

"Who knows with that crazy bitch! She wants to give him a fight. Maybe she will, maybe she won't."

"Do you have a lot on her?" Tamara asked.

"What do you mean?"

"Well, the sex you guys had together? Did it get kinky? Did she tell you about other affairs?"

"She was having a lesbian affair with her secretary when she was seeing me. She told me that. Plus we did some pretty weird shit."

"Do you have her phone number?"

"Yeah," he said, automatically patting his jacket pocket where his address book was. "What are you thinking?"

"Gimme," she said, holding out her hand.

Tentatively he took the book from his pocket. "What are you going to do?" he asked nervously.

"Get her off your back. Trust me," she said. She pointed at a phone in the corner of the room. "Is there another more private one?"

"The rest rooms."

She led the way. When they reached the phone in the little hall, she asked for Linda's number. He opened the book and told her. She smiled at him encouragingly, put a quarter in the phone and dialed the number.

"Miss Bell, my name is Henderson," she said, and winked at the nervous Danny. "I'm an attorney representing Daniel Perez? Yes. Well, I just wanted to let you know what I've advised my client to do. I've advised him to cooperate fully with your husband's attorney in return for anonymity. Yes, you could, call him a cocksucker. But while we're on the subject of homosexuality, he will of course not only recount the exploits you two shared, but the ones you told him about, such as your affair with your secretary. Well, I'm afraid calling me names won't help either. No, the only thing I can suggest is that you not oppose your husband in the divorce proceedings. I don't think your reputation could really withstand everything that would come up, particularly in view of the fact that my client said that he was even willing to embellish the facts a little. Talk about sex with animals and stuff like that. Of course I discouraged him immediately, telling him that would be perjury, but he's very angry and I don't know how much influence I have over him. I suggest you just follow my advice."

She held the receiver away from her ear and said, "Oh-oh, she hung up. A very angry lady that," and smiled sweetly at Danny.

He couldn't help laughing. "Do you think that'll work?" he asked.

"I'll bet you anything it will," she said with satisfaction.

He reached out and grabbed her, first hugging and then kissing her.

"Oh, *excuuuuuse* me!" a familiar-looking man said as he came out of the bathroom and dodged past them.

"Was that Steve Martin?" Danny said.

"Who cares?" Tamara said, kissing him again.

It was one of those evenings that made people forget that the Los Angeles air consisted in large part of noxious

switchboard. Sean had met him before. Billy. About twenty-two, short and already starting to go bald. He answered the order phones at night until ten or so as a part-time job.

"Hey, Billy," Sean said. "Nancy around?"

Billy looked back at the magazine he had been reading and shrugged. "She was here a little while ago."

"I'm supposed to pick up a check from her desk," Sean said.

Billy greeted this news with another shrug, so Sean pushed open the door and entered the hallway.

The light was on in Nancy's office, but when he went in he saw she wasn't there. He went around the desk and saw the envelope with his name neatly typed on it. Picking it up, he turned his head back toward the door and listened. Nothing.

He went to the filing cabinet and, gritting his teeth in an effort to be silent, carefully pulled open the drawer containing the files.

There they were. He saw his file, Danny's, and others. But no Alex Varney. He scrambled through again. Maybe it had been misfiled.

No Varney file.

Muffled footsteps in the hall. He pushed the drawer in fast, cringing at the noise. He turned, leaned back against the file cabinet, and began to open the envelope in his hands just as Nancy walked in.

"What are you doing, Sean?" she asked, giving him a hard look.

"Oh, hi," Sean said. He finished opening the envelope and pulled out the check. "Just wanted to see how much it was," he said.

She said nothing, just stood beside her desk and looked at him.

He looked down at the check and said, "Right. Well, thanks."

"You'd better hurry to that appointment," Nancy said. "The client is waiting."

"On my way," Sean said, moving past her.

He looked back as he went through the doorway. She had turned, frowning, to watch him.

Shit, he thought. That had been close. Maybe she was suspicious, but she couldn't have seen anything. She must have heard the drawer closing, but that could be put down to him leaning against the cabinet. All right, he told himself, calm down. It may have been enough to bother her, but not enough to hang him.

The apartment turned out to be a condominium in a small complex near Wilshire Boulevard. He found parking on the street and then pushed the outside buzzer. The lady didn't bother with the intercom, but he heard the gate unlock and entered.

He took the elevator up to the second floor, looking once more at the piece of paper with the address. 204.

He stopped outside the door and rang the bell.

"Come in," said a muffled voice.

He turned the door handle and pushed it open. The room was dimly lighted, but he saw a woman sitting in an armchair, half turned away from him.

"Good evening," he said, stepping toward the woman.

"Good evening, Sean," said the woman, and turned so that he could see her face.

Sean stop in midstride.

The blood drained from his face.

"Mrs. Lowell," he blurted out.

"Come in and sit down," Annette Lowell said. "We need to have a little chat."

Sean sat stiffly on an armchair opposite Susanne's

272

mother. Her idea of a chat was somewhat one-sided. She was talking and he was listening.

"My daughter is very precious to me, Sean," she said. She had a glass of cognac in her hand and twirled it as she spoke, looking down at the amber liquid every now and then, but mainly fastening her dark eyes on Sean's face. "I'll do anything to protect her. Literally anything. I hope you understand that."

Sean said nothing, although the color had returned to his face. She had found out about his occupation, she had said, inviting him to sit. She wanted to tell him the "facts of life."

"This is not going to be a long conversation," she continued. "I really only have one thing to tell you and that is that you will stop seeing my daughter as of now. This minute. You will not call her. You will not return her calls. You will not attempt to see her. Is *that* understood?"

Sean's confusion began to resolve into a kind of frozen strength. The prime question was, how this had happened? But that wasn't the point. How she had found out about his job and how she had got here, didn't really matter at the moment. What mattered was that she was trying to destroy the only thing of value in his life.

"That's between Susanne and me," he said stiffly. "We're both adults. It's not your decision to make."

"It's mine because I'm making it," she said remorselessly. "You will do as I say or I will tell her about your occupation as a male prostitute, a gigolo. I'd like to spare her that, but if I have to tell her I will."

"She already knows where I work," Sean shot back. "And it's not what you think it is."

For a moment Annette looked taken aback, but she gathered herself quickly and ploughed on. "This is why I have to take a hand. Susanne has always been stupid about men. You're not the first mistake she's made."

"Look," Sean said, attempting now to pacify her. "Let

273

me explain. It isn't how it looks. I've explained this to Susanne. I have this job for a purpose. I—"

"Everybody has a reason for what they do," she said malignantly, "even the lowliest addict and streetwalker. I'm not particularly interested in hearing yours. The facts speak for themselves." And then she got down to her prime area of concern. "Do you have any idea what publicity of your liaison with my daughter could do to my husband's political future? Do you think that after working so hard all these years I'm just going to stand by and see that happen?"

"I have done nothing wrong," Sean said. "And I would do nothing to hurt Susanne. You have to let me—"

"Stop!" she said, her voice cutting across the space between them like a sharp blade. "I'm not interested in discussing this further. You will either stop seeing Susanne, as I said, or I will destroy you with whatever means I have at my disposal."

Sean rose to his feet and glowered down at her. "You do what you have to do," he said. "But you're not going to come between us."

"Oh, yes, I will," she said. "You can count on it." And then she smiled, her expression far more threatening than the anger she had demonstrated before.

Sean felt a chill, but he forced himself to meet her eyes for a moment longer. Then he turned and stalked from the room.

He arrived at the restaurant where he was supposed to meet Susanne at 9:05. After a quick walk-through to make sure she wasn't already seated, he decided that he had beaten her there, and took a seat in the reception area.

He was still shaken from his ordeal with her mother. He vaguely remembered describing Annette to Susanne as "a formidable woman." Jesus, what an understatement! The

274

woman was a killer. And he was her intended victim . . .

Nothing Susanne had said, and she had said plenty of harsh things about her mother, had prepared him for the reality of the woman. She was frightening.

And how the hell had she found out about his work? She must have put someone on the job the day after meeting him. He must have made quite an impression at that dinner, Sean thought sardonically.

The hostess approached Sean, clipboard in hand, and a worried expression on her face as she surveyed the waiting crowd in the reception area. "We're still holding your table, but can't do it for much longer," she said. "It's 9:25 already."

"Let me make a phone call," Sean said, rising.

He went to the back of the restaurant toward the restrooms, where the public telephones were located.

Good thing Susanne had her own line, he thought as he dialed her number.

She answered immediately. "I've been trying to call you. All I've been getting is the damn answering machine," she said.

"I'm waiting at the restaurant. How come you didn't call here?" he asked, puzzled.

"At the . . . you're at the restaurant?" she said, her voice just as confused.

"Yes. We were supposed to meet at nine, right?"

"My mother said you called and cancelled. Something had come up."

"Your mother?" he said through a fog of incomprehension.

"Yes."

"Jesus," he said disgustedly. "When did she do that?"

"Two or three hours ago. I said I was going out with you and she said she almost forgot to tell me but that you called to cancel . . . what's going on here?"

"You'd better get down here. We can't talk over the

phone."

"God," Susanne said suddenly realizing what had happened. "She's at it, isn't she? I'll be there in fifteen or twenty minutes."

She hung up. Sean slammed the receiver down. The bitch had said she'd do anything and apparently she meant it.

Susanne arrived thirty minutes later. Sean had taken a table in the meantime and already started on the bottle of wine.

Susanne sat heavily in the seat opposite him, her face grim. "My mother came home just after we finished talking. She and I had a short conversation."

"She told you she saw me?"

"And what a scumbag you are."

"What did you say?"

"I told her to keep out of my fucking business."

Sean reached over and put his hand on hers. "I'm sorry that this happened," he said.

"God, she's such a bitch," Susanne said, her voice shaking. She was close to tears. "How can she do this to me?"

"She says she cares for your welfare," Sean said without irony. "Maybe the way it looks *is* bad. I tried to explain to her what I was doing at Debonaire, but she cut me off—wouldn't listen to a word I had to say."

"I told her," Susanne said. "I said you were there because friend of yours had been killed and you thought Debonaire had something to do with it. She laughed. She asked if I really believed that. She said even a screenwriter wouldn't get away with a story like that."

"I suppose she said a lot more too," Sean said gently.

"How can she be so hateful?" Susanne said, and this time tears did come into her eyes.

"Here," Sean said, pouring wine into a glass, "drink

276

some of this and try to relax. We'll figure out a way to handle this."

She gulped at the wine and then spluttered. "I'm sorry you have to put up with this. You don't deserve it. She said she'd ruin you if I didn't stop seeing you. Maybe you'd be better off . . ."

"You've got to be kidding," Sean said. "I'd be ruined without you! What can she do anyway? I don't have a career to ruin. No, come on, that's just an angry threat. We need to figure out how to handle her, not worry about her threats."

"You don't know her," Susanne said softly.

"Well, we have to do something," Sean said.

Susanne looked miserably at her plate. "Are you hungry?" she asked.

"No," he replied bitterly. "I seem to have lost my appetite."

"Me too. I'd like to get out of here. Maybe we could go for a walk?"

Sean signaled the waiter and asked for the check. After he paid, they left the restaurant and walked hand-in-hand along Sunset Plaza. They were silent at first, each lost in their own thoughts, neither of them noticing the expensive boutiques and trendy cafes on either side of the street.

"Maybe if we went and talked to her together?" Sean suggested. "Or talked to your father and asked him to intercede."

"He has no power over her in matters like this. In fact, not in much of anything," Susanne said. "And once she's made up her mind, no amount of talk will change it. She hears only what supports her position; everything else goes flying by."

An ocean breeze had blown the smog away and a couple of dozen stars flickered in the sky above them. Sean looked up and then sighed, "So what are we going to do?"

She didn't answer. Instead she swung him left down the

driveway beside Le Dome and they walked into the vast outdoor parking lot behind the Plaza. They stood at the edge, a steep hill below them, and looked down at the city lights. He put his arm around her and she leaned her head on his shoulder.

"I love you," she said in a muffled voice. "That's all that matters."

"I love you too," he said. "And it's all that matters to me as well."

She moved her head to look up at him. "You're willing to take whatever she can throw at us?"

"I'm willing to take what she throws at me. You're another matter. I'm not going to stand by and let her beat you up."

"I can handle it," she said. "I need to know if you can."

"Of course."

"Then nothing has changed," she said. "We'll do whatever we were going to do, even if I have to move out and get a job. Deal?"

"Deal," he said.

"Then for Christ's sake, I've been waiting all evening kiss me, you fool."

Chapter Eighteen

Nancy Hamilton hung up the telephone, a grim expression on her face. She swung her office chair around and stared out of the window. The sky seemed clear and the sunshine was brilliant, but that was just an illusion. It was early still. By the end of the day the particles of ozone that couldn't be seen now would have clustered together into a yellow haze, searing lungs and burning eyes. Which led her to the next analogy: little fires had a way of becoming infernos if they weren't detected and extinguished early. That seemed to be what was happening now.

She had three telephone calls to make in order to stop this fire from growing further. And to feel better about the tongue-lashing she had just endured. She moved her chair back around and picked up the telephone again.

The first was to Dirk.

"I was wrong," she said to him. "I want you back on that job. Do what we were told to do in the first place. I want Sean Parker thoroughly checked out. Background, friends, girlfriends, associates, finances, the works. Hire some help if you have to."

He asked a question and she said, "I need it yesterday."

The next call was to Ted. Danny answered the call, saying Ted had just run to the store. He d be back in minutes.

"You'll do. It involves both of you. Pass this message along to Ted. I don't care which of you handles it, but I want it handled today. I want Sean Parker out of there. Evicted by the end of the day. I'm about to fire him and he won't be able to afford the rent anyway."

In answer to his protest, she said, "It's your job at stake. And Ted's. He goes or you all go. No more work. Understood?"

When it was understood, she asked if Sean was there. "Please put him on the phone."

She tapped her fingers on the desk while she waited. She should have listened to Dirk's intuition. The entire matter was far more serious than she had suspected.

"Sean," she said when he came on the line, "I want to let you know that your services at Debonaire are no longer required. I don't believe we owe you any money, so this serves as immediate dismissal."

In answer to his question, she said, "Let's just say that you don't fit in. Your own ambivalence about the job has hindered your performance. Goodbye."

She hung up and smiled. There. She was feeling better already.

And then the phone rang again. She told the receptionist to put the caller through.

"Hi, what's up?" she said. She listened and added, "Yes, I got your messages. I was going to call you back this morning."

She listened.

"What?" Her voice was almost a shriek.

Danny cornered Ted as soon as he walked in the door and told him what Nancy had ordered.

"Shit! I like the guy," Ted said, carrying his bag of groceries into the kitchen and putting it on the counter.

"It's him or our jobs," Danny said seriously. "I like him too, but . . ." He held out his hands helplessly.

"Yeah, it's no choice," Ted said, opening the refrigerator and putting a carton of milk on the shelf. "Is he here?"

"Yep."

"Well, let's go do the deed," Ted said.

They went upstairs and Ted knocked on Sean's door.

"Come in."

Sean was sitting at a desk beside the window, writing on a pad. He turned to look at them, closed the pad and then looked back again. "Hey, guys. What's up?"

Ted automatically assumed the spokesman position. "I hear you've been fired from Debonaire."

"Good news sure flies," Sean said.

"Yeah, I'm sorry it happened. It's a bummer," Ted said.

Sean grimaced. "Not really. I didn't care too much for the job."

"Well," Ted began uncertainly, "the thing is, we're going to have to ask you to move out. I mean, without a job, you won't be able to pay the rent here, right?"

"I'm okay for now," Sean said, his voice changing. "I've been able to save a few bucks on the job."

"Yeah, but it won't last, and you'd be better off finding someplace cheaper, and we'd kind of like someone from the agency here."

"You're serious about this," Sean stated, looking at them both.

"Hey, man, it's for the best," Danny said.

Sean nodded. "Nancy Hamilton, right?"

"I'm sorry," Ted said, looking embarrassed. "We don't have any choice. It's you or our jobs."

"Why is she doing this to me?" Sean mused aloud.

"I think you pissed her off good," Danny said. "What did you do?"

"Nothing," Sean said bemusedly. "Everything at the agency has been relatively fine. Unless . . ."

"What?" Ted asked.

"No, it couldn't be," Sean said.

"Well, look, we're both sorry. We like you. If it was up to us, man . . ." Danny's voice trailed off.

281

"Hey, it's okay," Sean said. "I'll start looking for a place today and move out by the end of the month."

Ted cleared his throat. "Do you have any place you can stay now? Like with a friend?"

"Now? What do you mean?" Sean asked.

"Well, now. Like today," Ted said, not meeting his eyes.

"You want me to move out today? That's impossible," Sean protested.

"*We* don't want you to move out today," Ted said, "but if you don't move out by the end of the day, we'll all three of us be unemployed."

"You must have really pissed her off," Danny reiterated.

"What if I don't move? Legally I don't have to," Sean said, his belligerence growing.

"Look, I don't like this any more than you do," Ted said, his own irritation showing. "Why make more of a problem out of it than it is?"

"Shit!" Sean said, and lapsed into silence.

They stood there and watched him while he looked out the window. After a moment, he turned back.

"All right. I'm not into making trouble for you guys. I'll start making some calls. I could always move into a hotel for a couple of days, I guess."

"Hey, man, if you need a few bucks I could help you out," Danny said.

"No. No thanks. I'm okay for now," Sean replied, "but thanks. I appreciate it."

"Well, if there's anything we can help you with . . ." Ted said.

"No, I'm fine," Sean said.

"Well . . ." Ted said, and Danny started to move toward the door. "I'm sorry about this."

"It's okay," Sean said.

They started to leave.

"Ted?" Sean asked. Ted turned. "You could do one thing for me."

282

"What?"

"Tell me about the condo."

Ted's eyes flickered. "What condo?"

"You know, the address I had written down. You seemed to know it. What was that about? What is it?"

"What condo?" Danny said, standing in the doorway.

"It was a mistake," Ted said uncomfortably. "I misread the address. I thought it was someplace else."

"What place?" Sean asked.

"What condo?" Danny said again.

They both ignored him.

"It was a mistake," Ted said. "It was nothing." He turned, pushed past Danny, and left the room.

"What, the hell was all that about?" Danny asked.

"I was sent to meet someone, supposed to be a client, at a condo in Beverly Hills. Ted saw the address and seemed to know where it was, made a comment. Then when I asked about it, he clammed up, just like he did now."

Danny seemed to lose interest. "Well, maybe he went to the same client."

"That isn't the kind of comment he made," Sean said, half to himself.

"Yeah, well," Danny said. "Good luck, man." And left the room.

What was it Ted had said when he saw the address? Sean thought back, trying to recapture the moment. Something like surprise that he was being sent there. "You've come a long way fast." Yes, that was it. And when Sean had said he was meeting a client there, Ted had sounded surprised at that fact, then covered it up. What could it mean?

It meant something, because he was still covering it up. Of that Sean was sure. His reaction a few moments ago had been evasive, to say the least.

Next question: What did his firing and the subsequent harassment have to do with Annette Lowell's threats? She'd threatened to ruin him. Well, getting him fired was a good start. Getting him thrown out of his apartment had more nuisance value than anything else, but it followed the same line. Was she the impetus behind it? Had she called the agency and complained about him? Unlikely. Nancy would have brought it up.

All right, he thought, assuming that she did have something to do with it, what did that leave as possible conclusions? That she had some influence over Nancy? Some connection?

And then it struck him. Yes, there was a connection, one that in the light of events that followed he had completely forgotten and overlooked.

When he first met Susanne at her house he was delivering a package from Nancy addressed to A. Lowell. Annette! Jesus, there was a connection. But what was it? Some business deal? Or was it something innocent, like belonging to the same club?

Now that was worth looking into.

He looked at the telephone beside his bed, the thought occurring that he should call Susanne. But they had already arranged to meet for lunch in an hour or so and that was probably soon enough to talk to her. In the meantime, he'd better see about finding a place to stay.

He thought about it for a moment and decided to start with Oscar. See if his playwriting friend could put up with a roomie for a couple of days while he tried to scare up an apartment.

The thought occurred to him that he might have to look for a large one—one that he and Susanne could share. Well, he'd soon find out how things were going on her home front.

"She threatened to throw me out of the house without a dime," Susanne said.

They had bought sandwiches and were sitting in a park off Sunset Boulevard in Beverly Hills. There were a couple of elderly people nearby, some Hispanic nannies with small white children, and a young man practicing the graceful motions of tai-chi beneath a large oak tree.

"So what did you say?" Sean asked.

"I said that was fine. I'd move out immediately and move in with you. She said that wouldn't be very practical as you wouldn't have a place to stay after today as well."

"Goddamn!" Sean exclaimed. "It *was* her." And told Susanne the previous events of the day.

Susanne was stunned. "I can't believe this."

Sean didn't waste time trying to persuade her. "So what's your mother's connection with Debonaire?" he asked.

"I've no idea."

"The day I met you. The package I brought was for her. That was from Debonaire, or at least from Nancy. Any idea what was in it?"

"No. She gets deliveries like that all the time. It could have been anything."

They pondered over that a while, discussing the possibilities without resolving anything, and then Sean said, "So, anyway, how did your conversation end with her?"

"It was weird. She kind of backed down. We were yelling at each other. I said I'd see you anyway and that I'd move out, and then she got real calm and said that we were both angry and that maybe we should both just cool down and talk this over more rationally later. Very unlike her. I said there was nothing to talk over and stormed out of the house. And here I am."

Sean let out a deep breath. "What a mess," he said.

She rolled onto her back and stared up at the lattice of leaves overhanging them. "What are you going to do about a place?"

"Oscar. My friend. He's a playwright. He said I can move in with him for a couple of days till I find a place. It's not much. He has a Murphy bed in the living room, but it's convenient. In the Los Feliz-Hollywood area. Kind of on the border."

"And your stuff?"

"That can stay in the condo until I figure out what to do with it. I don't think the guys will complain; they feel bad enough about this as it is."

She turned to look at him, resting her head on her arm. "I'll help you find a place," she said firmly.

Sean reached out with a blade of grass and ran it along her arm. "Hey, don't worry about me. This is no big deal."

"I'm worrying about me," she said, smiling to alleviate any seriousness. "I may have to move in with you. I should at least get to check the place out."

"Would you? Move in with me?"

"All you'd have to do is ask."

"I'd love that," Sean said. "But I'm not going to ask until things settle down. Right now there's too much going on."

"That's fine," she said.

"The file was missing."

"What?"

"I went to the office and tried to get another look at that file on the guy Marina was trying to find. It's gone."

"So? Another dead end?"

"Yeah, but there's lots more to think about. All kinds of strange things are happening, aren't they? The tree's shaking."

"Well, as long as nothing falls on your head."

"It's a tough head," Sean said more confidently than he truly felt.

As Ted opened the door he only had time to catch a glimpse of a face he knew and then a beefy fist thumped into his stomach, knocking the wind out of him and sending him falling back to land in a seated position on the floor.

Gasping for breath, his face twisted in agony, he finally looked up to see the solid figure of Dirk Hunt standing over him. Slightly behind Dirk, looking down at him without a trace of expression on her face, was Nancy Hamilton.

Ted began to cough, then regained his self-control. "What the fuck's going on?" he managed to say, his hands still holding his stomach.

Before he could move, Dirk's boot swung between his elbow and his hip, the toe digging deep into his kidneys.

"Jesus!" Ted said, trying to roll out of the way of any further blows.

"All right, I think he has the idea," Nancy said, touching Dirk's arm.

She was, as always, immaculate, dressed in a deep red bownecked cardigan and a pleated rayon skirt. She wore high heels, which at this moment were roughly level with Ted's face.

He struggled up into a sitting position again. The pain in his side seemed to radiate through his body in time with his heart.

"What the hell is this all about?" he asked, his voice hoarse. "I told Sean to move, if that's what's bothering you."

Dirk grabbed him under the shoulder and pulled him up. He stood there, half bent, not wanting any more of this treatment. He had never cared for pain and now he was beginning to understand why.

For one wild moment he considered trying to take Dirk, but it passed. He was no fighter, and he'd seen Dirk in action before. The guy was remorseless, a machine dedicated to damage.

"I want the video," Nancy said.

"What video?"

Dirk hit him on the side of the head with his open palm. For a moment everything turned red, and then there was a ringing sound. He focused his eyes on Nancy.

"Sister Cecelia," Nancy said.

Ted thought as fast as he could under the circumstances. The one thing he hadn't thought of had happened. Cecelia

287

had gone to the agency and told them of his blackmail attempt. The stupid bitch! What if he really had copies of the tape with someone? What if Nancy had simply taken over the job of blackmailer, or joined forces with him? Why had she taken such a risk?

Now there was a thought, one that might save his ass.

"Hey, listen," he said. "No big deal. The chick's worth millions. Let me run the scam and we can split the profits. I admit I was wrong to do it freelance, but hey, we all make mistakes."

"I want the tape," Nancy said. "No deals."

"Look," Ted said, trying to force a winning smile. "I went to a lot of trouble over this. All I want is a piece of the action."

She nodded ever so slightly at Dirk and this time the meaty fist thudded against the side of his face.

Again the red flood overtook him as he spun around. He wasn't aware of falling, but found himself sitting on the floor again.

"This is getting boring," he heard himself say. And then he yelped as another boot took him in the ribs, sending him onto his back.

"Where are they, Ted?" Nancy's voice traveled over vast distances to reach him, echoing as if spoken through a tunnel.

He didn't want to tell her, but neither did he want more pain. He knew that if he didn't speak there would be more. Nancy was serious. Dirk was an animal. But the tapes were his future. They would provide the money that would give him his freedom. Freedom of choice, freedom of movement, action, lifestyle, everything.

He opened his eyes to see Dirk scowling down at him. The animal looked over at Nancy, as if to ask for further direction, and the thought occurred then to Ted that if he was dead, his freedom wouldn't amount to a damn. With that thought came a different level of fear. Beatings passed.

One could recover from them. It was more difficult to get over death. And these people could kill if they had to. He'd never known that until now, never realized the extent of the game in which he was involved, or who the players really were.

"All right," he groaned.

"Where are they?" Nancy asked.

"Upstairs. In my room." He forced himself to sit. God, he hurt. He didn't think he'd even be able to make it up the stairs.

"Where?" Nancy asked.

"Briefcase. In my closet."

She walked away, but Dirk stayed there, glowering down at him.

So much for a luxurious future, Ted thought miserably. He should have stuck to what he knew: hustling women for money and gifts. What was it his father used to call him? "Too big for your britches, sonny." Man, ain't that the truth. He was out of his league here, not prepared for it. Christ, he didn't even have another copy of the tape. He'd made only one other copy and he had given that to Cecelia. His comment to her about copies in a safe place was pure fabrication. He hadn't thought it necessary. He'd misjudged her, certain that she would just fold up under his pressure. Oh, boy.

Nancy came downstairs, the briefcase in her hand. She put it on a coffee table and said, "Combination?"

"Give me," he said, raising a hand weakly.

"Just tell me," she said sharply.

This was not the time to argue, he thought. "8-9-2."

She held up the vidoecassette and the audio tape. "Where's the copy?" she asked.

He attempted to think again. Should he say there was one? Would that help him? His thoughts were too ponderous to reach a conclusion. Stick with the truth. It was safest. Maybe.

Ted tried to shake his head. His brains felt as if they were rattling around in there. "There isn't one. That's it."

"You told her there was a copy in safekeeping somewhere," Nancy said dangerously.

"I lied. I swear. There isn't one. I didn't have time."

"God, you're not much of a blackmailer," Nancy said. "But if you're lying and a copy ever turns up . . ." She looked meaningfully at Dirk.

"No. I don't have one."

She stirred the contents of the briefcase with her hand, looking at his collection of drugs. "You're a walking pharmaceutical company, Ted. You should knock it off. It's turning your brain to mush. You'd never have thought of doing anything as stupid as this a year ago."

"Yeah, pretty stupid," Ted agreed. Sensation was returning to various parts of his body. Unfortunately, the sensation was pain. "So you're going to carry on, are you? Do it properly? How about a finder's fee?"

"You never give up hustling do you?" Nancy said. She shook her head in wonderment. "You poor, dumb fuck. You really picked the wrong one this time. Sister Cecelia. How do you think Her Holiness found out about the agency? Sister Cecelia French. My maiden name, French. *My* sister."

"Jesus Christ," Ted said pathetically.

Nancy started to move toward the door, then turned back. "By the way, Ted, you're fired." She nodded at Dirk. "Let him know that he's never to talk about the agency or its business to anyone ever. Give him a taste of the consequences if he ever thinks of blackmail again."

"My pleasure," Dirk said, speaking for the first time.

"Hey, I got the point," Ted said. "I—"

But before he could articulate his next thought, Dirk had pulled him up again and leveled another crushing blow to his ribs, followed quickly by another to the stomach.

Ted was helpless, too weakened to fight back, too disoriented to even move. Dirk grasped the neck of his shirt and straightened Ted up and drew his fist back, his target obviously the face.

"Here you go, pretty boy," he said, and smiled, and let his fist fly forward.

And then the door opened and Sean's voice said, "Hey, what the hell is going on here?"

The blow hit Ted in the mouth, but it had lost some of his momentum as Dirk turned. Still, he could taste blood.

Sean came barreling into the room at a run. He reached Dirk and grabbed his arm. "Enough," he said.

Dirk released his hold on Ted's shirt and let him sink back to his knees.

"Keep your face out of this," Dirk said, and tried to pull his arm away.

For the first time, Ted really noticed that not only was Sean good looking and tall, but that he was also well-built and obviously in good shape. Dirk must have noticed it too, because he darted a look at Nancy.

"Let it be," she said. "We've got what we wanted."

Sean released his hold on Dirk's arm, but watched him carefully. He knew a brawler when he saw one. The guy reminded him of some of the loggers up in Seattle. They'd come in after weeks in the woods, spoiling for it.

"As for you, Sean," Nancy said. "I suggest you forget about the young lady. You might soon be in Ted's position."

She turned and left, followed by Dirk, who gave Sean one last dirty look.

"Jesus," Sean said, crouching beside Ted. "Are you all right?"

"Do I look all right?" Ted said.

"Let me get you into a chair," Sean said, moving behind him and lifting him by the armpits.

Ted tried to stand, but his legs gave way. "A little shaky," he said.

Half-carrying him, Sean got Ted over to a chair, which he fell into with a deep groan.

291

Sean went to the kitchen, wet a towel, and brought it back. He dabbed at a streak of blood flowing from Ted's mouth.

"Forget that," Ted said. "I think the fucker broke my ribs."

"I'll call paramedics," Sean said, moving to the phone.

"No. Forget it. Don't. I'm okay," Ted said. "I've got a doctor I'll call. Get me a drink. A Scotch."

"What happened?" Sean said, heading for the liquor cabinet.

"I got beaten up," Ted said. "Oh, man, did I! I'm a fucker not a fighter."

"Yeah, well, that I can see," Sean said over his shoulder while he poured a healthy dose of whiskey into a tumbler. He brought it back and handed it to Ted.

Ted drank it and grimaced. "Jesus, that stings!"

"What was all that about?" Sean asked.

"I got fired," Ted said, taking another swallow. "Now we're both unemployed. I guess you don't have to move out right away."

Sean sat in a chair opposite him and leaned his elbows on his knees. "Get real, Ted. There's all sorts of shit happening here—and all of it has something to do with Debonaire. Tell me what happened."

The vaguely self-derisive look left Ted's eyes. "You get real," he said. "Do you see what happened to me? It's nothing compared to what would happen if I started talking to you or anyone else."

"Maybe I can help you," Sean said.

Ted slumped back in his seat. "It's over," he said dejectedly.

"For you, maybe," Sean said tightly. "What about the rest of us?"

"What are you talking about? You're out of it."

"Oh, no, I'm not. I'm just getting into it," Sean said emphatically. "So why don't you tell me what's really going on with Debonaire." He pointed at Ted's mouth. "This wasn't just about upsetting a client."

292

"What do *you* think's going on?" Ted asked craftily.

"I don't know," Sean said frankly. "All I know is that a friend of mine died suspiciously and that it had something to do with Debonaire. I plan to find out what."

"Who?"

"A girl by the name of Marina White. She worked for Panache, the women's escort service."

"I don't know her," Ted said. He rubbed his rib, pain showing on his face. "Listen, I don't know anything. And I've got to go and call a doctor."

"What was the videotape Nancy walked out of here with?" Sean asked. He'd noticed it in her hand.

"How the hell do I know. Maybe she rented a movie."

"All right then, tell me about the condo," Sean said.

"What condo?"

"You knew the address that I'd written down where I was supposed to meet a client. What was all that about?"

Ted gave him a hooded look. "I don't know what you're talking about," he said stubbornly.

The front door opened and Danny came in. He stopped in his tracks, looking at Ted. "Jesus, what happened to you?"

"Your friends from Debonaire," Sean said. "Nancy was here with some guy who worked Ted over."

Danny looked at Ted, then raised an eyebrow back at Sean. "Man, and I thought *you* pissed her off." he said.

Chapter Nineteen

"That's it, I'm out of it," Danny said emphatically. "I've had a good run, but it's over."

Ted had gone upstairs to lie on his bed. He had refused Sean and Danny's repeated offers to drive him to an emergency room for X-rays and treatment and instead had called his doctor friend, who promised to stop in and patch him up. Danny and Sean sat in the kitchen and drank coffee.

"When things get this rough, I know I'm in the wrong place, involved with the wrong people," Danny continued.

"Surely this isn't a big surprise to you?" Sean said, verging on the accusative. "You must have known what kind of person Nancy was, and her boyfriend . . . what's his name? Dirk?"

Danny met his stare without resentment. "Hey, I might just be a Mexican from the barrio, compadre, but I'm not stupid. I haven't known anything for sure, but it's been pretty obvious that Debonaire has had a few scams going. What did I care? As long as they didn't involve me and I didn't have to know about them." He shrugged expressively. "Look, we all fool ourselves in some way—compromise, you know. What I've been doing at Debonaire is illegal, right? But it doesn't hurt anyone and I could live with it in order to get the money I need. But now? Ted's upstairs all fucked up. And he's still too scared to talk about what it was really all about. Bad sign, man. Exit for

Danny sign, that's what it is."

"What are you going to do?" Sean asked.

Danny shrugged. "I got some money. I'll think about it. Maybe it's time for me to start my restaurant business. There's this woman I'm seeing who wants to help me. Her husband's connected and loaded. Maybe she can help me raise some more money."

Sean toyed with his spoon, twirling it in circles.

"What about you?" Danny said. "Why don't you just forget all this bullshit and get on with your life? Get back to your acting."

Sean looked up and smiled. "Listen, I don't want to sound like John Wayne here, but a man's gotta do what a man's gotta do. I have a dead friend. Maybe she deserved to die, but I doubt that. I don't think anyone really does. But I've got to find out what happened."

Danny grunted noncommittally. "I'm the one who's supposed to be the macho Latin around here. You're just a fucking actor. You're not even mentally equipped to deal with people like Nancy and Dirk, man, not to mention physically."

Sean twirled his spoon around. "I sure wish I could get into that condo and see what's really going on there."

"What is it with you, man? You can't stand a mystery?"

"I can't stand the idea of people getting away with murder," Sean said.

Danny sighed. "You know where it is?"

"Yeah, I went there."

"And nobody lives there?"

"It looked too spotless, like a showroom." Sean gave Danny a keen look. "Why? What are you thinking?"

Another heavy sigh from Danny. "This is none of my business. I should know better than to get involved," he said. He paused. "But I'll help you. Just on this one thing."

"What? How?" Sean asked.

"Tonight. I'll get you into the place," Danny said.

Dirk lumbered into the living room of their apartment to see Nancy talking on the telephone. More truthfully, she was listening; the other party was doing the talking. Which led him to guess who it was.

She sat on the couch, one leg half crossed under her, dressed in linen slacks and a blue cotton shirt, three silver bracelets on her left wrist, a Piaget watch on her right. She was barefoot.

He thought what a long way she had come since he had known her. Oh, she had always been beautiful, but the elegance and the confidence had come with the money. Whereas before she had been just another pretty small-town girl hooking in the big city, she was now a woman to be reckoned with. All in a few short years. He wished he could have said that it was because of him, but even he knew that wasn't true. It had all changed when she had once again come into contact with her family. Then had come the money and the funding for the agency. She had since outgrown him, no doubt about it.

Not that he minded all that much. He was still her lover, and she'd never had wandering eyes. Money and power were her interests, not other men. Not, he sometimes suspected, even himself. He was there to service her. If he did the job passably well, and ran her errands for her, she didn't complain. It was an arrangement that suited him. She was the most exciting woman he had ever met, and he was willing to put up with a lot for that privilege.

"All right," she said, hanging up the phone and turning to him.

"We've got another problem," she said, her mouth tight with displeasure.

"What?"

"Sean Parker. Do you have a man checking on him?"

"Yeah, I should get a report any time now. We'll know everything there is to know about him."

"Well, he knows more than he should about us," she said. "He's poking his nose too heavily into our business."

Dirk remembered how Sean had stood up to him and scowled. "That's two people who know too much. I didn't like leaving that asshole Ted with his tongue in his mouth. What's to stop him from talking?"

"He'll incriminate himself," Nancy said, but she frowned at the shortcomings in her argument. "You could be right, though. Maybe we should figure out a way to handle them both."

"How?"

"I'll think about it," she said. "Meantime, get on your guy's ass. I want that report on him. Friends, habits, background, the works, right?"

"That's what I asked for," Dirk said, resenting the repetitive orders.

"Well?" Nancy said sharply. "Get it. Now."

"What's happening between you and Susanne?" Kenneth Lowell asked, entering his wife's study.

Annette looked up from the papers she was studying on the oak desk and blinked two or three times, as if to bring her thoughts into the present. "What do you mean?"

"I heard the two of you arguing and Susanne looks upset."

"It's just boy trouble," Annette said.

Kenneth leaned against the doorjamb and crossed his arms. "And you're interfering?"

Annette leaned back in her chair and crossed her own arms. "She's an irresponsible child. She doesn't know what she's doing, or the consequences of her actions. I'm not going to stand by and see her get into untenable situations — situations that could prove embarrassing not only

297

for her but for all of us."

"For God's sake, she's a grown woman, and a smart one. When will you acknowledge that?" Kenneth said, more in a kind of wonder than with irritation.

Annette regarded her husband in a less kindly manner. She pushed herself forward, leaned her elbows on the desk and knitted her fingers. "Sometimes I think that *you* never grew up," she said. "You just don't seem to be able to see what is really important and what isn't."

"Yes," he said with distinguished irony. "I know your opinion of my ambitions. I keep telling you that they have nothing to do with maturity. Perhaps it is *your* drive that is immature, more suited to a young Turk than a middle-aged and wealthy woman who has already attained more than most people. Sometimes I wish that we could just enjoy our lives together without these imposed pressures."

"It's just starting," she said forcefully. "And I'm not going to let our willful daughter screw it up. I have been working for years to get us into this position. I've sacrificed and done things you will never know about to get you this far. Don't you understand? You are going to be a senator. And you will, believe me. Getting elected is a formality with the backing that's getting lined up. This is going to be real power, nothing like we've had before."

"Maybe you should run," he said, unimpressed by her fervor. "You want it more than I do. And I'm not interested in power as such. The only reason it interests me is because perhaps I'll be able to accomplish some needed changes, something that is difficult to do on the bench."

"Your idealism . . ." She let the words trail away, the implication obvious.

"Besides," he said, for the first time allowing a deep-seated anger to creep to the surface, "I have to live with some of the things you've done and they are not light burdens."

"But necessary," she snapped, with no sign of regret.

"Just as it's necessary to curb Susanne's indiscretions. I'm not going to let her get mixed up with the wrong people. Everything I've worked for is at stake. The wrong kind of publicity in the coming months could ruin it."

"And what about her happiness?" he asked, a languid sadness entering his voice.

"That's not the point at all," she said scornfully. "Besides, she's young, with all her years ahead of her. Everyone has to make their sacrifices. Why should she be an exception?"

"You could be asking too much," Kenneth warned.

"I'm doing it for you," she asserted.

"I don't believe that." He pushed himself away from the wall and turned to leave. Speaking over his shoulder as he walked out the door, he said, "Not for a moment."

Sean pressed the buzzer at the outer gate of the condominium building and waited. "No answer," he said.

"Hit it again," Danny said.

It was a cool evening. The moon was three-quarters full, a pale glow high in the sky over the quiet street.

"Okay," Danny said. He moved forward and withdrew a thin metal case from his jacket pocket. "I want you to stand a little behind me to the side, so that nobody in the street or on the path can see what I'm doing."

Sean complied then asked, "What *are* you doing?" as he watched Danny withdraw a thin metal rod from the case and insert it in the lock of the outer gate.

"It's called breaking and entering. And this one is a piece of cake," Danny said with a tight smile while he concentrated. "I used to run with a gang, man. Half of them had been in state prison before the age of twenty. They learned from the pros and they taught us. I've never forgotten my lessons, although I haven't had the chance to use them until now . . . There we go."

There was a "click" and Danny turned the handle on the

299

gate, swinging it open.

Two minutes later he was doing the same thing at the door of the condo. "This is easy shit," he said. "These people who live in Beverly Hills, if they knew how easy it was to get inside they wouldn't sleep."

He opened the door and stepped in, Sean close behind him. "Nice place," Danny said.

Sean led the way through the living room. "I just came in here and didn't look around. I want to check out the rest of it," he said.

"Let's look at the bedroom," Danny suggested.

They turned on the bedroom light and glanced around. The bed was immaculately made and there was no sign on the dresser or the chairs of the disorderliness found in a normal bedroom. Danny walked over to the dresser and opened drawers, glancing briefly at the contents. Then he looked into the mirror, and behind it.

He walked over next to the wall mirror opposite the bed. It was built into the wall and he ran his fingers around the edges. Then he tapped it, listening to the sounds while Sean watched curiously.

Danny stepped back, frowned, and said, "The mirror is opposite the bed. Why?"

Sean looked at him blankly then raised his eyebrows. "Do you think—"

"I've never seen it before, only read about it, but why not?" Danny asked, walking to the closet. He opened the doors and stepped in, turning on the light.

Almost immediately he began to tap his knuckles against the walls. "Yeah!" he said.

Sean popped his head into the closet to see Danny pushing a wall aside. "It's a door," Danny said.

Sean entered and looked over his shoulder at the tiny room. The mirror was transparent and they could see the bedroom, in particular the bed. And on this side of it whirred a VCR camera and tape recorder.

"Sweet," Danny said.

"Well, there's only one reason for that," Sean said. "These guys are running a blackmail operation."

"Looks like it," Danny agreed.

"Better grab the tapes," Sean said. "We're on them. They must be activated by the lights."

Danny leaned into the small room and turned the machines off and removed the video and audio tapes. Then they both backed out of the closet.

"So whose place is this?" Danny asked when they stood in the center of the room.

"Well, I'm not sure, but I think it's Debonaire's," Sean said. "I was led to believe that the woman I met here lived here, but I don't think that's the case. And Ted knew about this place. Maybe he's been featured on some of the films. Come to think of it, Nancy had a video tape in her hand when I walked in on them."

"Who was the woman you met here?" Danny asked.

"Some client. I don't know," Sean said. This was no time for a lengthy explanation about Susanne's mother.

"Well, it makes sense. Running a blackmail scam on the side. It's a natural next step."

"If your thoughts are larcenous, I suppose it is," Sean conceded.

Danny took a quick look around the room. "We'd better get out of here."

When they reached the street, Sean said, "I think it's time I tried another heart-to-heart with Ted."

They had come in separate cars and Danny started for his. "I've got a date. And like I told you, I've done all I'm going to do on this."

"I appreciate it," Sean said.

Danny unlocked his car door and then turned back to Sean. "By the way, it doesn't look like you have to move out now. Seems like all of us are without a job."

Sean nodded. He'd make a detour on the way home and

tell Oscar he wouldn't need to crash at his place. Then, if Ted wasn't drugged out on medication, he'd have a talk with him.

"See you later," Danny said from inside his car and started the engine.

Sean waved at him and walked across the street to his own automobile. As he drove toward Los Feliz he went over what he knew. It wasn't much, but it was tantalizing. Nancy Hamilton was involved in blackmail. Ted probably had something to do with it as well. There had been a falling out between them.

He realized he was making a dangerous assumption: that Debonaire owned the condominium they had just visited. The facts pointed to that but didn't prove it. Ted knew about the condo. Nancy had sent him to the condo to meet "a client"—Annette. How had that happened? All he could figure was that upon learning where he worked and deciding to confront him, Annette had called the agency, asked for a date with him, and said that she had wanted to meet somewhere private. Made sense in a way. She wouldn't have wanted to have the conversation at her home where they could be interrupted, particularly by Susanne. Or, if she actually knew Nancy, she hadn't even bothered to use the guise of a date but simply said she needed to talk to him. Why, however, hadn't she just called him and set up a meeting? Probably she had sought the added element of surprise. She was devious enough.

He took Sunset Boulevard, only half noticing the enormous billboards lining the Strip to promote new film releases. Traffic was light and he made good time into Hollywood, barely aware of the speed he was traveling, wrapped up in his thoughts.

So what had all this to do with Marina? Maybe she had discovered the blackmail, or, with her mention of murder, a killing related to the blackmail. It was the only conclusion he could come to based upon what he knew—which wasn't all that much.

And who could have been killed? He was more and more inclined to think it might have been the missing Alex Varney, the name on her list. He had disappeared without a trace. The fact that he was a loner and nobody was looking for him, including the police, only made it easier to conceive.

What were the chores on her list? "Check ownership," was one. Could that have been referring to Debonaire? Right now it seemed a definite possibility, and it was something he should do—investigate the ownership of the agency and the condo they had just visited. For all he knew, Nancy, as manager of Debonaire, was just a front for organized crime. It was certainly worth further investigation.

A couple of thin young male prostitutes stood on the corner of Las Palmas and Sunset, just visible outside a pool of shadows, ready to dive back in at the first sign of a patrol car. A sordid step below Debonaire in the vast scheme of things, but perhaps not all that different. Apparently Debonaire had its own shadowy pools, and he was only beginning to get an inkling of what they contained.

"May I come in? I'd like to talk to you," Annette said from Susanne's bedroom door.

Susanne put the book she was reading down on the bed beside her. "Of course you can," she said sarcastically. "As you're so fond of pointing out, this is your house. You shouldn't have to ask permission."

Annette's eyes reflected her displeasure, but she stepped in further, stopping at the end of the bed. She seemed to gather her thoughts, and when she spoke her tone was conciliatory. "Look, maybe we could take a different approach to this. It doesn't accomplish anything for us to be

303

at each other's throats all the time. I don't like it and you don't like it."

Susanne watched expectantly while Annette sat carefully on the bed. She had been approached by Annette under the guise of peace before and was not impressed. Her mother tended to use periods of truce to advance her own ground.

Annette sighed. "I sometimes forget how difficult things can be at your age." A reluctant smile. "It was a long time ago when I was that young."

"I'm not that young," Susanne said, not giving an inch, "I'll be twenty-six in a few months. In most quarters that's considered adulthood. And I'm not having a whole lot of difficulty with life, except in my relationship with you. And more than anything, that has to do with your perception of my age and maturity."

"Well, that may be true to a degree," Annette conceded. "I still think of you as my little girl, you know, particularly now that to all intents and purposes you are the only child."

"But I'm not," Susanne asserted stubbornly. "Not your little girl and not your only child. No matter what her condition, Marion is still your daughter."

"Yes, but my hopes died when . . . when her condition changed. They all rest with you now, as unfair as that may be."

For a moment Susanne relented. "Annette," she said more softly, "you have to live out your hopes and you have to let me live out mine. I can't live your dreams for you. Surely you can see that?"

"I think we both need a little distance," Annette said. "The recent pressures, the fact we see each other all the time . . . I think we've both lost perspective of each other. I'd like to make a proposal."

And here it comes, Susanne thought: the real motive behind all the conciliation and conversation. Her mental defenses reared up. "What?" she asked.

"I think one of the problems you face is that you're not sure what you want to do with your life," Annette said carefully. "That's quite understandable at your age. If I've been critical of that before, it's just impatience on my part. Anyway, I think it would be a wonderful idea if you took a trip, saw some new vistas, experienced some new cultures. Europe, for instance. In a different setting, away from the pressures of Los Angeles and (I must admit) the pressures I put on you, I think you'll gain a new understanding of where you are and where you want to be." She paused to give Susanne a measured look. "I'd pay all the expenses of course. Say, air fare and six months in Europe? What do you think?"

Susanne thought it was beautiful. Transparent, but beautiful. The maneuver was so obvious, she couldn't even feel angry. Instead, she decided to play her mother on the line for a while.

"I have a better idea," she said. "You see, as a matter of fact, I do know what I want to do, and you could help me."

"Oh?" Annette said apprehensively.

"Yes. I want to get into film production. To start with, I have a number of books I want to option. And to do that, I need money. Instead of spending money for me to travel overseas, *lend* me the money to option these properties." She smiled brightly, a saleswoman's smile. "Both of us will come out ahead."

"Oh," Annette said, but recovered quickly. "I still think you need some time to sort out your priorities. Why not take the trip and then, if you still feel inclined to pursue this career, I'll consider funding you when you return."

"My priorities are very clear," Susanne said firmly.

"Perhaps, but I don't think you're able to view all the alternatives while you're here," Annette argued. "Some distance, some time, and who knows what you'll come up

305

with."

Susanne tired of the game. "I'm not interested," she said. "Why don't we cut to the quick here. You want me away from here and away from Sean. That's what this is all about, right?"

"I'm only thinking of you," Annette said, her mouth turning down.

"You can stop thinking of me," Susanne said. "I'm old enough to think of myself, to be where I want to be and see who I want to see. Why don't you stop wasting our time?"

"I want you to stop seeing him," Annette said flatly.

Susanne shrugged, her expression fatalistic. "We've been through this. I'm not going to stop seeing him. I love him."

"You cannot just disobey me like that," Annette said, her voice finally rising, her face growing darker.

"I can," Susanne said quietly.

"I'm not going to just stand by and do nothing," Annette warned.

"Don't try and hurt Sean further." Susanne's voice was cutting. "I'll never forgive you for that. It will be the end of everything between us, I promise you."

"I will take whatever steps are necessary to stop you from this stupidity," Annette said, her voice cold.

She rose from the bed and glared down at her daughter.

They stared at each other, neither giving an inch.

"Then you'll have lost both your daughters," Susanne said.

Sean walked down the hallway to the condo, still smiling at Oscar's comments after his friend had managed to pry out of him that he was in love. They had ranged from "Love is always having to say you're sorry" to "It's a purely chemical reaction, and like any chemical formula, it's unstable and changes in time. Sanity will return."

306

They'd had a couple of beers at Oscar's apartment and Sean had surmised that his friend was secretly pleased that he wasn't going to stay there. Guests tended to cramp Oscar's free-wheeling style.

Oscar wasn't having a wonderful time of it. Since the collapse of the play, he'd been scrounging for work. Luckily, he'd landed a couple of scriptwriting assignments for television sitcoms—work he hated but that was necessary for survival. As usual, he would protest loudly, all the way to the bank.

Sean reached the door and put his key in the lock. He turned it, pushed the door open, and stepped in, feeling on the wall to his right for the light switch.

There was a noise to his right then. A fast step, a grunt, the sound of something whistling through the air toward him.

He had time only to see two burly shapes.

He tried to twist to one side and back, but he wasn't fast enough. He felt something strike the side of his head and then his vision began to blur and he felt himself lose balance, falling toward the floor.

Eyes half closed, he felt a boot kick his stomach and heard the air escape his lungs in a loud groan. And then in a rush of motion the men had jumped over him and were gone.

He lay there for a few minutes, engulfed in dizziness and nausea. Then slowly, head throbbing, he raised himself to his hands and knees and stayed in that position.

He shook his head to clear it, but it hurt, so he stopped and simply stared at the floor trying to focus. After a minute things grew clearer and he pushed himself back to his haunches. Then, carefully, holding the doorjamb for support, he rose to his feet and fumbled for the light.

The glare was like another blow, and he quickly narrowed his eyes and stood swaying there. After another moment, he looked around.

Everything seemed in place. No overturned furniture. The TV and stereo still there.

He walked precariously through the living room to the stairs and then cautiously took the upward climb. He looked in his bedroom. Nothing seemed to have been disturbed.

Danny's door was closed. He opened it, turned on the light and looked in. Just the usual clothes in a pile beside the bed.

God, he felt shaky! A new wave of dizziness engulfed him and he was tempted to just go and lie on his bed, but he decided to finish the inspection. Up another flight of stairs to Ted's room.

The door was open and the light fell into the hallway. He reached the door and peered in.

Ted was lying on his bed, his eyes closed. Beside him was a hypodermic syringe.

"Oh, God," Sean whispered, and staggered toward him.

He picked up the limp wrist and thought he felt the stirrings of a pulse. He grabbed for the telephone on the table beside the bed.

It seemed to take forever, but finally the 911 operator answered.

"I've got an unconscious drug overdose here," he said, feeling an awful sense of déjà vu, and gave the address.

And then the dizziness became too much and he felt himself fall toward the floor.

Chapter Twenty

They were different police this time, uniforms, dozens of them all over the house it seemed to a distraught and confused Sean, although in fact there were probably only three there at any one time. They were aggressive in that bland police manner, and suspicious. Ted had been carted off to a hospital, still unconscious, and Sean was the only one there to explain his version of what had happened.

It was when he also tried to explain the similarity of this incident to the circumstances under which Marina had died that their suspicions turned to him. "How come you're always around before someone OD's?" one of them asked bluntly.

Sean erupted at that point. "Listen, asshole," he said. "I'm a goddamned victim here as well. See this? It fucking hurts. I got attacked here." He pointed at the swollen portion of his skull. The policeman remained unimpressed, and even went so far as to point out how simple it was to self-inflict a blow.

He referred them to the Beverly Hills policeman, Lieutenant Roger Glenn, and it was only after one of them called him that their suspicions seemed to subside somewhat, although the same officer also called Oscar to find out if Sean had indeed been there earlier as he had claimed.

After what seemed like a couple of hours of this, Danny arrived home and corroborated his story about how Ted had been beaten up earlier that day by a man named Dirk, in the company of Nancy Hamilton. What neither of them mentioned, by mutually unspoken agreement, was Debonaire's blackmail operation and the possibility of Ted's involvement in it. Their little breaking-and-entering operation wouldn't have gone over well under the circumstances. Nor did they have any idea what Ted's involvement was and what consequences he would face if it were known. Grudgingly, however, the police began to accept his story.

When they finally left, Sean called the hospital to discover that Ted was in a coma, his condition described as critical, the prognosis unknown. He thought of calling Susanne, but it was too late by then and his head was throbbing mercilessly. Although he protested, Danny forced him to take some aspirin and encouraged him to get to bed.

"I got one thing for you," Danny said as Sean began to trudge from the living room. "My woman . . . I told her what had been going on and that you wanted to check ownership records and stuff. She gave me the name of her lawyer. He's not cheap, but he's fast and he has detectives that he works with. Here's his name and number." He handed Sean a piece of paper.

"Thanks. I'll call him tomorrow," Sean said.

"Well . . ." Danny said, looking away in embarrassment. "I guess I can help. Kick in a few bucks."

Sean smiled, even though it hurt his face. "I thought you didn't want to get involved?"

Danny inclined his head. "I guess I am involved. I think I'd like to find out what's going on. Anyway, forewarned is forearmed, right?"

"Right," Sean said. "And thanks."

"It's nothing," Danny said. "Now, for Chrissakes, go to bed. You look like you're going to fall over. I don't want to have to carry you upstairs."

"Yes," Sean said faintly, aware suddenly of his weakness.

He climbed the steps like a rickety octogenarian.

The curative powers of sleep were limited. When Sean awoke after a solid eight hours, his head still ached, although it was more irritating than truly painful. But his vision seemed fine and there was no dizziness when he clambered out of bed. He concluded that he had escaped a concussion.

As soon as he was awake enough, with a cup of coffee in his hands, he called Susanne and told her what had happened to Ted. She insisted on coming over immediately.

He sat in the kitchen and sipped his coffee thoughtfully, trying to reassess everything that had happened. One thing was obvious: Ted had somehow crossed Nancy Hamilton. That she was ultimately responsible for the attempt on his life last night (and in his mind, it was definitely an attempt, even though the police weren't convinced) was a distinct likelihood. And it was also obvious that it all had to do with blackmail.

He remembered the charity party he had gone to with Ted . . . the girl who had come up to Ted and called him a "blackmailing son of a bitch." Some senator's daughter. Dobbs. The setup at the condo, the videotape in Nancy's hand while her boyfriend was beating Ted up, it all led to blackmail—and some kind of falling out among thieves.

But what was the connection to Susanne's mother? For now he was more convinced than ever that there was a connection. Nancy's last words to him, "I suggest you forget about the young lady," proved that she knew exactly what was going on with Annette. Which in turn led him to believe that their connection was more than just casual. And if that were the case—

The telephone rang, interrupting his thought.

There was no sign of Danny. He was either still asleep or already out. Sean sighed and got up.

"Hello?"

"Stay away from the girl, and keep out of Debonaire's business," said a muffled male voice. "If you don't there'll be trouble for both of you. What happened to Ted could happen to you and the girl."

"Who is this?" Sean asked.

There was a click as the other party hung up.

Sean replaced the receiver, his heart thumping. Would they hurt Susanne? Was he wrong about Annette being involved somehow? But then why would they want him to stay away from her? On the other hand, why would they threaten to harm her? It was too confusing. There was only one thing he was certain of: if anything happened to her he would never forgive himself.

The buzzer sounded from the outer gate. He went to the intercom and Susanne's voice came over the speaker. He pressed the buzzer, then opened the door and stepped into the hallway to wait for her.

"Are you all right?" she asked as soon as she saw him. When she reached him she put her arms on his shoulders and peered at his head.

"I'm fine," he said and kissed her hungrily. "I feel like I haven't seen you for ages," he said.

"You have a lump on your head," she said, touching it.

"Ow! Don't," he said, surprised by the pain her touch caused.

"Poor baby," she said, smiling.

He put his arm around her shoulders and led her into the apartment. After pouring her a cup of coffee they sat at the table and he went over everything that had happened. She listened wide-eyed, interjecting with occasional questions and comments.

"And now I'm worried about you," he concluded.

"I can't believe this," she said. "How can my mother be involved with people like this? And how is she involved?"

"I don't know," Sean said. "We could always ask her,

312

I suppose."

Susanne shook her head. "Direct confrontation doesn't work with Annette. I think we need to find out more first."

Sean put his hand over hers. "Are you sure you want to?"

She saw the seriousness in his eyes and took a moment to consider his question before answering.

"This is your mother I'm talking about," he continued. "And I don't know what we're going to find out about her, or what we're going to have to do about it."

"Yes, I know," she said finally.

"I mean," he said uncertainly. "It could be nothing. Maybe Nancy is just doing a favor for her for some reason. Or maybe she is bringing some pressure to bear on Nancy to get her to put pressure on me. It could be quite innocent, but . . ."

"But you don't think it is," she finished for him.

Sean flicked his eyes away from hers. "I don't know."

"I want to know the truth," Susanne said, her voice firm. "If Annette is involved in any way, I want to know."

"Good," Sean said with a nod, "then we keep digging."

"Okay. So what's the next step?"

"Danny gave me the number of a lawyer who can look up ownership records. It'll probably be expensive, but I'd like to find out who is involved in Debonaire."

"So call him," Susanne said.

"I will. And then there's someone else I'd really like to talk to, although I don't know if it's possible." He told her about the girl's outburst against Ted at the recent charity event. "Someone at the table knew her. She's a senator's daughter. Dobbs."

"Emily Dobbs?" Susanne said incredulously.

"Yes, I think that was it. Do you know her?"

"I know her brother David. He's mentioned her. My mother tried to set us up. She's a friend of his father's. I met him too, actually, the senator."

313

"Can we get to her?"

She thought only for a second. "Through David, probably. Although we might have to tell him what's going on." She brightened up. "Which might not be a bad idea. He's a corporate attorney and could probably trace the Debonaire ownership for us as well. Save you some bucks."

"Let's do it," Sean said.

They met David and Emily Dobbs in a small coffee shop on Vermont Avenue. It was a recreation of the sixties, complete with a surly proprietor, bearded young men playing chess, and serious young girls in black leotards writing poetry in tattered notebooks.

David was calm, greeting Susanne warmly and Sean with an appraising look through thick spectacles. Emily, who looked a few years younger than her brother, was nervous, unable to stop twisting her hands together, and clearly distracted. All Susanne had said over the telephone was, "Look, we think Emily is being blackmailed and we know something about it. Let's get together and compare notes." David had said he knew nothing about it, but had agreed to approach his sister.

"So," David said when the steaming cups of cappuccino had been placed before them. "Emily and I had a little talk on the way over here." He shook his head. "Seems like she hung out with the wrong crowd and got into some trouble."

Sean and Susanne had agreed that she would talk to the girl, in the assumption that Emily would be more comfortable answering the questions of another female. She took the lead now. "You were being blackmailed?" she said.

Emily shook her head, not speaking.

"You weren't?" Susanne said, confusion in her voice. "I thought—"

"My father was being blackmailed," David said soberly.

314

"With something Emily was involved in." He took in their surprise and then said with lawyerly caution. "I think you should tell us what you know before we go on."

"I worked for this male escort agency," Sean said, picking up the ball. It was time for a demonstration of the beginnings of mutual trust. "I was suspicious about some of their activities and, in the course of snooping around, I found out that they had a blackmail operation going."

He told them about the condo in Beverly Hills and what he had found there. He also told them what had happened to Ted and to his friend Marina. He did not mention Annette.

"What did this guy Ted look like?" Emily asked, speaking for the first time.

"He's the guy you spoke to the other night," Sean said, mentioning the event he had attended.

"So, was he the one blackmailing you and your father?" Susanne asked.

"Probably," she said.

"We don't know who was behind it," David said, correcting her. "Apparently my father got a videotape in the mail. It showed Emily in a compromising position. He came to Emily in a rage and said she had finally ruined his political career, that because of this he was being forced to announce his retirement."

"You talked to him about it?" Sean asked.

"No. He won't talk about it. This is what he told Emily. He said he didn't know who was behind it but that 'they' wanted him out of office. He said he was enough of a political realist to know that if the tape was ever released to the media he wouldn't have a chance of reelection anyway. That's all."

"The tape?" Susanne said gently to Emily. "I guess it showed something sexual, huh?"

"Yes. It . . . it was bad," Emily said, her voice near a whisper, her eyes not meeting anyone's.

"Did it involve Ted?" Susanne asked.

"Yes. And . . . and someone else," Emily said. She twisted her hands on her lap and looked as if she was about to leap up from the table and run.

"It's okay," David said, gently touching his sister's shoulder.

"No, it's not," she said, tears in her eyes. "Daddy was always on my case for my behavior. This time I really blew it."

"We all make mistakes," Sean said, and immediately regretted it. The words were hollow.

Everyone looked uncomfortable for a moment and then Susanne said to David, "Will you help us? We need to trace the ownership of Debonaire. Is that easy to do?"

"That depends on whether the owner wants to be found or not, on how evasive the paper trail is. But there is always a paper trail to follow. Sure. I'll get on it right away. Today."

"There's also an affiliated female agency called Panache," Sean said.

"Anything else?" David asked.

Sean and Susanne looked at each other and shrugged. "We're following up some other leads," Sean said. "If you could do that fast, it could be a help."

"I'll do it through the company I work for," David said. "They have considerable resources and nobody will even notice that I'm using them."

"What do you want out of this?" Sean asked.

David smiled thinly. "All copies of the tape and the pressure off, of course. And maybe some justice."

Sean nodded. "Well, justice is what I'm after, so we'll see."

When Sean and Susanne were finally back in their car, Sean said, "I like him. He's a lot sharper than he looks."

"Mmm," Susanne said, her attention withdrawn.

"What?" Sean asked.

316

She looked up at him. "I was just thinking."

"That was obvious," he said with a smile. He didn't put the car in reverse but waited, watching her.

She shook her head angrily. "I don't like what I was thinking."

"Tell me."

She turned abruptly in her seat to face him. "When you look at a crime, you look at motive, right? In a crime like blackmail, you look at who stands to gain."

"Right?" he said, a question in his tone.

"Well," she said, struggling now, "I told you how my mother has guided my father's political career, right? Her ambitions for him?"

"Yes," he said, suddenly guessing what was coming, the comprehension entering his eyes.

"Right," she said with a fierce nod. "When Senator Dobbs leaves that seat vacant, guess who's going to run for it with full party backing. My father, that's who."

"Shit!" Sean said bitterly.

There was a message on the machine from Oscar when they returned to Sean's place. Instead of the normal lackadaisical comments, it was an urgent, "Call me, NOW!" And so Sean did.

"I need to see you," Oscar said. "What the fuck is going on?"

"What do you mean?" Sean asked.

"Can I come over?"

"Sure."

Sean stared at the silent telephone in his hand.

"What was that?" Susanne asked. She was leaning against the kitchen counter looking beautiful and worried.

"My friend Oscar. He's got a hair up his ass about something. He's coming over."

"Does it have anything to do with what's going on?"

"Who knows? He's worried about something."

Susanne pushed herself away from the counter and paced in front of it. "Sean, I feel like I'm sitting under the lip of a snow-covered cliff. This is beginning to look like an avalanche, and I don't know who the hell is going to get buried underneath it."

Sean walked over to her and took both her hands in his. "We can stop right now," he said. "Forget it all. Start creating something just for the two of us and to hell with the rest of it."

"What about your duty to your friend?"

"I love you more than duty," he said.

"You'd never forgive yourself," she said emphatically. "You have to see this through. *We* have to see it through. It seems that I have as much of a stake in it now as you do."

Fifteen minutes later Oscar arrived. In spite of his obvious concern, he gave Susanne an admiring glance but then he turned to Sean and said, "Can we talk?"

"Sure," Sean said.

Oscar glanced quickly at Susanne and then back at Sean. "It's all right," Sean said. "Go ahead. What's on your mind?"

They were sitting in the living room, Sean and Susanne on the couch, Oscar in an armchair opposite. "It's what's on *your* mind," Oscar said. "You're in the middle of something serious, and I don't know whether you know it or not."

"What happened?" Sean asked.

Oscar leaned, back in his chair and shook his head in perplexity. "I got a call this morning. An anonymous caller inviting me to become Judas. And you're the one to get crucified." He looked at Sean with an almost comically dramatic expression, waiting for a reaction.

"What are you talking about?" Sean asked.

"Well, you know when the cops called me and asked if

318

you'd been at my place, I said yes. Of course. Well, this dude, whoever he was, wanted me to change my story. Say that you hadn't. That I'd been confused. For this small service, I would receive $50,000 in the bank account of my choice, in whatever country I chose."

"You've got to be kidding," Sean said.

"Yeah. Your alibi torpedoed," Oscar said. "At least, that's what I assume the purpose was."

"That's ridiculous," Susanne said. "Whether he had an alibi or not is beside the point. Sean was attacked by the people who hurt Ted when he walked in. Nothing changes that."

"Maybe," Sean said thoughtfully. "Although the cops were quite willing to consider the fact that the lump on my head was self-inflicted. If it turned out that I'd been lying and wasn't where I said I was, they'd be more than willing to reexamine that theory."

"What's it all about?" Oscar asked, interest in his face now. He leaned forward, elbows on his knees.

"I got into trouble with the agency," Sean said. "I think now they want to get me into another kind of trouble." He explained a little of what was happening, just covering the surface details.

"Far out!" Oscar said enthusiastically. "Actor stumbles into plot and gets in over head. Great story!" He smiled at Susanne. "And a perfect love interest too."

Sean rolled his eyes. "Oscar sees everything in terms of story," he told Susanne. "The fact that our lives are in danger is totally insignificant in the big scheme of things. In fact, if we sacrificed them to make the story better, Oscar would be ecstatic."

"Art before life," Oscar said sanctimoniously.

"Tell me more about the call," Sean said, growing serious. "It was a man, you said. What was his voice like?"

"Nondescript. Muffled."

"So what did you say to him?"

319

"I asked how I'd get the money. What guarantees? He said it would be deposited in the account of my choice today. Then, after confirming it was there, I could call the police and change my story."

Sean whistled. "Expensive maneuver! Was anything else said?"

"No. That was it."

"What about your response? I mean, how did it end?"

Oscar lifted his hands and grimaced at what he obviously considered a stupid question. "Hell, naturally I said I'd think about it," he said. "I mean we're talking fifty grand here!"

When the laughter subsided, Sean said, "I'd like you to call the police and tell them about this."

"Yeah, I will," Oscar said. "I just wanted to check with you first. I had no idea what the hell you'd gotten yourself into." He turned to Susanne. "Sean's a nice guy and all, but sometimes I think he just fell off the back of the hay truck. Country kid in the big city."

"Oh, sure," Sean said. "Last year when I was broke for a while, Oscar had fifty bucks to his name and gave me thirty of them. And he calls me a soft touch."

"Okay, so you like each other," Susanne said, attempting to interject some mild reality. "What's our next step?"

"Food," Sean said. "I just realized I haven't eaten."

Oscar begged off, Susanne decided she was also hungry and they said their goodbyes, Oscar heading back over the hills to Los Feliz, Sean and Susanne down to Ventura Boulevard for some nouveau Mexican food.

Sean drove his Volkswagen out of the gates of the condominium complex and down the hill, feeling curiously satisfied. Oscar's revelation had proven that he was truly a target and somehow it satisfied him. Know thine enemy.

He told Susanne this, but she just looked troubled. "I'm just a Beverly Hills brat in the middle of a shooting war," she said. "I feel out of my depth."

320

"You don't seem to be doing too badly," Sean said, slowing before a sharp corner.

Suddenly there was a thump and a crunch and they hurtled forward against their seat belts.

"Jesus Christ!" Sean said, wrestling with the steering wheel.

Susanne let out a strangled yelp and grabbed the sides of her seat.

He looked in the rearview mirror and saw the white Cadillac that had rear-ended them. Its front window was shaded so he couldn't see the driver, but he was aware that the car was accelerating to hit him again.

"Hold on," he said, pressing his foot on the accelerator.

But a Volkswagen was no match for a Cadillac, and he darted a glance upward to see it closing the gap as he took the curve on two wheels.

He was just straightening the wheels out when the next thump came, sending his car into a sideways skid. He fought with the steering wheel and managed to gain control as the car reached the edge of the asphalt. Accelerating, he came out of the curve into a wider and straighter section of road.

He looked in the mirror again and saw the Caddy swing out and start to come alongside him.

"He's going to try and sideswipe me," he said, and without even thinking, slammed his foot on the brake as hard as he could.

The Volkswagen skidded to a halt and the Caddy shot ahead.

Sean saw its brake lights come on for just a second, and then it speeded up and continued down the hill. The reason soon became apparent: a line of three cars moving up the hill toward them.

Pulling over to the side, Sean finally released his hands from the steering wheel and slumped back in his seat.

"Are you all right?" Susanne asked.

"Yeah. You?"

"I'm fine," she said.

"They must have seen you in the car. They didn't care," Sean said in a wooden voice.

"They could have killed us," she said, her voice trembling with strain.

"They were trying to," Sean said. He rubbed both hands across his face. "You can't go home. I don't think I should either."

"Nothing will happen to me there," she said.

"I'm sure you're right, but I think it better if both of us stay out of sight until we figure out what's going on and what to do about it. I'd really feel better knowing where you were."

Susanne nodded at his logic. "Could we go back to your friend Oscar's place?"

"They know he's my friend. They called him, remember?"

"Do you realize that they must have found out from the police that you said you were with him? How else would they have known to call him?"

"Yes, the thought occurred to me," Sean said. He sat upright and started the engine. "I know where we'll go. Another friend. We can lie low there for a couple of days." He did a U-turn and started back up the hill.

Chapter Twenty-one

Doris Winston was pleased to see Sean and charmed by Susanne. Sean was happy to notice that the feeling was mutual. The two women took an instant liking to each other. "So you're the one who has Sean's heart in a tizzy," were Doris's first words. She smiled warmly at Susanne, who almost blushed.

Sean's first words were: "Last time you saw me, you warned that I could get into trouble and told me to call on you if I had to. Now I have to."

She simply nodded coolly and said, "Come inside."

They sat in the living room. She offered them tea but they both refused.

Doris crossed her hands over one knee and looked them over with those shrewd brown eyes. "How can I help?" she asked.

"We need a place to stay for a couple of days. Private. Somewhere we can't be found," Sean said.

Doris didn't even blink. "I have a guest room. You'd be very welcome to stay there. It's quite self-contained."

"I appreciate it," Sean said.

"What else do you need?" she asked.

"Access to a telephone, mainly."

"It's in your room, a separate line. I suppose all this has to do with what you were telling me last time, your little investigation?"

"Yes," Sean said, and proceeded to tell her what had

been happening.

"I think you'd be wise to stay here," Doris agreed when he concluded. "I don't think you should even go back to your apartment for clothes. It looks like you're in very deep water."

"My car is still at your place," Susanne said with a worried look to Sean.

"Just leave it for now," he said. "It's safe there."

"I'll have to call my parents," Susanne said uncertainly. "I know that sounds dumb, but I can't believe my mother really wants to see me hurt, and they would both worry if I disappeared."

"Why not call your father? Just tell him you're staying over with a friend," Sean suggested. "But don't say who or where."

"I can call him at his office," she said. "That would be the best way."

"We should also call your lawyer friend and let him know how to reach us," Sean said.

Doris rose. "Let me show you to your room. It sounds like you both have things to do."

She led them through the house to a spacious guest room at the rear. It was more than a room, actually, with its own bathroom, a tiny kitchenette with a hotplate and refrigerator, and French doors that opened up onto a small patio enclosed by vines and flowers.

"Oh, this is beautiful," Susanne said, standing at the doors.

"I have relatives and out-of-town guests occasionally, and I've grown to like my privacy," Doris explained. "This gives them theirs and me mine."

"It's perfect," Sean said. "Doris, I don't know how I'm going to be able to repay you for your kindness."

"Don't worry about it," she said dismissively, and moved on to practicalities. "There's no food here, so help yourself in the kitchen to anything you like. In fact, I'll have the

324

maid bring some staples like milk and coffee in here. And if there's anything you need, or if I can be of more concrete help, let me know."

She excused herself, leaving them alone. Sean looked longingly at the bed. "God, I'm exhausted," he said, surprised to suddenly notice it.

"Well, you've been knocked on the head and almost knocked off the road," Susanne said. "What do you expect?"

He sat on the edge of the bed and reached for the telephone. "I also need to call the hospital and see how Ted's doing. And call Danny and tell him I'm hiding out."

"Do you trust him?" Susanne asked cautiously.

"Danny? I think so. But I'm not going to tell him where we are, as much for his protection as ours."

"Good," she said, satisfied with that.

While he made the first call she went and stood on the patio. Some sweet scent drifted from the flowering vines to her right. An orange cat crossed the pathway and disappeared into bushes. It was a peaceful scene, such a contrast to what they had just been through.

She folded her arms across her chest and gripped her shoulders. She had never experienced violence in her sheltered life, and she found that it terrified her. She had been more frightened than she had let on in the car, looking down the hillside beside the road, knowing that if they had gone over they would not have survived. Only Sean's courage and quick thinking had saved them. She had never been that close to death before.

For some reason she thought of her sister. What incredible pressure had caused her to break down and withdraw like that? There was so much she didn't know about her. Her fears and loathings, the nightmares that haunted her enough to bring about insanity. She had never bothered to find out, was too involved in her own life. Of course, Marion had been self-involved herself, but that didn't excuse Susanne.

She turned and went back into the room. Sean was just hanging up. "Ted's still in a coma. They have him on lifesupport machines, still uncertain of the outcome."

Susanne just shook her head and sat beside him on the bed. "When this is all over, I want to go and visit my sister at the sanatorium in Santa Monica. I owe her that."

Sean stopped what he was doing and looked at her. Distant bells jangled in his mind. "What's the name of the sanatorium?" he asked slowly.

"Boswell," she said. She added dryly, "It's well known. Private, high fees, the upper crust of clientele. Only the best crazies go there."

"And your sister's name?"

"Marion."

Sean scrambled for his phone book, found a number and dialed it while Susanne curiously watched him.

"Sue? Hi, it's Sean . . . I'm fine . . . Listen, what was the name of the sanatorium that you said Marina went to for drug rehab?

"Right. Okay. I can't talk right now, I'm in a rush. I'll call you later, okay? Yeah, thanks, bye."

He hung up the phone and turned to Susanne.

"Bingo!" he said. "The connection."

Sean explained his reasoning to a puzzled Susanne. "There were items on Marina's list of things to check. They didn't mean anything to me at the time. But knowing she was at Boswell, and that your sister is at Boswell, makes a few of those items very clear. One of the things was 'Marion again.' What the hell did that mean? How about it means to see Marion at the sanatorium again? Another was to make preliminary contact with AL. I thought it was Al, like in Albert. But think! Whose initials are those? A period, L period."

326

"My God!" Susanne said. "My mother! Annette Lowell."

"Right," Sean said, a self-satisfied smile on his face. "Marina met your sister, found out something, and wanted to contact your mother. Marina told her friend that she was onto something big in terms of money. Could it have been blackmail? Did she find out something about a murder? There was mention of researching all members of family. Your family? It's starting to fall into place."

"But who could have been murdered?" Susanne asked.

"I told you," Sean said. "There was a guy at Debonaire that Marina wanted me to find out about. But he's disappeared. Gone. Nobody knows where he is. Guy by the name of Alex Varney."

"What?" Susanne said, her mouth dropping open.

"I tried to find out where—" Sean began, but she cut him off.

"Alex Varney?!"

"Yeah."

Susanne gripped his arm tightly, her face a shade paler. "Do you remember the guy I told you about that I thought I was in love with. How he went after my sister and my mother intervened and paid him off?"

"You're kidding!" Sean said, realizing exactly where she was heading.

She shook her head. "I'm not. *Alex Varney.*"

"Jesus!" Sean said, a half a dozen expressions flitting across his face.

"What the hell does all this mean?" Susanne asked, her only expression one of mystification now.

Sean shook his head. "I'm not sure. But I don't like where it's heading. The pieces are coming together."

"He disappeared," Susanne stated. "My mother said she paid him off. Maybe he just took the money and ran. Maybe that was part of the deal."

"He left everything he owned, Susanne. I mean, maybe he had so much money from the payoff that it didn't

327

matter, but . . ."

"You think that your friend's talk of a murder, that it was him, don't you?" she asked, her voice rising.

"Susanne, calm down," he said soothingly. "It could be, but it's only one theory."

"Jesus!" she said disgustedly. "I'm not mad at you. I'm mad at the facts. It's logical. It's almost certain, Sean. This guy was killed. Your friend found out about it somehow at the sanatorium. It had something to do with Marion and my mother. The guy worked at Debonaire, maybe your friend knew him. You said she worked in the business too."

"The facts could lead to any number of conclusions," Sean said. "Maybe Nancy Hamilton was blackmailing your mother!"

"Then why is she helping my mother get rid of you?"

Sean grimaced. "I don't know," he said.

Susanne began to get that disgusted look on her face again. It was as if her thoughts were too ugly, too dreadful to be faced, yet they had to be. She hated the entire process.

"What is it?" Sean asked.

"There's one fact that scares me, the coincidence of it," she said. "When Alex Varney disappeared . . . that's when my sister had her breakdown. I can only think that something terrible must have happened, something she knew of or saw. What could be terrible enough to make her lose her sanity?"

Sean made his decision, the only logical remaining course of action. He put his hand over hers and said, "We have to go and see your sister."

Like a shell-shocked victim, Susanne nodded numbly and said in a hollow voice, "I know."

"Alex probably fit in nicely with my sense of rebellion," Susanne was saying as they drove down Wilshire Boulevard toward Santa Monica. "He was everything all those nice and pretty boys my mother kept fixing me up with weren't. He had this veneer of sophistication, but you could tell he'd come from the street. There was this underlying cynicism, a fuck-you edge to the guy that attracted me. And I think Annette spotted it immediately. She probably came from the same street."

"So it was hate at first sight between the two of them?" Sean asked.

"Absolutely. And then when he saw Marion and immediately dropped me and started chasing her, Annette went after him like a hunting dog after possum. The guy didn't stand a chance. He might have been street smart, but she's made of iron. There was a cloud of dust, but I never had any doubt about who'd be left standing and who'd be left behind."

"And she's the one who told you he worked for Debonaire?"

"No! She never told me that. Just that he was a gigolo and made his living off women."

"Did he ever say anything about that to you?" Sean asked, moving into the right lane to take the 26th Street exit.

Susanne thought for a moment. "No, he didn't. But it made sense afterward. I remembered how whenever we went out to a party or charity event, he seemed to know an inordinate number of elderly women. You know, we'd go to a party and there'd be ladies smiling knowingly across the room at him. I was so naive, I thought it was just because he was attractive!"

"I can understand why it was such a shock when I told you where I was working," Sean said.

"Yes, but only because I wasn't thinking. My feelings had taken charge," she said ruminatively. "What happened with him was such a betrayal to me. Then when you said what you did, the same emotions surfaced. It was like an emotional replay. Intellectually, of course, it wasn't the same thing at all, but it takes a while to let the emotions simmer down and allow judgement to resurface."

She was talking fast, glancing out of the window every now and then. Sean smiled and said, "You're nervous, aren't you?"

"Yes," she said. "Scared shitless."

The Boswell Sanatorium was northwest of San Vicente Boulevard on a huge tract of land overlooking Santa Monica Canyon. They saw the building from behind enormous iron gates. It sat back across green lawns, an institutional mansion, perhaps a large house that had been added onto from all sides. The grounds were surrounded by a tall metal fence, spiked on top. In the distance, they could see people sitting on benches and walking across the lawns.

Susanne pressed the buzzer on the speaker and announced herself. There was a long pause and then the female voice said, "Do you have an appointment?"

"No, I don't," Susanne said.

"I have strict orders that this patient is not allowed visitors," the voice said.

"I'm immediate family. Her sister," Susanne said. "I don't think there'd be a problem with that."

"Well, it says no visitors," the woman repeated uncertainly.

"Why don't you let me in and I'll speak to whoever is in charge," Susanne said sweetly, grimacing at Sean.

"Well . . ."

"Thank you," Susanne said.

Well, all right," the wavering voice said, and a moment later the gate began to swing open.

They drove up a long, roughly sealed driveway and pulled up in front of the ornate double wooden doors in front of the house.

330

"Imposing place," Sean said. "Reminds me of a prison."

"It is," Susanne said grimly. "The last time I was here that was perfectly clear to me. The guards are called orderlies and nurses, the doctors are the wardens."

Sean got out of the car opened the door for Susanne. As she stepped out, a woman in white nursing uniform stepped out of the double doors and looked down at them. Susanne smiled at her.

"I'm Susanne Lowell," she said brightly.

"Please come with me," the woman said.

She led them through the doors into a gloomy hallway and then into an office. A tall, thin man sat behind a desk. He had long, thin hair that flopped over his forehead and thick glasses that magnified his eyes. He looked up at them, then back down at a folder on his desk.

"Uh, I'm Dr. Carter," he said, not looking up. "Dr. Emira isn't here this afternoon and Marion Lowell is his patient. I see that there's an order here that he signed forbidding visitation except from Mrs. Annette Lowell."

"That's my mother," Susanne said. "She's the one who suggested I come and see my sister Marion. She thought it might do her some good. I understand she spoke to Dr. Emira about it and he suggested it."

"Oh, I see," Dr. Carter said. "Well, it probably could help. I see in the file that the patient has been making progress and that lately she has been formulating words. Not complete sentences, mind you, but words. At least she is coming out of the shell in which she's been hiding." He peered over his glasses at Sean. "And you are?"

Sean came up with an appropriate answer. "Oh, I'm Susanne's fiancé. We all grew up together. Marion was one of my best friends."

"Well, I'm sure some positive reinforcement couldn't hurt," Dr. Carter said, his lanky body rising from behind the desk. "I'll take you to her room."

They walked along a hall and through what had once

331

been a living room. Half a dozen people sat there, two watching television, one leafing rapidly through a magazine, a couple staring blankly at nothing, and one apparently sleeping. Not one appeared to notice them as they passed.

"As you can see, we like to keep the surroundings natural and unassuming," Carter said over his shoulder. Then, as if wishing to disassociate himself from them, he increased his pace, forging ahead.

Finally, after another long corridor, Carter stopped in front of a door. "This is her room," he said. "I'll announce you and then leave. Whatever you do, don't get her upset. If she starts to get that way, please leave and come back to my office."

"Fine," Susanne said.

He opened the door and assumed a hearty cheerfulness. "And how are we today, Marion? I have some visitors for you."

She sat in an armchair beside a window, staring out at an expanse of lawn dotted with trees. She did not turn or acknowledge their presence in any way.

"Well," Carter said uncomfortably, "no stress, remember?" and left.

Although taller than Susanne, Marion had the same brown hair and hazel eyes as her sister. But whereas Susanne was bright and vibrant, this woman was pale and limp, her hair lank, her mouth slack.

Susanne straightened her shoulders, walked over and dropped to a crouch beside the chair. She took her sister's hand in hers and tried to find life in her eyes. "Marion? It's me, Susanne. I've come to see you."

Marion's eyes finally moved down to her, but they registered nothing. No recognition, no emotion whatsoever.

"How are you?" Susanne asked. "Are they looking after you well here?"

Marion turned her head and looked out the window

332

again.

Susanne glanced at Sean and he saw the beginnings of tears in her eyes. He understood how painful it had to be for her to see her sister in this condition.

He also crouched beside Marion. "Marion, my name is Sean. I'm a friend," he said, his voice firm and intense. "I love your sister, Marion."

The girl's eyes drifted slowly down to him and for a moment they seemed clouded with a passing puzzlement, but almost immediately they became bovine and passive again.

"Marion, we need your help. Susanne and I need your help," he said with the same intensity. "I think you can understand us and I want you to help us. Do you understand?"

If she did, she wasn't showing it.

He took her hand from Susanne's and gripped her other one as well. Then he half stood and pushed his face close to hers, staring directly into her eyes.

"Tell us what happened to Alex Varney," he said. "Tell us about Alex."

She closed her eyes and pulled her head back, as if to escape his stare.

"Tell us about Alex," he repeated, shaking her hands in his.

She opened her eyes again, and for a moment that blank stare met his. Then she turned her gaze to the window.

"Help us, Marion," Sean pleaded. "Something happened to Alex, didn't it? Something terrible. You have to tell us."

There was no response and he shook his head in frustration. "Do you remember Marina?" he asked. "Marina was my friend, too. For her sake, you must tell me about Alex."

Nothing.

He looked over at Susanne. There were definitely tears

in her eyes now as she watched her sister's placid face.

"Marion," she said, emotion clogging her voice, "won't you talk to us? Please."

"It's useless," Sean said.

"It's like she's trapped somewhere," Susanne said. "Somewhere in the past."

Susanne rose and leaned down to kiss her sister's cheek. She ran her hand over Marion's hair. "Oh, Marion, please get better," she said. Then she stood and looked down at this childlike adult.

"Let's go," she said finally. "We're not doing any good here."

Sean rose, debated whether to try one more time to talk to the girl and then decided against it. He wasn't getting anywhere and didn't have the tools to change the situation.

Once again, Susanne stroked her sister's hair. "I love you, Marion. I'll come and see you again," she said and turned.

Sean took her arm and led her to the door. Tears stained her cheeks and he could feel her pain. Momentarily he was angry at himself for putting her through this. It had led nowhere and served only to upset and sadden her.

And then, as they reached the door, a voice came from behind them.

"Mommy."

They both whirled around.

She was sitting exactly as they left her, still looking at the window. They looked at each other, then back at her, neither quite believing what they had heard.

Susanne's voice quivered with emotion. "Mommy?"

And then they actually saw her speak, as she repeated the word in that childish voice, "Mommy."

Susanne moved toward her, but some instinct made Sean grab her arm and restrain her. He shook his head.

"Mommy what?" Susanne asked from where she stood.

Marion slowly turned her head from the window and

334

looked at her sister. Her eyes were puzzled, searching.

"Mommy killed Alex," she said.

She stood and faced them. And raised her right arm, holding her thumb upright and her index finger pointed at them, just like a child mimicking a gun.

"Bang! Bang!" she said.

And then the frozen mask on her face began to dissolve and she started to scream.

Sean's immediate impulse was to turn, which he started to do. "I'll get the doctor," he said.

"No!" Susanne said sharply. "They'll just sedate her."

She ran over to her sister who now had both her hands covering her mouth, revealing only her terrified eyes. Susanne put her arms around her and began to stroke her head.

"It's all right, Marion. It's all going to be all right, I promise," she said in a soothing litany. "It's okay, honey. It's okay."

The screams miraculously began to subside, replaced by choked sobs. And then Marion put her arms around her sister and held her as tightly as she could and cried against her shoulder.

Chapter Twenty-two

They drove away from the sanatorium in silence, each looking into their own thoughts. Marion had finally calmed down, but she had not spoken again, withdrawing almost immediately back into her private world, tormented by demons neither of them could even conceive of. They had left without seeing the doctor again.

"It could never be proven," Sean said finally.

"One catatonic witness? No, it couldn't," Susanne said. "Do you believe her?"

"Yes."

"Does your mother own a gun?"

"I suppose so. I remember some years ago she took shooting lessons." She grew silent, then added bitterly, "Self-protection, she said. Protecting what's hers, as always."

They lapsed into silence again until Susanne said, "What are we going to do?"

Sean shrugged. "I don't know. I think we're going to go back to Doris's and get some sleep. That's as far ahead as I can think."

"You must be exhausted," Susanne said.

He suddenly realized how tightly he was holding the steering wheel, feeling the strain in the muscles of his back and neck. His head had also begun to throb again. Consciously, he relaxed.

"I'm so sorry, Susanne," he said miserably.

She reached a hand out to touch his leg. "If you feel responsible for any of this, don't. Whatever it was that happened was long before I knew you. It seems that you've been the necessary catalyst to bring it all to the surface. And that's something that needs doing, no matter how unpleasant the consequences."

"Whatever it was," he repeated thoughtfully, "if your mother indeed killed Alex Varney, my guess is that Marion must have been there, must have seen the whole thing, and that it was too much for her to bear."

Susanne made the gun figure with her hand and said, "Bang, bang. Why would she make something like that up? She must have seen it."

"I don't know what to do?" Sean said.

"Sleep," Susanne said. She felt exhausted as well, emotionally drained, as if the turbulence of an entire lifetime had been crowded into this one day. "That was the best suggestion. We'll take a fresh look at everything tomorrow."

It was dark by the time they arrived at Doris's house in Beverly Hills. She offered them dinner but they refused, saying they were tired. For some reason neither felt like telling her about what they had just discovered. It was as if the reality was too harsh for even them to comprehend; to talk about it to another at this stage seemed unfitting, even futile. It had no meaning, no context in their lives as yet.

Doris was immediately sensitive to their mood. "There's a small bar in the kitchenette above the sink, if you want a nightcap," she said understandingly. "And if there's anything else you need, just let me know."

What Sean needed was a shower, and he took one, standing under the fierce hot needles of water for almost twenty minutes, letting them pound against his head and shoulders, beating relaxation into him. When he was finished, Susanne was sitting on the bed, a glass of sherry in her hand.

"I poured one for you," she said, handing him a glass from the bedside table.

They sipped their drinks contemplatively, hardly saying anything to each other. When they went to bed their love-making was so tender, it was almost devoid of passion. It was a reaffirmation of their feelings, and with it they created a sanctuary that encompassed and revitalized them. No matter what evils the world contained, for these moments they found themselves a safe port, a loving refuge that nothing could violate.

Sean woke at eleven after sleeping for twelve hours, a dreamless, motionless sleep that left him feeling alert and energetic. His head no longer hurt and his muscles no longer ached.

Susanne wasn't in the room, so he got up and showered again. When he came out, she was sitting at the small table in the dining nook, two hot breakfasts of eggs and bacon, toast and coffee, set out before her.

Sean was ravenous and attacked the food as if he hadn't eaten for days. Susanne watched in wonder. "Well, they say sex is good for the appetite," she said when he finished.

Only then did she mention that David Dobbs had called. "About half an hour ago. He said he'd found out some information about Debonaire but didn't want to discuss it over the phone. He'll be here at any minute."

The events of the previous day descended like a cloud around Sean's head. For a brief time he'd been able to put them aside. Now they were once again intruding, demanding to be dealt with.

There wasn't much time for him to adjust to reality. About two minutes later, Doris knocked on their door and said David was waiting for them in the living room.

He sat the couch in a three-piece suit, a briefcase on the

floor beside him. After a brief greeting, he sighed and said, "I found out what you wanted to know and more. And I don't know if you want to know it."

"Tell us," Susanne said stiffly. She sat upright in a chair opposite him, while Sean sat beside him on the couch.

"I've traced the ownership of Debonaire. Believe me, it wasn't easy, there were layers of layers of paper covering it up. Debonaire is co-owned by Nancy Hamilton and by Companionship, Inc., as is Panache; Companionship is owned by Playlife, which also owns a whole chain of pornographic 976 telephone services; Playlife is owned by something else, and so on and so on. Parent company upon parent, a very complicated family tree. But we got down to the source of it all."

He took off his glasses and rubbed them on the sleeve of his jacket, then put them back on. "The holding company for all of this is registered in the Cayman Islands — offshore, as we call it. And that's where it gets tricky. Privacy is the commodity the islands offer investors, and they don't like to violate it. Luckily, I've done business there before for a client and had a man in place in a certain ministry there. My company had paid him very well to do some similar work for us before, so he was not averse to snooping around. I'm afraid he'll be sending a bill."

He gave them a half-apologetic look, but Sean said, "That's fine. So what did you find?"

"I found sole ownership. Another corporation, of course, but with a sole owner." He looked at Susanne and cleared his throat. "Your mother, Annette Lowell. She owns it all."

"Right," Sean said, and looked at Susanne who was slowly nodding her head.

"You don't seem surprised," said a bewildered David. "I couldn't believe it."

"No, I don't suppose we are," Sean said. "There were too many fingers pointing in that direction."

"And talking about fingers," David continued, "she has

339

her fingers in dozens of pies, some of them barely legal, or at least skirting the edges of propriety. Then there are some that are just too bizarre to believe. I mean, she even has an interest in an evangelical group."

"But there's nothing criminal about any of this, is there?" Sean asked.

"Legally? No. At least none of this paperwork proves criminal action." He cleared his throat again and looked away from Susanne. "It did occur to me that if my father was being blackmailed by Debonaire, that it's possible your mother was behind it. I understand your father's going to run for the vacant seat."

"Yes, we thought of that," Susanne said. "I'd say now that it's a virtual certainty that she's behind it all, including the murder of Sean's friend. And she may have been, probably was, directly involved in yet another murder."

"Good God," David said.

"Yes," Susanne said.

There was an awkward pause and then Susanne stood. "Sean can fill you in. If you don't mind, I'm going outside. I need to be alone for a few minutes, okay?"

"Of course," David said.

Sean nodded. They both watched her walk from the room.

"What's she going to do?" David asked, turning to Sean. "I mean, what are you going to do? This is her mother, for God's sake!"

"I don't know," Sean said. "And right now, I guess she doesn't either."

Susanne sat on a bench in the small patio behind their room. There was a rustle of birds moving among leaves in the vines above, and a sudden burst of bright song. The orange cat appeared out of nowhere and rubbed against her leg. Getting no response, the animal stalked away and

340

lay in a pool of sunlight.

What was she going to do? She had no idea. She didn't have the wisdom of Solomon or the faith of Abraham. She just had herself and a mother who had committed unspeakably evil acts. Strangely, she felt no hatred toward her mother, not even the usual sense of antagonism, only a deep sadness.

The alternatives were few. She could forget the whole thing and persuade Sean to do the same. Out of love for her, he wouldn't need much persuasion.

She could confront her mother with what she knew and see where that led.

She could tell her father what she knew, and see where that led.

She could go to the authorities with what she knew, and it was obvious where that would lead: investigation, scandal, the ruin of her father's political ambitions, possibly prison for her mother. Of course, her father's ambitions were virtually nonexistent; they were really Annette's ambitions. As for scandal and all the rest of it . . . well, crimes had been committed. If they were proved, why should their family be exempt from the consequences? Because they were wealthy and powerful? That went against everything she had ever believed in. Her father had taught her about justice, the rule of law that kept society from falling into chaos. And she had formed her own opinions about right and wrong and responsibility.

But this was her mother! Flesh and blood from which she had been born. She had begun life in that womb, suckled on that breast, been given shelter and belongings by that person. But people had to be responsible for what they did. She believed that with every fiber of her being. It was not only just, but compassionate. Not for the victims, but for the individual who had committed harmful acts it was also the only hope of redemption. To face up to what had been done and make amends.

341

She rose and walked briskly back into the living room. David was standing, briefcase in hand, shaking hands with Sean.

"Wait," she said.

They both turned to look into her determined face.

"You're a lawyer," she said to David. "Sean's told you what's going on. What do we have? Do we have proof of any kind? Anything that would stand up in a court? Do we even have enough to go to the police with."

David shook his head. "I was just telling Sean that you don't have proof. You have conjecture. You have no proof that she killed this guy Varney. You have no proof that she had anything to do with Sean's old girlfriend, or even that she was murdered. And no proof that she was involved in the attempt on the life of the guy Sean lived with. You have enough circumstantial stuff to take to a sympathetic policeman, enough to give him cause to investigate further, but that's all. I'm convinced, but a court wouldn't be. You probably don't even have enough to justify a search warrant, let alone an arrest."

"Then we need proof," she said, sitting on the edge of the couch.

"What do you have in mind?" Sean asked.

"There might be something in writing, something in my mother's files. She has a small room off her study. The room itself is a vault, with a combination lock on the outside. Inside are steel file cabinets, all locked of course. I've no idea where she keeps the keys. But I know the combination to the vault room. I could at least get us in there."

"Danny!" Sean said.

David smiled pleasantly at them. "I don't think I heard the beginnings of conspiratorial criminal action, but I'd better leave before I do. After all, you guys might need a lawyer and I won't be much help if I'm in jail with you."

"Thank you so much for what you've done," Susanne

said, hugging him and kissing his cheek.

David blushed and said it was nothing.

When he left, Susanne asked Sean what he meant by Danny.

"The guy is a wizard with locks. He shouldn't have any problem with file cabinets, steel or not."

"We need to get Annette out of the house," Susanne said.

"Call her. Tell her I've been making accusations and you need to talk to her. Say you'll be waiting to meet her somewhere. Somewhere some distance from your house. Like the Denny's on Sunset near the Hollywood Freeway."

"She'll just tell me to come home," Susanne said. "Talk to her there."

"Okay, I'll call her," Sean said. "Say I have proof that she killed Alex. Ask if she wants to buy it. She'll believe that."

"Yes, she would," Susanne said.

"Where's Doris?" Sean asked.

"She went out."

Sean suddenly stopped his burst of creative enthusiasm. "Are you sure about this?" he asked. "You've thought it through?"

"Yes, I'm sure," she said.

"What made you decide?"

"Because it's right. Because we have to find the truth, regardless of the consequences. If we didn't, I'd never be able to live with myself. And, ultimately, you and I would never be able to live with each other."

Sean clasped her in a hug. "That was exactly my conclusion. And that's one of the many reasons I love you."

"This is called breaking and entering," Danny said nervously as the three of them drove toward Annette's house.

"Don't worry about it. I'll make sure we share a cell," Sean said lightly.

343

Danny had come as soon as Sean had called, and had immediately agreed to help upon hearing the circumstances. His concerns now, Sean realized, were just automatic.

He had also called Annette. She hadn't commented on what he said other than to agree to meet him. Right now she was probably traveling in exactly the opposite direction in which they were going.

He looked anxiously at Susanne in the seat beside him. In spite of her resolve, she too was nervous and hadn't spoken much in the car. He wanted to tell her that it was going to be all right, even to tell her that it was okay with him if she wanted to change her mind. But he couldn't do that. It wasn't okay with either of them. They had made the right decision, and like everyone involved they would have to face the consequences.

Finally, after what seemed an interminable drive, they reached the house. Susanne had her automatic gate opener and they entered the long driveway. No other cars in sight, Sean noted as he pulled up in front of the house. They had already established that her father would probably be at work. "If not," Susanne said, "he'll probably be in his study and won't hear a thing."

Susanne took a key from her purse and opened the front door and walked in casually. In spite of the fact that she lived here, Susanne felt an urge to tiptoe—skulk in like the thief she was.

"Her study is down here toward the back," she said, leading the way. She came to a closed door and opened it, stepping in, the two men close behind her.

"Well, this *is* a surprise," Annette said.

She was sitting behind her desk, papers before her, a Tiffany lamp casting a glow.

They all stopped, frozen in place.

"Now you're here, you might as well come in," Annette said coolly.

"You're supposed to be meeting Sean," Susanne blurted out.

"I sent someone else to *meet* him," she said, endowing the word with a nasty edge. "What are you doing here?"

Nobody spoke and then Annette smiled grimly. "I see. Get me out of the house on a fool's errand and come and ransack my office. Perhaps I should call the police. This is intent to burglarize, I presume."

"I wouldn't do that," Sean said. "Not until we've talked."

"Oh, yes, you accused me of killing someone. Alex Varney. I think you'd have a difficult time proving that. It's ludicrous. Mr. Varney has traveled to parts unknown."

"And responsible to some degree for the death of Marina White and the attempt to murder Ted Marshall. We know that you own Debonaire and Panache and all the other fringe companies."

"Proof?" she asked scornfully. "There's nothing illegal about my business interests. And besides, you'd have a hard time getting the paperwork to prove even that. I think you're wasting my time and my daughter's." She looked at Susanne. "You don't believe any of this nonsense, do you? He's just trying to get even because I told him to stay away from you."

"I believe it all," Susanne said.

Annette's mouth tightened. "You've always thought the worst of me," she said.

Susanne stepped farther into the room and stopped a few feet from her mother. "How could you do these things?" she asked.

Annette blinked. "I have done nothing," she said.

"I know you killed Alex," Susanne said.

"Know? How could you?"

"A witness," Susanne said.

Annette smiled. "That's impossible, Susanne."

Susanne shook her head. "Miraculous, but not impossible. Marion told me. You shot him. She saw you."

345

Her words hung between them. Annette's face grew visibly paler, and her eyes held Susanne's as if unable to tear away.

"That's impossible," she repeated finally.

"We saw her yesterday. Sean and I. She spoke. She told us." Susanne's words traveled with the force of projectiles across the distance between them.

"That couldn't have happened," Annette said again, this time more softly, her voice uncertain.

"No, it's true," Susanne said, the volume of her voice dropping too. "She spoke and she is going to get better and she is going to speak again."

They could see Annette's thoughts. They ran across her face like shadows. She shook her head and said, "Nobody would believe her. She is certifiably insane. That's why she's there. She's crazy."

"Made that way by you," Susanne said. "By what she saw."

There was silence then. Mother and daughter regarded each other implacably. Sean didn't dare move. This was between them. It had virtually nothing to do with him now.

Annette was the first to break the silence. "What are you planning to do with these wild accusations?"

"I'm going to tell the police," Susanne said.

"There is no proof, nothing that would stand up. All you'd accomplish by doing that is to ruin everything I've tried to do for your father. If you loved him, you wouldn't even consider this rash action."

"That won't work," Susanne said with a tight smile. "I'm going to do what is right."

Casually, Annette opened a drawer from her desk and withdrew a revolver.

She pointed it at Sean and Danny. "Come closer, you two. I need to think. I need time to think."

"What are you going to do, Annette? Kill them both?"

346

Susanne asked, no fear in her voice, just disbelief.

"They were attempting to rob me," Annette said thoughtfully.

"And what about me, Mother? Would you kill me too? Your last remaining daughter?"

Annette looked at her without speaking.

"You'd have to kill me too, Annette," Kenneth Lowell said, stepping into the room.

He wore a rumpled robe over gray slacks and a white shirt. There were slippers on his feet and his hair was tousled.

"It's gone too far," he said, walking over to her desk. He stopped beside Susanne and put an arm around her shoulder. "I'm sorry, I should have stopped it long ago."

"You knew?" Susanne asked, her voice hoarse. "About the murders, the blackmailing? You knew all that was happening?"

"No," he said, dropping his arm. "I knew about the murder of Alex Varney. But I didn't know Annette had killed him. Oh, I suspected it, but I didn't want to believe it."

"I don't understand," Susanne said.

"You are talking too much. Don't say anything else," Annette said to Kenneth. "Nothing can be proved. Why doesn't everyone just walk out of here."

"No," her husband said. "It's going to end now." He turned to his daughter. "I arrived home after the shooting. Varney was dead on the floor, right about where I'm standing. Marion was unconscious on the floor, the gun beside her when I walked in. Your mother said Marion had killed Varney. I wanted to call the police, but she persuaded me not to, for our daughter's sake. Instead I called in a favor with a Vietnamese refugee I had helped sponsor over here, and he disposed of the body at sea. I didn't know then that my little girl would never wake up from the horror she had witnessed."

347

He turned to his wife, his eyes and voice sad. "And there have been other killings? And blackmail?"

"There is no evidence of that," she said, her voice rising. "If Marion recovers it would be her word against mine. And nothing else can ever be proved, including the overdose of that little bitch who was trying to blackmail me."

He shook his head. "That's up to the police and the courts to decide. I made a mistake before. I won't do it again. I've ignored your sickness for too long, never had the courage to face it *or* you, for that matter. I'll take the consequences, just as you must."

"You can't do that!" she shouted, rage entering her voice. "Do you know what I've done for you? Do you know how long and hard I've worked for you? The machine I've got in place? You're going to be senator, maybe more."

"I don't want it," he said tiredly. He moved then and slumped into the chair opposite her. "I never really did."

"But it's all been for you," she said, almost pleading. "I've got two dozen businesses spread across the state. The fundraising machinery is incredible. My family, I've even had them working for you. I've placed my two younger sisters in positions to directly help you."

"Sisters?" he said. "What sisters?"

"Yes," she said impatiently. "Nancy and Cecelia. Nancy was directly responsible for Dobbs announcing his retirement. Cecelia is one of the most influential evangelists in the state, the damn country. By endorsing you, she can carry thousands of votes and produce thousands of campaigners. Don't you see? Everything is finally in place! All my work, my dreams, my energy! Don't you see what I've done for you?"

"I told you once before that I didn't believe it was really for me. Now I'm certain," Kenneth said. He held out his hand. "Give me the gun, Annette. We'll take care of this. We'll get you help. It will all work out."

"No!" she screamed, her face livid now, her hand tightening on the gun and jerking it up.

Without turning, Kenneth said quietly, "Please leave me with my wife now."

Susanne stood frozen in horror by everything she had heard. The reality of Annette's condition was worse than her imaginings. It was nightmarish, hellish. She could feel compassion for her mother, but she also knew she was looking at an evil that few people see.

"Come on," Sean said, stepping up and taking her arm. His priority was to get her out of this room and away from the madwoman with a gun in her hand.

Danny had already sidled to the door and stepped through it.

"Come on," Sean said again, tugging at her.

Mutely, she allowed him to lead her into the hallway. He put his arm around her, supporting her. "Let's go outside for a minute," he said. "You need some air."

They went out the front door and her legs suddenly felt if they were melting. She sank to a sitting position on the step. Sean sat beside her, his arm still around her shoulders, and pulled her head against him. She began to sob then, her chest heaving with huge dry sobs, and then the tears began to flow down her face.

Danny stood beside the car as if he couldn't wait to leave.

Kenneth Lowell came slowly out of the house and stood silently on the step behind them. When Susanne became aware of his presence she got up and threw her arms around him, still sobbing.

The sound of the gunshot almost threw them apart. Sean jumped to his feet, exchanged a shocked glance with Susanne, and the two of them sprinted back into the house.

Sean reached the door to the office first and skidded to a halt.

Annette Lowell lay across her desk, the gun in her hand,

349

a spreading pool of blood covering the papers.

Sean turned and caught Susanne just as she entered. Her hand flew up to her mouth, as if to strangle a scream.

"No!" he said, whirling her quickly around and leading her away.

Through the front door they could see Kenneth standing exactly where they had left him.

As they approached him he turned and held his hands out to Susanne in a helpless, pitiful gesture and said, his voice pleading, "I loved her, you see. I loved her in spite of it all."

And then Susanne found the strength to take her father in her arms and hold him while he cried like a child against her shoulder.

They met two days later at Doris's house. Danny, Sean, and Susanne sat with her on a patio beside the swimming pool and drank coffee, comparing notes and filling in the blanks.

Now that they had a dead body, the police had moved quickly. Nancy Hamilton and Dirk were picked up; they proved only too eager to incriminate each other.

Debonaire's activities were vaster than expected, as were those of its sister organization, Panache.

"They had blackmail tapes on all kinds of people," Sean said. "Even the mayor was featured in one of the films. They were mainly political figures, or their spouses or children, as was the case with Emily Dobbs. They were never blackmailed for money, only for favors, mainly having to do with the political future of Susanne's father. Also things like construction permits relating to Annette's development businesses."

Susanne said, "She used her sisters, my aunts, whom I never even knew. She set Nancy up in business after she came to Los Angeles and she helped Cecelia get started as

350

an evangelist some years earlier. She didn't do it out of the goodness of her heart, however. It was all part of an obsessive dream she had to set my father up in politics. A mad obsession."

Ted was still in a coma, his future uncertain.

Marion had already been taken from the sanatorium and brought to the house, where she was under the care of a private doctor. The prognosis was good. "It won't take long," he promised.

Kenneth had immediately resigned from the bench. No charges were filed against him. There seemed no point. Susanne was working with him, managing her mother's business empire, liquidating all the vaguely legal businesses and redirecting the funds. "I'll take a year to get it all in order, then get to my own dream of making movies," she said.

"And what about you, Danny?" Doris asked, as they watched Sean and Susanne stroll hand-in-hand on a path between beds of brilliant flowers.

"I'm going into the restaurant business," he said. "There's this woman, she's going to help me raise the financing."

"Someone special?"

"Yes, she is," Danny said, smiling at the thought. "She says she won't leave her husband, but I think I'll just keep asking."

He looked at the two in the garden. An orange cat appeared on the path and rubbed against Susanne's leg. She picked it up and held it against her chest.

"What about them?" Danny asked. "After all this, are they going to be all right?"

Doris smiled. "Yes, they are. They are two very special young people. And they will help her family get through this, too. You see, they love each other very much. That will give them all the strength and joy they need to persevere."

"Yes," Danny said. "I once thought I didn't need love. It seems that everyone in this world does."

The cat jumped out of Susanne's arms. Although they could not hear what she said, they saw Sean laugh and pull her toward him and kiss her.